PRAISE FOR THE NOVELS OF BARBARA DAVIS

"Fans of Tana French, Alena Dillon, and Hannah Mary McKinnon will adore Davis's multilayered tale of intrigue, romance, and long-held biases set straight."

—*Booklist*

"*The Last of the Moon Girls* is reminiscent of two of my all-time favorites, Sarah Addison Allen's *Garden Spells* [and] Alice Hoffman's *Practical Magic*, because it's witchy, full of plant magic, and painfully human."

—Kristin Fields, bestselling author of *A Lily in the Light*

"A story of love, hope, redemption, and rediscovering who you were meant to be . . . Will resonate with readers who love a tale full of heart and soul."

—Camille Di Maio, bestselling author of *The Memory of Us* and *The Beautiful Strangers*

"Infused with honesty, friendship, and a touch of romance. Davis creates nuanced and well-developed characters . . . A carefully woven tale that the reader won't soon forget."

—Emily Cavanagh, author of *The Bloom Girls* and *This Bright Beauty*

"Brimming with compassion and a refreshingly grown-up romance . . . An uplifting tale about starting over and how letting go of our nevers just might be the only thing that lets us move forward."

—Emily Carpenter, author of *Until the Day I Die*

"Heartfelt and beautifully written."

—Diane Chamberlain, *USA Today* bestselling author of *Pretending to Dance*

"A beautifully crafted page-turner . . . Part contemporary women's fiction, part historical novel, the plot moves seamlessly back and forth in time to unlock family secrets that bind four generations of women . . . This novel has it all."
— Barbara Claypole White, bestselling author of *Echoes of Family*

"Everything I love in a novel . . . Elegant and haunting."
— Erika Marks, author of *The Last Treasure*

"A book about love and loss and finding your way forward. I could not read it fast enough!"
— Anita Hughes, author of *Christmas in Paris*

"One of the best books out there, and Davis is genuinely proving herself to be one of the strongest new voices of epic romance."
— RT Book Reviews (4½ stars)

"Davis has a gift for developing flawed characters and their emotionally wrenching dilemmas . . . A very satisfying tale."
— Historical Novel Society

"A beautifully layered story."
— Karen White, *New York Times* bestselling author of *Flight Patterns*

THE
KEEPER
OF
HAPPY
ENDINGS

OTHER BOOKS BY BARBARA DAVIS

THE

KEEPER

OF

HAPPY

ENDINGS

BARBARA DAVIS

LAKE UNION
PUBLISHING

Text copyright © 2021 by Barbara Davis
All rights reserved.

Published by Lake Union Publishing, Seattle

www.apub.com

Amazon, the Amazon logo, and Lake Union Publishing are trademarks of Amazon.com, Inc., or its affiliates.

ISBN-13: 9781542021470
ISBN-10: 1542021472

Cover design by Faceout Studio, Tim Green

Printed in the United States of America

*This book is dedicated to the millions of health-care
workers around the world
who have risked their own personal safety
to care for our loved ones in 2020 and beyond—heroes,
each and every one.*

There are all sorts of heroes, and almost none of them will ever have something shiny pinned to their chests.

—Soline Roussel, the Keeper of Happy Endings

We are the chosen, handmaids of La Mère Divine, *descended from an ancient line, called upon to further the cause of love and true happiness. We are* les tisseuses de sorts . . . *the Spell Weavers.*

—Esmée Roussel, the Dress Witch

AUTHOR'S NOTE

Though this story features historical events, this is a work of fiction. Names, characters, organizations, events, dates, and incidents are products of my imagination or used fictitiously.

PROLOGUE

Soline

*Faith is the essential ingredient. If one loses
faith in la* magie, *one has lost everything.*

—Esmée Roussel, the Dress Witch

13 September 1976—Boston

I have always grieved the ends of things. The final notes of a song as
they ebb into silence. The curtain falling at the end of a play. The last
snowflake. Goodbyes.

So many goodbyes.

They all seem so long ago now, and yet the collective rawness still
chafes. I've had too much wine tonight, I think. It has made me morose.
Or perhaps I've simply had too much life, too much sadness—too many
scars. Still, I find myself drawn to those scars, a map of wounds that
takes me neither forward nor back.

I've brought the box down from the closet again and laid it on the
bed. It isn't heavy in the physical sense, but the memories inside carry a
different kind of weight, the kind that sits heavily on the heart.

It's made of sturdy stuff, thick gray cardboard with metal fittings at
the corners and a heavy cord threaded through as a handle. I hold my
breath as I lift the lid and fold back layers of crumpled tissue to gaze at

the dress within. It has aged over the years—like me. The packet of letters is there too—most in French, a few in English—tied with a length of ribbon. These I will read later, as I often do on nights like this, when the empty places in my life stretch like shadows all around me. There is an order to this ritual of mine, a sequence I never vary. When so much has been uprooted—so many things lost—one must seek comfort in rituals. Even the sad ones.

I lift out the dress and hold it in my arms, the way one holds a baby or a promise—close and perhaps a little too fiercely. I step to the mirror, and for an instant she looks back at me, the girl I was before Hitler came to Paris, full of hope and naive dreams. But an instant later, she's gone. In her place is the woman I've become. Worn and alone. Dreamless. My gaze slides back to the box, to the brown leather case lying at the bottom, and I feel my heart squeeze, remembering the first time I saw it. *For safekeeping,* he said as he pressed it into my hands on that last morning.

I unzip the case for the hundredth time, running my fingers over the tortoiseshell comb and matching shoehorn, the shaving brush and razor. Such personal things. And he'd given them to me. I remove the cut-glass flask from its band of brown elastic—long since empty—and unscrew the cap, yearning for a whiff of the bright, clean scent I've engraved on my memory. A blend of seawater and the peel of fresh limes.

Anson.

Only this time, for the first time, there is no hint of him. For thirty years I've been lifting this empty bottle to my nose, taking comfort in the only thing of him left to me—his scent. And now even that is gone.

I wait for tears, but none come. I suppose I'm beyond them now. Emptied. And perhaps it's just as well. I return the flask and zip the case closed. My eyes stray to the packet of letters, usually the final step in my sorry little ritual. I will not read them tonight. Or ever again, I think.

It's time to let go. Time to let it *all* go.

I return the shaving case to the box, then fold the dress and lay it inside, arranging the sleeves tenderly across the bodice—the way I've seen bodies laid out at funerals. Fitting, I suppose. I caress the fabric one last time, then fold the tissue over it all and lower the lid.

Adieu, Anson, mon amour. C'est la fin.

ONE

RORY

May 26, 1985—Boston

It couldn't be Sunday. Not already.

Rory smacked the snooze button and fell back onto her pillow, wishing the day away, but five minutes later the alarm shrilled again, which could mean only one thing. Somehow, another week had been swallowed whole, gone in a blur of takeout and old movies, interminable nights immersed in other people's happy endings.

A pulpy paperback thumped to the floor as she threw back the covers and put her feet on the floor. Kathleen Woodiwiss's *A Rose in Winter*, finished last night around 4:00 a.m. She stared at it, splayed open at her feet like a felled bird. She'd never been a fan of romance novels. Now she couldn't devour them fast enough, a guilty pleasure that made her vaguely ashamed, like gambling or a porn addiction.

She scooped up the novel and tossed it into a wicker basket filled with a dozen more just like it, waiting to be taken to Goodwill. There was another box by the front door and a third in her trunk. *Junk food for the brain,* her mother called them. But her eyes were already sliding to the stack of new titles on the nightstand. Tonight, Johanna Lindsey's latest awaited.

She poked through the jumble of unopened mail beside the bed, including the master's program course catalog she'd been doing her best to avoid, finally locating the steel-and-gold Rolex her mother had given her when she finished undergrad. As expected, it had stopped running, the date in the little magnifying bubble off by three days. She reset the time and slid it onto her wrist, then set her sights on a mug of strong coffee. No way was she facing today without caffeine.

In the kitchen, she eyed her surroundings with a creeping sense of overwhelm; the sink full of dishes, the brimming trash can, the remnants of last night's takeout from Eastern Paradise still sitting on the counter. She'd meant to tidy up after dinner, but then *Random Harvest* came on and she hadn't been able to tear herself away until Greer Garson and Ronald Colman were finally reunited. By the time she stopped blubbering, she'd forgotten about the kitchen. And now there wasn't time if she was going to make it across town by eleven.

She toyed with calling to cancel as she splashed half-and-half into her mug—a sore throat or a migraine, a messy case of food poisoning—but she'd already bailed twice this month, which meant she had to do this.

In the shower, she rehearsed for the grilling she knew was coming: questions about her studies, her hobbies, her plans for the future. The questions never changed, and it was getting harder and harder to pretend she cared about any of it. The truth was, she had no hobbies to speak of, dreaded the idea of returning to school, and her plans for the future were in serious doubt. But she would put on a brave face and say the right things, because that's what was expected of her. And because the alternative—a deep dive into the black hole that had become her life—was simply too exhausting to contemplate.

She padded to the bedroom, toweling her hair as she went, doing her best to resist the familiar pull from her nightstand. It was a ritual she'd begun of late, starting each day with one or two of Hux's letters, but there wasn't time this morning. And yet she found herself opening the bottom drawer, lifting out the box she kept there. Forty-three envelopes addressed in his thin, sprawling script, a lifeline tethering her to him, keeping her from hitting bottom.

The first had arrived in her mailbox just five hours after his flight left Logan. He'd sent it overnight delivery, to make sure it arrived on the right day. He'd written another while sitting at the gate and one more while on the plane. They'd come nearly every day at first before leveling off to one or two a week. And then they'd simply stopped coming.

She glanced at the photo beside the bed, taken at a restaurant on the cape the weekend after he'd proposed. Dr. Matthew Edward Huxley—Hux to everyone who knew him. She missed his face, his laugh, his silly jokes and off-key singing, his love of all things trivia and his perfect scrambled eggs.

They'd met at a charity event for Tufts' new neonatal intensive-care wing. His smile had made her go weak at the knees, but it was who he was underneath that smile that actually sealed the deal.

The child of two special needs teachers, he had learned the value of service early on and by example. But during his freshman year at UNC, a logging truck had jumped the median on I-40 and hit his parents' car head-on. He quit school after the funeral, rudderless and bitter, and spent a summer on the Outer Banks, playing beach bum with a pack of surfers and numbing himself with Captain Morgan.

Eventually, he'd pulled himself together, returning to UNC, then going on to medical school. His plan had been to specialize in internal medicine, but after one week of pediatric rounds, those plans had changed. When his residency was over, he had signed with Doctors Without Borders to provide care to children in South Sudan, as a way of honoring his parents' memory.

It was one of the things she loved most about him. His story was far from perfect; no trust fund or country-club upbringing for Matthew Huxley. He'd gone through some things—things that had rocked him to the core—but he'd found his footing and a way to give back. It was hard to see him off when the time came, but she was proud of the work he had committed to doing, even if his letters were difficult to read.

In one he'd admitted to taking up smoking. *Everyone here smokes like a fiend. Maybe to keep their hands from shaking. We're all so incredibly tired.* In another, he'd written about a journalist named Teresa who was there doing a story for the BBC and how she kept him connected to the outside world. He wrote about the work too, about endless days in makeshift surgeries, children maimed, orphaned, terrified. It was worse than he'd ever imagined, but it was making him a better doctor—tougher but more compassionate.

The pace was grueling, the emotional trauma more than he could adequately express on paper. *We're so spoiled in the US. We can't comprehend the sheer scope of lawlessness and barbarity, the gut-wrenching need that exists in other places. The lack of basic humanity. What we do, me, all of us, it's a drop in the bucket when you see what's happening here.*

That was the last one.

One week, two, a third passing with her own letters unanswered. And then one day she was listening to NPR and the reason became clear. The US was confirming that a band of armed rebels had abducted three workers in an early-morning raid in South Sudan, including an American physician, a nurse from New Zealand, and a British journalist on assignment for the BBC and *World* magazine.

It had taken several days to confirm what she already knew—that Hux was the captured American—but there were no leads. Nothing on the truck witnesses saw driving away. No description of the men who'd forced them out of the clinic at gunpoint. And not a word from anyone claiming responsibility, which typically happened in the first forty-eight hours. They had simply vanished.

Five months later, she was still waiting. According to the State Department, every resource was being brought to bear, every lead being followed, not that there'd been many. A late-night raid had been carried out on an abandoned shack in Libya eight weeks ago, after someone reported seeing a woman fitting the description of the missing journalist, but by the time they went in, the shack was empty, the occupants long gone.

The official line from the State Department was that they were *continuing to work with various humanitarian agencies to locate all personnel and secure their safe return*, but the truth was that information had dried up, meaning prospects for a positive outcome were growing more and more doubtful.

Rory stared at the box, longing to lift out one or two letters and crawl back into bed, but she had somewhere to be. Two somewheres, actually, if she counted her promise to meet Lisette this afternoon at Sugar Kisses.

Twenty minutes later, she grabbed her purse and keys, checking her reflection one last time. White slacks and a sleeveless button-down in pale peach silk. Damp hair scraped into a ponytail. A single coat of mascara, another of lip gloss, and simple diamond studs. Far from up to standard, but when it came to her mother, nothing ever was.

TWO

RORY

The aromas of blueberry scones and freshly ground coffee greeted Rory as she let herself in. She caught the whir of her mother's juicer from the kitchen as she kicked off her flats and stationed them near the door—facing out, in case she needed to beat a hasty retreat. Heaven knew, it wouldn't be the first time.

As usual, the house was immaculate, a study in monied good taste with its plush beige carpets and carefully matched furniture. And the correct art on the walls, of course—bowls of fruit and pitchers of over-blown poppies, hanging in heavy gilt frames. Not an item askew or a speck of dust to be seen.

It had looked like this even when she was little, thanks to her mother's militant rules about cleanliness. No shoes beyond the foyer. No hands on the walls. No food or drink beyond the dining room—unless there was a party. And there were plenty of parties. Tea parties, cocktail parties, dinner parties, and of course the fundraisers for her mother's pet charities, each catered to perfection, then painstakingly cleared by a crew of professionals kept on speed dial.

She found her mother in the kitchen, pouring fresh-squeezed orange juice into a cut-glass pitcher, her signature gold charm bracelet tinkling as she worked. She looked crisp and tidy in khakis and a starched white blouse, her heavy gold waves pulled back in a low *Town & Country* ponytail. As usual, her makeup was flawless, subtle eyes, lightly rouged cheeks, a hint of frosty peach gloss on her lips. At forty-two, she was still capable of turning heads.

She looked up when Rory entered. "There you are," she said, performing a quick but thorough inventory of her daughter. "I was beginning to think you weren't coming again. Is your hair wet?"

"I didn't have time to blow it out. What do you need me to do?"

"Everything's done, and I hope not cold." She handed Rory a plate of perfectly sliced melon and a bowl brimming with strawberries. "Take those out to the table. I'll bring the rest."

Rory took the fruit and headed for the terrace. It was a perfect morning, the sky a dizzying blue, the breeze ripe with the promise of an early summer. Below, Boston stretched in all directions, a jumble of crooked streets and tumbling rooftops. Storrow Drive with its endless ribbon of traffic, the Esplanade sprawling leafy and green, the shining stretch of the Charles River, dotted with bright little sailboats.

She adored the city with all its contradictions, its rich colonial history and vibrant melting-pot culture. Art, food, music, and science, all rubbing elbows and vying for attention. But there was something about seeing it like this, away from the bustle and noise, that had always felt a little magical when she was growing up, as if she might suddenly grow wings with which to fly away.

She used to dream of flying away a lot when she was a girl, of being someone else, living another life. One that was her own. A career that had nothing to do with her mother. A husband who was nothing like her father. She'd almost done it too.

Almost.

11

The word felt like a stone in her chest, the weight of it always with her, making simple tasks like going to the market or meeting a friend feel almost overwhelming. It wasn't normal, this need to retreat from the world. But it wasn't new either. She had always leaned toward the introverted end of the spectrum, doing her best to avoid dinner parties and other social events, not to mention the attention that came with being the daughter of one of Boston's most prominent social and philanthropic elites.

Never a hair out of place, never a faux pas made—that was Camilla Lowell Grant. The right clothes, the right home, the right art. The right everything, if you didn't count the chronically unfaithful husband and the intractable daughter. Still, Camilla bore her burdens admirably. Most of the time.

Rory took in the table as she set down the fruit plates. It looked like something out of *Victoria* magazine: crisp white islet laid with her grandmother's Royal Albert china, linen napkins flawlessly folded beside each place setting. And in the center, a bowl of waxy white gardenias—her mother's signature flower. Perfection, as usual.

The brunch tradition had begun on her twelfth birthday and had quickly become a weekly event. The menu varied from week to week— fresh fruit and some sort of pastry baked from scratch, toast points with smoked salmon and creamy Boursin cheese, flawlessly turned omelets made with whatever was in season, and the one constant: mimosas made with freshly squeezed orange juice and perfectly chilled Veuve Clicquot.

It was meant to be a time for catching up, but lately, their tête-à-têtes had become increasingly tense as her mother found new and not-so-subtle ways to suggest it might be time to move on with her life.

Rory fingered the ruby ring on her left hand, a small oval with a tiny nick at the bottom. It was the ring Hux's father had used to propose to his mother, all he'd been able to afford as a soldier returning from the Korean War. Hux had promised to take her shopping for a proper ring, but he'd wanted to use his mother's ring to actually pop the question. Touched by his sentimentality, she had opted to keep the original, thrilled that he would entrust her with something so precious. Now his mother's ring was all she had.

She pushed the thought away when Camilla appeared carrying two plates. "Mushroom and asparagus frittatas," she announced, setting down the plates with a flourish.

"It looks delicious," Rory said, taking her usual chair. Her mother had never been the domestic type, but she certainly knew her way around a kitchen.

Camilla slid several catalogs from beneath her arm and handed them to Rory before settling across from her. "They came last week, but you skipped out on brunch. I was tempted to tell the postwoman I didn't know anyone named Rory, but did she have anything for my daughter, Aurora."

Rory managed a dry smile. "You need some new material, Mother. That joke's getting old."

"Rory is a boy's name. *Your* name is Aurora. And it's a beautiful name. A lady's name."

"An *old* lady's name," Rory shot back. "And it was Daddy who shortened it. It obviously never bothered him."

Camilla responded with a huff. "You have to be *around* to be bothered."

Rory picked up her fork, poking listlessly at her frittata. It was true. Her father's interests had always lain elsewhere. She had no idea how many affairs there'd been, though she suspected her mother could provide an exact tally. She'd kept careful tabs on the women who moved in and out of Geoffrey Grant's life over the years, carefully adding each name to the collection, like quarters to a swear jar.

Why she'd never divorced him was beyond Rory, though she suspected the weekend at Doral with his twenty-eight-year-old receptionist might have proven the coup de grâce if he hadn't ended up dying in her bed first. It was the type of scandal from which most society wives never quite recovered, a cliché of the most delicious and disastrous variety, but for Camilla, it became the crown jewel in her collection of betrayals, a badge of honor, purchased with her pride.

"Aren't you eating?"

Rory picked up a strawberry, nibbling dutifully. Camilla had pulled the bottle of Veuve from the ice and was wrestling with the cork. After a few minutes, Rory reached across the table and took the bottle from her. "Let me have that before you take out someone's eye."

The cork came free with a hollow pop. Rory poured champagne into a pair of flutes and topped both with a splash of orange juice.

They touched glasses wordlessly, out of habit, then turned their attention to the food. Camilla did most of the talking, with only a minimum of input required on Rory's part. Gossip about plastic surgery and rumored divorces. A friend's upcoming trip to Ireland. What was coming to the Boston Opera House next season. The theme for the holiday charity ball she was organizing again this year. Eventually the small talk ran out and the conversation wandered into familiar if uncomfortable territory.

"I ran into Dinah Marshall the other day when I was dropping off my watch to be repaired. Denise, her youngest, is heading to Boston College in the fall. She's going to study music. The harp, I think. I told her you were back to Tufts in August to finish up your master's. And then perhaps on to Paris next summer for that internship we talked about. She asked me to pass along her congratulations."

"Denise plays the piano," Rory answered flatly. "Patricia plays the harp."

"Yes, of course. Piano." Camilla lifted her napkin, dabbing daintily at her mouth. "And what about you? Are you excited about going back?"

Rory reached for the champagne bottle and topped off her glass, forgoing the orange juice this time. She sipped slowly, then raised her eyes to her mother. "I'm not excited about anything."

Camilla sighed as she slid a scone onto her plate. "Are you pouting, Aurora?"

"I'm twenty-three years old, Mother. I don't pout."

"Really? What do you call what's happening now?"

Rory put down her mimosa and sat up very straight. "We haven't seen each other in three weeks. Were you not even going to ask about Hux?"

Camilla blinked at her. "Of course I was."

"When? We've finished breakfast. We've talked about Vicky Foster's face-lift, the appalling food in the UK, your plans for the holiday ball, and Dinah Marshall's daughter going back to school. Yet you couldn't find time to slip my fiancé's name into the conversation."

"Really, you can't expect me to just blurt out something like that over breakfast."

"What does breakfast have to do with it?"

The corners of Camilla's mouth turned down in a nearly perfect pout. "I was being delicate."

"Delicate?" The word set Rory's teeth on edge, as if good table manners were an excuse for not giving a damn. "I don't need you to be delicate, Mother. I need you to care. But you don't. You never have."

Camilla's eyes widened. "What a thing to say."

"You never liked him. From day one, you acted like he was some phase I'd grow out of, the way you hoped I'd grow out of liking soccer."

"That isn't true."

"It absolutely is. You didn't like his looks, or his surfing, or the fact that he left private practice. But the real problem is you don't like that he's from a little beach town in North Carolina that no one's ever heard of. That his parents taught high school instead of organizing card games and dinner parties."

There it was, her mother's patented look of indignation—the squared shoulders and tilted chin, the cool glare aimed straight down her perfect patrician nose. "That's an awful thing to imply."

"I didn't imply it. I said it straight out. Most mothers would consider someone like Hux a great catch, but not you. You want someone with the right last name and a *Mayflower* sticker on their steamer trunk, and now that Hux is missing, you see the chance for a do-over. Though I'm not sure why you think your marital track record qualifies you to choose anyone else's husband."

Camilla went still, her face frozen, as if she'd received a slap she hadn't seen coming.

"I'm sorry," Rory blurted. "I didn't mean—"

"Of course you did."

Rory blew out a breath, angry with herself for striking such a low blow. "I'm sorry. I was just lashing out and you got in the way."

Camilla's expression morphed into one of concern. "Has there been . . . news?"

"No. No news. Never mind. I don't want to talk about it."

"Then what *do* you want to talk about? I have no idea what's happening in your life these days. You don't return my phone calls. You turn down my invitations for dinner. You've skipped brunch two weeks in a row. What have you been up to?"

Rory stared into her glass, her throat suddenly thick. "Waiting, mostly."

"Sweetheart . . ." Camilla reached across the table, brushing Rory's bangs out of her eyes.

"Don't," Rory snapped, jerking her head away. "I don't want you to feel sorry for me."

"Then what do you want? I'm worried about you. You spend your days with your nose buried in one of those awful books or glued to the television, watching some old black-and-white tearjerker until all hours. We talked about this. It isn't healthy."

"I'm fine. I just . . ." She looked away, wanting desperately not to be having this discussion again. "I just need time."

"Sweetheart, it's been five months."

Rory shot her a look. "I wasn't aware that there was a time limit."

"That isn't what I meant. I only mean that whatever has happened to Matthew, whether he's alive somewhere or—" She broke off, as if weighing her next words carefully. "You're still here, Aurora. Still alive. You have to go on, no matter what."

Rory swallowed the sting of tears. She wanted to believe Hux was alive somewhere, that he would come home to her one day, but the dread was always there, like an invisible hand hovering at her shoulder. Would tomorrow be the day she got the news? How would it happen? A letter? A phone call? Would someone knock on her door? She'd never screwed up the courage to ask. Asking would have made it too real, and it was already real enough.

"What if I can't go on?" she asked quietly.

"Don't be silly. Of course you can. It's what the Grants do."

Rory smothered a sigh, wishing she could make her understand. "I just don't care. About anything." She looked at her mother, so cool and well groomed, unflappable. "You have no idea what that's like, do you? To wake up in the morning and not have the will to put your feet on the floor, to shower and dress and go out into the world where everywhere you look, life is galloping off without you. You've never lost someone you cared about. And don't say Daddy. We both know it's not the same thing."

Camilla opened her mouth, then closed it again, as if rethinking her initial response. "You have no idea what I've lost, Aurora," she said finally.

Rory narrowed her eyes, surprised by Camilla's cryptic tone. There was so much about her mother's life she didn't know. So much she'd sealed off or refused to talk about. "*Was* there someone?" she asked softly. "Someone before Daddy?"

"I was eighteen when I married your father. There wasn't time for anyone else."

"Okay, then. Not before. But later . . . during?"

Camilla stared at her, aghast. "Certainly not!"

"Then *what*? What don't I know?"

Camilla waved a hand, clearly ready to change the subject. "Nothing. It doesn't matter now. But for the record, mothers are human too. We've had lives and been disappointed. We bleed like everyone else. But we have responsibilities, duties to fulfill and appearances to maintain. And so we keep moving forward."

"Except I can't see forward. I can't see anything. It's like the future's just . . . gone."

"You need to get out, Aurora, to be around people. There's a cocktail thing happening at Marcos next week. One of Cassandra Maitland's private dos for some new cellist she's discovered. Why don't you come with me? We could go to Rosella for hair and nails in the morning, get those bangs of yours trimmed, then pick up something fun for you to wear. There's nothing like a good splurge before a party to lift your spirits. And it'll do you good to see some of the old crowd, to feel normal again."

Rory eyed her coolly. "Normal?"

"Please don't look at me like that. You can't just keep hiding. I'm worried about you. Maybe it's time . . . to talk to someone?"

Rory stiffened. "You think I'm crazy?"

Camilla folded her napkin carefully before setting it aside. "I think you're having trouble coping with what's happened, and that talking to someone about it might be helpful." She paused, then added gently, "Someone you trust."

Rory sat quietly, absorbing the sting of her mother's words. "I'm sorry," she said finally. "About before and what I said. It's just . . . Hux." Her throat tightened around his name. "I spent two hours on the phone again Friday, most of it on hold. It's always the same runaround. *We're doing everything in our power.* But it isn't true. How *can* it be when they don't even know where he is?"

Camilla responded with another of her customary huffs. "How is that even possible? Surely we have people who specialize in this sort of thing. Ambassadors. Diplomats. The president, for heaven's sake."

A familiar stone lodged in Rory's chest, the same stone that always lodged there when she let herself think about the unthinkable. "It's starting to feel like he isn't coming back."

"Hush, now," Camilla said, reaching for her hand. "None of that talk. You must keep your chin up and be brave."

Rory gulped back a flood of tears, recalling her freshman year of high school, when she'd vowed never to show her face in school again after failing to make the swim team. Camilla had wrapped her up tightly, whispering those same words against her ear. *You must keep your chin up and be brave.* But she didn't feel brave. She felt numb. Lost and exhausted.

"I read somewhere that the longer he's missing, the lower the odds of him being found alive." She reclaimed her hand to wipe her eyes. "I'm starting to lose hope."

"Stop that, now. I mean it. You mustn't dwell on such thoughts. You'll feel better when school starts in the fall and you're back to your old routine. Classes and activities with your friends. It'll help fill your time."

Rory thought of the class catalog on her nightstand and nodded, because it was what was expected of her. A stiff upper lip and back to school to finish her MFA, then the internship if her mother had her way, perhaps a curator position someday. So different from the future she and Hux had planned when his time with DWB was over.

"You know," Camilla said hesitantly, "I was thinking it might be a good idea for you to move back home until things are . . . settled. It's just me rattling around the house now, and your room is just like you left it."

"Move back home?"

"I could look after you, cook for you. You wouldn't have to worry about anything but your studies."

Studies. School. The meeting with Lisette!

"Oh no. What time is it?" Rory glanced at her watch. "I have to go."

"What—now?"

"Janelle Turner's little sister signed up for summer session, and I promised I'd meet her to drop off a couple of my old textbooks."

"Today? When you knew we were having brunch?"

"I know. I'm sorry. But she's got to be in Braintree by three for her parents' anniversary party, and classes start tomorrow. It was the only time we could make it work."

"But you barely ate anything. At least let me fix you a plate."

"Thanks," Rory said, pushing to her feet. "I'm good. But I hate to leave you with all this."

"It's not like I have anything else to do. Will I see you next week?"

Something, the crease between Camilla's finely penciled brows or the downward turn of her mouth, tugged at Rory's conscience. "Yes. Next Sunday. I promise." She was about to leave when she bent down and dropped a kiss on her mother's cheek. "I really am sorry about before. About the marriage thing. I shouldn't have said it."

Camilla shrugged. "No, you shouldn't have. But you weren't wrong. Now go. Meet your friend."

THREE

RORY

Rory glanced at her watch as she stepped out of Sugar Kisses and into the crush of pedestrians moving along the sidewalk on Newbury Street. Her meeting with Lisette had taken longer than expected, and she'd have to hoof it if she was going to get to her car in time to avoid a parking ticket.

At the corner, as she waited for the signal to change, her thoughts turned to this morning's conversation with her mother. She'd said things she promised herself she would never say—even if they *were* true—and she had touched a nerve.

But it wasn't just her mother's indignation that had piqued her curiosity. There had been a moment while she was talking about Hux, about what it was like to lose someone, when her mother had closed her eyes and gone perfectly still, as if warding off an unwelcome memory. A rare moment of vulnerability from a woman who was never vulnerable.

We bleed like everyone else.

Except in Camilla Grant's case, it wasn't really true. At least not that Rory'd ever seen. When she was a child, her mother had seemed to be carved of marble, pure and fine and cool to the touch, Hiram Powers's *The Greek Slave* but with the bronze spine of Rodin's *Eve*. Impervious—or so she'd thought. But that moment this morning, that look on her face. *You have no idea what I've lost, Aurora.* What had she meant? Not a lover, apparently. Not that she would have blamed her mother for seeking comfort outside her marriage. She couldn't remember her parents sharing a room, let alone a bed. How lonely she must have been.

Finally, the signal changed, and the crowd at the curb began to shuffle forward. She was preparing to step into the crosswalk when an old row house on the opposite corner caught her eye and she halted.

As row houses went, it was nothing special—three stories of weathered red brick with a rounded corner tower and a witch-hat turret overlooking the road. Newbury Street was lined with dozens just like it. For that matter, so were half the streets in Boston. But there was something about this one that felt different enough to stop her in her tracks.

Curtainless windows filmed with grit. An overgrown strip of grass out front. Bits of trash blown up around the cracked front stoop. It was vacant; she was sure of it. And yet, she had the strangest feeling that she was being watched from one of the upper windows.

She was contemplating a closer look when a passing police car reminded her that six blocks away, the meter was running. She didn't have time to indulge her curiosity. But as she continued down Newbury Street, she found herself glancing over her shoulder with a pang of regret. It was a peculiar sensation, like leaving a party just as things were getting interesting. Something told her the row house wasn't finished with her yet.

It was nearly four by the time Rory finally returned home. She had narrowly avoided a parking ticket, which she decided to take as a good omen. These days, she had to take her wins where she found them. She took off her makeup, then stripped out of her brunch clothes, swapping them for sweats and a T-shirt. The bedroom TV was on, as it always was, but with the sound turned way down. Cary Grant and Katharine Hepburn. *Bringing Up Baby.* It was another quirk she'd developed, leaving the television on day and night. It gave the illusion of company and helped buffer the silence, which was too easily filled with dark thoughts.

I think you're having trouble coping with what's happened.

Her mother's words echoed annoyingly. Of course she was having trouble coping. Her fiancé had vanished without a trace. And pouring out her troubles to a stranger who mumbled, *"Yes, I see,"* at regular intervals wasn't going to change that.

In the kitchen, she worked around discarded takeout containers and a sink full of dirty dishes as she popped a bowl of canned minestrone into the microwave. Was this her life now? Living on canned soup and takeout while the dishes piled up? Stacks of romance novels and weekly skirmishes with her mother?

If she wasn't careful, she'd end up like one of those women whose entire life revolved around the care and feeding of her eighteen cats. Hyperbole? Maybe. But it certainly wasn't out of the realm of possibility. She'd need to get some cats, though. And a few floral-print housedresses. Maybe a pair of fuzzy slippers.

She closed her eyes, shutting out the depressing images. She'd grown up privileged, the quintessential trust-fund baby. Cars, clothes, designer everything. Elite summer camps and the very best schools. She'd wanted for nothing—except a life of her own. Growing up, she had dreamed about escaping her mother's gravitational pull to chart a course of her own. And she'd been on the verge of making it happen. Then Hux disappeared, and it all fell apart.

Where would she be today—this very minute—if she'd followed through on Hux's advice to chase her dream? A gallery of her own, for up-and-coming artists. Unheard Of, she was going to call it. Hux had been the impetus behind the name. In fact, the whole idea had been his.

They'd gone to hear a new band at one of the local pubs and ended up staying till last call. The streets were quiet, and they'd opted to walk rather than hail a cab. Hux had curled an arm about her shoulder, his warmth welcome against the chilly autumn night. She'd slowed as they passed a small gallery, pausing to admire one of the pieces in the window.

"You like art," Hux had observed, sounding unusually serious. "You study art. Your degree is in art. How is it you don't *make* art?"

She grinned up at him mischievously. "Who says I don't?"

"Wait. You paint?"

"Paint? No. I've experimented a little with textiles, but just as a hobby. Just as well. Art can be a messy business, and my mother could never abide a mess in the house. If she has her way, I'll follow in her footsteps and become a historian or conservator. Respectable and tidy."

"And if you had *your* way?"

She blinked at him, dismayed to realize he was waiting for an answer, and even more dismayed to realize she didn't have one. No one had ever asked what *she* wanted. She'd been given options, from her mother mostly, like a menu for Chinese takeout. Choose one from column A and one from column B. Column A being marriage to a *suitable* man, children, and a tasteful home, and Column B having to do with her career. Strictly speaking, none of the Grants had to work, but in families with old names and even older money, not making oneself useful in some conspicuous way was considered vulgar. They weren't from Palm Beach, after all.

"I really don't know," she'd answered at last. "I suppose I'd have a little studio somewhere. A real one overlooking the sea, and I'd make beautiful seascapes out of all kinds of fabrics."

"That's an actual thing?"

"It's called textile art. Think of a combination of sculpture and painting, done with bits of fabric. I started playing around with it when I was a kid. I loved the beach, but my parents never had time to take

24

me. So I made my own beaches—out of fabric scraps. I still play around with it sometimes, but with school, it's hard to find the time."

"Why didn't I know anything about this?"

She shrugged, suddenly shy. "It's just a hobby."

He'd pulled her close, pressing a kiss to her forehead. "You, Rory Grant, are full of surprises." They'd begun to walk again, her hand tucked into his jacket pocket. "So why haven't I ever seen any of your work? I don't recall seeing anything like what you just described hanging in your apartment."

"There's one in the spare room. And a few more in the closet."

"The spare room you won't let me go into?"

"Because it's a mess. I used to use it as a studio when I was selling them."

He stopped walking and turned to face her. "I thought you said it was just a hobby."

She shrugged. "It is—or was. Like I said, no time. But a friend took some pictures once and showed them to an interior designer she knows. He took seven pieces on consignment and sold them in two weeks."

"Aha! Another piece of the story emerges. So when do I get a look? Or don't I rate?"

His enthusiasm sent little whorls of pleasure dancing in Rory's chest. She was usually squeamish about mentioning her art, but it felt good to have someone take her seriously. "If you're really interested I can arrange a private showing—unless you're in a hurry to get home."

"What? Now?"

She reached for his hand. "Come with me."

Fifteen minutes later, they were standing in front of Finn's, one of Boston's most exclusive seafood restaurants, gazing at a beautifully lit seascape in the front window.

She stood quietly, trying to see the piece as Hux would—for the first time. A torturous sea and rock-strewn shore, a low, leaden sky. She had chosen the fabrics with painstaking care. Watered silk and bits of crushed taffeta, denim and twill and crepe de chine, tulle and foamy bits of lace, carefully layered to create a sense of movement and depth.

It had taken nearly six months to finish and had fetched a whopping $700. Not that she cared about the money. Unlike most artists, she had that luxury. For her, what mattered was that it was hanging in the window of a prominent restaurant, her initials in the lower right-hand corner, for all of Boston to see.

"You really did this?" he asked, his eyes still riveted to the window. "It's incredible. It feels like I could walk right into those waves. And the sky . . ." His face was half in shadow when he finally turned to look at her, but the half she could see was smiling. "Rory, this is more than just a hobby. It's a gift. Were they all like this one?"

"Similar, but this is my favorite. It's called *North of November*."

"I still can't believe it. You should have pieces in galleries all over town."

She laughed. "If only."

"What?"

"You don't just *put* your work in a gallery, Hux. Especially if you're a nobody. A new artist has a better chance of winning the lottery than getting into a decent show. In fact, I'm pretty sure the only reason this one ended up here is because my last name is Grant. The owner thought it would ingratiate him with my mother. He certainly read that one wrong."

"Your mother isn't supportive of your art?"

"That's the problem. She doesn't see it as art. At least not proper art."

"What is *proper* art?"

"The masters. Rembrandt. Raphael. Caravaggio."

"They've all been dead for hundreds of years."

"Exactly."

He frowned, shaking his head. "So you have to be dead for your work to be worthy? That hardly seems fair."

"It's not. But there we are. Unless you've sold well at auction, no one wants to take a chance on your work. If I had my way, I'd see to it that there were galleries dedicated entirely to artists no one's ever heard of."

"Would you?"

"Yes."

"Then open one. Right here in Boston."

She stared at him as the idea began to take shape. A showcase for artists no one had ever heard of. She had no idea how to go about it, and her mother would absolutely hate the idea. Still, it was hard to ignore the sudden flutter of excitement she felt at the thought.

"Do you really think I could?"

"Why not? You have the resources, the connections, the dream."

"What if that's all it is? A dream?"

He'd wound an arm around her shoulder, pulling her close enough to drop a kiss on the top of her head. "Dreams are like waves, babe. You have to wait for the right one to come along, the one that has your name on it. And then when it does, you have to get up and ride it. This dream has your name all over it."

She'd believed it then. But did she still?

Her dream of being a textile artist had actually begun as a fetish for vintage clothing. Not because she loved clothes. She'd never cared about fashion. It was fabric that captivated her, the way it moved and felt and behaved. Watered silks and pebbly knits, crisp organdy, diaphanous lace, nubby tweeds and lamb-soft worsteds, each with a texture and personality all its own.

Her first attempt had been crude and unsophisticated, but a passion for creation had already found its way into her blood, driving her to perfect her craft with practice and new techniques. What had started as a fetish had become a quiet obsession, resulting in a series of pieces dubbed the Storm Watch Collection.

Her mother had referred to them as her arts and crafts projects, but the owner of the interior design shop had been enthusiastic enough to put several pieces in his window. By summer's end, he'd sold the entire collection, including the one hanging in the window of Finn's.

When the call came that *North of November* had sold and would hang in a public place, she was so excited that she'd burst into her mother's study without knocking. Camilla had smiled indulgently at the news, declaring herself not a bit surprised. It was a pretty piece, and tourists loved that sort of thing. She hadn't meant to be condescending, but the remark stung more than Rory ever let on. After that, she'd worked less and less on her art. Until Hux had rekindled her creative flame with talk of a gallery. But when he disappeared, the flame had gone out.

By the time the microwave dinged, Rory had lost interest in her soup. Instead, she headed for the spare room she had set up as a makeshift studio. She hadn't set foot inside since Hux vanished, too frantic to work at first and then later, unable to look at anything that reminded her of him.

The room felt smaller than she remembered, cluttered and a little overwhelming, with the faint tang of fabric glue still hanging in the air. A desk strewn with art supply catalogs occupied one corner; an easel used for sketching filled another. Shelves piled with fabric swatches lined one wall, and under the window sat the secondhand Bernina she'd bought early on but rarely used after discovering she preferred hand stitching. All collecting dust now.

Her eyes slid to the unframed piece behind the desk—an enormous wave purling around the eastern wall of a stoic granite lighthouse. It was her personal favorite, inspired by a photo she'd seen once and never forgotten. She had titled it *Fearless*, because that's how it felt. Stoic and indomitable.

There were four more in the closet, part of the new collection she'd been working on when Hux disappeared. Not long ago—had it really only been five months?—she'd imagined them hanging on a gallery wall—on *her* gallery wall. Now she couldn't imagine anything.

Moving deeper into the room, she stood before two large needle-work frames, where a pair of unfinished pieces had languished for months. She ran her fingers over one, recalling the hours of felting required to create each whirl and eddy. She wouldn't finish them now. School would start in the fall, and there wouldn't be time. And there really wasn't much point.

Out of nowhere, the row house on Newbury Street sprang to mind. It had been such a peculiar moment—as if she'd felt a tap on her shoulder and turned to find an old friend standing there. It was nothing like the cold, angular places she'd looked at last year, but suddenly she knew it would be perfect for the gallery, brimming with history and old Boston charm and, once filled with the kind of pieces she envisioned, the perfect marriage of old and new.

Unheard Of.

The name, like a whisper, seemed to stir to life, like a thing coming awake after a heavy sleep. Was she actually considering this? Moving forward with plans she'd laid to rest months ago? And what about Hux? Was it selfish to contemplate such a thing while his life—their lives *together*—still hung in the balance? But she could feel it, the plans she believed long dead, slowly coming to life.

This dream has your name all over it.

Before she could check the impulse, she opened the desk drawer, shuffling through the contents until she found a business card for Brett Gleason, the real estate agent she'd hired last year to scout properties. She stared at it, wrestling with the urge to pick up the phone. What harm could there be in checking it out? It wasn't like it would amount to anything; there wasn't even a sign up. It was simply a matter of satisfying her curiosity, she told herself as she picked up the phone and punched in the number.

~

Two days later, Brett called back with information. Rory was carrying a plate of scrambled eggs to the living room when the phone rang. She froze, as she did any time the phone rang now. Was this it? Was there news? She set down the plate, ran her eyes around the room, looking for the cordless. Her heart was pounding by the time she found it.

"Hello?"

"Hey, it's Brett."

The breath went out of her at the sound of his voice. "I didn't expect to hear from you this soon. Were you able to find out anything?"

"I did, as a matter of fact. According to city records, the property is owned by one Soline Roussel. Apparently, she operated a bridal shop there until it burned a few years back. They gutted it after the fire, right down to the lath, started renovations but never finished. It's been empty ever since. No recent MLS listings, though, which means she probably isn't looking to unload it. It's odd that she'd let it sit empty rather than leasing it. With a little work, the place could be a real cash cow."

Rory sagged onto the couch, grappling with possible responses. Just how far did she want to take this?

"Rory? You still there?"

"Yes, I'm here."

"Are you really thinking about doing this?"

"I don't know. Maybe."

"Well then, this is great news. I always thought it was a great idea. But after all the places we looked at last summer, why this one?"

"I don't know. I saw it and I just knew. It was like it was sitting there, waiting for me."

"One of those women's intuition things?"

"Yeah, I guess. Would you be willing to contact her about a possible lease?"

There was a brief stretch of silence, the sound of a phone ringing in the background. "I can certainly do that," Brett replied finally. "But I've got to be straight with you. We scouted at least twenty properties, and you passed on every one of them. If I'm going to go sleuthing around and lean on this woman, I need to know you're actually ready to move."

It was a fair statement and absolutely true. She had turned down every property he'd shown her. Not because she couldn't have made them work or because she was squeamish about committing but because none of them had felt right. But this one—a building she'd never noticed until yesterday and had never set foot in—did.

"Rory?"

"I'm ready to move."

FOUR

SOLINE

*We may forsake The Work, but The Work will
never forsake us. It will fight to keep us, throwing itself into our path, again and again, until
at long last, we pay attention. This is what it
means to be chosen.*

—*Esmée Roussel, the Dress Witch*

29 May 1985—Boston

I'm startled when my phone rings at precisely 8:00 a.m. I don't get
calls anymore, or at least not many, and when I do, they seldom come
before I've finished my coffee. I let the phone ring as I fill the carafe and
push down the plunger of the press, hoping whoever it is will hang up.
There's no one I want to talk to.

The phone keeps ringing. I lift up the receiver and immediately
hang it up. Seconds later, it rings again. I hang up again, without a
word, hoping whoever it is will get the message and leave me alone.
When it begins to ring a third time, I snatch the receiver from its cradle.

"I don't want to buy anything!"

I am about to slam the receiver back down when I catch a sharp
bark of laughter. It's a familiar sound and a surprisingly pleasant one,

even at this uncaffeinated time of day. My solicitor, and friend too, I suppose, who I've not spoken to in months.

"Daniel Ballantine—is that you?"

"Yes, it's me. And I'm not calling to get you to buy anything. I'm calling to ask if you're interested in *selling* something. Or to be more specific, leasing something."

"What are you talking about?"

"I had a call last night. We've had an inquiry on the Fairfield property."

I feel as though a blast of cold air has just hit the back of my neck. "Someone wants my shop?"

There's a pause, the polite but uncomfortable sort. "Well, it hasn't been a shop for years now, but someone's interested in your building, yes."

"Who?"

"The agent didn't mention his client by name, but if the guy found me, he's obviously done his homework. Brett Gleason's his name, with Back Bay Land Group. They've asked for a sit-down."

"It's not for sale *or* lease."

Daniel makes the noise he makes when he's frustrated with me, half grunt, half sigh. "Soline, it's been three years—more than three, actually—and we both know reopening isn't in the cards. The fire caused a lot of damage, and what with everything . . ."

Everything.

I hold out my free hand, palm up, staring at it. The shiny pink skin, mottled with bits of waxy white, the slight clawlike curling of the fingers. The other hand, the one holding the phone, is a little better, but not much, the result of second-degree burns sustained when a cigarette I left burning set my bridal shop on fire. There were splints, physical therapy, a series of grueling surgeries. More splints. Followed by more therapy. Until the doctors all agreed there was nothing more to be done.

"You mean my hands?" I say quietly.

"I mean everything, Soline. You came here alone and worked your ass off, built a name for yourself out of nothing. People will never forget the name Roussel and what it stood for. But you're retired now. Why leave the place sitting empty? We're talking top dollar in the current leasing market."

"I don't need the money."

"No. You certainly don't. But you don't need the memories either. Maybe it's time to let go of them and move on."

His words touch off a spark in me. "You think that's all it will take? I sign a contract, someone else moves in, and it all goes away?"

Daniel sighs. "I didn't mean it like that. I know what you've been through and that there are reasons you're reluctant to let go. But you wouldn't *be* letting it go. Not completely. Though, truthfully, I'm not sure holding on is serving you at this point."

I scowl at the coffee press, cursing him under my breath. Why did he have to call now, when I've been doing so well pretending to be numb? "I don't want to talk about this now."

"Just promise me you'll think about it."

I heave a sigh, weary of being hectored. "All right."

"All right, you'll lease it?"

"All right, I'll think about it."

"I'll call you tomorrow."

"Not tomorrow," I snap. "The day after."

"All right. The day after."

I hang up the phone and go back to my cold coffee. I have to start over now. I remove the plunger and toss the tepid slop into the sink. I know Daniel has my best interests at heart, and not only because I pay him to. But there are parts of my story even he doesn't know, parts I have put away for good. And after so many years, what does it matter? People like me—like the Roussels—are a dying breed, our gifts of little value to a world that no longer believes in *la magie*.

For generations, my family has been part of a kind of *conte de fée*—a fairy tale. Though perhaps *fairy tale* is the wrong term. Fairy tales have happy endings. Fables are meant as cautionary tales, lessons intended to teach us about life and its consequences. And over the years, the Roussels have learned much about consequences.

There are many names for what we are. Gypsies, hexers, white witches, and shamans. In England we're called *cunning folk*, though I've always hated the term. Perhaps because it conjures thoughts of slick-handed cheats, waiting to separate the unsuspecting passerby from the few pennies in his pocket, the charlatans with their phony magic and vulgar showmanship, making up fortunes and doling out platitudes. We are not those people. For us, The Work is sacred, a vocation.

In France, where I come from, we are *les tisseuses de sort*—Spell Weavers—which is at least closer to the truth. We possess certain skills, talents with things like charms and herbs, cards and stones—or in our case, needle and thread. There are not many of us left these days, or at least not many who depend on *the craft* for their living. But there are a few still, if one knows where to look. And for a time, I was one of them, like my mother and her mother before her, living in the narrow, twisty lanes of Paris discreetly known as the craft district.

We were the Roussels, a family of dressmakers—bridal designers to be precise—but with a particular specialty. The bride who wears a Roussel gown on her wedding day is guaranteed a happy ending. We are the chosen, or so the story goes. Handmaidens of *La Mère Divine*—the Divine Mother. And like all handmaidens, we're meant to be content with our solitary lot, to sacrifice our happiness in service to others. Like the holy Catholic sisters, the black-and-whites as *Tante* Lilou called them, we are taught from a tender age that happy endings are for other people.

A gift, *Maman* claimed, though looking back, I'm not convinced it was ever worth the price. And yes, there was a price. With *magie*, something must always be rendered. And the Roussels have learned only too well the price for disobedience.

A *maléfice*—a curse passed down through the generations—because one of us, some foolish Roussel whose name has long been forgotten, once used *la magie* to steal another woman's husband, breaking the first tenet of our creed: do no harm.

A myth, probably, though I suspect like all myths, some thread of truth runs through it. And a thing repeated often enough takes on a truth of its own, like the steady drip of water carves its way through stone. And so the curse has been drilled into us, into my mother and hers, and hers before that, warning us against the unhappy fate of those who have strayed from their calling. Our hearts are to remain locked up tight, closed to temptations that might cause us to forget our true purpose—to ensure the happiness of others. So goes the Roussel catechism. But the heart often demands its own way, and the Roussels have fallen prey to both love and its consequences.

Superstition, some might say. But I've seen the evidence myself, or at least heard of it. Giselle, my mother's mother, deserted by her failed-artist husband after giving birth to a second daughter. *Tante* Lilou, widowed when her handsome Brit husband rolled his car into a ditch the day they returned from honeymooning in Greece. *Maman*, abandoned by her mysterious young lover when she turned up pregnant. And me, of course. But that is a story for another time.

For now, let us return to *The Work. Maman* called it sacred, a vocation carved into our hearts long before we were born. That, too, is like the Catholic sisters, I suppose, though we take no formal vows. Our name is our vow. Our blood is our vow. Our work—charms painstakingly sewn into the seam of a white silk gown—is our vow. And we are well paid for our work.

In Paris, where fashion and name-dropping go hand in hand, we were relative nobodies. The name Roussel wasn't likely to be heard in the fashionable salons, where the *bon ton* sipped champagne and nibbled *tarte tropézienne*. Such distinctions were reserved for the likes of Chanel, Lanvin, and Patou. But in the more discreet corners of the city, where women with certain skills were paid to keep other women's secrets, *Maman*, born Esmée Roussel, daughter of Giselle Roussel, was known as *La Sorcière de la Robe*.

The Dress Witch.

The name passed to her when my *grand-mère* died and was to be mine when *Maman* finally laid down her needle. But it wasn't a name I ever wanted for myself. I had inherited my mother's gift with a needle and far exceeded her abilities in design, but I could never match her when it came to spell work. I had no patience for such things. Because my thoughts—my *dreams*—lay elsewhere.

Maman did her best to rid me of them. She was a harsh taskmaster, quick to scold and slow to praise. To her, I was selfish and ungrateful, a wildling who would come to harm one day if I didn't stop my silly dreaming and bend myself to my calling. *Un rêveur*, she would bark when my mind would wander and the distraction came out in my hands. *Daydreamer.* I deserved it, of course. I was a daydreamer. As starry-eyed and fanciful as any young girl should be.

And like any other young girl, I kept my dreams in a book. Not the one I used to record *Maman*'s teachings but an entirely different sort of book. One with blank white pages just waiting to be filled with my very own designs. Pages and pages of clothes I would create one day and put my name on. Dresses and suits and stunning evening gowns in every color of the rainbow. Ocher and azure and aubergine.

Such were the colors of my girlhood dreams. Alas, we women seldom get the life we would choose for ourselves. Instead, our lot is chosen *for* us, by those who claim to know best, and before we know it, we've been shaped into someone we don't recognize, remade in someone else's image. For the Roussels, this is especially true.

For seventy years, we kept a salon in the Rue Legendre, with a small apartment above for living. It wasn't much as salons go, small but smart, with shuttered windows and a purple door to distinguish it from its neighbors. Purple is the color of our kind, the color of *la magie*—of magick. We could have afforded to put on a better show, a fancy sign or smart canvas awnings, but our clients valued discretion almost as much as they valued *Maman*'s gift with a needle. And who could blame them? No woman—a French one least of all—wants it known that she requires help with *les choses de cœur*. Many did require it, though. Still, many *were* turned away, deemed a poor match with their chosen grooms and therefore ill-suited for a binding.

One did not simply walk in off the street and commission a gown from *Maman*. To become a Roussel bride, three things were required: a referral from a previous client, a vow of discretion, and absolute honesty. And even then there was no guarantee that the prospective bride would be found worthy. There was a process, tests that must be passed, questions asked and answered, and of course the readings, all of which took place in *Maman*'s little sitting room at the back of the shop.

The would-be client would arrive at the appointed time. Alone. Never with her mother in tow. A tray of refreshments always awaited—a plate of biscuits and sweet dark chocolate served in thin china cups. The bride would settle into her chair with her refreshments. *Maman* would smile her disarming smile over the rim of her cup, and the questions would begin.

How long have you known your young man? How did you meet? Does his mother approve of you? Does yours approve of him? Have you discussed having children? Have the two of you been intimate? Does he please you physically? Has he ever been unfaithful to you? Have you been unfaithful to him?

Occasionally, they would try to lie, but it did them no good. *Maman* could smell a lie before it left someone's mouth. And the price of a lie was to be turned away.

After the questions, she would move on to the true test. The women were instructed to bring a personal article of their own to the interview and also one belonging to their fiancés: a hairbrush or a ring, something each used and touched every day. *Maman* would hold the items in her hands one at a time, letting her eyes go soft and her breath go deep, until the images began to come up. Echoes, she called them. Of what has been and what is to come.

It will sound strange to you, like make-believe. It was stranger still to watch it through a keyhole when I was a little girl, spying on things I did not yet understand. And then one day, *Maman* explained. Every soul creates an echo. Like a fingerprint or signature that becomes infused in the things around us. Who we are. Where we belong. What we're meant to bring to the world. No two echoes are alike. They are ours and ours alone. But they're incomplete—one half of a perfect whole. Like a mirror without a reflection. And so each echo is constantly seeking its other half, to complete itself. That is what we look for in a reading, a sign that the lovers' echoes are a match.

Nearly two-thirds of the brides who sought *Maman*'s help were turned away, and no amount of money could entice her to change her mind. These were critical considerations, after all. It was her reputation on the line, and she must be careful of it. One failure could ruin her, ruin all the Roussels.

I was twelve when she began to school me in earnest. A year earlier than her *maman* began with her. When I asked why, she said there wasn't time to wait. I would need to be ready when the time came. I didn't understand then. I wouldn't for several years. But I did as I was told. And so began my lessons at the knee of the Dress Witch.

My training consisted of three parts. The first was *divination*, which, according to *Maman*, was where any *sorcière* worth her salt should focus first. It is known by other names. Scrying, dousing, invocation. Naming it one rather than the other makes no difference. *La magie* is a supple thing, powerful yet pliant, adaptable to many forms and uses. Smell. Sound. Sight. Touch. Even taste can be used if the practitioner is sufficiently schooled. For the Roussels, it is touch and the ability to channel a person's story—one's echoes—through our fingertips.

When it comes to spells—and to happiness—there is no such thing as one size fits all. Good magick, *effective* magick, is about knowing your client's story, who they are and how they live their lives, what makes them tick. To be effective, you must get at the truth.

We would work every day after the shop closed, with items *Maman* found or picked up cheap at one of the secondhand stalls. She taught me to go quiet inside, to soften my gaze and slow my breath—so very, very slow—until everything fell away and the images shimmered to the surface. Loves, losses, babies, weddings, accidents, illnesses, flicking past my eyes like pages in a scrapbook. Afterward, *Maman* would quiz me to see if my readings matched hers.

I was terrible at first, overwhelmed by the kinds of things that came up. I was young and found being privy to the intimate details of a stranger's life uncomfortable, as if I'd been peering through their blinds or reading their diaries. *Maman* would simply roll her eyes. *The echoes do not lie,* she would remind me. *They are a person's memoir, stripped of fancy and self-delusion, the raw and unvarnished truth, and those truths are the foundation for everything else.*

By *everything else*, she meant charm crafting.

A particular charm must be created for each Roussel bride, the words carefully chosen and shaped into a kind of verse, meant to dissolve specific impediments and ensure a happy outcome. The writing of a binding charm is considered sacred work and is to be entered into reverently. Never in haste and never, ever with the intent to bend the will of another. Both lovers must come willingly to the union and must have full faith in the charm's binding power. Faith is the cornerstone of *all* magick. Without it, even the most powerful charm is useless.

When the charm is complete, it is sewn into the dress, discreetly worked into the seam that will lay closest to the bride's heart. The words should be wrought in white silk thread, the stitches nearly invisible to the naked eye, as a guard against copying and misappropriation. Binding spells call on powerful magick, and in careless hands can do harm that is difficult if not impossible to reverse. But in skilled hands, a thoughtfully worked binding assures both protection and happiness. On the wedding day, when the lovers exchange vows, their union is said to be *envoûtée*—spellbound.

This part of the training came hard for me. I was impatient, which made me clumsy, perhaps because I found the work so achingly dull. I longed to make dresses, beautiful, shimmering gowns like the ones pictured in *La Joie des Modes*. But *Maman* refused to let me do more than pin a hem or trace a pattern until I had mastered charm crafting.

I thought her terribly unfair. At fifteen I was already as good with a needle as she, perhaps better, and had a sketchbook full of ideas I ached to bring to life. Voluminous princess skirts, tightly nipped waists, bead-encrusted bodices, and wide satin bows with sashes so long they skimmed the floor. They were gowns meant to celebrate the female form, offering glimpses of shoulder and back and bosom.

Maman detested them all, pronouncing them fanciful and vulgar, fit only for the stage. Her opinion stung more than I let on, but one day after yet another harsh critique, I informed her that her shapeless confections were *très démodé*—dreary and outdated. No woman, I snapped sullenly—not even the ones who need *our* help—wanted to walk down the aisle in a dress that looked as if it had been fashioned from her mother's best tablecloth, and certainly not at the prices we were charging.

She responded as I knew she would, by pointing out that our clients weren't paying for fashion but peace of mind. Still, I scorned the idea that a Roussel bride should have to choose between fashion and *la magie*. I saw no reason they couldn't have both. If she would only let me make up a few of my dresses and display them in the salon, she would see that I was right. But *Maman* was not persuaded. And so I began to sew in secret, working every night after her light went out, dreaming of the day women would walk down the aisle in gowns bearing my name on the label.

Now, years later and an ocean away from where I began, the memories are still raw, but it was work that helped put me back together again after Paris and all that came after. Daniel is right. Despite it all, I managed to make a name for myself and carried on the Roussel legacy in a way I hoped would make *Maman* proud. With my shop, I found my feet. And I found *myself*. Selling it, no matter how long it's been sitting empty, would be like letting go of all of that—like letting go of me—and I don't know if I'm ready for that.

FIVE

SOLINE

*Always, there must be free will. It is not for us
to impose our beliefs on others or to endeavor
to persuade one to the practices of our faith. We
do not seek those who need our help. Rather,
they must seek us and request our assistance.*

—*Esmée Roussel, the Dress Witch*

31 May 1985—Boston

This time, Daniel waits until after breakfast to call. I consider letting it
ring but know it's pointless. He'll only show up at my door with a box of
my favorite truffles. After so many years, he knows how to get around me.

I take my time refilling my coffee cup while the phone continues to
ring. Seven times. Eight. Nine. I still don't know what I'm going to say.
I haven't allowed myself to think about it since his first call. But now I
have to think about it, because he knows I'm here—where else would I
be?—and he isn't giving up.

"You're becoming a nuisance," I growl when I finally pick up.

"What if it wasn't me?" There's a smile in his voice and a hint of
annoyance that I've made him wait.

"Who else would be calling me?"

"True enough. Have you thought about what you might want to do?"

I take a sip of my coffee, wincing as it goes down, hot and strong. What I *want* to do is turn back the clock, go back to a time when I still had dreams, before my heart froze over. "No," I say flatly. "I haven't had time."

"I know a little more than I did the last time we spoke. The agent called again yesterday. His client's been looking for a space to open a gallery. They're definitely thinking lease rather than sale, which means you wouldn't actually be letting go of the place. You'd just be . . . sharing it. For a good cause."

I let out a sigh. "There's property all over this city. Why does he have to have mine?"

"It's a she, actually, though the agent still wouldn't drop her name. He did tell me the gallery would showcase up-and-coming artists. She's even got a name. She wants to call it Unheard Of."

I run the name around in my head. Clever. Intriguing. Of course it's a woman. "You should have told him it wasn't available when he called the first time," I snap, annoyed that life seems determined to throw me back into the past when all I want is to be left alone.

"I'm not your guard dog," Daniel says in the voice he reserves for me when I'm being exasperating. "I'm your lawyer. My job is to offer counsel when there's a serious opportunity on the table. And this one *is* serious. They know about the fire, that repairs were never completed. Gleason says she doesn't care. Apparently, they've been looking for a space for almost a year, but nothing he showed her measured up. Eventually, she shelved the idea. Then she spotted the row house and just knew it was *the* one. Her exact words. She said it was as if the building had been waiting for her."

Waiting for her . . .

The words seem to vibrate in my chest, the way a tuning fork resonates when struck. "She thinks the building—my building—has been waiting for her?"

44

"That's what he said. Who knows with these artsy types."

"I'm an artsy type," I remind him dryly.

"Of course you are. So maybe you and this want-to-be gallery owner are kindred spirits. Should I set up a meeting?"

"I didn't say that."

"I know, but maybe she's right. Maybe the building has been waiting for her. Maybe you have too. They're only talking about a lease. And you'd know it was being used for something meaningful. For art."

"Stop your wheedling, Daniel. I'm not a child."

To his credit, he remains silent. The truth is I can be rather childlike at times. Sullen and immovable. And yes, difficult. I suppose that's what comes from a life that's denied you everything you ever wanted. But now it's someone else doing the wanting. Someone with a dream. Someone who believes in art and artists. Do I really want to play the spoiler?

"Soline?" Daniel prods finally.

"Set up a meeting."

There's a beat of startled silence. "For what day?"

"You pick the day. I won't be there."

"You don't want to meet this mystery woman?"

"No." My answer comes so fast it surprises even me. I've never cared much for the business end of things. That's why I have a solicitor. Daniel can oversee the negotiations and finalize the deal if one is reached, then send the necessary paperwork by courier. I can bear that much, as long as I don't have to sit through it all with a smile on my face and pretend I don't remember the stitch-by-stitch unraveling of my life. Because I do.

I remember the day I learned the Nazis would come. I remember where I was and what I was wearing. I remember what *Maman* was wearing and what she said. And I remember not wanting to believe any of it. It was impossible. But *Maman* knew better and had quietly begun hoarding what we would need—what *I* would need—and on my sixteenth birthday, she decided it was time to prepare me for what was coming.

SIX

SOLINE

A crucifix around your neck and a charme
magique *in your pocket may keep away the
witch hunters, but they are worthless against
the Nazis.*

—*Esmée Roussel, the Dress Witch*

17 September 1939—Paris

It's near closing time, and I'm tidying up the workroom, complaining
about the bolts of fabric beginning to pile up in the corners, when
Maman's sewing machine goes quiet.

"There will come a time," she says gravely, "when we'll need more
than flour and sugar to survive."

My mother has never been given to dramatics. She is a woman who
lives her life in the cool and careful middle, with no time for theatrics,
so this dire prediction, delivered out of the blue, takes me by surprise.

I blink at her. "Who said anything about flour?"

She reaches over and clicks off the radio, then folds her hands in
her lap. "It's time for me to say a few things, Soline, and I want you to
listen."

This alone is enough to put me on my guard. *Maman* is not a talker, unless it's to point out an uneven hem or shabbily cut pattern. But war changes things. My belly tightens when I meet her eyes, dark like my own with a fringe of black lashes that are suddenly and inexplicably spiked with tears.

She points to the empty chair beside her worktable. "Come sit by me and listen."

Her tears, so rare, terrify me. "What is it?"

"There are changes coming," she begins. "Dark times that will test us all. Even now, the winds are blowing." She is fingering the gold crucifix she has taken to wearing every day, a new habit, like the garnet beads she keeps in her apron pocket and works absently when her hands happen to be free.

Oui, Maman carries a rosary. And wears a crucifix. It isn't uncommon for our kind to practice a blend of Catholicism and *la magie des esprits*. She doesn't attend mass or make confession, but she goes to the church now and then to light a candle—as a kind of hedge against *malchance*.

Perhaps it's to do with the early days of the church, when our feast days were assumed into the Christian calendar in an effort to herd women like us into the *one true faith*. Or a holdover from darker times, when being anything but Catholic might result in one being bound to a stake and set alight. Whatever the reason, many of the *gifted* in France continue to straddle the line between saints and spirits. Especially the women.

The female sex has always been troublesome for those in power, because we see things, know things. And now *Maman* knows something. And so I sit quietly, waiting.

"The Germans again," she says harshly, picking up the thread of the conversation. "Led by *un fou*—a madman with a shadow on his soul. He will take everything. And what he cannot take, he will destroy." She pauses, laying a hand on my arm. "You must be ready, So-So."

She rarely touches me. And she never calls me So-So. It was one of my *tante* Lilou's pet names for me and has always set her teeth on edge. Her sudden show of tenderness sends a chill through me.

"How do you know this?"

"I've lived it before. And not so long ago. Now it's coming again." She squeezes her eyes tight, as if trying to rid herself of the images. "It will be no little thing, this war. Barbarity the world has never seen, and so will not see coming." Her head comes up, her gaze riveted to my face. "You will need to be strong, *ma fille*. And careful."

She looks pale suddenly, her dark eyes bead-hard as she forces me to meet them. How have I not noticed the new sharpness in her face, the thinning of her once-full mouth? She's frightened, and I have never seen her frightened.

There's something she isn't saying, something that frightens her more than the prospect of war. Suddenly, I'm frightened too. "When, *Maman*?"

"A year, perhaps more. But I've been preparing, laying up stores against what's to come. It will be harder and harder to get things. Food. Clothes. Even shoes. Money won't matter because there won't be anything to buy and no one to buy it from. That's why the workroom is jammed. And the pantry downstairs. So you'll have what you need when the time comes. Things you can barter." Her hand creeps back to the crucifix. "I'm afraid for you."

The words hang in the air between us. Heavy. Solitary. "Only for me?"

Her eyes remain steady, her emotions unguarded for the first time in my memory. Fear. Sorrow. And a silent apology. Suddenly, I understand what she isn't saying and what I haven't let myself see until now. The hollow cheeks and shadowed eyes, the cough I sometimes hear in the night. *Maman* is sick and will be gone soon.

SEVEN

Soline

For more than two hundred years, there has been a Dress Witch, the keeper of our secret and the teacher of our craft. Our gift, though taught, is at its roots hereditary, the title passed from one generation to the next. When the mother lays down her needle, the daughter takes it up. And so goes The Work.

—*Esmée Roussel, the Dress Witch*

17 January 1940—Paris

For now at least, nothing seems to be happening. The tables at the sidewalk cafés are still full, the coffeehouses humming with artists and philosophers, sipping endless cups of black coffee, gnawing on life like a bone. The chefs keep cooking, and the wine keeps flowing, the cinemas draw their usual crowds, and fashion continues to be the chief pastime of Parisian women. More importantly—at least for the Roussels—young lovers continue to marry.

Maman says it's to do with Hitler's troops sweeping through Europe like a plague of locusts. The prospect of soldiers on our streets is making everyone nervous, and brides are desperate to get down the aisle before the worst comes to pass.

Every day now, we wake to reports of new atrocities. A woman who had fled Berlin with her aging parents told *Maman* about the night she witnessed dozens of Jews from her neighborhood being rounded up for the camps, their synagogues burned, their businesses destroyed, the streets where they lived and worked littered with shards of broken glass. *Kristallnacht*, they called it—the Night of Broken Glass. We'd heard about it, of course, on the radio, but not the way she told it.

And this morning, there are reports of mothers putting their children on trains, giving them up to strangers in order to save them from what's coming. *Maman* has been sobbing on and off for hours. She's declining rapidly now, so thin the bones of her face have begun to show through her skin, and her cough worsens every day. She refuses to see a doctor, assuring me with alarming calm that it will make no difference. There is no longer any pretense between us. She's dying, and all I can do is watch.

"Will it be much longer?" I ask as she clicks off the radio and settles back against her pillows. "Before they come to Paris, I mean."

She turns her head, coughing into a handkerchief, a broken rattling that leaves her winded and pale. "They're closer every day now. They won't stop until they have it all."

Her answer comes as no surprise. It's what they're saying on *Radio Londres* too. "They've already taken half of Europe. Why do they need Paris?"

"They want to *purge* all of Europe—to *purify* it. Many will die. And the ones who don't will lose everything."

I nod, because there's no longer any doubt about her being right. Every day brings fresh horrors. Raids and roundups. Trains crisscrossing Europe, loaded with prisoners bound for the camps. Communists. Jews. Roma.

"Will no one be safe, then?"

"Those willing to turn a blind eye and go along, but only those. Some will even profit from it. For the rest, they will come with their scythes, cutting down anyone who stands in their way. And I won't be here. There will be no one to protect you."

I want to tell her she's wrong, that she'll get well and everything will be fine, but we both know better. And so I say nothing.

"I've had a letter from Lilou," she says abruptly.

The news leaves me speechless. *Maman* has never forgiven her sister for falling in love with an Englishman and running off to get married. He was wealthy and dashing, with a flat in London and a house in the country where he kept horses and sheep. I found it all terribly romantic. *Maman* felt quite differently and had shown little emotion when a letter arrived telling us Lilou's husband was dead. She had torn the letter to pieces and thrown it into the fire, muttering that it had all been inevitable, and it served her right for abandoning us. Now, more than a decade later, it seems there has been another letter.

"I didn't know you and Lilou were writing letters."

"War changes things," *Maman* replies stiffly. "And there were . . . things to say."

"You told her you were sick?"

"She said you should come."

I stare at her. "To London?"

"It's still possible. But not for long." She surprises me by reaching for my hand, her knuckles white as her fingers close around mine. "I want you to go, Soline. I want you to be safe. And you won't be in Paris. No one will. You must go. Tomorrow."

"Without you?"

Her eyes flutter closed. "*Oui, ma fille.* Without me."

"But how—"

She shakes her head, cutting me off. "You can't stay, Soline. I was a fool to think a pantry full of coffee and sugar could keep you safe. It won't. Nothing will if they decide to come for you."

The panic in her eyes is so raw, I feel the hairs on the back of my neck prickle. I narrow my gaze, certain she knows something I don't. "What reason could they have to come for *me, Maman*?"

Her eyes glitter, fever mixed with fear. "Don't you see? They don't need a reason! But they'll find one. People always find a way to justify their hate—and give others an excuse to fall in line. They put words in people's mouths, plant them like viruses, then watch them spread. People here in Paris—people we *know*—will be infected. And when the fever spreads, they'll point the finger at anyone they think might save them. Please, I beg you, go to Lilou."

"How can I go?" The words spill out more sharply than I intend, but she is asking the impossible. We've never been close—not the way most mothers and daughters are—but she's my mother. I can't just abandon her. "You're so weak you can't get down the stairs, and you can barely feed yourself. If I go, there will be no one to take care of you."

"You must, Soline. You must go. Now."

"What about The Work? Someone has to be here to do The Work."

She lets out a sigh, clearly weary of arguing. "There won't be any work, Soline. There will be no brides because there will be no grooms. The men will be gone. All of them."

I feel the air go out of my lungs. I've heard stories about the last war, the shortage of marriageable men after, because they went off to fight and never came home. I never imagined it happening again. But of course, she's right. Referrals have already slowed to a trickle, and it will only get worse. And then what? Still, I can't do what she's asking.

"I won't leave you here by yourself."

"You little fool!" Her eyes flash as she catches me by the wrist. "Do you think it will matter if you're here when my time comes? That you can somehow stop what's happening to me? You can't. There is no magick for this. Or for what's coming. There's nothing left for you here."

I turn away from her, stung by her harshness. Ours has always been an awkward relationship, filled with chilly truces and prickly silence, her disapproval always there, like a current running between us, because I'm a reminder of past mistakes.

Once upon a time, I had a father, a man who managed at least once to woo Esmée Roussel to his bed. I don't know his name. I only know that he was a musician attending school in Paris and that he left without marrying her. *Maman* has never spoken of him, and Lilou was strangely silent on the subject, despite my curiosity. And so he has remained a shadow, a nameless lapse in judgment for which a baby girl was the penance.

I remember Lilou telling me once that *Maman* had been one of the most beautiful girls in Paris and that it had to do with the Roma blood running through our veins. She said it was what gave the Roussels the look of gypsies—and what gave us our magick—and that *Maman* had gotten more than her share of both. Perhaps it's true. Perhaps *Maman* was beautiful once, but bitterness has hardened her, something I vowed would never happen to me. And yet I see her sometimes, when I stand at the mirror, the me I might become if I'm not careful, cold and brittle and so very solitary. But Lilou is there sometimes too, looking back, asking me what I will make of my life.

Lilou, who lopped off her hair and rouged her lips and called me *ma pêche*. Who followed her heart and married her Brit and left Paris far behind her. She was different from *Maman* in every way it was possible to be different, and I adored her. She wasn't fond of rules and didn't believe in regrets—or sin, which she claimed was a ruse to make women apologize for what they wanted. How I longed to be like her when I was a girl, to look the world straight in the eye and dare its opinion, to follow my own dreams and chase my own wishes. And perhaps I will one day—but not while *Maman* needs me.

EIGHT

RORY

Rory held her breath as she stepped into the row house's murky interior. The power wasn't due to be turned on until tomorrow, but as of 6:00 p.m. last night, the place was hers—lock, stock, and lease payment.

She couldn't stay long. She was due at her mother's for brunch at eleven. But the freshly cut set of keys Daniel Ballantine had handed her yesterday had been burning a hole in her pocket. Now that it was light, she was here to soak up the atmosphere and savor the moment.

A wash of dull light filtered in through the gritty front window, creating a murky underwater atmosphere. Rory squinted, willing her eyes to adjust as she wandered about the front room. In its current condition, the place could hardly be considered glamorous, though it had once been home to one of the most exclusive bridal salons in Boston, owned by a Parisian dressmaker known for her exquisite taste and avant-garde designs.

If she'd ever had a second thought, which she hadn't, the building's history would have been enough to make her take the leap, the idea that once upon a time the row house had been a place where taffeta, organza, and creamy satins had been used to create something lasting and beautiful. It felt like a sign, as if fate had in fact sent a wave with her name on it. Perhaps that's why Soline Roussel hadn't sold the building after the fire, because it was meant for her—for the gallery.

Things had moved relatively quickly once the decision was made. After several rounds of phone tag and one very brief showing, she'd made an offer, requiring yet another round of phone tag before finally being accepted. She'd been a nervous wreck waiting for the papers to be drawn up, afraid her mysterious new landlady would change her mind and back out of their deal. Thankfully, everything had gone as planned—or almost everything. She'd been hoping to finally meet the elusive Ms. Roussel at the signing, but as usual, her attorney had acted on her behalf.

She'd asked Daniel for Ms. Roussel's phone number when the business was done or an address where she might send a thank-you note, but he had quickly nixed the idea, explaining that his client was an extremely private person and preferred to leave matters of business to him. All future inquiries would be handled through his office.

Rory doubted there would be need for future inquiries. She was ready to get the renovations started. The fire damage was largely confined to the second-floor apartment, where the blaze had actually started, but smoke and water had left their marks down here too. The roof and dormers, along with the windows on the upper floors, had been replaced soon after the fire, but after the initial gutting, work on the interior had been abandoned, leaving the place little more than a shell, stripped to the lath and littered with drop cloths, abandoned tools, and discarded paint pails overflowing with trash.

The contractor she'd hired to do the renovations—a friend of Brett's—estimated the first-floor work could be completed in ninety days, give or take. After that, she'd need several weeks to furnish the place and complete the art installations. If all went well, an October opening might be doable. November at the latest.

A bloom of anticipation warmed her as she imagined the finished product. Glossy black floors and discreet lighting, soft gray walls lined with beautifully framed art. Black lacquer plinths. Acrylic vitrines. Well-placed benches for lingering and conversation. And later, upstairs, rooms for readings, lectures, perhaps even a workshop now and then.

She eyed the staircase with its black marble newels and art deco ironwork. Like everything else, it would require some TLC, but thank goodness they hadn't torn it out. She ran a palm over the cool black marble, the almost sensuous curve of the iron railing, envisioning it all dramatically lit from above, mirrored in shadow on the wall behind— very film noir.

For a moment, she toyed with the idea of going upstairs for a quick poke around, but there wasn't time. Not that she was in a hurry to tell her mother she wouldn't be heading back to school in the fall. She'd been skirting the issue for several weeks, determined to keep her decision quiet until the lease was signed. But now it was time to face the music.

Maybe she'd come back after brunch, clean the windows, and round up the trash before the workmen showed up tomorrow. It would give her something to look forward to. She was turning away, her hand still on the stair railing, when she felt it—or thought she felt it. A subtle vibration coursing through her fingers and up her arm, like the hum of a tuning fork running through her bones. Stranger still were the quicksilver flashes she'd experienced as she squeezed her eyes shut, like heat lightning, imprinting the backs of her lids with a strange jumble of images.

She jerked her hand back, rubbing her bare arm. A shock? But how? The power had been off for years. Against her better judgment, she touched the railing again with the flats of her fingers, fast, as if testing an iron or a burner on a stove. Nothing.

Had she imagined it? She was sure the contractor had checked the wiring as part of his walk-through, and she didn't recall him finding any problems. Just the same, she'd ask him to take a second look. The last thing she needed was an electrical fire or, worse, someone getting electrocuted on opening night.

Opening night.

Just thinking the words set little wings fluttering in her belly as she picked up her purse and moved to the door. Because it made her think of Hux and his belief in her vision. His voice had been in her head all morning, while she brushed her teeth, while she stirred cream into her coffee, while driving over. And she heard it again as she locked the door behind her.

Dreams are like waves, babe. You have to wait for the right one to come along, the one that has your name on it. And then when it does, you have to get up and ride it.

Her mother was already on the terrace when she arrived. She glanced up from her issue of *Town & Country* as Rory approached, her penciled brows lifting a notch.

"Aurora. You're nearly on time."

Rory offered the barest of nods. "Good morning to you too."

"I just meant I haven't brought the food out because I didn't expect you yet. I have a spinach and tomato strata warming in the oven. And those little zucchini muffins you like." She laid down her magazine and stood. "Go ahead and open the Veuve, and I'll bring out the food."

Rory went to work on the champagne cork, hoping her news might sit better after a little lubrication. She'd spent the drive over rehearsing what she was going to say, only to conclude that it didn't matter. There was simply no good way to break this news.

Moments later, Camilla returned carrying a pitcher of orange juice. "I think we're ready to sit."

Rory started guiltily, nearly overturning one of the champagne flutes. Camilla eyed her curiously. "Are you all right? You seem distracted."

"I'm fine. Let's eat."

A silence fell as they filled their plates. Finally, Camilla lifted her glass. "To sunny Sunday mornings!"

Rory raised her glass obediently, going through the motions. She could feel her mother's eyes on her, assessing, inquisitive. Finally, Camilla lowered her knife. "Are you certain you're all right, Aurora? You don't seem to be yourself."

"I'm fine." She reached for her glass, took another sip. "Any progress on the holiday event?"

Camilla blinked at her, clearly surprised. "Well, yes, actually. I've been toying with a Gatsby theme. You know, Roaring Twenties costumes, a nice jazz band. Lots of feathers and sequins for decorations. Black and gold and cream. Very elegant, of course."

"Of course. Will you go as a flapper?"

Camilla's laugh echoed across the terrace, light and almost girlish. "Certainly not. No one wants to see that. I was thinking of a pinstripe suit and spats, maybe a wide fedora. What do you think? I could go as a mobster, and you could be my moll. Lots of fringe and a boa. And those bright-red cupid lips."

"Sounds fun. But you could still pull off the flapper. You've certainly got the legs for it."

Camilla rolled her eyes. "Don't be ridiculous. I'm long past the age for flashing one's knees." She paused, scooping up several bright-red berries. "And what about you? Did you manage to get your classes lined up for the fall?"

And here it was. The moment of truth. Rory reached for her glass, finishing it off in one go. "Not exactly, no."

"But, honey, you promised—"

"I'm not going back in the fall," she blurted. So much for a tactful opening line. "I've decided to go ahead with my plans for the gallery instead."

Camilla lowered her spoon, sending several berries skittering across the tablecloth. "The gallery? I thought—"

"I know. I did too. Then I saw this building, an old row house on the corner of Newbury and Fairfield, and I knew it was what I was supposed to do."

Camilla let out a sigh. "Aurora, we've talked about this. You have no business experience. And no real experience in the art world yet. You need to finish school before you jump into something like this. Bulk up your credentials so you'll have something to fall back on."

"In case I fail, you mean."

"Well, yes. And don't look at me like that. Have you any idea how many galleries fail in their first year?"

"No, but I'm sure you're about to tell me."

"I don't want you to become a statistic, Aurora. And you will if you pursue this." She shook her head, as if bewildered. "You didn't say a word about this the last time you were here. Now, just like that, you're thinking of quitting school?"

Rory lifted her chin. "I don't need your permission."

Camilla was clearly taken aback but kept her voice even. "No. You're over eighteen, and you have your own money. Your father made sure of that. But I'm asking you to slow down and do your homework and to finish your schooling while you're doing it. A master's degree is a real accomplishment, something you can be proud of no matter what you decide to do down the road. And Paris. You've always wanted to go, and it's the kind of thing that looks good on a résumé. Who knows what the future holds for you? Maybe it is this gallery of yours. Or maybe it isn't. Just wait a little, that's all I'm saying."

Rory wet her lips, once, twice. "I signed the lease last night."

Camilla's face went blank. "Oh, Aurora. Tell me you didn't."

"I'm sorry. I don't want to go back to school. Or go to Paris. I want to do this, to follow my dream."

"Your dream." Camilla shook her head dismissively. "Until a year ago, I never heard you utter the word *gallery*. And then it was only because Matthew put the idea in your head. He thinks because you have a trust fund, it doesn't matter if you fail. He doesn't know a thing about the art world, but he's filled your head with this silly notion—a gallery for artists no one has ever heard of. You gave it up once. Now you're running back to it because you don't know what to do with yourself."

"That isn't true. But even if it were, why does it matter? Why can't I just want what I want? Why does everything I do have to pass some kind of test with you?"

"This isn't about me, Aurora. It isn't even about you. It's about Matthew. You're trying to prove something to someone who isn't even here, because you're miserable and afraid. You don't know the first thing about running a gallery—or what happens when you step out on a limb and fall. But I do. You're nowhere near ready to take on something like this, and if you'd slow down for a minute, you'd see that."

The words rankled more than Rory cared to admit. It had all happened so fast, and with no due diligence to speak of. What if her mother was right? What if she had jumped into the deep end of the pool because of something Hux said once, because she couldn't bear the thought that she might never see him again?

"You haven't thought this through, Aurora. Let me contact Steven Mercer and have him make a call or two. It might cost you a little something—rash decisions generally do—but the man knows his way around a contract. I don't care what you signed. He'll get you out of it."

Rory stiffened, infuriated by her mother's cool assurance. "I don't *want* to get out of it."

Camilla leaned forward, gripping the edge of the table with both hands. "What if you can't make a go of it? Have you thought about that? Or do you intend to keep throwing money at it until you've burned through your trust fund?"

Rory sagged back into her chair. "Your faith in me is overwhelming."

Camilla's face softened. "It has nothing to do with my faith in you. I just don't want to see you disappointed, and I'm afraid you will be. It's a big thing to open a gallery. And an even bigger thing if you're not ready. Statistically—"

"Yes, yes. You already said that. I promise if I go belly-up, I'll move away and change my name. I won't embarrass you. And who knows, maybe I'll finally make you proud."

For a moment, Camilla looked genuinely startled. "You've always made me proud, Aurora. Always."

Rory held her gaze. "Have I?"

"Of course you have."

"Then be happy for me. After all these hideous months, something good is finally happening. Celebrate with me. Please."

Camilla nodded coolly, a reluctant gesture of defeat. She reached for the bottle of Veuve and refilled both their glasses, then after a splash of orange juice, held up her mimosa. "To my daughter—the gallery owner."

"Thank you," Rory said over the rim of her glass. It was hardly a ringing endorsement, but then she hadn't expected one. They'd reached a kind of armistice, though, and for now that would do. It's what their relationship had always been, an endless cycle of arrows and olive branches. "I know it isn't what you wanted for me. But it's what *I* want for me."

Camilla's smile faded. "You've always been so much braver than me."

It was a strange admission. Not a confession—her mother didn't believe in confessions—but an unexpected compliment.

"I promise you, it's nothing to do with being brave. In fact, I'm terrified that everything you just said is true. That I'm not ready. That I'm doing it for the wrong reason. But this gallery is the first thing I've cared about in months. Yes, it happened fast. And yes, it's a huge risk, but it's a reason to get out of bed in the morning. And getting out of bed was starting to feel much harder than it should." She paused, realizing for the first time just how true those words were. "It isn't just a matter of wanting this. I need it."

"Then I suppose you'd better tell me about this row house of yours. I'm afraid the strata's ice-cold. Should I pop it in to reheat?"

"No, it's fine. Let's just eat."

Camilla scooped out a portion for herself, then held out her hand for Rory's plate. "I think it's still a little warm. The cheese is still stretchy. Now, tell me about this place you found. Where is it? What's it like?"

"It's right off Newbury, next to DeLuca's. Red brick with a lovely turret and a big bay window in front. It needs some work, though. There was a fire a few years ago, and the repairs were never finished."

"So it's been empty all this time?"

"It has. The owner decided not to reopen after the fire but held on to the building. The contractor says an autumn opening is doable. We'll tackle the ground floor first, then start on the upper floors once we're open. Oh, and there's this amazing staircase, black marble and wrought iron. Very dramatic. I'm thinking pale gray and mother-of-pearl, low lighting, glossy black floors."

Camilla looked up from her plate. "Sounds like you've put a lot of thought into this."

"I always knew the kind of feel I wanted. Clean. Monochromatic. The minute I saw the row house, I knew it would be a perfect fit. I just got that feeling, you know?"

Camilla arched a brow as she spooned a few more strawberries onto her plate. "What feeling would that be?"

"I don't know. Like it was meant to be, I guess. I probably walked past the place a hundred times and never noticed it. Then a few weeks ago, on my way home from meeting Lisette, it just jumped out at me. I swear it was like magic."

"What was it before?"

"A bridal shop. The woman who owns it is named Soline Roussel. I was hoping to meet her when I signed the lease, but she didn't show. Her lawyer says she doesn't go out much anymore."

Camilla frowned, as if searching her memory. "I think I know her."

"You *know* Soline Roussel?"

"I'm sorry. I meant I know who she is. Everyone did in my day. From Paris, or so she claimed. I don't remember the name of her shop, something French, but she had quite a clientele, as I recall. She was famous for her bows."

"Her bows?"

"Her trademark, you might say. The Roussel Bow. All her dresses had them in some shape or form. At the waist, the shoulders, the bustle. She was quite *à la mode* back then, with her accent and her elegant little shop, promising that her dresses would bring good luck."

Rory glanced up, intrigued. "Good luck?"

"That was the talk—some nonsense about her dresses guaranteeing a happy marriage. She made them all by hand, a custom-made good-luck charm for each and every bride. A great gimmick, I suppose, if you can make people believe it. But then, most brides will believe anything. Throw in the French thing and you'll have them eating out of your hand. And she did. My friends were all wild for her dresses."

"But not you?"

Camilla shrugged. "What I wanted was immaterial. A local salon would never have done."

"Why?"

"I was a Lowell, darling. Nothing but a proper gown from Paris would do for a Lowell. And so off to Paris we went, to visit *Maison Dior*. We left Boston with two trunks and came back with seven."

"Dior," Rory breathed. She'd never cared about fashion, but even she knew a wedding dress from The House of Dior was worthy of awe. "I wish the photos hadn't all been ruined. You must have looked gorgeous."

Camilla sniffed dismissively. "It was white, and French, and so tight I thought I would pass out before I got down the aisle, but it did the job."

The job.

Those two words conveyed all anyone needed to know about Camilla's feelings regarding the holy state of matrimony. They also signaled that it was time to steer the conversation back to safer waters.

"What else do you know about Soline Roussel?"

"Not much. Why?"

"Well, it's quite a story, isn't it? Enchanted wedding dresses and happily-ever-afters. And then her business being destroyed by fire. I wonder why she never reopened. I got the feeling from her lawyer that she's something of a recluse. It's sad."

"I remember the fire—or at least the news about it. It was right around the time your father died. I don't recall how it started, but I remember hearing that she ended up in the hospital with some pretty bad burns."

Burns. That would explain her desire for privacy. "Do you know what happened to her? Later, I mean."

"I don't. You know how the news is. They only care about the tragedy. The aftermath is never quite as exciting. Anyway, she's renting you her building, which is all that matters."

Rory nodded half-heartedly. It was true. Soline Roussel's story shouldn't matter, but it did somehow. Perhaps because Rory had come to understand how the loss of something precious could completely unravel a life.

NINE

RORY

June 19, 1985—Boston

Rory sagged onto the bottom step with her legal pad, weary but happy to be able to check another item off her to-do list. The contractor's men had delivered the scaffolding required to begin work on the ceiling; she'd scrubbed all the windows, hauled out the remaining trash, done a walk-through with the electrician, and contacted someone to come look at the furnace. Not bad for two o'clock.

There was plenty to do if she was going to be ready by fall. She'd need to start lining up artists, create a marketing plan and an event calendar, figure out what drafting a press release entailed, and brainstorm ideas for the grand opening. The learning curve would be steep, and there would almost certainly be missteps, but come hell or high water, she planned to make a go of it. No one would be able to say Unheard Of was just a trust-fund-fueled vanity exercise.

Rory's stomach let out a groan, reminding her that she'd skipped lunch. She ran down the legal pad one more time, concluding that she'd done what she could for now. She'd head home, grab a sandwich and a shower, then get to work on the brochure copy.

She had just finished locking up and was hunting for her purse when she spotted what appeared to be a small door cut into the dark wood paneling of the staircase's outer wall. She'd never noticed it before, but there it was, with a small hole where, presumably, a knob had once been. After a few tugs, the door yielded, revealing a low, inky crawl space. There was no switch or string, no light anywhere that Rory could find. Going down on one knee, she squinted into the opening, trying not to think about what might have taken up residence under the stairs of a building that had been abandoned for almost four years.

The floor was bare wood, gritty with dust, but at least nothing seemed to be moving. She held her breath, not sure what she expected to find as she groped about blindly. She came up empty on her first attempt, but on the second try her knuckles grazed what felt like a large, flattish box.

It took some doing, but she finally managed to extricate the box and drag it into her lap. It was an old dress box, similar to the elaborate hatboxes women used to carry when they traveled. This one was fashioned of heavy gray cardboard, with metal fittings at the corners to avoid crushing and a length of badly frayed cord threaded through as a handle, so it could be carried like a suitcase.

There appeared to be a bit of writing in one corner. She wiped at the grime with the heel of her hand until a single line of cursive finally emerged—*Madame Roussel, Paris.* Apparently, Soline Roussel had owned a shop in Paris and had brought this box with her all the way to Boston. But what was it doing under the stairs?

She willed herself to go slowly as she worked the cord free, then gently lifted the lid. There were several sheets of tissue paper, crumpled and yellow with age. One by one, she peeled them away, breath held until an expanse of creamy white lace came into view.

It was like something from a fairy tale: a sweetheart neckline encrusted with iridescent crystals and tiny seed pearls, sleeves of slashed organza, as filmy as a pair of dragonfly wings, folded almost tenderly over one another. Clearly vintage and, judging by the quality of the beadwork, almost certainly hand sewn.

Rory eyed it longingly, itching to explore its landscape, frothy lace and tissue-thin silk, the cool, nubby texture of the beading. And yet she hesitated. Disturbing it now, after it had languished so long in the dark, felt wrong somehow, like casually handling the contents of Tutankhamun's tomb. But that was silly. If the dress meant anything to anyone, it wouldn't be here, shut up in a box covered with dust.

The gown gave a little sigh as she lifted it out of its box, as if relieved to at last be free. The paneled organza skirts unfurled like flower petals as Rory gave them a gentle shake, luminous and frothy. Even the back was stunning, with corset-style lacing and a wide satin bow with sashes that trailed all the way to the floor.

The Roussel Bow.

She was beginning to see why Soline Roussel had made such a name for herself. It was the most beautiful thing she'd ever seen—or imagined. A dress fit for a princess—albeit a very small princess. The sleeves, clearly meant to be full length, fell a good six inches shy of her wrist, and the waist was ridiculously tiny. A custom-made gown, then, and not a mark on it, so probably never worn. What had happened to the bride who was meant to wear it?

The question unsettled her more than she cared to admit. Perhaps because every scenario she imagined was more heart-wrenching than the last. Illness. Betrayal. Death. And they all ended the same way—with a wedding that never happened.

Rory closed her eyes, willing the thoughts away. Whatever the story—and there was almost certainly a story attached to the dress—it was someone *else's* story. It wasn't a sign or an omen. It had nothing to do with her. The smart thing to do would be to put it and the box back where she'd found them.

But as she rearranged the sheets of tissue, she discovered a packet of letters at the bottom of the box and a zippered leather case, monogrammed in gold. A shaving kit, she realized as she picked it up, the kind men used for travel. The calfskin was scuffed and the monogram had begun to wear, but it had clearly been expensive.

She unzipped it, letting it fall open like a book. On one side was a shaving brush and a silver-handled razor; on the other, a tortoiseshell comb, matching shoehorn, and an empty flask meant to hold cologne. She traced a finger over what remained of the monogram—A.W.P. Andrew? Allen? She would likely never know. Unless the packet of letters offered some clue.

She slid them free of their ribbon, counting as she fanned out the envelopes. Eighteen in all. None was stamped or properly addressed, though several bore the words *Mademoiselle Roussel* across the front. Hand-delivered, then, rather than mailed. And kept together, presumably for sentimental reasons. Love letters from A.W.P.?

She selected one at random, teasing a single sheet of blue vellum from its envelope. It was written in French. A disappointment, since she'd long since forgotten the French she'd learned her freshman year at Tufts. But she could read the date: *17 décembre 1942*. December, forty-two years ago. She tried another and then another. Both bore similar dates and were also in French. Finally, toward the bottom of the packet, she discovered a handful written in English. The first was dated August 4, 1964.

> Dearest Mademoiselle Roussel,
> It's been almost a year since David and I exchanged our vows, and though you asked me to wait for our one-year anniversary, I find I cannot wait a day longer to express my gratitude for your kindness when I

came to you with my troubles. Your generosity still astonishes me. To walk down the aisle in one of your gowns was more than a poor girl from the south side of Boston could ever have hoped for. But more importantly, David has had the most miraculous recovery from his accident. It's so astonishing his doctors can hardly believe it, let alone explain it. It took everything in me not to tell them that it had to do with your dress. They would think me quite mad, and a year ago I would have agreed. But now I know I have you and your charm to thank for my happy ending. And for our baby, who will arrive in the new year. If there is ever any way I can repay your kindness, you need only ask.

With my deepest gratitude,
Kathleen P. Shore

Rory reread the letter several times, picking up something new with each pass. A poor girl from the south side of Boston. A miraculous recovery from an accident. A wedding dress given credit for a happy ending. A charm of some kind. It was inconceivable. But wasn't it exactly what her mother had said at brunch last week? Enchanted gowns. Guaranteed happy endings. Was such a thing actually possible?

Kathleen Shore certainly seemed to think so.

Another letter chosen at random read much the same, though it was dated two years later. A young bride writing on her one-year anniversary, thanking Ms. Roussel for the resolution of some tricky financial problem just one month after walking down the aisle in one of her lucky gowns. A third bride wrote of being able to forgive her groom for a reckless infidelity on the eve of their wedding. A fourth had recovered from a chronic illness doctors believed would see her using a wheelchair within two or three years.

Each letter seemed more fantastic than the last. And each credited her astonishing good fortune to Soline Roussel's special *skills* as a dressmaker. It seemed reasonable to assume those written in French contained similar stories. Eighteen brides. Eighteen letters. Eighteen happy endings kept in an old dress box.

Rory gathered the letters together, retying them before returning them to the box. A stack of letters spanning decades, a bridal gown worthy of a princess, and a man's shaving kit. The whole thing had the feel of an unfinished story. A sad, unfinished story.

TEN

RORY

June 20, 1985—Boston

Rory was used to waking with a book beside her, but this morning it was a letter she found lying open amid the rumpled sheets. She folded it carefully and placed it on the nightstand with the others. She'd read them all again last night. Or at least those written in English. They were all variations of the same story: health recovered, fortunes repaired, careers saved, feuds mended, lost things found. And all as a result of a Roussel gown. Or so the grateful brides believed.

Her eyes slid to the dress box on the chest beneath the window. The easy thing would have been to put it back under the stairs, where it wouldn't make her think about weddings that never happened. Instead, she'd taken it home, uncomfortable with relegating it to the dark again. It was silly, she knew, but she couldn't get past something her mother had said.

A custom-made good-luck charm for each and every bride.

She crossed to the box and lifted the lid, trailing a hand along one sheer sleeve. So lovely, and clearly not off-the-rack, since Mademoiselle Roussel didn't do off-the-rack. It had been *created* for someone, *belonged* to someone. But to whom? And how was the shaving kit connected? There was always a chance that it wasn't, but it didn't seem likely.

And where did the letters fit in? They'd obviously been important at some point, and yet they'd been shut up under the stairs along with the other things, abandoned when the shop closed. Unless . . . Was it possible Soline Roussel didn't know they'd survived the fire?

Rory started a pot of coffee, then dialed Daniel Ballantine's number. She was surprised when his receptionist put her straight through.

"Ms. Grant. I wasn't expecting to hear from you so soon. I hope there isn't a problem."

"No. Not exactly. But I need to get in touch with Ms. Roussel. I know you said she doesn't like to be bothered, but it's rather important. I was hoping I could persuade you to give me her number."

"I'm afraid not. As I've said, all her business goes through me."

"It's Rory, please. And this isn't business. It's a personal matter. I promise not to pester her. I just need to speak to her this once."

"Concerning what, if you don't mind my asking?"

Rory wasn't sure how much to reveal and how much to keep to herself. "I'd prefer not to share that with anyone but Ms. Roussel, if you don't mind. It's rather . . . delicate."

"The best I can do is pass along your number," he said finally. "Though I doubt it will get you anywhere. Ms. Roussel isn't a fan of the telephone. She barely talks to me."

"All right, then. Tell her I found something that might belong to her—a box."

"What kind of box?"

Once again, Rory was reluctant to reveal too much. "Just tell her I found a box. If it's important, she'll know."

"All right. I'll pass it along. But don't be surprised if you don't hear back."

Two hours later, the phone rang. Rory abandoned the to-do list she'd been working on and grabbed the handset. "Hello?"

There was a stretch of silence, then finally a woman's voice. "I'm calling for Miss Grant."

Rory's pulse ticked up. "This is Aurora."

"My name is Soline Roussel. I've had a call from my attorney, Daniel Ballantine. He said you . . . found something. A box."

"In the space under the stairs, yes. I don't know how it ended up there, but I thought you might like to have it back."

Another pause, briefer this time, and then the words came tumbling out. "I didn't know . . . I thought . . . Yes. Yes, I'd like to have it back."

"I'd be happy to bring it to you if you'll give me your address."

"No. I couldn't . . . I don't receive guests."

Rory swallowed her disappointment. She'd been hoping to finally meet the elusive mademoiselle. Apparently that wasn't going to happen. "I could deliver it to Mr. Ballantine's office if you'd like, and he could get it to you."

"Thank you, no. Daniel's sweet, but he can be a bit of a nag, and I prefer not to have to answer a lot of questions. The contents of the box are . . . well, they're rather personal, as I'm sure you've guessed."

"Is there somewhere else, then? The gallery . . . I'm sorry . . . the row house?"

"There's a patisserie on the next street over, called Bisous Sucrés. Do you know it? I could meet you there at one thirty."

"Sugar Kisses," Rory translated. "Yes, of course. I'll be there."

She felt a ripple of excitement as she hung up the phone. She was finally going to meet Soline Roussel.

Rory seesawed her Audi into a cramped parking space along Boylston Street, dropped several quarters in the meter, and set off down the sidewalk with the dress box in her arms.

After a few minutes, the patisserie's familiar black-and-white awning came into view. Its proper name, Bisous Sucrés, was splashed across the canvas in loopy gold script, with its lowercase English translation bracketed beneath in hot pink. As usual, business was booming.

Rory navigated the crowded bistro tables in the courtyard, scanning faces until she realized she had no idea who she was looking for. In her excitement, she'd forgotten to ask Ms. Roussel how to recognize her. Then she remembered her mother's mention of burns. Presumably, there would be scars.

The heady aromas of chocolate, cherries, and rich dark coffee greeted her as she pushed through the front door. The line at the counter snaked nearly to the door. Rory sidled past, peering around the dress box. Families. Tourists. Students bent over textbooks. But no one who fit her invented image of Soline Roussel, who she now pictured as a fragile octogenarian with burn scars and an uncomfortable gaze.

Her eyes suddenly connected with those of a woman sitting alone near the back of the shop. Her dark hair was swept up in a glossy chignon, and she wore a smart suit of crimson knit, with black velvet cuffs and shiny gold toggles running down the front. At her throat, a checked scarf of red, white, and black was arranged cravat-style and fastened with a pearl stickpin. She looked startled as their eyes met, as if briefly struck by a wave of panic. After a moment, she seemed to compose herself and inclined her head ever so slightly.

Rory shifted the box to her hip and made her way to the table, not noticing until the last moment that there was a mug and plate in front of the empty chair. "I'm sorry," she blurted. "I thought—"

"Miss Grant?"

Rory recognized the voice from the phone, smoky and low. French. But she was so young—late fifties, perhaps older, but not much. And absolutely beautiful with porcelain-pale skin and a perfect red bow of a mouth. Not a scar to be seen. "You're . . . Ms. Roussel?"

"I am." She gestured with her chin toward the empty chair.

Rory set the box on the corner of the table and took a seat. She couldn't stop staring.

"I took the liberty of ordering you a little something—as a thank-you."

Rory glanced at the table, where a *mille feuille* and a *café au lait* sat waiting for her. "Thank you. I love their pastries. But you really didn't have to, Ms. Roussel. I was happy to come."

"Soline, please. You have questions, I'm sure."

Rory blinked at her, caught off guard by the matter-of-fact invitation. She had no idea how to begin.

Soline seemed to sense her awkwardness. "Your name is Aurora. A beautiful name. In France we say *Aurore*. It means goddess of the dawn."

Rory couldn't help smiling. It sounded so lovely when she said it. Not matronly at all. "I go by Rory," she said sheepishly. "My mother hates it."

Soline's lips twitched, the flicker of a smile. "Mothers like the names they give us." Her smile faded as her gaze settled on the dress box. "You opened the box, yes?"

Rory ducked her head. "I did. I'm sorry. I was just so surprised to find it. I couldn't imagine why . . ."

"Ask what you want to ask," Soline prompted when Rory went quiet.

Rory was surprised by her abrupt tone and by the fact that she hadn't so much as touched the box. Instead, she sat stiffly, her hands folded primly beneath the table, as if braced for an interrogation.

"The dress," Rory began tentatively. "It's one of yours?"

"Yes."

"And the other . . . things?"

"They belong to me as well."

"The dress is so beautiful, like something from a fairy tale." She paused, not sure how to proceed. "It looks . . . brand-new."

"It *is* new. And very old."

"You mean it was never worn."

Soline dropped her gaze. "*Oui.*"

The single word posed more questions than it answered. Why had the dress never been worn? Infidelity? Or a tragedy of some sort? She thought of the letters, all penned by grateful brides who'd received the fabled happy ending. But it seemed the owner of the fairy-tale dress had had no such luck. Why?

"I read some of the letters."

"Did you?"

Rory nodded. "The ones that were in English. I couldn't read the others."

"The recent ones were written to me. The others are from women my mother sewed for a long time ago, back in Paris." She paused, swallowing as she looked away. "She died not long after the Nazis came. When people heard the news, the letters started showing up."

"And you kept them all these years."

"To remember her by, yes. And to remind myself that once upon a time, there were happy endings in Paris and that my mother played a part in a few of them."

Rory laid a hand on the box. "With dresses like this one?"

She managed a thin smile, not quite bitter but almost. "No fairy tale is complete without a proper dress, *chérie.*"

"But not just any dress," Rory pressed, sensing evasion in the response. "A Roussel dress. There's something special about them, isn't there? Something that makes them lucky?"

"Drink your *café*, *Aurore*. Before it gets cold."

Rory lifted her mug obediently. "I'm sorry for prying. I'm just trying to understand what I read. All those grateful brides with such amazing turns of luck. And they all seemed to be thanking *you*, as if somehow you'd *made* it happen. I know what people used to say—my mother told me—and the letters seem to be saying the same thing, that your dresses are . . . magical."

The corners of Soline's mouth curled, lending her a faintly feline air. "Any businesswoman worth her salt knows the value of a good gimmick. Toothpaste that makes you kissable. Shiny floors that make you the envy of your neighbors. Brides want fairy tales, so that's what I gave them."

Rory eyed her skeptically. "You're saying your dresses had nothing to do with what was in those letters?"

"I'm saying people have ways of clinging to ideas that make the world seem nicer than it is. And perhaps that's to be expected. When life is hard, it helps to cling to illusion. I suppose the letters were that for me once. But life has taught me that even in fairy tales, the heroine must make her *own* magic—or not, as the case may be."

"But you kept them. You could have thrown them away, but you didn't."

Soline pulled in a deep breath and let it out very slowly. "There was so much ugliness back then, so much heartache and loss everywhere you looked. The letters were a way to remember the good."

"And yet they wound up in a box under the stairs."

There was an uncomfortable beat of silence, but finally Soline replied. "Before she died, my mother told me there is a time for holding on and a time for letting go and that I needed to learn the difference. I didn't understand then, but there came a time—a moment—when I knew I had to let go of those broken pieces of my life. In the end, I couldn't bear to part with them. I thought if I hid them from myself, put them where I wouldn't see them every day, it would be enough."

Rory studied her over the rim of her mug. Beneath the flawless style and carefully applied cosmetics, there was an air of tragedy that reminded her of Camilla. "Was it?"

"It must seem silly to you, clinging to such painful reminders, but they were all I had left of that part of my life. Of Paris and the life I thought I would have."

The life I thought I would have. Rory rolled the words around in her head. They might just as easily have come out of her mouth. "No," she said finally. "It doesn't seem silly at all. We all have our own ways of coping."

"And you, *chérie*?" Soline asked, her eyes suddenly keen. "Are you . . . coping?"

Rory shifted in her chair, unsettled by both the question and Soline's steady regard. "I think we're all trying to cope, one way or another." She'd been aiming for nonchalance but missed badly. Time to change the subject. "I was sorry to hear about your shop. About the fire, I mean. Did you never think of reopening?"

Soline looked down at her lap, as if weighing her answer. "Life has a way of letting us know when something's over. It's not always pleasant, but it's always obvious if we're paying attention. I spent half my life reaching for things that weren't meant to be mine—and paying dearly for it. At some point, one must read the signs."

Rory sipped her coffee, wondering about the kinds of things Soline had reached for and why they hadn't been meant for her.

"You have other questions," Soline said brusquely. "Go on, then, ask them. I owe you that, I suppose."

Rory found her bluntness both unsettling and refreshing, a welcome change after so many careful conversations with her mother. "The shaving kit. It's connected to the dress, isn't it? It belonged to the groom?"

"An ambulance driver who was killed in the war."

"And the dress is yours."

Tears suddenly pooled in Soline's eyes. "It was meant to be, yes."

"I'm sorry. I shouldn't have pressed you."

Soline gave her head a little shake, as if annoyed with herself. "I'm sorry to get soppy. It's just . . . after the fire . . . They said everything was lost. I never expected to see it again."

"Please don't apologize. I'm the one who should be sorry for pressing you. Please forgive me."

"*C'est oublié*," she murmured, reaching for a napkin and carefully blotting her eyes. "It's forgotten."

Rory tried not to stare. Until that moment, Soline's hands had been in her lap, but now she saw the gloves: black kid, with tiny jet buttons at each wrist, and glaringly out of place in the middle of June.

Scars. Not her face. On her hands.

She averted her eyes, pretending not to notice. "Before I forget, I want to thank you for letting me lease the row house. I had actually given up the idea of opening the gallery. And then one day I was crossing the street and there it was. I was crushed when Daniel said it wasn't available. I'm so glad you changed your mind."

Soline rolled her eyes. "Mr. Ballantine knows how to get around me. He told me about your gallery for new artists. He knew it would soften the ground. When will you open?"

Rory found herself breathing a sigh of relief as the conversation shifted to safer territory. "October, if all goes well. I'd love for you to see it when it's finished. Maybe you could come to the opening. I'd be honored to have you there."

Soline's shoulders stiffened. "Thank you, no. I don't go out much these days, and I haven't been back to the shop since the night of the fire."

"Not once in four years?"

Soline shrugged. "Memories, you know. It's . . . hard."

"I'm so sorry. About . . . everything."

"Never mind all that. Pity is my poison." She pushed to her feet then, surprisingly petite despite her sleek black heels. "Thank you again,

Aurore. It was kind of you to go to the trouble. I wish you *bonne chance* with your gallery."

She picked up her handbag. Rory watched as she fumbled with the strap, her gloved fingers stiff and clumsy. After several attempts, she managed to get the strap up onto her shoulder, but the dress box was nearly as big as she was. She'd be lucky to make it out of the café, let alone navigate the crowded sidewalk.

"If you'd like, I can walk you to your car."

"Thank you. That won't be necessary. I don't drive anymore. But my town house is close."

"Then let me give you a lift. The box—"

"I've already been enough trouble, and I'm quite capable of walking."

Rory eyed Soline's shoes with skepticism. Boston's frost-heaved sidewalks—the by-product of decades of harsh New England winters—could be challenging in flats. Pencil-thin heels coupled with a box she'd barely be able to see over spelled disaster.

"It's no trouble," she assured Soline as she pushed to her feet and grabbed the box from the table. "I'm parked right up the street."

Soline nodded, but her discomfort was plain. "Yes, all right."

Rory held the door open as they stepped out onto the sidewalk. She couldn't explain her sudden solicitousness. Soline Roussel wasn't remotely feeble. And yet there was an air of fragility about her, like a broken bit of porcelain whose pieces hadn't been properly mended. If she were jostled too roughly, she might break into a million pieces. And Rory knew only too well what that felt like.

ELEVEN

RORY

Soline sat stiffly in the passenger seat, hidden behind a pair of Hepburn-esque dark glasses, her purse clutched tightly on her knees. She hadn't spoken since rattling off her Beacon Hill address. Rory glanced at her as she turned onto Cedar Street and let off the gas.

"Which house?"

"That one," she said, pointing. "The red door. Just drop me here. I'll be fine."

Rory pulled up to the curb and cut the engine. "I'll carry the box inside for you."

Before Soline could protest, Rory was out of the car, retrieving the dress box from the back seat. Soline struggled with her seat belt a moment but eventually climbed out of the car and sailed past, keys at the ready.

Rory fell in behind her, eyeing the house's Georgian facade as they moved up the walk. Weathered red brick, glossy black shutters, a pair of chimneys at each end. And in one of Boston's most desirable neighborhoods. Apparently, Soline had done quite well for herself.

After some fumbling with the key, Soline pushed inside, leaving Rory to follow her into a spacious entry hall dominated by an ornate pedestal table and a French empire chandelier. She shed her sunglasses, depositing them on the table along with her handbag, and immediately set to work on her gloves.

Rory looked on uncomfortably until it became obvious that Soline wasn't making much progress. "Those buttons look tricky. Why don't I help you?"

Soline's shoulders sagged, like a flower wilting all at once. She said nothing as she held out her hands. Rory set down the box and unbuttoned both gloves, then met Soline's gaze. "Would you like me to . . ."

Soline nodded. "But don't pull them off by the fingers. Peel them back. Slowly."

Rory did as she'd been instructed, holding her breath as she eased back the leather. There was an audible sigh as the first glove came free, though whether hers or Soline's, she couldn't be sure. When the second hand was presented she set to work again, aware that Soline's lower lip was now caught between her teeth. Clearly, embarrassment wasn't all she was suffering.

When the job was done, Rory laid the gloves on the table, limp now and turned inside out, like the molted skins of some enormous insect. The thought sent a shudder through her, and she looked away, back to Soline, who'd begun to massage her hands with long, repetitive strokes. They were waxy white in places, puckered and pink in others, the fingers curled and faintly clawlike. Rory averted her gaze, not wanting to appear rude.

"Go on," Soline said evenly. "Look at them."

A lump formed in Rory's throat as she surveyed the damage. The contracted palms and thickened scar tissue, the slightly webbed appearance of the fingers. Useless to a woman who made her living with a needle and thread.

"It happened in the fire," Soline explained. "But of course, you've guessed that."

Rory nodded. "I did wonder why you were wearing gloves in June."

"Scars make people uncomfortable, so I cover them when I'm in public, which isn't often anymore. It's easier to keep out of people's way than to endure their pity. It isn't their fault. They *are* rather awful to look at."

It was on the tip of Rory's tongue to say she was sorry, but she caught herself. No pity. "That's why you never reopened the shop," she said instead. "Because of your hands."

"For a while, I thought I might be able to go back. I wanted to believe the doctors could work some sort of a miracle. I think they believed it too, in the beginning. But there was too much damage."

"Is it . . . painful?"

"Not in the way you're probably thinking. They're numb, mostly. Scar tissue has no nerve endings. But there's a thing called *contracture* that happens with deep burns, especially to the hands. As the scar tissue forms, it draws the fingers inward or twists them sideways." She held up her hands again, inviting Rory to look more closely. Most of the nails were gone from her right hand, leaving the fingertips shiny and flat.

"I'm one of the lucky ones, if you can believe that. There isn't a lot of pain involved, but when I wear the gloves for too long, my fingers are stretched, which makes the joints ache. Like arthritis, I suppose."

"Isn't there . . . Can't they operate or something?"

She'd begun to massage them again, alternately applying pressure to each palm with the balls of her thumbs, wincing as she worked at the scarred flesh. "I've had six operations. Debridement, tendon repair, skin grafts. And every kind of splint known to man. Then came the therapy. Pressure therapy. Stretching therapy." She shrugged. "Eventually, one reaches the end of the road. They gave me exercises to help with flexibility and range of motion. I did them for a while, when I thought there was a chance, but I stopped eventually. I didn't see the point once I knew I'd never pick up a needle again."

Rory hated the finality in her voice. "Couldn't you hire someone to do the sewing?"

Soline's gaze slid to the box at Rory's feet. "Not with my dresses. The work is delicate, very . . . specialized."

"But couldn't you train someone? An apprentice or something?"

"The work I do can't be taught and must be done by hand—by me."

"My mother remembers your shop. She said it was the most elegant bridal salon in town. I wish I could have seen it before—" Rory caught herself. "I'm so sorry. I only meant it must have been lovely."

Soline stepped away, then paused, glancing over her shoulder. "Follow me, and bring the box."

They passed through a large parlor with slate-gray walls and a long sofa upholstered in caramel-colored leather, then through a set of french doors into a small study.

It was a warm, welcoming room, though sparsely furnished. An antique writing desk, a reading chair, and a small table in front of the fireplace, shelves lined with old books bound in jewel-toned leather. But it was the opposite wall that captured Rory's attention: a montage of photographs mounted in identical black frames. Photos, newspaper clippings, magazine covers, and several rough pencil sketches of Soline's designs. She let the dress box slide to the floor and inched closer, scanning the captions, many of which stretched back thirty years.

Ooh là là! A Taste of Paris Arrives in Back Bay.

Bridal Couture Comes to Boston.

The Roussel Bow: A Must-Have For This Year's Bride.

The photos were wonderful—Soline hovering over a frothy creation with a mouthful of pins; perched on a ladder, pulling a bolt of cloth from a shelf; tweaking a large taffeta bow at the waist of a whip-thin blonde. Rory lingered over that one a moment, studying Soline's hands. Long, tapered fingers and neatly manicured nails. Beautiful and so capable—but ruined now.

The most recent photo was of the salon itself, taken four years ago for a spread in *Boston Bride*—less than a year before the fire. It was strange to see it as it had been then, elegantly furnished in shades of pewter and cream. Everything carefully chosen—and very French. Or at least what she'd always imagined French decor to look like.

There was also a shot of the large bay window, taken from the street. The salon name was lettered on the glass in elegant gold script, but she couldn't make it out. She turned to Soline. "What does it say?"

"*L'Aiguille Enchantée*," Soline answered softly. "It means the Charmed Needle."

"The Charmed Needle," Rory repeated with a dreamy air. Even the name smacked of magic. "A perfect name for a shop that sells fairy-tale dresses and happy endings."

"Make-believe," Soline shot back. "Silliness passed down through generations of Roussels."

"You don't believe in fairy tales?"

"Not for a long time now."

Rory peered at Soline's reflection, captured in the glass of the picture frame. "But you did once?"

"Fairy tales can be dangerous, *Aurore*. It's easy to forget they're not real. And then, before we know it, we're lost in them. Which is why we must learn to let go of what's gone and live with what is."

Rory felt a shiver run down her neck. Soline had been referring to her own loss, of course—of A.W.P. But the words could just as easily have been meant for her. There was no denying the similarities in their stories. Their passion for the creative, their lost loves, their penchant for withdrawing from the world—and now the row house.

A coincidence? Or had some invisible hand nudged her into the path of this tragic woman and her forsaken dress? A cautionary tale, perhaps, about what happened when one clung too desperately to the hope of a happy ending?

"A.W.P. . . . ," Rory said quietly.

"His name was Anson."

"Anson, then. Do you still . . . Have you forgotten his face?"

"I thought I might. But no, I haven't forgotten." She pulled in a breath, letting it out slowly. "I saw him everywhere at first. On the street, hailing a cab. At the bar in a crowded restaurant. Through the window of a barber shop. He was everywhere—and nowhere."

"Does it still happen?"

"Sometimes."

The response filled Rory with a vague dread. "How do you bear it?"

Soline lowered her lashes. "We all have our ghosts, *chérie*. Faces that belong to our past. Except they don't always stay in the past. Sometimes they reappear when we least expect them. That's why I put the box under the stairs. Because I *couldn't* bear it."

Rory understood that kind of pain, the ache that waited for you every night when you closed your eyes and was still there in the morning when you woke. The empty place where your heart should be. Before she could check herself, her eyes had filled with tears.

Soline narrowed her gaze, clearly alarmed. "*Chérie*, what is it? Are you unwell?"

"No. I'm fine. But I should go."

"Something's wrong."

"No. Really. I shouldn't have pestered you." She nearly tripped over the dress box as she sidled past Soline toward the door. "You don't need to show me out. I can find my way."

"*Aurore . . .*"

Rory kept moving, desperate to reach the front door before she was reduced to a pathetic puddle. She'd gotten what she wanted. She'd been determined to learn Soline Roussel's story, and she had. Now, as she beat a hasty retreat, she couldn't help wondering if she'd been given a glimpse of her own in the bargain.

TWELVE

Soline

We traffic in the promise of happily-ever-after, but not all are destined for such fairy-tale endings. Some are unable, others unwilling, and still more have been taught they are undeserving. It is up to the Spell Weaver to discern which is which.

—*Esmée Roussel, the Dress Witch*

20 June 1985—Boston

I close my eyes as the first sip of wine goes down. Louis Jadot Gevrey-Chambertin. It's a guilty pleasure of mine. Chocolate and ripe cherry, chalky on the tongue, velvety on the way down. Plush and pricey. It's funny, I had to come all the way to America to learn to appreciate French wines—*Maman* never had wine in the house—but I have learned to appreciate them. Perhaps a little more than is good for me. But it helps with my hands. With the pain. And with . . . other things. Or at least, I pretend it does.

Today's events have shaken me. For reasons I understand too well and for others I do not understand at all. I don't often have guests in my home. In fact, I never have guests in my home. No dinners, or cocktail parties, or lunches with friends. No friends. *Oui*, I know how awful that sounds. How sad and pathetic. But I don't want pity. It's a choice I made years ago. After the fire. It seems my whole life is marked as either *before the fire* or *after the fire*. Not that there's been much of a life since that terrible night. Again, my choice.

I can't remember when I last had company. A year? No, longer than that. And then it was only Daniel and his wife the Christmas before last. I'm comfortable alone—or at least used to it. Still, I was surprised by the pang of regret I felt when I heard the front door close behind that girl. But then, so much about today has surprised me. A phone call from a stranger. A packet of old letters. The dress. *Mon dieu* . . . the dress. Memories I've been hiding from for more years than I care to admit. And now they've found me. Because Aurora Grant found me.

Rory—the girl who has resurrected my past.

When she entered the patisserie, for the tiniest moment I thought I knew her. One of my clients perhaps. Or a bride I'd turned down. There was something familiar about her, a connection I sensed the instant our eyes met. And yet, as she drew closer, I saw that I was wrong. I didn't know her.

Except I *did* recognize her. She was me. Or a shadow of me when I was her age. Lost. Grieving. Desperate for a glint of light at the end of a very dark tunnel. She was lovely. A sharp, pretty face and a pink-and-cream complexion. Eyes the color of the sky when a storm approaches, neither blue nor gray, and a mane of honey-hued waves forever falling across her face—a clever way to hide from the world.

I understand that part, not wanting the world to see your sadness. You think you're the only one, singled out by fate to suffer. You're not, of course, but it feels that way. The rest of the world is moving forward, living their lives and dreaming their dreams, while you're frozen, forever suspended in that terrible moment when your world stopped turning and the ground suddenly fell away. You exist in a void, where everything's empty and endlessly dark, until little by little the light becomes unbearable.

She wanted to know my story, wanted me to open the box then and there, and was disappointed when she saw that I wouldn't. Still, she'd gone out of her way to do me a good turn. I felt obliged to satisfy at least part of her curiosity.

She was delicate with her questions, careful of my feelings. There's a particular brand of sympathy that comes with shared sorrow. An invisible thread that connects us, wound to wound. Why else would I have let her drive me home? And then that awful business with the gloves—when I invited her to look at my hands.

I can still see the look on her face when I held them out. Tenderness rather than pity. I could have kissed her for that. And then later, when her eyes filled with tears and she rushed out of the house, I wanted to go after her, to put my arms around her and let her cry her poor heart out. There's a story there. A sad one, I think. So sad she couldn't hide it, though she did try.

I don't know what's happened to Aurora Grant to make her sad. I only know that something has. But she's young. There's time for her to escape the void. Her gallery will be her lifeline. As the shop was mine. I like the idea of it, a gallery for undiscovered artists. And the title—Unheard Of. I like the girl, too, and what she said about the building—that it felt like it had been waiting for her. Perhaps it's right that her lifeline should begin where mine ended. Fate has taken up our threads and woven them together. Not seamless, perhaps, but inextricable now.

I top off my wineglass and return to the study, lingering in front of the wall of framed photographs. I rarely look at them these days—even now, the loss is hard—but this afternoon, when Rory was here, I found myself peering over her shoulder, trying to see them as she did, for the very first time. She was staring at a photo of the front window, asking if I still remembered Anson's face, when I suddenly caught our reflections in the frame's glass. She was looking back at me, and for a fraction of an instant, Anson seemed to be standing there too, his face superimposed over hers. Then I blinked and he was gone, leaving only our faces in the glass. It was only a fluke, a trick of the light and memory, but it felt so real at that moment, so startlingly and achingly real.

The dress box is still on the floor where she left it. I carry it to the chair and sit with it in my lap for a time. I don't need to open it. I know what's inside: pieces of my past threatening to burrow into my heart like wounded things. Reminders of my lost happy endings. I thought them gone, relegated to the dark space beneath the stairs, then reduced to ash. But they've been exhumed now, and I have no choice but to remember.

I feel my breath catch as I lift the lid and peel back the tissue. The dress is just as I remember, shimmery and frothy white. I run my hands over the beading, recalling long nights spent sewing in secret. *Maman* would never have approved had she known. She would have thought it a terrible waste, since there were precious few grooms left in France by the time I finished it. Still, I brought it with me when I left. Because I had dreams of my own happy ending. One day I would wear my lovely dress with its clever enchantment, and I would prove *Maman* wrong. I would prove all the Roussels wrong. It nearly worked too. Instead, I lost everything.

Tears scorch my throat as I set the box aside and turn out the light. I thought I was ready, but I'm not.

My wineglass dangles from my fingers as I make my way down the hall to my bedroom. I'm tired, and my head aches. I forget how loud public places are and how much they take out of me. My thoughts drift to the plastic vial in the nightstand, a prescription one of my doctors wrote the day I left the hospital, to help manage the pain. I stopped taking them after a week. They made me feel so heavy. But the vial is still there, an insurance policy should the nights get too long or the days too empty. I think of them now and then. Sometimes I even take them out, pour them into my palm, imagine swallowing them all at once. I won't, of course. I have other things on my mind tonight.

I undress in the dark and climb into bed, my thoughts wandering back to Rory. If I were to read her the way *Maman* taught me, what would I see? She would be easy, I think. She's like me in that way too—or how I used to be. Wide open to the world. *Maman* used to scold me for it. She said I could never hide anything, that my face would always give me away.

It was true once, but I've learned over the years to hide a great many things from the world. From myself too, I suppose. Pain has a way of hardening us, each new heartbreak laying down a fresh layer of protection, like the nacre of a pearl, until we think ourselves impenetrable, immune to both our present and our past.

What fools we are to believe it.

THIRTEEN

Soline

The temptation may arise to use la magie for selfish ends. But such transgressions will always bring an ill wind, which will then be visited upon future generations.

—*Esmée Roussel, the Dress Witch*

11 December 1942—Paris

Two and a half years of Nazi occupation have decimated Paris.

I will never forget the morning they came. I heard the soldiers before I saw them, like the distant roll of thunder as I hurried along the Rue Legendre, and made my way to the Place de la Concorde. I don't know what I expected as I turned onto the Champs-Élysées. War, I suppose. Panicked Parisians taking to the streets in one last attempt to stave off the invaders. Soldiers brandishing weapons and taking prisoners. Guns. Bombs. Fire. Blood. The chaos of war.

But there was no chaos. In fact, there had been a strange and sinister order to it all, a steely precision that was almost breathtaking. Motorcycles, horses, columns of tanks and armored cars, and thousands upon thousands of soldiers moving in lockstep, immaculate in their helmets and gray-green uniforms. As for Parisians taking to the streets, there had been none of that either. Instead, onlookers lined the sidewalks, silent and slack-jawed, awed by the machine that was swallowing their city whole. Or what remained of it at that point.

The wealthy and well connected had been pouring out of Paris for weeks: cars, trains, horse-drawn carts clogging the roads, bound for the coast as *l'exode* began in earnest. Shops had closed. Hotels had emptied. Theaters went dark. Even the market stalls had gone quiet in anticipation of the invasion. And finally, in June of 1940, it came to pass. Hitler's Wehrmacht entered Paris without firing a shot, and by late afternoon, swastikas flew over the Arc de Triomphe and the Tour Eiffel.

Life has been a blur since that terrible day. Curfews are in effect and strictly enforced. German street signs have replaced French ones, and clocks are now set to German time, a thumb in the eye of a city already demoralized. Not even our time is our own now.

French newspapers have been shut down, and all radios must be tuned to German propaganda stations. There are posters, too, tacked up all over, urging us to see our occupiers as friends. As if we can't feel them steadily tightening their grip around our throats.

Ration cards have been issued for food and clothing, resulting in endless queues for the barest of necessities. Paris has become a city obsessed with food. Finding it, affording it, making it stretch. Women spend the better part of their days in search of an egg or a soupbone, while magazines teach us how to stretch butter with gelatin and make a cake without eggs. *Maman*'s careful hoarding means we suffer less than most, but our stores are thinning at an alarming rate.

Getting around is also difficult. There's no petrol to be had, leaving only bicycles and the Métro. Or walking, which is what I usually do. Nazi soldiers are everywhere, in the cafés and the shops, drinking our wine and clearing our shelves, loitering on corners and chatting up our women, as if everything in France is theirs for the taking, which I suppose it is. But no one suffers more than the Jews.

In addition to having their property and possessions seized, the *Statut des Juifs* prohibits them from working in certain professions, going to the theater, shopping in most stores, and even owning radios. All Jews over the age of six must wear a yellow star printed with the word *Juif* over their heart, to more easily mark them for persecution. For this honor, they are made to use an entire month's cloth ration. Some defy the new law, though they do so at great risk. Those caught or denounced by Nazi sympathizers are beaten or worse.

And the roundups have begun. Thousands of Jews, mostly women and children, detained for days, without food or water, shipped first to the holding camp at Drancy before eventually being stuffed into cattle cars and taken away. Operation Spring Breeze, one of the roundups was called, organized and carried out by the French police.

By our *own* police.

But it was only the beginning. Details of the death camps have begun to leak out. Whispers of gas chambers and ovens, shallow trenches filled with bodies. All over Europe, Jews are being erased. And the French government is helping to do it.

We get our news—the *real* news—the way most Parisians do, from banned BBC broadcasts on *Radio Londres* or from whatever underground paper is being quietly passed from hand to hand. Like everything else these days, being caught means severe punishment.

Maman has been taking the news especially hard, which surprises me a little. I've never known her to be weepy, but after two years of the *boches*, we are all worn to a raveling. Her illness has taken a firm hold now, her fits of coughing so severe she's forced to submit to nightly sleeping draughts in order to rest. And there are the blood-flecked handkerchiefs I pretended not to know about until she could no longer hide them from me. Now, as another winter sets in with no fuel for warmth, her condition has become dire.

What little work there is has fallen to me now. It's fittings mostly, but I'm grateful for anything that fills the days. And then in the evenings, when the blackout curtains are drawn and *Maman* is asleep, I continue to work on my dress, though I doubt she will live long enough to see it finished.

One night, she calls me to her room and tells me to pull up a chair. It's painful to see the changes that have come over her. We're all thinner these days, but *Maman*'s thinness is of a crueler variety, a slow ravaging that has left the skin stretched taut over the bones of her face. And yet, her eyes are bright and hectic as they move over me.

"Sit," she says, swatting my hand when I reach out to touch her forehead. "I have something to tell you. Something I should have told you years ago."

"You should be resting," I reply, hoping to put her off. I don't want to talk about death. Or Nazis. Or how hard things are going to get. We've spoken of little else lately. "We can talk later. After you've had some sleep."

"What I have to say cannot wait until tomorrow."

I nod, waiting.

"Go to my dresser. In the top drawer, near the back, you'll find a box. Bring it to me."

The box is where she said it would be, a jeweler's case of dark-green velvet about the size of my palm. I carry it back to the bed and return to my chair, watching with a kind of fascination as she presses the case to her chest with inexplicable tenderness. When her gaze finally lifts to mine, it's as if she'd forgotten I was there.

Her hands tremble as she fumbles with the lid. In the end, she gives up and hands it back to me. "Open it, please."

I do as I'm told, not realizing I'm holding my breath until it escapes all at once. Inside is a pillow-shaped locket engraved with a pair of lilies. I find *Maman*'s eyes. She blinks slowly, offering the slightest of nods.

It takes a moment to locate the catch, but finally I'm staring at the face of a stranger. He's handsome in a sharp, brooding way, with high cheekbones, deep-set eyes, and a head of thick, dark curls. His mouth is full, almost feminine, tilted up at the corners, as if trying to suppress a smile.

"His name was Erich Freede," *Maman* says softly. "He was a student at the Conservatoire de Paris the summer before you were born."

She falls silent then, though I can feel her gaze on me as I continue to stare at the photograph. Eventually, her words sink in. *The summer before you were born.* I look up, a question caught like a bone in my throat.

"He was your father."

Father. The word sounds foreign on her lips, but her gaze never wavers.

"Why are you telling me this now?"

"Because we've never spoken of him. We must do that now."

I've always been curious about the man who'd managed to find a chink in my mother's armor, but suddenly I don't want to talk about him or why she's suddenly decided to have this conversation.

"He was on his way to a rehearsal when we met. I was delivering a dress on Rue de Madrid, near the school. It had rained all morning and the streets were full of puddles. I was waiting to cross at the corner when a car sped past, soaking me with muddy water. I was horrified when I looked down at the dress box. It was soaking wet and filthy, and all I could think was, Maman *will murder me if this dress is ruined.* And then he was there, holding out a handkerchief."

"Erich," I say, pronouncing the name slowly, getting used to the feel of it.

"Yes. Erich." A rare smile softens the lines illness has etched into her face. "He was wearing a white summer suit that looked like it had been made for him and black-and-white brogues so shiny, I could have used them to powder my nose. One of the smart set, with his straw boater and immaculately knotted tie. And there I was, dripping like a wet cat."

"And he fell in love with you then and there," I supply, reading the rest in her eyes.

Her expression goes soft and dreamy. "We both did. He was so handsome that when he asked me my name, I couldn't remember. It was as if my mind had suddenly been wiped clean, as if nothing had happened to me before that moment. He helped me clean up the box, then bent down to wipe the mud off my shoes. I was so flustered I knocked his hat off into the street, and before we knew it, neither of us could stop laughing. He gave me his coat to cover my wet clothes and walked me the rest of the way."

I find myself smiling. It's a side of *Maman* I have never imagined— a young woman on the brink of a grand passion. "What happened after you delivered the dress?"

"We spent every spare moment together, usually in some park or other. It wasn't much, but it was enough. He would bring a blanket and food, and I'd make some excuse about where I was going. We'd eat, and then he would play his violin for me. He played so beautifully, as if he were telling a story every time he picked up his bow. I went to a few of his concerts at the school. All those musicians playing together on one stage, and all I could hear was him. Or at least it seemed that way to me."

"How long did it last?"

"Seven months and thirteen days."

The swiftness and precision of her answer surprises me. "What happened?"

"He finished his schooling. It was time to go home."

"Home?"

She closes her eyes, wincing. "Berlin."

Her anguish is palpable and so uncharacteristic. Perhaps because I thought her incapable of such feelings. "I'm sorry he left you, *Maman*."

Her eyes open slowly, dark and bottomless. "It was me," she whispers. "I ended it."

"You? Why?"

"He wanted me to go back to Germany with him, to marry him. But your grandmother forbid it. Even when I told her there was going to be a baby."

"Because of the shop?"

"Because of the war," she replies quietly. "Erich was a German. A *boche*, as they were known then—and still are, I suppose. My mother never forgave them for the Somme. So many of our boys were killed there, slaughtered in the trenches by the thousands. She couldn't forgive it. Many couldn't. She said marrying a German would bring far more shame than a bastard child."

"So that was it? You just let him leave?"

She nods, pulling in a phlegmy breath. "His parents were dead, and his sisters had gone to live with an aunt while he attended school. It was time to go back to his responsibilities. I could have made him stay," she whispers thickly. "If I had told him about you, he would have stayed."

I stare at her, stunned. "You never told him you were pregnant?"

She turns her face away. "It would only have made things harder for us both. We had . . . responsibilities."

I blink at her, trying to understand. It isn't that I've missed having a father—you can't miss what you've never had—but her argument makes no sense. "What could be more responsible than marrying the father of your child?"

"It wasn't as easy as that. There was the shop to think about. I couldn't leave *Maman* with only Lilou to help. Not when I knew she wouldn't stay. Even when we were girls, my sister had one foot out the door. And then there were the stories—all the broken Roussel hearts, the ones who defied the rules of our calling and suffered for it. *Maman* said mine would be next and that when it happened, I couldn't come back." A pair of tears squeezes from between her clenched lids, leaving thin silver tracks in their wake. "I would be on my own—like my mother was after Lilou was born."

"So you kept your secret and broke Erich's heart instead."

"I was afraid."

The admission brings a lump to my throat. "And you never saw him again?"

She shakes her head, slowly, painfully. "I had a letter once, begging me to reconsider. I was afraid I would weaken, so I threw it in the fire. Lilou was livid with me. She never understood duty. And I . . ." Her eyes drift from mine. "I never understood anything else."

"I'm so sorry," I say softly, because I am. But I'm angry too. That I'd never had the chance to know this man who told stories with his violin or the woman my mother had been then, the one who'd fallen in love with a stranger on a street corner. I would have liked that woman. But the years have transformed her into someone else—into an unhappy echo of the very mother who had forced her to deny her heart. It seems a terrible irony as I sit listening to her story, and I wonder if she realizes it, too, and if that's why she's decided to tell me her story.

"It must have broken your heart to let him go," I say gently. And then a thought suddenly occurs. "Is that why you're telling me now, because you want me to help you find him?"

Her tears come suddenly and noisily, like a dam breaking, and I can't think of anything to say. I have no experience in offering her comfort and I'm apparently doing it badly. "I'm so sorry, *Maman*. Whatever I said, I'm sorry."

"He was Jewish," she sobs raggedly. "Erich Freede was Jewish."

I stare at her, struggling to connect the words with the anguish in her eyes. It takes a moment, but finally I understand. A Jew. In Germany.

"The Nazis," I say quietly. "*Mon dieu*."

She closes her eyes, dragging in another sob. "The stories . . . The camps . . . I can't bear to think of it."

I glance at the locket in my hand, recalling the day one of *Maman*'s clients shared her account of *Kristallnacht*, how she had closed the shop and gone to her room and not come out until morning. And how, when she heard about the Vél' d'Hiv roundup on the radio, she had wept uncontrollably and refused to eat for days. She hadn't been crying for humanity; she'd been crying for Erich Freede, because she'd never stopped loving him.

It was why she'd been hanging on every word of the daily BBC broadcasts, scouring every line of the contraband newspapers that sometimes found their way into our letter box. And perhaps why she's taken to feverishly fingering her rosary of late—a hedge against evil.

"Have you . . . had news of him?"

"No." She covers her mouth, eyes clenched as a fresh pair of tears spills down her cheeks. "For years, I've imagined him playing all the great halls in Europe, holding audiences in the palm of his hand. It was a way of holding on to him, imagining him happy after everything that happened, and now . . . I don't know where he is. I don't know if he's alive or dead."

My heart aches as I watch her speak, but I'm afraid too. Her breathing is thick and raspy, her lips blanched of color as she labors to breathe. "Please, *Maman*. You mustn't upset yourself."

"If only I hadn't listened to my mother . . . If I'd told him about you and asked him to stay, he might be safe now."

"You don't know that, *Maman*. Jews are being rounded up here too. We're doing it. The French."

She struggles up from her pillow, clutching at my hand. "But it might have been different. Don't you see? If he had remained in Paris, I would have been able to warn him. Instead, I broke his heart . . . and now I've killed him."

I press her back against her pillows, hushing her like a child in the throes of a nightmare. I tell her to close her eyes and I stroke her hair, trying to recall a time when the roles were reversed and she was the one to comfort me. I can't. She's never been that kind of mother. Still, I can't deny her that small bit of tenderness. Not when her heart is breaking.

I sit on the edge of her bed, waiting for her to quiet, and think of the *maléfice*—the curse. *Maman*'s mother had warned her that loving Erich Freede would lead to heartbreak. But how was that different from her current anguish, wondering if the man she loved was hiding somewhere, like a cornered animal, or imprisoned at the mercy of monsters at one of the camps? If that's what comes of protecting your heart, I want no part of it.

Maman withdraws her hand from mine, brushing impatiently at her tears. "I wanted you to have the locket because I want you to have a part of your father. And because I need you to do something."

I nod mutely.

"You will leave Paris one day. Take the locket when you go. Take him away from this place with all its terrible memories. Promise me you will."

"Leave Paris?" I stare at her, stunned. "But where would I go? Paris is my home."

"Not anymore. And you will leave. You must."

"But the shop. The work. You always said—"

"I said a lot of things. I taught you to live for the work, because that's what I was taught, but I was wrong. I was wrong about so much."

"*Maman*—"

"Let me speak!"

I open my mouth, then close it again. It will do me no good to argue.

"I've always kept you at arm's length. No, don't shake your head. We both know it's true. But you don't know why." She drags in a breath, rattling and wet. "You were so like him, Soline. So much it hurt to look at you. You have my eyes, my hair, my mouth, but you have always had his heart. He was a dreamer—*un rêveur*. He had such plans for us." She pauses to drag in a shuddering breath. "I took that from him—and I was reminded of it every time I looked at you."

Something in my chest lets go as I process her words. For years, I've wondered what I had done to deserve her wintery brand of motherhood, hoping to find something, anything that might thaw her toward me. Now I understand that there was nothing. There's a strange relief in knowing.

I lay my hand over hers. "I think you should rest. Your medicine—"

Her eyes flash feverishly. "Be quiet and listen. A chance is coming for you, Soline. One that will take you away from here. You must take it."

"It's too late to go to Lilou. London is in the crosshairs too."

"Not Lilou. Farther away. And for good."

"But the shop . . ."

She shakes her head, silencing me. "That's over now. The Nazis have seen to that. They'll scorch the earth before they're finished. But you will start again. In a new place."

An uneasy churning has begun beneath my ribs. "How do you know this?"

Her eyes flash again. "How do you think? I took the hairbrush from your bureau while you were gone to the butcher."

"You performed a reading . . . on me?"

"Not fully. You came back too soon. But I saw enough."

The admission astonishes me. She's always been so adamant about the dangers of using *la magie* to meddle in our own affairs. "But you always said—"

"Yes, yes." She sighs, flapping a bony hand. "I know what I said, but I bent the rules. There are times when we must know which way the wind will blow, and it will blow you far away, *ma fille*. Far from Paris and all this madness. But you will not escape unscathed. There will be hardship and heartbreak along the way. You must hold tight to your faith, Soline, whatever comes."

I look at her, bewildered. The Roussels have no faith, as such. We have our needles and our thread. That is our faith—The Work. "Please don't speak in riddles, *Maman*."

"My faith was tested once, when I was a little older than you. I failed." She stops, craning her neck to pull in a breath. "I had no faith in what could be—a life of my own and love. Because I was not a dreamer. And so I followed the path marked out for me. But you, So-So . . . you have such dreams. And you're gifted. More gifted than I ever was."

For a moment, I can't even blink. I've waited so long for even the tiniest crumb of recognition, proof that she saw me at all. Now, suddenly . . . praise. I want to weep, but I know *Maman* will not like it. "I had a good teacher," I say instead.

She waves the words away, impatient to finish what she has to say. "This chance I spoke of . . . it will test your heart. It might even break it. But the most precious gifts always come at the highest price. I learned this too late . . . which is why I'm telling you now. You must—"

She breaks off, clutching a handkerchief to her mouth to muffle a sudden bout of coughing. By the time the spasms finally stop she's ashen and shaking, her lips faintly blue. I reach for her hand, the birdlike bones fragile beneath my fingers, and it suddenly strikes me how seldom I've seen them quiet over the years. Always with a needle, a tape, a pair of shears. Stitching, pinning, hemming. But soon her illness will still them for good.

My eyes well before I can look away. She catches me by the sleeve, and for an instant, I glimpse a softness in her face. "No tears, *mon tendre*. Not for me. You will need them later. So many changes are coming, and you must be ready."

I do as I'm told and blot my eyes on my sleeve, but her grave predictions have me rattled. "You're frightening me with all this dire talk, *Maman*. Can't you just tell me what you know?" But the moment the words leave my mouth, I regret them. "Never mind," I say quickly. "You're tired. You mustn't talk any more tonight."

She turns her head away, and for a moment, I think she's crying, but when she looks at me again, her eyes are dry. When she finally speaks, her voice is slushy and thick. "Here is what I know, *ma fille*. There is a grief worse than death. It is the grief of a life half-lived. Not because you don't know what could have been—but because you do. You realize too late that it was there for the taking—right there in your hands—and you let it slip away. Because you let something—or someone—keep you apart. But when your time comes, you can do it differently, *ma fille*. And it will come. But you must keep him alive, So-So." She pauses, pressing a fist to her breast. "Here, in your heart. And never give up on what can be true for you. As long as you keep his beautiful face in your heart, he will never truly be lost. There will always be a way back."

She's rambling now, hovering on the edge of sleep, confusing her past with my future. Her sleeping draught is taking effect. "Rest now, *Maman*. Close your eyes and rest."

Her eyes remain locked on my face, suddenly wide and fever bright. "There are times for holding on in this life, So-So, and times for letting go. You must learn to know the difference—and trust your heart enough to let it break. It's a hard thing, this holding on. But that's where the faith comes in. Do you understand?"

I nod, because finally I think I do. I glance at the locket, still open in my lap. Erich Freede's dark eyes stare back at me. *Keep his face . . . his beautiful face . . . always in your heart.* Yes. For *Maman*'s sake, I will.

"Sleep now," I say softly.

She lets go of my hand and closes her eyes, settling into her pillows with a long, spongy sigh. I linger briefly, digesting all that has passed between us, wishing it could have come sooner, stunned that it's come at all. The silence stretches. I stand, then turn to go.

"Leave him with me," she calls softly, her voice thin and childlike. "Just for a little while."

I close the locket and press it into her palm, curling her fingers around it, then bend down to place a kiss on her forehead. It's an act I've never performed before—and will never perform again.

The next morning, I enter her room to find that she has slipped away. She lies quiet against her pillows, her face pale in death. But beautiful, too, as if slipping her skin has at long last freed her to be happy. Her hand lies open against the sheets, the locket and her rosary lying loose in her palm. I put the rosary in her bureau, then fasten the locket around my neck. The weight of it between my breasts feels foreign. My father. A stranger. But I've made a promise, and I will keep it.

I feel no surprise at finding her gone, only a dull wave of sadness as I pull the bedroom door closed behind me. I knew in my bones that our talk last night was meant to be a kind of goodbye.

As usual, *Maman* has had the last word.

FOURTEEN

SOLINE

We do not create love from thin air, using philters or glamours or any other manner of manipulation. We do not create love at all. We merely shepherd its expression and assure its survival.

—*Esmée Roussel, the Dress Witch*

3 March 1943—Paris

I have closed the shop for good, not that anyone noticed.

Maman was buried quietly in a cardboard casket covered with cloth, because there was no wood for a proper coffin. Flowers appeared on the stoop, small posies tied with bits of ribbon or twine. And of course, the letters—dozens of envelopes pushed through the shop's letter box, heartfelt remembrances from brides *Maman* helped find happiness over the years. So many seeming miracles, accomplished with a handful of stitches and a little bit of magick.

I've saved some of the letters, bundling them together with a length of ribbon. They're *Maman*'s legacy to me—a collection of her happy endings. It helps to read them now and then, to know she will be remembered. But life must go on. Death is everywhere these days. On the radio and in the papers, in the camps and on the battlefields, the prisons and field hospitals. To most, Esmée Roussel is just one more missing face in the queues, but I feel her absence keenly.

For as long as I can remember, she has been the voice in my ear, directing my work, shaping my thoughts—shaping *me*. And with her gone, I suddenly feel unshaped. I've never been much more than Esmée Roussel's daughter. Suddenly, I'm not even that.

After years of clandestine work, I have finally finished my dress—a Soline Roussel original—but there seems little point in starting another. As *Maman* predicted, there are no brides in Paris because there are no grooms. Unless one counts the *boche*, which I do not.

My life has simply lost its rhythm. I have no one to cook for, sew for, care for, and I'm at a loss to see what comes next. My world, never more than a few miles wide, has shrunk to a handful of rooms, with entire weeks passing when I do not venture outside. But my hoard of supplies has dwindled alarmingly. It is time to rejoin the living in the food queues.

It's a drizzly Wednesday morning. I grab my umbrella and my ration cards and head to the shops. It's a meat day, and the queue at the butcher's is already spilling out into the street, thin faces all in a row, sharp with hunger and mistrust. I take my place among them, sharing my umbrella with the woman behind me.

It's impossible to ignore the talk rippling up and down the queue. Murmurs of diphtheria and the tuberculosis that killed *Maman*. Children with rickets. Babies born too weak to survive. People dropping dead of starvation in Poland. And the question no one speaks aloud—how long before it's us?

But worse than the threat of hunger, for me at least, is the smothering weight of boredom. I need something to fill my days, some way to be useful again, or I'll run mad. A few of the couture houses are still open: Lelong, Grès, Schiaparelli. But they're dressing the Nazi wives now, and *Maman* wouldn't approve of me having a hand in that. Not that I'd ever get my foot in any of those doors. Sadly, I haven't the slightest idea what else I might be fit for.

And then one morning, I ride *Maman*'s old bicycle to Neuilly-sur-Seine, on the outskirts of the city, to trade two skeins of lace—more prized than beef on the black market and twice as hard to find—for some butter and a handful of eggs. I'm near the American Hospital when a trio of ambulances grinding up the street sends a shiver through me. Sirens aren't uncommon on the streets of Paris—far from it—but I don't think any of us has gotten used to that jarring, plaintive wail. We all know what it means. More butchered men. More widows.

I watch, transfixed, as they pass through the hospital gate and into the large front courtyard. There's a clamor as the sirens die, a bustle of slamming doors and swarming uniforms as the drivers spill out to unload their cargo.

Hospitals all over France are overflowing. We've all heard the horror stories: doctors performing amputations from sunup to sundown, nurses so overwhelmed they often collapse from lack of sleep, volunteers changing linens and manning bedpans—anything to lighten the load.

Before I realize what I'm doing, I've abandoned my bicycle in the shade of a chestnut tree and am marching toward the courtyard. After two years of caring for *Maman*, changing her linens and helping her bathe, washing her bloody handkerchiefs and dosing out her sleeping draughts, I'm no stranger to the baser duties of nursing. Suddenly, I see a way to fill my days and be useful.

No one notices me. There's so much going on, men scurrying in every direction, orders being shouted as the American drivers scramble to unload the casualties. Bandaged eyes. A shattered jaw. A leg grotesquely twisted. A palm-size bit of shrapnel jutting from a hastily dressed chest wound. A boy no older than me with a blood-soaked stump where his right arm should have been.

A wave of nausea washes over me as I take it all in, the courtyard tilting dizzily as I fight to keep down my breakfast. I cover my mouth, willing the faintness to pass as I search for the shortest route back to my bike. And yet, I can't seem to make my feet move. I just stand there, paralyzed and clammy, caught between the overwhelming urge to flee and the need to render whatever aid I might be capable of.

In the end, the choice is made *for* me. One of the drivers—the one who seems to be in charge—suddenly notices me standing very still amid the chaos.

"Tell Alice we've got seven total," he barks at me. "Three critical."

Alice?

I blink at him, then turn to peer over my shoulder. When I find no one there, I turn back to him and blink again.

"*Parlez-vous anglais?*" he snaps in nearly perfect French.

"*Oui.* I mean, yes. Yes, I do."

He narrows his eyes, surveying me from head to heel. There isn't much to see. I haven't bothered with my appearance since the shop closed, and I've bothered even less today. I'm wearing a pair of old culottes, practical when one must get around on a bicycle, and a plain white blouse with one of *Maman's* cardigans over it.

"Are you a volunteer here?" he asks, in English now.

I look around awkwardly, then blurt the first word that comes into my head. "*Oui.*"

"Then get a move on. Seven and three."

He turns away before I can ask him anything else and resumes barking orders. With my eyes averted, I pick my way around several stretchers and head for the entrance. There's no guard posted, I realize, no sign of a German anywhere, which seems odd. You can't go a block without tripping over a Nazi these days.

Inside, the chaos is more controlled, somber and antiseptic, like a hive where every inmate knows its purpose and goes about it with grim determination. Nurses, dull-eyed with fatigue, bustling about in their crisp whites and practical shoes. Volunteers crisscrossing the receiving area with carts and basins and armloads of linens. Soldiers in wheelchairs, clustered in corners and along walls, rehashing the glories of battle or smoking cigarettes and staring into space.

It's overwhelming but exhilarating, too, to be standing in the middle of so much activity. Paris has fallen under a kind of spell since the Nazis arrived, as if the city itself has gone into hibernation, hoping to sleep until the nightmare is over. But the doctors and nurses, and even the volunteers, can't afford to hibernate. They're on a mission, and suddenly I desperately want to be part of it.

I catch the eye of a nurse with a head full of coppery curls beneath her starched cap. "I'm supposed to talk to Alice," I say tentatively.

"There," she responds with a hike of her thumb. "The one with the clipboard. If you run, you might just catch her."

I catch up with Alice as she's about to push through a set of double doors. "*Excusez-moi.*"

She turns, gray eyes wide beneath iron-colored brows. For an instant, she looks genuinely amused. "You must be new. No one says *excuse me* around here. What do you need?"

"A man outside—the one in charge of the ambulances—sent me to say *seven total, three critical.*"

The steely brows shoot up, all traces of amusement gone. "Right."

And with that, she's off, snapping out orders in a voice that can be heard long after the doors swing shut behind her. Moments later, the first stretchers appear, accompanied by a flurry of low voices and scuffing feet. I watch uneasily as they disappear through a different set of doors marked TRIAGE, wondering how many, if any, will go home to their families.

The bustle quiets once the wounded have been dispatched, and I suddenly feel exposed and out of place. Before I can ask who I should talk to about volunteering, a woman I recognize as the mother of one of *Maman's* brides spots me and makes her way over. She wears no makeup, and her usually impeccable coif has been reduced to a few hastily applied pins.

"You're Madame Roussel's girl, Soline." Her face softens when I nod. "I heard about your *maman. Je suis désolée.*"

"*Merci*, Madame Laval."

"Please. It's just Adeline these days. Have you come to help the boys, then?"

"I have. But I don't know where to go."

She pats my arm and gives me a little wink. "Come with me."

I assume she's taking me to an office somewhere, where I will speak to whomever is in charge and fill out some papers. Instead, she leads me to a corner piled with cardboard boxes. She lifts three from one of the stacks and drops them into my arms.

"Take those to the storeroom, through there and to the right, and come back for more."

"Are you . . . in charge?"

"In charge?" She throws her graying head back and laughs. "*Bonté divine!* Dr. Jack is in charge here, and make no mistake. I'm just doing my bit, same as everyone else. Now, off with you. And mind where you go. It wouldn't do to blunder into the surgery on your first day."

I do as I'm told and find myself in a narrow corridor lit with light bulbs that have been painted blue to comply with blackout restrictions. The combined smells of alcohol and iodine grow sharper as I move down the hallway, in search of a sign that reads STORAGE ROOM.

There are so many doors, most of them unmarked, and I imagine myself walking through the wrong one or, worse, being called out for trespassing where I don't belong. But no one seems to pay me the least bit of attention, too busy with their own tasks to notice a confused new face in the crowd.

"Are you lost?"

I start guiltily, nearly dropping my boxes as I whirl around. It's the ambulance driver who barked at me in the courtyard. He seems taller than he did outdoors, broad-shouldered and lean in his uniform khakis, blond and tan the way only an American can be.

"I'm afraid I am," I admit, embarrassed to be caught flustered for the second time by this man who seems to have command of himself and everything around him. "It's my first day, and I'm . . ."

My words trickle to a halt. There's a smear of blood on his shoulder, dark but not quite dry, and another one on the side of his neck, just below his ear, and all I can think is: *Is it the blood of the boy with half an arm or the man with the metal sticking out of his chest?*

Suddenly, my mouth is full of saliva, and the room begins to sway. Overhead, the blue-painted light bulbs seem to dim. Still, I can't look away from the blood, as if it represents all the dead boys in France. All the ache, and loss, and horror.

The American seems to sense my distress and quickly relieves me of the boxes. "Are you going to be sick?"

The words seem to come from a long way off, as if spoken underwater, but eventually they register. *Sick. Am I going to be sick?* I turn my head and pull in a lungful of air, ashamed of my weakness in front of this stoic man.

"I don't . . . know," I manage thickly. "I think . . ."

Before I can finish, he has hold of my elbow and is steering me back up the corridor. We stop in front of a narrow door marked LAVATORY. He opens it and pushes me inside. "Go ahead. Don't fight it. It'll only drag things out."

I blink at him a moment, then fold myself over the toilet and bring up the remains of my breakfast. It's over soon enough, but my legs are shaking miserably, and my face is clammy with sweat. To my horror, I begin to cry.

I hear him turn on the tap, then feel something cool and wet being pressed into my hand. A handkerchief. I wipe my mouth, then blot my eyes. He takes the handkerchief and rinses it out, then carefully folds it and hands it back. "Hold this on the back of your neck. It'll help."

"I'm so sorry."

"What for?"

I shake my head, blinking away a fresh rush of tears. "I'm not usually squeamish, but I saw the blood on your uniform, and it reminded me of the boy you brought in, the one with half his arm gone, and all I could think was, *How many there are just like him now*. And how many more who would feel lucky to have only lost an arm."

"You're new," he says quietly.

I nod, wiping my eyes again. "I don't know how I even ended up here. I left home on my bicycle this morning to barter for some eggs."

I'm surprised when he barks out a laugh. It's the opposite of what I'm expecting, but I suppose my response wasn't what he'd been expecting either, and I suddenly find myself laughing too.

"You'll get used to it," he says when we've laughed ourselves out. "Okay, not used to it, but better able to cope. In the meantime, remember that everyone in this place had a first day."

I look away. "Not like this one."

He leans in with a sly smile. "Can I tell you a secret?"

"What?"

"I've been doing this for almost a year, and I still toss my cookies at least once a week."

I don't know whether to believe him or not, but I'm grateful for his kindness and am about to say so when I'm interrupted by a conspicuous cough.

"Let's go, Romeo," a voice calls gruffly from the hallway. "Time to move out."

Romeo.

I feel my face go red. This disembodied voice—whoever he is—thinks he's interrupting a *rendez-vous romantique*, which is what anyone coming across a young French girl and a handsome American huddled in a bathroom would think.

Romeo blows out a breath. "Yeah, yeah." For the first time, I notice how tired he looks. "Tell Patrick I'll be right there." He waits until he's sure we're alone again, then smiles sheepishly. "Sorry. Duty calls."

"Of course." I hold out the soggy handkerchief, awkward again.

He glances at it and grins. "Hang on to it. I'll be back."

I watch him go, then turn on the tap to rinse out the handkerchief. It's made of fine cotton, expensive, with a thin satin stripe woven through at the edge. My hands go quiet when I see the bit of red in one corner. For a moment I think it's blood, then realize it's a monogram. It seems strange, like finding a silver tea service in the middle of a battlefield. What kind of soldier carries monogrammed handkerchiefs? I hold it to the light, peering at the letters picked out in fancy script—A.W.P.

I spend the rest of the day looking for his face in the corridors and wondering what the letters stand for.

FIFTEEN

Soline

Before proceeding, one must be certain the lovers are destined for happiness. It is not a matter of attraction. Rather, it is a question of capacity. The potential to be happy must be there in both parties. If it is not, no charm, however skillfully worked, can guarantee a happy outcome.

—Esmée Roussel, the Dress Witch

10 March 1943—Paris

A week has passed with no sign of my American Romeo. I bring the handkerchief with me to work every day, hoping for a chance to return it. Not because I'm worried he might need it—a man who carries a monogrammed handkerchief in a war zone will have plenty more just like it—but because I want him to know I'm still here, that I haven't quit.

In fact, I'm getting used to the place, the smells and sights, the long hours and war-battered faces. I give sponge baths and fill water pitchers, deliver meals and empty bedpans. I even help write letters to sweethearts. The hardest part has been learning my way around, to know which doors are off-limits and which are allowed, which ward holds which type of casualty, and the quickest way to get to the mess when I finally get a break. And that's where I am when I finally see him again—Romeo.

I've just finished a letter for a Canadian airman with two broken arms when I look up from my coffee cup and see him in the doorway. I can tell from his expression that he's been there awhile, watching me, and I feel my cheeks color.

My pulse skitters as our eyes meet. He's smiling that big American smile of his, lounging against the doorframe with his arms folded across his chest. When I return his smile, he drops his arms and heads for my table. There's a bandage on his forehead, a bruise at his temple.

"You're still here," he says, grinning. "I wasn't sure you would be."

"You're hurt."

He shrugs, rubbing a hand along his jaw. "One of the field hospitals got caught short, and I was stuck for a few days. Things got a little hairy one night, but we managed. Anyway, it looks like you've settled in for the long haul."

"I had no choice. I owe you a handkerchief."

His blue-green eyes flash mischievously. "My plan worked, then. I'm glad."

I feel timid suddenly, and breathless, and giddy, and I find myself wondering if this was how *Maman* felt the day she met Erich Freede. "The monogram," I ask shyly. "A.W.P. What does it stand for?"

"Anson. My name is Anson William Purcell. Now you."

"I'm Soline Roussel."

"Pleased to meet you, Soline Roussel." He holds out a hand. I take it, briefly startled by the warmth of his fingers. "So how are things? Easier now that you've found your footing?"

"A little, yes. One of the other volunteers has taken me under her wing. She knew my mother before she passed away and has been very kind."

117

His grin disappears, his face softening. "I'm sorry about your mother. When did she die?"

"Three months ago now, I think. I'm losing track of the days. We had a small bridal salon in the Rue Legendre, but she got sick and the *boche* came. I thought since I had nursed her, I would be prepared. But that first day, seeing those poor boys . . . I wasn't ready."

"Of course you weren't, but you stayed anyway. That was brave."

I peer at the red-and-green American Field Service patch on his sleeve. I've heard stories about the American drivers, how many of them had joined up before the United States even entered the war and had come over at their own expense, earning them the nickname the Gentlemen Volunteers.

"There's a lot of talk about the drivers. They say you volunteer to come and that you actually pay your own way. Is it true?"

He makes a face. "It's not as big a deal as it sounds. Most of us are rich boys from Princeton and Yale, looking for adventure."

"Which are you?"

"Yale. Like my old man and his old man. Or was."

"You left university to do this? Why?"

He shrugs, but there's something evasive about the gesture, as if the subject makes him uncomfortable. "I wanted to do my part. And I liked the AFS's motto—*that freedom and mercy shall not perish from this earth*." Another shrug. "Anyway, here I am."

"Your family must be proud."

"My mother's been gone almost three years, so it's just my sister and my father now. And *proud* isn't exactly the word I'd use. The Purcells have always been navy men, and I was expected to fall in line. My father was set to pull the required strings to get me into Officer Candidate School when I graduated, but I didn't want that. Any more than I wanted to get roped into the family business. Needless to say, he was pretty steamed when I told him I'd quit school to sign up."

I survey the damage to his face. We've all heard stories of AFS drivers killed in the line of duty or detained and questioned by the Gestapo for aiding escaped prisoners. "Perhaps he's just concerned for your safety and thinks you'd be safer as an officer in the American navy."

The corners of his mouth twitch with something like a grimace. "No, I've just spoiled his plans."

"Are you . . . being careful?"

He tips his head to one side, studying me in return. "Does it matter to you that I'm careful?"

My cheeks go hot. He's nothing to me and isn't likely to be, but I tell myself it's a perfectly valid question. "I think it must matter to your father and sister."

His smile slips, replaced by something flinty and unreadable. "There isn't time to be careful. You do what you're sent to do. If you're lucky, you get back in one piece so you can do it all over again the next day."

"How do you do it? Aren't you afraid?"

"Every single day."

"But you do it anyway."

"Same as you."

I shake my head, unwilling to concede that his work and mine are in any way similar. "You save lives. I change sheets and write letters."

"Don't think for a minute that writing a letter to a soldier's mother or sweetheart isn't saving his life. It's a lifeline, a reason to keep going." He pauses, running a hand through his thatch of blond hair. His expression is deadly earnest. "We're all doing what we can, Soline, and we're all scared silly. But we show up every day, because it's important stuff. All of it—all of us—important."

I'm trying to think of something to say when I hear my name. I turn to find Adeline standing in the doorway, pointing to her wristwatch. I throw her a nod and stand. "I have to go."

Anson pushes to his feet, catching my hand. "I'll miss you, Soline Roussel."

His voice, low and warm, makes my pulse quicken. "Don't be silly. You can't miss someone you don't know."

He shoots me a roguish grin. "You're Soline Roussel from Paris, France. You're kind and beautiful, and once upon a time you and your mother owned a bridal salon. Now you spend your time nursing soldiers. I'm Anson Purcell, Yale dropout. My family is from Newport, Rhode Island. My father is named Owen, and he builds racing yachts. My mother's name was Lydia. My sister is Cynthia—Thia for short—and she wants to be a French Impressionist when she grows up. There. Now we know each other, which means I can miss you properly."

Something warm and unfamiliar spirals in my belly. My world has been one of women, brides and their mothers, *Maman*. No one has ever flirted with me, but I recognize it when I hear it, and I can't blame him. It's easier than talking about war and death. But I've been warned about Americans, all disarming smiles and apple pie. I take an awkward step back, pulling my hand free.

"I have to go. The patients need their lunch." I turn toward the door, then glance back at him over my shoulder. "Try to be careful."

I feel curiously removed from my body as I walk away, as if my feet aren't quite touching the floor. Adeline is waiting with an arched brow and a sly cat's grin.

"And what was that about?"

"Nothing," I reply quickly. A lie. Because even in that moment of flushed confusion, I know it was the very opposite of nothing. "He lent me a handkerchief on my first day, and I was just saying thank you."

"Over coffee?"

I reach for an explanation but quickly give up. Nothing I say will wipe the grin off her face. "It was nothing, Adeline. He was kind to me."

She chuckles knowingly. "They usually are—*kind*. But be careful, *chérie*. This isn't the cinema. The hero, however handsome, isn't always a safe bet."

"Do you think he's a hero?" I ask, sounding every bit as dreamy as I feel.

"Well, if he isn't, he certainly looks the part. And the AFS must think so. They're terribly picky about who they accept. Then, I suppose they have to be. It takes a special breed to do what they do. Which is why you should be careful with your heart, little girl. Attachments are dangerous things in wartime."

I nod obediently, but in my bones, I know it's too late. An attachment has already been formed, at least for me.

Adeline claps her work-reddened hands as we approach the orthopedic ward, where a cart stacked with metal mess trays awaits. "*Voilà! C'est très bien.* We'll feed the men, and then you and I will have some lunch, and you can tell me about this handkerchief."

I don't know where I would be without Adeline. She's helped me find my footing, introducing me to the other volunteers and stepping in to smooth over my blunders.

I remember one day in particular. We had a flurry of casualties come in and everyone was scurrying to make up fresh beds. I'd just left the laundry with an armload of linens and was coming around a corner when I blundered into the hospital's resident physician in charge—Dr. Jack, as he's known—soaking him with a scalding cup of coffee.

Sumner Jackson's temper is a frequent topic of discussion among the nurses. But as I looked up at him that day, at his dripping white coat and thundercloud face, I realized the rumors hadn't done him justice. He was tall and broad with thick shoulders, heavy brows that sat low over his eyes, and a nose that reminded me more of a prizefighter than a surgeon.

I gulped out an apology in French, then in English, then in French again, all the while trying to keep my armload of sheets from tumbling to the floor. As usual, Adeline appeared to rescue me, explaining that I was new and still a little clumsy. I held my breath while he looked me over with his dark, flat eyes.

Finally, in place of his scowl, the hint of a smile appeared. "Mademoiselle, it is my considered medical opinion that coffee, while highly effective when taken internally, is of little value when applied to the skin. Perhaps a little slower around the corners in future."

And with that, he stepped around me and moved off down the hall, leaving me with knocking knees and an armload of coffee-spattered sheets.

In the weeks since, I have learned a great deal about Sumner Jackson, about his personal mission and the extraordinary lengths he has undertaken to make sure no German soldier ever occupies one of our beds. The patients we tend are either French, Canadian, English, or American. For the most part, we've stopped paying attention to their nationalities. All we know is that the beds are full and so are the bedpans.

Some of the men—boys, really, not much older than I—are from prison camps and are sent back when they're well enough. Others, the worst of them, are shipped home, too mutilated to return to the battlefield. And some die. Sometimes after seeming to make a full recovery. It's always a shock to arrive in the morning and find a bed empty or already occupied by an unfamiliar face. The stories are always the same. *A sudden turn for the worse. Sepsis. Hemorrhage. The doctors did all they could.* It's always so sudden, so horribly and tragically unexpected.

In the beginning I asked questions, but no one seemed to want to talk about those empty beds. The living are what the doctors and nurses are about. And as I have quickly learned, it is what I need to be about, too, if I want to remain at the hospital. I'm to do as I'm told without question or comment and keep my nose out of matters outside my purview.

And so I do as I'm told. I keep my head down and make myself useful, seeing to meals, stocking supplies, fetching and carrying whatever needs fetching and carrying. But my favorite duty is writing letters for soldiers who can't write for themselves. Perhaps it's to do with what Anson said in the mess that day—that writing letters saves lives too.

The words I take down are often sad, but they're always brave. It's hard sometimes not to cry as I write, knowing that somewhere there's a mother or a wife or a fiancée who would soon read them and would weep with a mixture of gratitude and anguish. Maimed but safe. Blind but spared. Alive but forever changed.

There was no way of knowing when or even *if* the letters would arrive. Personal correspondence would sit in a pile for days, even weeks, waiting to be inspected by the censors. Finally, after being cleared, they were put on a ship or a plane and with any luck would reach their destination in four to six weeks. If they arrived at all.

Still, the men write—some of them every day—glossing over the muddy, bloody grind of war with false assurances and newsy bits of this and that. It's hope they're sending home, a slender thread tethering them to someone across the sea. To mothers and wives and sweethearts all enduring a hell of their own. Weeks without word. Prayers gone unanswered. Letters that never come.

And telegrams that do.

SIXTEEN

RORY

June 23, 1985—Boston

Rory grimaced as she wrestled her curls into a ponytail. She looked like she had during exam week, hollow-eyed and pale after pulling too many all-nighters.

It had been three days since her meeting with Soline, and she couldn't shake the feeling that their chance acquaintance had been meant as a kind of wake-up call, a reminder that life rarely unfolded the way it did in novels. Love *didn't* conquer all, heroes *weren't* invincible, and lovers rarely rode off into the sunset together. Broken hearts stayed broken.

She glanced at her watch, then back at her face. She wished she'd gotten up early enough to at least blow out her hair. Or better yet, phone her mother to say something had come up and she couldn't make brunch, but it was too late for that now. The Veuve was already on ice, and she was going to be late. Again.

She was on her hands and knees, rooting under the bed for her left shoe, when the doorbell rang. She headed for the door, expecting a child with braids selling Girl Scout cookies or a pair of well-dressed young men handing out religious tracts. Instead, she found Soline Roussel standing in the hall, holding a white pastry box tied with Sugar Kisses' familiar black-and-white logo.

"*Bonjour*," Soline said brightly. "I hope you're hungry."

Rory opened her mouth, but nothing would come out. She couldn't have been more flustered if she'd opened the door and found Princess Di in the hall. "What are you doing here?" she managed, stepping aside to let Soline enter.

"It's your turn."

"My turn to what?"

"To tell me your story. I told you mine; now it's your turn to tell me yours."

"I don't have a story."

Soline arched a nearly black brow. "No?"

Rory felt her cheeks go hot under the pointed gaze. There was something troubling about those dark-chocolate eyes, a combination of warmth and steeliness that made her feel agonizingly transparent. "How did you know where to find me?"

"Monsieur Ballantine was kind enough to give me your address." She smiled then, creating a fan of tiny lines at the corners of her eyes. "You see? I know my way around him too."

"But . . . why?"

Soline's expression softened. "The last time we met, you left my house in tears, *chérie*. I don't know why, but I'd like to."

Rory smothered a groan. To say the memory was cringeworthy would be the understatement of the year. "I'm sorry about that. My life's kind of upside down right now, and it just hit me all of a sudden. I apologize for rushing out like that, without thanking you or saying a proper goodbye. It was rude."

"It was no such thing. But I didn't come for an apology. I came to make sure you were all right. I've been worrying about you these last few days, and it occurred to me that I didn't have to. I could come and see for myself that you were all right."

Rory dropped her gaze, embarrassed that this reclusive woman had felt the need to schlep across town to check on her. "You didn't have to come. Really. I'm fine."

"You don't have to pretend with me, Rory. It's all right to be sad."

Rory's head came up slowly. The words, so different from her mother's well-meaning stoicism, seemed to unlock something in her chest, like a door suddenly swinging open.

"Do you have coffee?" Soline asked when the silence grew awkward.

"Coffee?"

"I brought breakfast. *Pain au chocolat* and *chausson aux pommes*."

Rory blinked at her, nodding slowly. "Yes, I have coffee."

Rory led Soline to the kitchen, hoping she wouldn't notice the basket of unfolded laundry on the couch or the jumble of snow boots still sitting in front of the coat closet. They hadn't had snow since March.

In the kitchen, she gathered the containers from last night's takeout and slid them into the trash, then set about consolidating the dirty dishes in the sink. After a few minutes, she gave up. A sink full of dirty dishes was a sink full of dirty dishes, no matter how neatly they were stacked.

"Sorry about the mess," she said as she finished measuring out the coffee. "I don't spend a lot of time in the kitchen these days. Cooking for one isn't much fun, so it's mostly takeout now, and things sort of pile up."

"It's true," Soline said, grabbing a knife from the nearby block to snip the twine on the pastry box. "Cooking for one isn't fun. But one must eat, and not always from cartons. Have you plates for the pastries?"

"In the cabinet to your left. There should be napkins there too."

She watched as Soline worked her gloves off and began transferring pastries to a plate. She had no idea what her landlady was doing in her kitchen, but she suddenly realized she was glad. Though she did wonder how Soline had managed to get all the way to the South End without a car. "Please tell me you didn't carry that box on the T and then walk all the way from the station."

"Of course not. I took a taxi. Come and sit." She waited for Rory to join her at the table, then slid the plate of pastries toward her. "*Que désirez-vous?*"

Rory found herself wishing she'd paid better attention in French class. "I'm sorry. I don't speak much French—well, any French, actually."

"I asked: What is your pleasure?"

"Right. The apple, I think."

"And I will have the *chocolat*." Soline slid a croissant onto her plate, then shook out her napkin and laid it in her lap. "All right," she said finally, licking powdered sugar from her fingers. "What happened?"

"What do you mean?"

Soline cocked her head, one brow raised. "Are we going to play games, you and I?"

"I still don't understand what you're doing here. Why do you care?"

"Why do you think?"

"Because it's my turn?"

"Partly, yes. But it's more than that. You remind me of someone I knew once."

"Who?"

"Me," Soline said, pausing to sip her coffee. "Life has done something to you, taken something from you. I don't know what or how long ago, but you can't find your feet again. This gallery of yours, you want to pretend it will fill the hole life has carved in you. But deep down, you know it can't. And you're afraid nothing ever will."

Rory swallowed, her throat suddenly dry. It was true. Every word. But how? "Did Brett say something to Daniel? Is that how you know all this?"

"No, of course not."

"Then how?"

Soline's smile was both brief and wistful as she lowered her mug. "We're kindred spirits, you and I. Strangers who share a common past."

Rory wasn't sure what she'd expected, but it wasn't this. "I don't understand."

"We're all a collection of our stories, *chérie*. Our joys and sorrows. Our loves and losses. That is who we are, a tally of all our agonies and ecstasies. Sometimes the agonies leave a mark, like a bruise on the soul. We do our best to hide them from the world, and from ourselves too. Because we're afraid of being fragile. Of being damaged. That's what makes us kindred spirits, Rory—our bruises."

A chill crept up the back of Rory's neck. Coming from anyone else, the words might have seemed ridiculous, the kind of woo-woo stuff one might hear from a palm reader at the fair. But she'd felt it too, hadn't she? The eerie overlap of Soline's story with her own.

"It's just so hard to get my head around. The way we met, the way your story feels so . . . familiar." An unexpected rush of tears suddenly clogged her throat. She turned her head, wiping at her eyes. "I'm sorry. We've seen each other twice, and I've managed to burst into tears both times." She sniffed noisily, shaking her head in disgust. "What an idiot you must think me."

"What happened, Rory?"

"My fiancé," she whispered finally. "His name is Hux. Well, it's Matthew, actually, but everyone calls him Hux. Nine months ago, he left for South Sudan, to work with Doctors Without Borders. He wrote to me all the time, two or three times a week, like clockwork. And then all of a sudden, the letters stopped. It took a few weeks—there was some confusion about his next of kin—but they finally confirmed that he and several colleagues had been abducted."

Soline's hand went to her throat. "*Mon pauvre enfant.* Was he . . ."

Rory stared at the wadded napkin in her fist. "I don't know. No one does. There wasn't a ransom demand, and there's been no news for months." She paused when her voice began to wobble and cleared her throat. "They have no idea where he is or who has him. Or if he's even alive."

"How long has it been?"

"Six months. I lie awake every night, imagining a thousand different scenarios, terrible things. And yet, I can't make myself believe he's gone. I know it's crazy, but I feel like I would know if he'd been killed, that I would have sensed it somehow. Does that sound silly?"

"Not to me."

The empathy in her voice was like balm on a wound. *Kindred spirits.* Perhaps they were. "I've been reading a lot of books," she blurted. "The kind where the hero always wins and love always triumphs. It's like an addiction. But they're not real. In real life, things turn out badly."

"That's why you wanted to know my story," Soline said gently. "You were hoping for a happy ending. A real one this time."

"Like I said, silly."

"No. I know what it is to wait, to not know. You grab on to anything to get through another day."

Rory dragged the elastic from her hair, blowing out a breath as she raked a hand through the heavy waves. "I'm such a mess. Sometimes I think I'd rather . . ."

"Know the worst?" Soline supplied quietly.

Rory clamped a hand over her mouth, ashamed of the thought. "It's terrible, isn't it? To even think something like that. It's just, this limbo is torture. When you got the news, were you—" She stopped, realizing they'd never spoken of it. "How *did* you get the news?"

Soline sat very still, her eyes suddenly clouded. "There was a telegram saying he'd gone missing. They found his ambulance abandoned . . . and a lot of blood. Someone reported seeing German soldiers marching him into the woods at gunpoint."

Rory felt herself go pale. "I'm sorry. I shouldn't have asked. It's just that people talk about closure, about it being easier once you know, and I was wondering . . ."

"No," Soline said before Rory could get the rest out. "It wasn't easier. At least not for me. We tell ourselves we want to know. But when the truth finally comes, and it isn't what we'd hoped for, we'd give anything to go back to that place of waiting, where even a flicker of hope still exists."

"The other day, you said there comes a time when we have to let go of what's gone. But how do you know when that time is?"

Soline's face softened. "I was speaking of myself, *chérie*. Only of myself."

"But how *did* you know?"

Her eyes dipped for a fraction of a second before coming back to Rory's. "In the beginning, I couldn't believe it. I was certain there'd been a mistake. And even after . . . For years, I would take out Anson's shaving kit and open the empty cologne bottle, because I swore I could still smell him, like a cool breeze coming in off the sea. And then one night, I couldn't smell him anymore. He was just . . . gone. That's when I put the box away, when I realized there was nothing left to hold on to. But it's different for you. You have time, Rory."

"Time for what?"

"Time to have faith."

Rory cleared her throat, determined to stave off another rush of tears. "What you said before, about the gallery filling the hole in my life . . . It's true. It was Hux's idea for me to open the gallery, and I was so excited. Then, when they told me he was missing, I stopped caring about everything—until I saw your building. It felt like fate was sending me a message. But sometimes I wonder if it's just a way to hold on to him, by doing the thing he wanted me to do."

"Do you have a picture of him?"

"I keep one on my nightstand."

"May I see it?"

"Yes, of course. I'll go get it."

Moments later, Rory returned with the photograph. It was a shot of them standing arm in arm, beaming like the newly engaged lovers they'd been when it was taken. "He asked me to marry him the day before it was taken. We drove out to the cape to celebrate."

"You're beautiful together," Soline said, studying the photo. "And just look at that smile. You make him happy."

Rory found herself smiling too. "It's mutual. I never felt like I fit anywhere until we met. Everyone had all these ideas about who I was supposed to be. The only thing Hux ever wanted me to be was me. He made it okay to want what I want." She paused to look at the photo when Soline handed it back, pressing her fingertips to the glass. "Now that he's gone, I'm afraid . . ."

"That you'll lose yourself again?"

Rory's head came up slowly. "Yes."

"Then don't let him be gone."

"Don't . . . *let* him?"

"The night my mother died, she gave me a locket with my father's picture in it. I never knew him, but she asked me to keep him alive for her sake—here." She paused, pressing a hand to her heart. "She said to keep someone in your heart is to keep them alive forever. You can do that for Hux, Rory."

"Is that what you did with Anson—kept him alive in your heart?"

"I tried."

"Was there ever anyone else? After, I mean."

Soline smiled sadly. "There is only so much room in a woman's heart, *chérie*. Anson filled all of mine."

Rory nodded. The thought of anyone taking Hux's place was simply unfathomable. "Sometimes it's all I can do to look at his picture. Was it like that for you?"

"I don't have any pictures."

"None?"

"We met during the war, at the hospital where I volunteered. There was no time for pictures."

Rory was about to respond when the living room phone rang. Her eyes shot to the clock above the sink, suddenly remembering that she should have been at her mother's an hour ago. "That'll be my mother," she said, pushing back from the table. "We were supposed to have brunch this morning."

After a brief search, Rory located the cordless and braced for the inevitable.

"Why are you still at home?" Camilla demanded, skipping right past hello. "Brunch is ruined."

"I'm sorry. I got caught up in something and lost track of time."

"What was so important that you couldn't pick up the phone and let me know?"

Rory bit her lip. The surest way to blow up their tentative truce would be to admit she'd forgotten their brunch date because Soline had shown up with pastries. "It was just some gallery stuff."

"You don't open for months. Whatever it was had to be done today?"

"I said I'm sorry. I was ready to walk out the door and I got sidetracked."

"You sound funny," Camilla said abruptly. "Stuffy. Like you're getting sick."

"Do I?" She couldn't very well admit she'd been blubbering. Instead, she seized on the excuse with both hands. "You know, I think I might be. My throat's a little raw. I was thinking about making some tea and crawling back in bed."

"That's a good idea. Do you have soup?"

"Um . . . yeah, I think so."

"And tea?"

"Yes, I have tea."

"Put some honey in the tea. It'll help your throat."

"Okay, I will. Thanks. And I'm sorry about brunch."

"Never mind that. Just get some rest. I'll check on you later."

Soline appeared as Rory ended the call, carrying her gloves and handbag. "I boxed up the remaining pastries and put the cups and plates in the sink."

"You're going?"

"You had plans. You should have said."

"No! It was just brunch with my mother. We do it every Sunday."

"And you let me spoil it."

"Not really. In fact, I was dreading it. My mother and I . . . Well, let's just say it's been a little strained lately. She doesn't think much of my gallery idea. Or my art or anything else I care about."

Soline's brows shot up. "You never told me you were an artist."

"Oh, I'm not. It's just something I used to play around with. When Hux went missing, I gave it up. I haven't set foot in the spare room in months."

"You keep a studio here?"

"A studio? No. It's just an extra room where I kept my supplies."

"May I see this nonstudio of yours?"

Rory hesitated, uncomfortable with the idea of showing someone as accomplished as Soline her work. But how could she say no to a woman who'd taken a cab across town to make sure she was okay? "Sure, I guess. If you want."

At the end of the hall, she pushed the door open and waved Soline in. "Like I said, I haven't been in here in a while, so it's kind of a mess."

Soline stepped past her into the room, skirting bins filled with tools and bits of fabric. She appeared to be about to say something when her eyes lit on the seascape hanging behind the desk. "Oh, Rory . . ." Her head came around, her expression one of wonder. "You did this?"

Rory nodded shyly.

"It's exquisite. Like a painting but with fabric. Are there more?"

"Four in the closet and two more on the frames behind you."

Soline rolled her eyes. "The closet. *Mon dieu.*" She wandered over to the unfinished piece on the nearest frame—a small schooner listing precariously on a dark and angry sea. "The stitching is so fine, nearly invisible. By hand, yes?"

"Yes."

"Who taught you to sew like this?"

"No one. I taught myself."

"Astonishing. And they'll go up in the gallery when they're finished?"

"Oh, no. This is just a hobby."

Soline frowned. "Don't you want your work to be seen, your name to be known?"

The question made Rory uncomfortable. Instead of answering, she countered with one of her own. "Is that what you wanted? For people to know your name?"

Soline stepped away, studying the fabric swatches littering the worktable. "Once," she said finally. "When I was a girl. I used to dream of having my own label. I was going to turn heads all over Paris. But then the war happened, and Anson . . ."

"But you *did* it. You have an entire wall of magazine articles and newspaper clippings to prove it. You have a gift, and you used it to make people happy. You'll always have that to be proud of."

"And you have this, Rory. Don't ever say it's nothing. It's the very opposite of nothing. Adding beauty to the world isn't vanity, *chérie.* It's a calling."

A calling.

The word stayed with Rory as she pulled the door closed and led Soline back to the living room. Soline checked her watch, then collected her handbag and gloves from the coffee table. "Thank you for sharing your work with me, and please think about what I said. You have a gift, Rory, and gifts are meant to be shared."

"You don't need to go. I'll make a fresh pot of coffee and we can talk some more."

Soline smiled indulgently. "Don't be silly. You don't want to listen to an old woman prattle all afternoon. Besides, I asked the driver to come back and collect me. He's probably out there waiting. I wanted to see that you were all right, and I have." Her smile deepened as she crooked a finger under Rory's chin. "*Une gentille fille.* Such a sweet girl. Remember what I said—about keeping Matthew in your heart. Until you know for sure, there is still hope. And hope costs us nothing."

SEVENTEEN

RORY

Rory looked around the apartment, admiring her handiwork. After Soline left, she'd decided to put on some music, roll up her sleeves, and get the apartment in order. She'd made a good job of it too, even managing to haul several boxes of giveaway books to her car. Not bad for someone who was supposed to be coming down with a cold.

In the kitchen, she poked around in the pantry. Pasta, but no sauce. Cheerios, but no milk. Peanut butter, but no bread. Which left take-out—again. Soline was right. It was time to stop eating out of cartons. She'd make a list tomorrow and hit the market, but for now, Gerardo's would have to do. She placed a delivery order for eggplant Parm and an antipasto, then decided she had time to start a load of whites and grab a quick shower before dinner arrived.

She was surprised to hear the doorbell ring just fifteen minutes later. Apparently it was a slow night at Gerardo's. She grabbed a twenty from her purse, then clicked off the stereo, abruptly silencing the primal thump of Duran Duran's "The Wild Boys."

"That was fast," she said, pulling back the door. "Sundays must—"

The words died in Rory's throat. Instead of the delivery boy from Gerardo's, Camilla stood blinking back at her, a CVS bag dangling from her wrist and a large orange Tupperware container tucked into the crook of one arm. She swept Rory with narrowed eyes, lingering on the twenty-dollar bill in her hand.

"Are you having a party?"

Rory stuffed the twenty into her pocket with a sigh. "No, I'm not having a party. I was just playing some music while I cleaned up a little."

"I made soup with the little stars, like I used to when you were little. *Sick soup*, you used to call it. But I see you've made a miraculous recovery."

Rory sighed. Camilla swept past her, charm bracelet jangling in her wake. Rory had no choice but to follow her to the kitchen.

"I told you I had soup."

"You told me you *thought* you had soup," Camilla replied sullenly. "And I didn't want you having to fuss if you weren't feeling well." She ran an eye over her daughter as she began emptying the contents of the CVS bag. Cough drops. Vicks. NyQuil. A thermometer. "I don't suppose you actually need any of this."

Rory dropped her gaze. "I'm sorry."

"Why, Aurora? Why tell me you're sick when you're not? Is spending time with me so terrible?"

Rory swallowed another sigh. What was she supposed to say? Admitting she'd blown off brunch because her landlady showed up with a box from Sugar Kisses wasn't likely to sit well. Best to leave Soline out of it.

"I felt bad about getting sidetracked, so when you mentioned that I sounded sick, I just . . . went with it."

"Went with it," Camilla repeated dryly. "Are you hungry, at least?"

"I actually just ordered takeout."

"Right."

Camilla grabbed the soup container and opened the refrigerator. For a moment, she stood staring at the contents. A package of onion bagels, two sticks of butter, a single can of Sunkist, and a nearly empty jar of olives. She turned finally, a pale brow crooked in disapproval. "You haven't any food."

"I know. That's why the takeout. I was planning on hitting the market tomorrow."

"Don't you cook anymore?" She pulled open the pantry door, running her eyes over the thinly stocked shelves. "Look at this. Cheerios and canned soup. It's a wonder you're *not* sick eating like this." Her gaze settled on the pastry box. She lifted the lid, peering inside. "*Pain au chocolat.* Very nice. I see you weren't too distracted to go to the bakery this morning."

"I didn't go to the bakery," Rory countered, weary of being scolded. "Soline brought them."

Camilla's face went blank.

"My landlady," Rory supplied. "She stopped by this morning just as I was about to leave."

"Your landlady showed up out of the blue. With pastries."

"Yes."

"And that's what sidetracked you?"

"We started talking."

"About what? You barely know her."

"Hux. The gallery. My art."

"I see."

There it was—the cool, affronted look her mother pulled out whenever she felt slighted. Rory counted to ten, refusing to take the bait.

"You're talking about your life to strangers now, instead of your own mother?"

"We have things in common."

Camilla closed the pantry door and stood with both hands on her hips. "What could you possibly have in common? The woman has to be in her eighties."

"She's nowhere near eighty. And we do have things in common. She lost someone she loved in the war, an ambulance driver who went missing."

"Aurora . . ."

"She knows what it's like to hear the phone ring and wonder if today's the day you find out your prayers weren't answered, to feel your heart tear open when you see other people being happy, to bury yourself in work because you can't stand to be alone with your grief. She understands me needing to open the gallery. She even likes my art."

Camilla took a step forward, laying a hand on Rory's arm. "What's going on, Aurora? You're genuinely starting to worry me."

"Please, not this again."

"Yes. This again. You sound . . . I don't know what. You skip out on brunch again, then lie about being sick. Now you're talking about your *art*? What am I supposed to think? You've quit school. You live like a hermit. No one hears from you anymore. All you seem to care about is this gallery of yours. And this woman you've suddenly decided to befriend. I feel like I don't know you anymore."

"Maybe you *never* knew me."

Camilla's eyes widened. "Never knew you? I raised you."

"No, Mother. You molded me—or tried to. And now that I'm doing what I want, you suddenly don't know me. That's what this is about. Not school or what's in my refrigerator. It's about me not being who *you* want me to be. Not liking the things you like or living the way you live. But none of those things are important to me, because I'm not like you."

Camilla stiffened. "Sometimes I think you have too much of your father in you."

139

Of course. It had to be about her father. Because one way or another, *everything* was about her father. "Can we please leave Daddy out of this? I don't know *who* I'm like. Or why I have to be *like* anyone. Can't I just be me?"

"Of course you can. I've never stopped you from doing what you wanted."

"Stopped me?" Rory snapped. "No. You never stopped me. But you've never been shy about voicing your opinion anytime I strayed from the blueprint you had for me. The clothes I wore. The sports I played. Even the people I hung around with. When I told you Hux proposed, you asked if I said yes just to spite you."

"I'm your mother, Aurora. It's my *job* to shape you—to keep you from making the same mistakes I did."

"Are we talking about Daddy again?"

Camilla looked down at the neatly stacked rings on her left hand: wedding ring, engagement ring, the three-carat eternity band her husband's secretary had picked out for their twentieth anniversary. Three years after Geoffrey Grant's death, she still wore them. "You said something the other day about my track record with marriage. It made me think. Maybe I'm just not wired for love. Or happiness. Some people aren't, you know."

Rory found herself frowning. She wasn't sure what she'd expected her to say, but it certainly wasn't that. "Not wired for love? That's a strange thing to say."

Camilla smiled sadly. "Not when you look at the history. The Lowells aren't exactly known for their stellar marriages." She glanced at her rings again, spinning them absently. When she brought her eyes back to Rory the smile had gone brittle. "But we do look good on the society page, which is what's really important. Or so my mother always said."

It was Rory's turn to wonder what was going on. Camilla rarely spoke of her family and never of her mother. Not even when prompted. Now, quite unexpectedly, she had introduced her into the conversation.

"You never talk about your parents, about your childhood or growing up."

Camilla turned away, lining up the newly purchased cold remedies on the counter.

"Your mother," Rory pressed. "Was she . . . *wired* for love?"

"No," Camilla said simply and without hesitation. "I don't think she was."

"Did you fight?"

"Like us, you mean? No, we didn't fight. No one fought with Gwendolyn Lowell."

Gwendolyn. Rory rolled the name around in her head, realizing just how seldom she'd heard it growing up. "Why didn't anyone fight with her?"

"Because she was never wrong. About anything. And woe to anyone who crossed her. Especially my father. He was forty-seven when he died. A heart attack. I used to wonder if he died to get away from her. I was furious with him for leaving me alone with her."

"Maybe it's genetic," Rory said quietly. "Not being wired for love, I mean. Maybe it's passed from mother to daughter, like blue eyes or curly hair."

"It doesn't work that way, Aurora."

"You said it yourself—the Lowells aren't known for their stellar marriages. What if Hux—"

"For heaven's sake, Aurora. You are *not* a Lowell!"

Rory blinked at her. "What?"

Camilla closed her eyes as a pair of red splotches appeared on her cheeks. "You're a *Grant*, Aurora. Aurora Millicent *Grant*. My mother and her . . . *wiring* . . . have nothing to do with you."

"I didn't mean to upset you."

Camilla ran a hand over her already perfect hair, then smoothed the front of her blouse. "I'm sorry for snapping. It's just that my relationship with my mother was . . . complicated."

"Is that why you never talk about her?"

"I don't talk about her because there's nothing to talk *about*. She paid for my schooling, exposed me to art and music, arranged for dance lessons, elocution lessons, lessons on which fork to use. Everything she was required to do—and nothing more."

"You didn't mention love," Rory pointed out. "Were you loved?"

"I was groomed," Camilla replied carefully. "Trained to live up to the position I'd been given as a Lowell, to do and be exactly what was expected of me."

Something about her use of the word *given* made Rory bristle. She was starting to see why her mother avoided the subject of family. "And did you? Live up to it, I mean?"

"Almost never."

The words hung between them as Rory stood studying her. It was startling to discover this unexpected chink in her mother's armor, a raw place in her childhood that had never quite healed. Perhaps they could find common ground after all. "I'm sorry," she said softly.

Camilla shook her head, her eyes clouded with emotion. She was hurting and doing her damnedest to pretend she wasn't. "I didn't mean it the way it came out. It was years ago, when I was just a girl. Everything's a drama when you're a little girl. Please forget I said it."

Rory was torn between pressing her for more and letting the matter drop. Today's clash had started like all the others, but something new had crept into the conversation. Something that might finally explain the tension always simmering just beneath the surface of their relationship.

"You don't have to pretend with me," she told Camilla, aware that she was repeating Soline's words almost exactly. "It's okay to be sad. Or mad. Or both."

Camilla forced a smile. "It's nothing. Really. Spilled milk, as they say."

Rory reached for her hand. "We don't have to talk about it now. We don't *ever* have to talk about it if you don't want to. But I'm here if you ever want someone to just listen."

The doorbell rang before Camilla could answer, but her relief was plain. "You have company," she said, reclaiming her hand. "I'll go."

"It's just my dinner. Eggplant Parm and an antipasto from Gerardo's. Stay. We can split it."

Camilla shook her head, her face already shuttered as she sidled past. "I'm sure you have work to do. Enjoy your eggplant."

"You're not interfering. Stay and let me make up for this morning."

"I'm fine," she tossed over her shoulder as she opened the door and pushed past the startled delivery boy. "Fine. Really."

Rory paid for her food and carried the bag to the kitchen, convinced that her mother was anything but fine.

EIGHTEEN

SOLINE

Every heart has a signature, a unique echo that ripples out into the world. And every echo has a match. When those echoes connect, they become so attuned that even if they be separated, they continue to seek one another.

—Esmée Roussel, the Dress Witch

23 June 1985—Boston

I stare out the window as I seed a tomato. Perhaps I'll eat on the terrace and watch the sun go down. But even as the thought flits through my head, I know I won't. I'm in one of my moods tonight, the kind that calls for an especially good bottle of wine. I reach for my glass and take a deep mouthful, still brooding over this morning's conversation with Aurora.

I wanted to check on her, to make sure she was all right, and I'm glad I went. She needs looking after just now, and a little cherishing too. More, I think, than even she knows.

She was surprised when I told her she reminded me of myself, and a little embarrassed, too, to be seen so clearly. But I was telling the truth. The girl—she is still a girl to me—is in a dark place, a limbo of uncertainty and darkness, where no light can get through. She's so much in love with her young man. Hux—what kind of name is that for a boy? But it's what she calls him, so it's how I'll try to think of him too. He's certainly a handsome one. American in all the best ways. And a good heart into the bargain. She's lucky to have found him.

It's true, I tell myself. She is. But I wonder. Can it really be called lucky to find someone whose heartbeat matches your own, only to lose them?

Her story is so much a mirror of my own that it was hard to sit across from her and listen. Like Anson, her Hux was trying to do good, volunteering to do work most aren't brave enough to undertake. And like Anson, he appears to have paid a price for his courage. Perhaps the ultimate price.

I pick up my wineglass and swallow the rest, waiting for the slow wash of warmth to bloom in my belly, my chest, but it isn't enough. I refill the glass and abandon my salad, no longer hungry. Instead, I take both glass and bottle to my study and sit down at my desk, fumbling through the middle drawer for the engraved cigarette case and lighter I keep there—gifts from an old friend.

It takes several tries to get the thing to light—my hands are a little shaky tonight—but finally the cigarette is lit. I pull in a lungful of smoke, holding it there until I feel dizzy. It's been a while since I felt the need to smoke. It's been a while since I felt a lot of things.

Erich Freede stares back at me from an enameled frame on the desk. Father, stranger, lover of Esmée Roussel. Fate unknown. I've had the photo from *Maman*'s locket enlarged and look at it often, because I promised her I would. And today, I told *Aurore*—no, she prefers Rory—to do the same with Hux, to hold him in her heart. I hope it will help. I have no photograph of Anson. No image to cherish. But I do have something.

My eyes slide to the dress box, still sitting where I left it that first night. I can feel the pull of it, the whisper of its contents coaxing me to revisit the old sorrows. I've resisted until now, like a wound I can't bear to reawaken. But the wine and cigarettes are like old friends, reminding me of the many nights spent weeping over the remnants of my dreams. Holding his shaving kit, savoring the smell of him. Untying the packet of letters and reading them one by one. I'd fancied myself a kind of historian—*le gardien des fins heureuses*—the keeper of happy endings. Except for my own, of course. But I *was* happy for a while—we both were—at a time when there was very little happiness to go around.

The war ground on, until all of Paris felt gray and dead. My days at the hospital were long and taxing, a blur of haunted faces and broken lives that seemed to go on forever. But through it all, there was Anson.

He was forever making excuses to hang around the mess, hoping to catch me on a break or at lunch. I confess, I made a few unnecessary trips there myself, particularly after new casualties arrived and he was likely to be about. We would sip terrible coffee and make small talk about music and movies, until the mess finally emptied and his hand would steal across the table and find mine.

We fancied ourselves discreet, convinced that no one else knew of our blooming affection. There were rules about fraternization, but in those days, when life felt so precious and precarious, no one had the heart to come between young lovers.

Eventually, we became more brazen, slipping away whenever we could for a quick bite or a walk. We took turns telling our stories. I couldn't tell him everything, of course—*Maman* had brought me up to be careful of our gifts—but I told him what I could, how brides would come from miles away for a Roussel gown, about the letters people left when she died. And I talked about having my own salon when the war was over and the beautiful dresses I would make.

Anson talked about growing up as Newport royalty, about parties at the yacht club, boarding school in Boston, endless summers spent sailing with friends. And he talked about his family, about his father, who came home a hero after being wounded in World War I and promptly seized the reins of the family business from his older brother; his mother, Lydia, who died after a harrowing battle with pneumonia; his little sister, who painted and wrote songs and wanted to be famous one day and live in a garret in Paris; the boats his family had built for generations, sailboats famous for winning something called the America's Cup.

But my favorite topic that summer was Anson himself, hearing how he grew up, how he'd been packed off to boarding school at the age of eight, how he learned to race himself and became the captain of his own team, then gave up sailing entirely after an ugly fight with his father—and the argument he and his father had the day he announced he was leaving school to join the AFS.

I could listen to him talk for hours, but we never had hours. Our duties meant we had to settle for stolen moments when our shifts happened to allow, and it seemed petty to complain when so many were sacrificing so much.

Then one day, he told me he had arranged a night off for us both. I didn't ask how or whom he had spoken to. I didn't care. He took me to a café. Not one of the noisy places frequented by the *boche* but a quaint brasserie on Rue Saint-Benoît that had music and candles on the table. We were shown to a booth in one of the back corners. Anson ordered a bottle of good red wine, which went to his head after only one glass. And we ate such food, no doubt procured through the black market. There was a velvety pink soup with bits of lobster, roasted pork with apples and onions, and for dessert, an almond merengue torte. It was the grandest meal I'd ever eaten and must have cost Anson a fortune, but for those few brief hours, we could forget the war and simply be together.

He walked me home after, our fingers twined warmly. I don't think my feet touched the ground the entire way. When we reached the door, I fumbled with my key, my hands suddenly damp. Finally, it slid home, but as I reached for the knob, he caught my hand, and his eyes found mine in the darkness. He whispered my name, touched my face, then pressed his lips to mine with maddening slowness.

The night fell away as I swayed into him, until there was only his pulse and mine—his echo and mine. It felt like déjà vu, like finding something I didn't know I had lost. And I never wanted it to end. It had to, of course. There were rules for good girls. But the touch paper had been lit in earnest.

By the end of the summer, I was in love with Anson Purcell. And he was in love with me.

NINETEEN

Soline

*To ensure a happy ending, a bride must be
willing to give her whole heart to the man she
marries. Her spine, however, must at all times
remain her own.*

—Esmée Roussel, the Dress Witch

14 August 1943—Paris

Things have been getting tighter and tighter at the hospital. Food has
begun to dwindle, despite the supplies the Americans continue to send.
Our numbers swelled horribly as we entered the summer months. Nearly
five hundred counting wounded and staff—all needing to be fed three
times a day.

The mood has changed too. There are growing concerns that we will
be shut down, our patients sent to the camps—or worse. The Germans
are becoming impatient, suspicious that somehow the hospital—Dr. Jack
in particular—is involved in aiding the Resistance to help soldiers and
French Jews evade capture.

Things got worse last month after an entire unit of American airmen
managed to avoid capture when their planes were shot down. The Germans
stepped up their efforts, mounting a sweeping search of the area, but the

men appear to have vanished. Rewards are now posted for anyone having knowledge of groups or persons suspected of aiding them. Neighbors have begun turning on one another, offering up information—some of it true, much of it false—in exchange for a franc or two.

Even the hospital has fallen under suspicion. Rumors spread through the corridors like a brushfire, and suddenly the subject no one has wanted to talk about—the suspicious number of sudden deaths and empty beds—is all anyone can talk about, though only in hushed tones. We're all on edge. Collaborators are everywhere these days, snooping for information that might earn them a fat reward. There's talk of a spy in our midst, someone pretending to fight for the cause who's actually in league with the Nazis. And so we're all on our guard, for fear one wrong word will land the Gestapo on our doorsteps.

It's whispered that Dr. Jack will be arrested any day and that he keeps a suitcase packed, so he'll be ready when the time comes. Meanwhile, we do our best to go about our business—because what else is there to do? The soldiers keep coming, every day, a steady stream. Wounded. Broken. Hollowed out.

We're all frightfully tired, and time passes slowly despite the bustle. Perhaps it's how infrequently I see Anson these days that makes me feel so restless. After weeks of deliciously clandestine moments—breathless kisses stolen in the storage room or the back row of the cinema, quiet dinners and endless talk about what we'll do when the war ends—he has suddenly grown distant.

I understand that his job is critical. The war never stops—not even for young lovers—but lately, Anson's work has been keeping him away from the hospital for longer and longer stretches. And then, when I do see him, it's impossible not to mark the change in him. He seems edgy and distracted, always glancing over his shoulder, as if he expects to find someone on his heels. He's become evasive with me, vague and even distant. And he's begun to disappear for days at a time. When he finally reappears, he offers some flimsy excuse, and I do my best to believe.

But this morning, I saw him talking to one of the nurses. Elise is her name. She's older than I am and a good deal more worldly, with full lips and a deep, throaty laugh. They were huddled together on the stairs, their heads bent so close her mouth nearly grazed the side of Anson's neck as she slipped what looked like a note into his jacket pocket. I must have made some sort of sound, because he turned suddenly and saw me watching.

He stepped away, but it was too late. I couldn't unsee what I'd seen. Or hide my tears from Adeline when I came around the corner and careened into her. She didn't seem surprised when I told her what I'd seen. She said she always thought him too handsome for his own good and that it was best that I learn the truth before things went too far. But for me, things have already gone too far.

A few hours ago, I saw him duck out the door. He hesitated when he saw me, an awkward, unfathomable plea in his eyes. I turned away. If he wanted Elise, he could have her. At least that's what I told myself.

Now he's back from wherever he's been, wearing that furtive expression again as he slips down the murky flight of stairs that leads to the cellar. I know where he's going—and why. It's the perfect place for a rendezvous, dark and secluded with its maze of crates and boxes. The thought of him meeting Elise there, catching them together, turns my limbs to jelly. And yet, I can't help myself. I wait a few seconds, then follow him down.

I hold my breath, watching as he moves to the bottom of the stairs, then disappears into the murky warren below. After a few moments, he switches on a pocket torch. The beam makes him easier to follow, and I keep to the shadows, winding through the labyrinth of crates and cartons. Cabbages. Turnips. Potatoes. Ersatz coffee. Even crates of cheap red wine. Finally, his footsteps go quiet and I hear the faint jangle of keys, then the groan of dry hinges.

I creep forward again, close enough to see a dingy slice of light appear between the open door and its frame. I can't see much through the opening, a naked bulb overhead and a small cot with a blanket folded at the foot.

Anson's shadow looms against the bare stone wall. In the quiet, I hear the zipper of his jacket and then a rustling sound, like clothes being stripped off. I take an abrupt step back, then another. I thought I wanted to know the truth, to see it with my own eyes, but suddenly I find I can't bear it.

I feel sick to my stomach and ashamed. I've been such a fool, such a stupid, lovesick fool. I turn to go back the way I came, but in the dark, I blunder into a stack of crates. The sound echoes like a shot in the quiet.

I see Anson's shadow go still, then straighten. An instant later, he appears in the doorway, briefly silhouetted. "Who's there?"

He waits, head cocked. I cover my mouth with both hands, willing myself to be silent. Part of me wants to confront him, to tell him I know what he's up to, but I can't bear the thought of being caught skulking in the dark.

"Show yourself," he growls. His voice is strange, wary and thick with menace. "Now."

I've never seen him angry, and it frightens me to think of his reaction should he discover me here. I squeeze my eyes shut, willing myself to be invisible as the scuff of his boots moves closer. I'm wedged between two stacks of crates, caught like a rabbit in a snare. I release a sigh of relief when I hear him move past. But seconds later, he reverses course and I feel the bite of his fingers on my arm.

He yanks me from my hiding place, a wine bottle clutched in his fist, raised high and ready to strike. I'm stunned by the look on his face, his features contorted with a mix of fear and rage. He's almost unrecognizable.

He clamps a hand over my mouth and yanks me backward against him, still poised to wield the wine bottle. I can feel the energy in him, coiled, lethal. A sob bubbles up in my throat.

The muscles in his arms go slack, but his grip remains firm as he jerks me around to face him. Seconds tick by as we lock eyes in the darkness. Eventually, I feel the tightly coiled energy in him begin to unspool. He lowers the bottle, then holds a finger to his lips, commanding me to be silent.

I'm half marched, half dragged to the small room he's just left. It's not much bigger than a closet and is furnished as a crude kind of living space. In addition to the cot, there's a small sink and a cracked mirror, a narrow chest of drawers, and a battered leather case fitted with what looks like a homemade radio. But it's the empty leather pouch and the scattering of official-looking documents on the table that hold my attention. *Cartes d'identité*—French identity papers, birth certificates, ration cards for both food and clothing.

A dozen questions crowd into my head, but before I can open my mouth, Anson's fingers bite deeper into my arm and I'm pulled around to face him. "What are you doing down here?"

I stare at him, stunned that he can ask such a thing of me when he's the one sneaking around in the dark. But the glint in his eyes withers me, and I find myself explaining. "I saw you with Elise, whispering in the hall. I saw her slip a note into your pocket, and I thought . . ." I swallow the rest, letting my eyes slide away. "I needed to know if it was true."

He eyes me with astonishment. "That's why you followed me down here? Because you thought I had a date with Elise?"

I look away, shocked to realize there might be something worse than catching Anson with another woman. I shift my gaze back to the papers on the table. Most are yellowed with age and deeply creased. A few are marred with stains, splotches, the occasional torn corner. Who do they belong to, and what are they doing down here?

I reach for one of the documents, a certificate of birth, but Anson catches my wrist. "Don't touch," he hisses. His eyes, stripped of color in the cold light of the overhead bulb, send a chill through me.

My thoughts skitter to those suddenly empty beds, seemingly recovered men dying without warning in the middle of the night and with greater and greater frequency of late. To the rumors of a traitor in our midst—a spy reporting back to the Gestapo. We've all feigned ignorance, because it's safer than admitting what we all suspect, that those men hadn't died at all, that somehow they'd been smuggled out of the hospital right under our noses. That Dr. Jack is somehow at the back of it all, and the Germans know it and are just waiting for proof before they make their arrest.

Is that what Anson is doing in the basement? Helping Sumner Jackson smuggle Americans and Brits out of France and using forged papers to do it? If so, why not tell me? Surely he knows I can be trusted. A wave of dread washes through me as another thought occurs—a terrible thought. What if Anson is the spy we've all been worried about, and he's actually been helping the Gestapo gather evidence? The possibility makes the back of my neck go clammy. Has he been working for the Nazis the whole time, pretending to be a hero? Pretending . . . everything?

"Those papers," I say, nodding toward the table. "Please tell me you're not doing anything wrong with them, that you're not . . ." I let the words trail, unable to finish the rest.

He studies me, his expression unreadable. The moment spins out, and we stand eye to eye as I wait for his answer, as if we're poised at the edge of some terrible precipice, waiting to see who will jump first.

"Just tell me you're not working for *them*," I say thickly. "Please."

A muscle begins to tick in his jaw. "That's what you think?"

"I don't know *what* I think, Anson. You're sneaking around down here with a flashlight, raking through papers that clearly aren't yours." I'm talking fast now, hating the words as they leave my mouth. I want so badly to be wrong, but what if I'm not?

When he reaches for my hand I pull away. He stares at me, astonished. "You're afraid of me?"

"There's been so much talk. And you've been acting so strangely . . ."

He takes a step back, raking a hand through his hair. "You think I'm the spy? And now that you've stumbled onto my little secret, I'll be forced to—what? Strangle you? Slit your throat?" His eyes are flinty as they lock with mine, but there's hurt there too, as if I'd drawn back my hand and physically struck him. "After all this time," he says finally. "After everything we've shared, *that's* who you think I am?"

"Anson . . ."

"I think I liked it better when you suspected me of going behind your back with Elise. I think she'd prefer it, too, to being called a Nazi."

"I didn't call either one of you a Nazi. But what am I supposed to think?"

"You're supposed to trust me."

I lift my chin. "The way you trusted me?"

He blows out a long breath, and I suddenly see how tired he is. "It's got nothing to do with trust," he says wearily. "It's to do with being careful. If I'm caught . . . I couldn't put you in that kind of danger. I never meant for you to know any of this."

"But I do know. Or at least I think I do. So you might as well tell me the rest."

He shakes his head. "No."

"The men," I press, determined to confirm what now seems plain. "The ones who died so suddenly. All those empty beds. They didn't die, did they?"

"Leave it alone, Soline. Please. Go back upstairs and forget you saw any of this."

I shake my head, refusing to be put off. I need to know it all, about the work he's doing and the risks he's taking. "It was you," I press again. "You helped them get away. Using papers like these. It was you."

He blows out a breath, annoyed by my persistence. "It was a lot of people. An entire cell risking their lives to save a handful of men. Airmen mostly, along with a few friends of the Resistance who managed to get themselves into the Gestapo's crosshairs. There's a man who does the papers, an artist turned forger, if you can believe that." He pauses, pointing to the documents on the table. "This is his work. We give them new names and get them across the border into Spain, then on to England, even to the

States now and then. Sometimes we need a guy's bed before we can safely move him down the line, so we hide him—down here."

I glance around the tiny room again, the sparse furnishings and contraband radio, the crude facilities. All this time, Anson has been risking his life to help others escape the Nazis—soldiers fighting to pry France from Hitler's grip, agitators and fellow resisters in danger of arrest.

My thoughts wander to Erich Freede, the man my mother had loved but let go, of the family he might have gone on to have in Germany. A wife, children with whom I share blood and history, and I find myself praying that someone like Anson helped them get out in time.

"You could have told me," I say softly. "I would have kept your secret."

"Except it isn't just *my* secret to keep. It belongs to all of us, Soline. Everyone who works for the Resistance. And it's up to all of us to keep it."

"Well, now it belongs to me too," I say flatly. "But I want to do more than just keep the secret. Let me be a part of what you're doing, Anson. Let me help."

"I can't let you do that."

"Please. I don't know what I can do, but there must be something."

"No."

"I'll go to Dr. Jack, then," I tell him. "I'll ask him to let me help. And you needn't pretend he doesn't know about all of this. Nothing happens here that he doesn't sanction."

Anson's face remains stony. "Soline, I won't—"

I press the flats of my fingers to his lips, cutting him off. "Don't tell me no, Anson. Tell me what I can do."

TWENTY

SOLINE

*Without faith, even our work is doomed to
fail. Faith is everything.*

—*Esmée Roussel, the Dress Witch*

27 August 1943—Paris

I've been stunned to learn what a handful of brave men and women has
been able to accomplish under the watchful eyes of the *boche*. While
Paris crawls with Göring's Gestapo, Dr. Jack and his staff have been
quietly waging their own war against *Herr* Hitler. And I have become
a part of it.

If anyone had ever hinted that I would be involved in such a thing,
I would have accused them of drinking too much wine. But I find
it gives me a fresh sense of purpose, a way to feel less a victim while
the Nazis overrun our city. And I fancy *Maman* looking down on my
clandestine activities with approval, if only for the sake of Erich Freede.

It also helps me feel closer to Anson, to know his cause is my cause,
that we're passionate about the same things. We talk more and more
about the future these days. We do not speak of forever—the war makes
such talk feel imprudent—but we talk about our tomorrows. Places we
mean to go and things we mean to do. And in these sweet, silly musings,

we are always together. For now, it is enough. As *Maman* used to say, the work must come first.

I've received quite the education since that day in the cellar, about the various specialties within the Resistance: clandestine radio operations, sabotage of supply transports, printing and distribution of underground newspapers, even the movement of weapons and explosives. Each cell operates independently of one another. Our work is less daring than the blowing up of bridges and railroads, but it's no less dangerous. To smuggle downed Allied airmen out of France requires intricate planning and many hands.

The process begins with falsified death certificates and carefully forged identity papers for each escapee and employs a vast network of couriers—many of them women like me—and a series of safe houses along a carefully guarded route over the Pyrenees, into northern Spain, and then on to the port of Lisbon.

That is Anson's work, transporting the men when moving day finally arrives. I dread those nights when he kisses me goodbye and promises to return safely, because we both know he can't guarantee anything of the sort. We all seem to be living on borrowed time these days, daring fate to catch us out, wondering not *if* our time will come but how and where. It doesn't help that the hospital gates stand directly opposite the German headquarters and that guards are posted day and night.

But I have work of my own now—as a courier. Finally, after nearly two weeks of training, I'm being given real assignments. I've never thought of myself as particularly brave, but what I'm doing feels right. Not just for Paris but for Anson. Helping the cause, even a little, means helping him.

He was adamant that I not report to him, and so I've been assigned to Elise, whose fiancé, I've learned, has been sent to work in a German munitions factory as part of the forced-service edict. She's brusque and all business, but not unkind, and she has trained me well.

I work as a liaison, conveying information to other members of our cell: a rendezvous schedule hidden in a tin of coffee, a drop-off point scribbled on a scrap of paper used to wrap a wedge of cheese. Sometimes the exchange is verbal, a seemingly innocent inquiry about an aunt's recent bout of flu or a question about the Métro timetable. I'm to recite the line exactly as given, memorize the reply, and report back to Elise. I never know what any of it means, but that's by design. In the event that I'm picked up and questioned, I can't reveal anything because I don't *know* anything.

But today, I've been trusted with something new. I'm to collect a pouch of papers from a man Elise referred to only as The Painter. She told me to fill a basket with wine, bread, and cheese and then pedal *Maman*'s bike to a garret in the Rue des Saints-Pères.

I'm nervous as I pull up in front of the dingy apartment building. My instructions are to appear as if I'm meeting a lover for an afternoon assignation. I take out a compact and a tube of lipstick, as I've been taught, and make a show of primping, all the while using the mirror to make sure I haven't been followed.

It's the first thing they teach you: how to make sure you aren't tailed and what to do if you are. What to look for on the street. How to melt into a crowd. How to get rid of anything that might tie you back to the cell. But nothing looks out of the ordinary.

I chain up my bike, loop the basket over my arm, and climb the skinny flight of steps to the third floor. Three sharp knocks on the door. No more. No less. There's the clicking of locks, and the door cracks open, revealing one eye and a heavy brow.

"*J'espère que tu as faim,*" I say, precisely as instructed. *I hope you're hungry.*

The door inches back. Three-quarters of a face now. The eye narrows as it runs over me. Eventually, the door opens enough to let me in.

It's a tiny apartment, two rooms crowded with tables and lamps, made even more claustrophobic by heavy blackout curtains, which are closed though it's the middle of the day. There is a distinct reek to the place. Chemical fumes mixed with unwashed male bodies, scorched acorn coffee, and cigarette smoke.

I remember my instructions while I wait. I'm to say nothing unless specifically addressed, to make no comment or question anything I see. The less I know, the better. But it's hard to curb my curiosity about what appears to be a kind of assembly line. There are small tables set up along the far wall, stocked with an assortment of inks, writing implements, seals, stamps, and glues.

I count four men in all—the one who answered my knock and three others bent over various tables. No one speaks, and yet it's clear who's in charge. He's seated at the farthest table, surrounded by the tools of his trade—The Painter. There's something almost desperate in the way he hunches over his work, stained fingers twitching with small, frenetic strokes, inventing human beings with paper and ink.

He lifts his head, craning his neck to work out a kink. Our eyes lock briefly. He's surprisingly young, not much older than I am, with a long face, round wire spectacles, and a chin full of dark stubble. The moment is over quickly. He returns to his work, and the man who let me in returns, handing me an oilskin pouch. I don't look inside or say a word. I simply tuck the pouch into the back of my skirt and cover it with my cardigan. No money changes hands. The Painter takes nothing for his work. Like the rest of us, he cares only about the cause.

When enough time has passed, I empty my basket, leaving the wine and food behind, and muss my hair and lipstick a little, in case anyone happens to notice me leaving. And then I'm outside in the sunshine again, pedaling away with a packet of forged documents tucked into my waistband.

It's a relief to get back to the hospital and finally hand off the smuggled pouch to Elise. She's matter-of-fact in her praise, which isn't unusual. She's not the effusive type, but there's something unsettling about the way she won't meet my eyes. And then she tells me. Anson has failed to return from last night's mission.

The news nearly knocks me to the ground. Elise makes me sit down and brings me a cup of coffee. There's no pretense that Anson and I are merely work colleagues. She's just a woman, comforting another woman, and I'm grateful. She tells me it isn't unusual—a hundred things could have happened—and she's sure he'll be back anytime now. But I can hear in her voice that she's worried, and as I go back to my duties, my mind runs to worst-case scenarios, to Anson shot dead or herded onto a train bound for one of the camps.

Working with the Resistance means expecting the worst, accepting that capture, torture, even death is inevitable. But I cannot and will not accept those inevitabilities for Anson. He must be safe. He must be. But the day drags into evening, and there's still no word, no sign of him anywhere. I think of *Maman*, her hands busy with her beads as she spoke of Erich Freede, and I suddenly understand. At such moments, we will trust anything, believe anything that allows us to hold on to hope.

Adeline senses that something is wrong. I insist it's only a headache, and there's no need to go home, but she continues to press me until I agree to at least go to the mess and eat something.

I taste nothing as I try to swallow some soup. Adeline is beside me, insisting that I go home and get some rest, when he's suddenly there in the doorway. I nearly drop my spoon, gulping down tears I mustn't let spill. He looks spent, his eyes heavy and smudged with shadows, but he meets my gaze across the busy hall, holding it in a way that says everything I need to hear.

I'm safe. I'm sorry. I love you.

I stand on wobbly legs and duck into the nearest lavatory to sob out my relief. When I find him again, someone has brought him a cup of coffee. It's black, not light and sweet the way he likes it, but he doesn't seem to notice. I see Elise catch his eye from across the room, brows raised. He shakes his head almost imperceptibly. I wonder what it means but know better than to ask him anything with so many people around.

Later, when the mess is empty and Anson has finished his second sandwich, I ask him what happened. I know it's breaking the rules, but I don't care.

"Where have you been?"

He shakes his head. "I can't."

"I thought you were dead," I whisper raggedly. "Or gone to one of the camps. Don't tell me you can't."

"I need to talk to Sumner," he says blankly, as if I haven't spoken at all. "Where is he?"

His stare is empty, devoid of warmth or affection. He's in Resistance mode—*clandestinité*—that stoic corner of his heart where there is no room for me. Or for anything that doesn't involve the cause.

"Four new casualties arrived a few hours ago," I tell him, trying to keep my voice even. "I heard someone mention a double amputation, but he might be out by now."

Anson nods, then drains his coffee cup and stands. "We need to talk. But I have to do this first. Go home and sleep. I'll come later."

I frown at this breach of the rules. It was a precaution we had agreed on when I joined the cell: he would never, under any circumstance, come to the apartment on Rue Legendre. So far as the outside world knew, we were colleagues and nothing more. For my protection, he'd explained, so there was never a chance of leading trouble to my door. But something has changed his mind, and I'm frightened.

"I thought we needed to be careful about them learning my address."

His eyes darken. "We're past that now."

"Why?"

"Because they already have it."

A shiver runs through me, like a cold finger sliding down my spine. "The Gestapo knows where I live?"

"They know everything, Soline."

TWENTY-ONE

SOLINE

Much can go awry between the asking and the doing, for that is when a union is most at risk—before the charm has been woven and the vows exchanged. The Spell Weaver must be on her guard against any and all tempests, and there will almost certainly be tempests.

—Esmée Roussel, the Dress Witch

27 August 1943—Paris

I feel like a character in a spy novel as I glance over my shoulder, then slide the heavy brass shop key into the lock. No sign of a black Mercedes-Benz—the Gestapo's vehicle of choice—parked anywhere on the street. No man in a gray suit and black fedora loitering in a nearby doorway.

They tell us what to look for. They also tell us what to expect if we're arrested. Beatings, being shackled and hung upside down, or forced into a tub of frigid water, held under until you nearly drown, then repeated again and again. The *baignoire*, it's called—*the bath*.

It's also common to pick up and question a suspect's female loved ones—mothers, sisters, lovers—and interrogate them for hours. One technique, said to be highly effective, is to threaten to send them to one of the *specialty* brothels favored by German soldiers. The prospect makes me shudder as I push inside and bolt the door behind me.

I come home only to bathe and sleep now. The apartment hasn't felt like home since *Maman* died, and with the blackout curtains drawn, the rooms feel claustrophobic and unsettlingly empty.

I go up to bathe, then try to lie down, but my thoughts keep churning back to Anson's words. *They know everything.* Eventually, I give up and get dressed. I try to scare up something to eat, but I've been taking most of my meals at the hospital, and there isn't much in the larder.

I've just unearthed a tin of stale crackers and a jar of jam when I hear the bell ring downstairs, three sharp, shrill pulses. It's Anson, of course, but the sound still startles me. It seems an eternity since anyone's rung that bell.

He's peering over his shoulder when I pull back the door, scanning the street for danger. For a moment I forget myself and reach for his hand. He flinches, flashing a silent warning as he ducks past me. I bolt the door behind him, then watch as he tests the knob, not once but twice.

He groans as he drops into the nearest chair, clutching the small canvas satchel he often carries when he leaves the hospital—his *passport*, as he calls it, because the AFS emblem on the flap keeps the Nazis at bay.

If possible, he looks even wearier than when I left him at the hospital. But there's more than just exhaustion weighing on him. There's a barely tamped-down panic in his eyes, something I've never seen. "Anson, what is it? What's happened?"

He rakes a hand through his hair, as if torn. "I shouldn't be here. We agreed—"

"I don't care what we agreed. I care about where you've been. And you're here now. If you were followed, the damage is done. Tell me what's happened."

He nods, then drops his head in his hands with a groan. "I ran into trouble last night."

My heart does a little gallop. "What kind of trouble?"

"The kind I've been dreading since the day you followed me down to the basement."

"Tell me. Please."

He's eerily stoic as he pours out his story, as if reciting it from memory. He'd set out just after dark, to shuttle a man wanted by the SS to the next in a series of safe houses. The man's *carte d'identité* identified him as Marcel Landray, farm laborer, born 1919 in Chauvigny, France. But none of it was true. In truth, he was Raimond Lavoie, a fugitive wanted for printing anti-Nazi propaganda and engaging in degenerate behavior—*boche* code for homosexual activity.

He'd already spent a month in a safe house, driven underground after being denounced by a neighbor in exchange for a few francs and a pat on the head from the SS. Capture would have meant transport to one of the camps, Dachau probably, or Buchenwald, where he would have been made to wear a pink triangle on his shirt—until he was eventually gassed, beaten, or starved to death. Remaining in France had been out of the question.

The handoff went as planned, but on the way back the engine had overheated, forcing Anson to pull off and wait for the radiator to cool. He was found by the French police at two in the morning, five hours past curfew, on a road where an ambulance with the AFS had no business being. They took him in for questioning. His cover story, arranged in advance, was that he had snuck away from the hospital to rendezvous with a sweetheart and had lost track of time. He gave them a name—Micheline Paget—and an address, neither of which fooled the police. A short time later, two men in gray-green uniforms arrived at the jail, Gestapo under orders from Major General Karl Oberg—known to many as the Butcher of Paris—to rid the city of resisters by any means necessary. They didn't want to talk about Micheline Paget. They wanted to talk about Sumner Jackson.

Anson goes quiet. I cover his hand with mine. "Why don't you sleep a little? Just an hour, and then you can tell me the rest."

He shakes his head but lets his eyes close. "I didn't give them anything."

"Of course you didn't."

I reach up to smooth the crease from his brow, but he pushes my hand away. "I didn't have to tell them anything, Soline. They already knew it all—or most of it. The forged papers, the safe houses, the airmen we've moved. They know Sumner's involved."

"But how?"

He offers a half-hearted shrug. "Someone inside, one of Oberg's informants probably, watching us for months and waiting for one of us to slip up. And I was the one. It's only a matter of time now."

"This isn't your fault, Anson. You just said you didn't give them anything. How can you even—"

The anguish in his eyes is so raw I'm almost relieved when he looks away. "They as much as said it, Soline. They're coming for Dr. Jack. For all of us, I suppose. Oberg won't quit until he's got what he needs, and he doesn't care how he gets it. Which leaves me with a choice to make."

Of all the things he's said, this frightens me most. "What kind of choice?"

"One I don't know *how* to make—or live with."

Suddenly I can't breathe. I lace my fingers through his, trying not to think of whips and shackles and tubs of icy water. But the question must be asked. "Did they . . . hurt you? I've heard the stories about what they do to make people talk."

"No." His eyes are dull and unfocused, his voice queerly flat. "It wasn't like that." He pauses, looking down at our hands, mine small and pale, his tan and work roughened. "The Germans have an arrangement with the hospital higher-ups; they leave us alone so long as we don't make waves and spare them the expense of treating wounded Brits and Americans. It's the only reason Sumner hasn't been taken yet. Beating information out of me would have looked bad—so they threatened me instead."

"With what?"

"With you."

My mouth works mutely, trying to digest the two words. "With me? I don't understand. How do they even know who I am?"

"I told you. They know everything. Last night wasn't about finding out what *I* know. It was about telling me what *they* know. They know we're getting forged papers, but not *where* we're getting them. They also know we're using a network of couriers."

"And they know I'm one of them," I supply quietly.

"No. At least I don't think they do. But they do know about us, that we're . . ."

Lovers. The word hangs unspoken in the air between us. Not strictly true—not in the physical sense of the word—but true in every way that matters.

"Is love a crime now too?"

"No," he says, standing abruptly. "But it's . . . useful."

I stare at him, rolling the word around in my head. *Useful.* And then suddenly it falls into place. They didn't have to threaten him. All they had to do was threaten me.

"You have to leave, Soline. There's no way around it."

I get to my feet slowly, silently. They tell us what can happen, and we say we understand. But somehow we've all managed to convince ourselves it won't happen to us. That as long as we're careful, there will be no late-night knock at our door, no boots following as we slip down an empty alley, no neatly typed list with our name on it. We believe it until we can't believe it anymore.

"Do you understand, Soline?"

I nod numbly. "You're saying I have to leave the hospital."

"I'm saying you have to leave France."

It takes a moment for the words to penetrate, and even then I can't make sense of them. "Leave . . . France?"

"It isn't safe for you here."

I wet my lips, my mouth suddenly dry. "But where will we go?"

He looks at me, unblinking. "Not we, Soline. You."

The moment seems to slow, spooling out between us. I've heard people describe the moment they received bad news—they felt the blood drain from their face or the air leave their lungs—and for me, in this moment, every bit of that is true.

Leave France without him? He can't possibly have just suggested such a thing. But when I look at him again I realize he has, and that he means it.

"I won't go," I tell him flatly. "Not without you."

"I can't leave now, Soline. Surely you know that. There's too much left to do, too many people depending on me."

"You're one person, Anson. They can do without one person. And what about the Gestapo? You think once I'm gone, they'll just leave you alone? They won't. You *know* they won't."

"Of course they won't. But if you're safe, it won't matter what they do to me."

"It will matter to me!"

He heaves a sigh, so very tired. "I need you to do this. Please."

"I can't go, Anson. I can't leave without you."

"I've already arranged it."

I blink at him, astonished. "Without talking to *me*?"

"There wasn't time. I've spoken with Sumner. You go tomorrow. A safe house first, then out through Spain, like the rest."

"No."

"Soline, we talked about this."

"Not like this, we didn't! We talked about going together. When the war was over. It was never supposed to be just me. Are you trying to get rid of me? Is that what this is, a way to get me out of your hair?"

It's an unfair thing to say. A horrible thing. But I've just had the legs knocked out from under me, and I want to hurt him as he has hurt me. I turn my back, wiping my tears on my sleeve.

"Soline."

I stiffen when he touches me but don't resist when he turns me around to face him. He hooks my chin with his fingers, forcing me to look at him. "I need you to do this. I need it for me. Do you understand?"

He drops his hands to my shoulders when I try to pull away, holding me in place. "I can't quit, Soline. What I'm doing—what we're all doing—is too important. As long as Sumner's in, so am I. That's just how it is. But I won't be able to keep myself safe while I'm worried about you getting picked up. And you will if you stay. Because they know all they have to do is tell me they have you, and I'll tell them everything."

"You wouldn't."

"But I would," he says quietly. "Without thinking twice."

Suddenly I understand. It isn't just me he's afraid for. It's the cause, the lives that would hang in the balance if I were to be arrested—because if he was forced to choose, he would choose me. But I wouldn't want that.

"Promise me that no matter what happens, you won't give in to them. Not for me."

"I have to know you're safe, Soline. So I can work."

I turn my head, blinking back tears. The decision has been made. The plans we made, the future we thought we would have together, are over. *We're* over.

"You can do this," he says gently. "You'll be with our people. Your papers will be ready in a few hours. You leave at dawn."

Dawn. Ten hours.

I look at him, eyes pleading. "Let me stay. I'll leave the hospital. I'll go out to the country, somewhere they can't find me. Please."

"I can't. I need to know you're safe and taken care of. It's done. But we still have tonight."

His words are like a knife, slicing into my flesh. "I don't want tonight. I want forever. I know we never said it, but I thought you did too. Now, after everything, I'm supposed to just walk away, not knowing where I'll end up or if I'll ever see you again."

He stares at me, his face a stunned blank. "That's what you think? That I plan to just hand you off and that's that? We're through?"

"It happens," I whisper, thinking of *Maman* and Erich Freede. "People get . . . separated."

"That isn't going to happen to us."

"You can't know that."

"But I do. I've arranged to get you to the States, though it won't be easy for you. I've written a letter for you to mail when you get to Lisbon—to my father. I told him we'll be getting married as soon as I'm home—if that's all right with you."

"Married . . ." The word is like a pair of wings unfurling in my chest, threatening to lift me off the ground. I've never said it aloud, but I've dreamed it hundreds of times. "Yes," I whisper hoarsely. "Yes, it's all right with me. But are you sure it's what you want? When I said forever, I wasn't asking . . . Are you *sure* you want to marry me?"

"I was sure ten minutes after I met you, Soline. I love you."

Love.

I've been so careful about not using that word. Until tonight. Not because I don't feel it but because I feel it so keenly. Perhaps *Maman* has made me superstitious with her talk of curses. I can't help thinking of Lilou—widowed two weeks after speaking her vows—because she dared to love. But it's been said now and cannot be unsaid, even if I wished it. Nor can it be allowed to hang between us, unanswered.

"I love you too," I say thickly. "More than I ever thought I could let myself love anyone. And I want to marry you. But are you sure this is right? What will your father say when I show up on his doorstep, a stranger, expecting to move into his home?"

"I explained it all in the letter. Or as much as I *can* explain. He doesn't know what I'm doing over here. And he can't. No one can. I mean that, Soline. No matter what you hear or how bad things sound, you can't breathe a word about what we've been doing. Too many people would be put at risk. The safety of one person can never be allowed to jeopardize the entire cell. Do you understand?"

"Yes."

"For now, all my father needs to know is that I drive an ambulance, I'm crazy about you, and I plan to make you a Purcell the minute I'm back on American soil."

He grins at me, taking both my hands in his. "I can't wait to show you where I grew up and introduce you to everyone. My sister will fall in love with you the minute you open your mouth. She's a sucker for all things French."

I manage a smile, but there's something niggling at the back of my brain, a talk we had once about his father, how he could be a hard man at times, with strong ideas about respectability and duty, and I can't help wondering if those ideas extend to his son's choice of a wife.

Anson frowns, trying to read my expression. "Please don't be sad. I'll be home before you know it, and then we can start a real life together. But until then, I'll know you're safe."

"And what about you? You'll still be here—with *them*."

He cups my face, kissing me tenderly. "Nothing will keep me from getting home if I know you're waiting for me."

"But how are you managing this? It's all we can do to get men over the border, let alone to America."

"The Purcells have been navy men since the days of John Paul Jones—until me, that is. Anyway, I dropped dear Pater's name and called in a few favors. I doubt he'll be any too happy about it—he prefers to wield the power in the family—but that's a fight for another day."

"I'm afraid," I say softly.

"I know. But you're brave too." He kisses me again, and I can taste my tears on his lips, bitterness and salt, and suddenly every moment, every touch, is precious. Because they're all I will have to take with me when the sun comes up again.

He pulls away, holding me at arm's length. "I should go. You need to pack a few things, bare-necessity stuff. One small case. And then you should try to sleep. I'll be back before dawn."

"What about you? You're exhausted."

"I'll go back to the hospital, try to grab a few hours."

I reach for his hand. "Stay with me. Please."

"You know I can't." His voice is thick, his eyes churning like a hungry sea. "We're not . . ." He swallows hard and tries to step away. "There are rules, Soline."

I shake my head because suddenly it all seems absurd. Men are being shot in the street and butchered on battlefields, women and children packed into trains like cattle and shipped to death camps. But *this*—two people in love, spending what might be their last night together—is against the rules. I can't make sense of it. And then I remember something I heard Lilou say to my mother the night she ran away to marry her Brit. *I refuse to let someone else's rules cheat me of my bit of joy.*

I refuse too.

"I don't care about the rules," I murmur, pulling him back to me. "It's our last night. Please don't make me spend it alone."

He says nothing as I lead him up the stairs. There's a moment of hesitation when we reach the top. Whether his or mine, I can't say, but it passes quickly and the decision is made, the point of denial behind us.

I feel shy suddenly and leave the light off. Until this moment, our rendezvous have consisted of brief, stolen moments, hurried embraces and feverish kisses. But tonight there's no reason to hurry. I don't know if I will be his first—I don't *want* to know—but he will be mine.

I unbutton his shirt and push it back from his shoulders, letting it slide to the floor. I reach for his belt next, working with shaky fingers.

He stands very still, his eyes on my face, and I wonder if he senses my nervousness. I've seen men without their clothes—I've bathed hundreds at the hospital—but I hadn't been in love with any of *them*.

Finally, it's Anson's turn to undress me. I shiver as my blouse falls away, his fingertips like a whisper against my skin. There's a kind of reverence in his voice as he murmurs my name, his eyes filled with such tenderness that my throat catches with an unexpected rush of tears.

Moments later, my clothes are on the floor and I'm standing there naked, chilly and trembling all over. I catch my reflection in the bureau mirror and wish I'd remembered to turn off the hall light too. I've lost weight since the war began and my body looks sharp in the glass, sinewy and pale, and I worry that I'm a disappointment. And then Anson is behind me, wrapping an arm about my waist, bending his mouth to the curve of my shoulder. I close my eyes, abandoning myself to the moment. I want only him. His breath. His hands. His skin.

He leads me to the bed, pulling me down with him onto the sheets. He smells of sweat and the strong carbolic soap they use at the hospital, earthy and astringent. Male. Our breaths mingle warm and wet as we find each other in the darkness, his hands insistent and everywhere, as if trying to map my body with his touch. And yet he's in no hurry, content to savor the moment—to savor *me*—and I let him, lost in the bittersweet magic of these few brief hours before we must say goodbye.

I wait until Anson's breathing grows even, then slip from the bed. It will be light soon, and there's packing to be done. I know about the journey that awaits me. I won't need much—plain clothes that are easy to move in, sturdy shoes with low heels, a few personal items. But there are other things too, things I can't leave behind.

I'm careful not to wake Anson as I move about in the darkness, gathering *Maman*'s rosary, the locket containing Erich Freede's photo, the packet of letters I saved after *Maman* died. They're her legacy to me, a reminder that once upon a time, there had been happy endings and, just maybe, there would be again.

Downstairs, in the workroom, I flip on the light and stand staring at the dress I began sewing a seeming lifetime ago. It's been finished for months, languishing in a darkened workroom, denied its moment of triumph. But the dreams I had when I began it were very different from the dreams I have now. I'm leaving Paris—for good it seems—and there's something I must do before the sun comes up.

I gather what I need: a white candle, a pen and paper, a bowl of water, another of salt, a needle, a spool of white thread—and the dress. I light the candle and close my eyes, then slowly begin to breathe, waiting for something to come up. I scribble a few words, cross them out, begin again, wishing I'd paid better attention to *Maman*'s instruction about charm writing. There's so little time, and I still have the stitching to do. I try again.

Finally, I'm ready to begin. But my hands are damp, and I have trouble holding on to the needle. *Maman*'s voice is in my head, scolding. *You haven't prepared properly before beginning. Your charm is clumsy and overly broad. Your stitchwork is abominable.* Every word is true, but at last I lay down my needle and survey my handiwork.

> Over distance, over time,
> Whatever trials might come,
> May the echoes of these two young hearts
> Be forever joined as one.

The untidy needlework is bad enough, but I've managed to prick myself several times in the process, leaving tiny smears of blood on the lining of the bodice. It feels like an omen. I feed the remaining thread to the candle and snuff out the flame. The work isn't up to *Maman*'s standards, but I've done my best. The rest is in fate's hands.

TWENTY-TWO

Soline

*To be effective, one must know one's treatments
and when to use them. A charm is a spell used
to create opportunities . . . a series of serendipi-
ties meant to help fate along, while a fascination or glamour is an instrument of deception
meant to distort natural events.*

—*Esmée Roussel, the Dress Witch*

28 August 1943—Paris

I'm already dressed, sitting in a chair near the window when Anson
stirs. His eyes open heavily, the corners of his mouth lifting in that lazy
American smile I've come to love. I try to smile back, but I can't manage
it. All I can think about are the minutes ticking away.

He dresses in the dark, then follows me to the kitchen. I scrounge the
last of the coffee *Maman* hoarded before the war, managing two nearly full
cups. It's stale but better than nothing, and helps wash down the crackers
and jam that serve as our breakfast.

Anson drains his cup in one go and carries it to the sink. "It's time,"
he says grimly. "The sun will be up soon."

I nod, not trusting my voice. I'm afraid that if I open my mouth, I'll beg him to let me stay, and we've covered that territory already.

He nods in return. "I'll wait for you downstairs."

I take one last walk through the apartment, checking windows and turning out lights. Ridiculous, since I'm leaving everything behind. What does it matter if someone comes in? It isn't mine anymore. I close the door to my bedroom and go downstairs.

Anson is standing near the door, peering through the split in the blackout curtains. He turns as I reach the bottom of the stairs, frowning at my empty hands. "Where's your suitcase?"

I point to the dress box near his feet.

He glances at it, then back at me. "A cardboard box?"

"It's a dress box," I correct, as if that explains everything.

"Soline, you can't carry that. You need a proper suitcase."

"I don't have a proper suitcase."

"Well, that won't work. You need something sturdy. Something you can carry easily." He scrapes a hand through his hair. "Don't you have *anything* else?"

"I'm taking this."

He glances at his watch, then nods grudgingly. "All right. Let's go. Don't talk. Just keep your head down and keep walking. No matter what happens, keep walking and don't stop until you get to the hospital. Your ride will be waiting."

My stomach plummets to my shoes. "Aren't you my ride?"

His eyes slide away. "No."

"Why? It's what you do. You're the driver."

"Not this time."

I stare at him in disbelief. "You should have said. If I'd known—"

He silences me with a look. "You know how this works, Soline. The rules are in place to protect the cell. I'm too close to this one—too close to *you*. I used my connections to set it all in motion, but I have to step away when we get to the hospital. For everyone's safety. Do you understand?"

He's wearing that expression he gets sometimes, as if he'd flipped a switch and turned off his emotions. I've seen it before, but never directed at me. I incline my head stiffly, mimicking his stoniness.

"The driver will have your papers. You need to memorize all the information. Dates. Places. Everything. From now on—at least until you reach the States—you're Yvonne Dufort from Chartres. Say it."

"Yvonne Dufort," I repeat numbly. "From Chartres."

"Good girl. You're going to be fine. Now kiss me. There won't be time later."

I let him pull me into his arms but stand stiffly, the dress box between us. I don't want to kiss him. I want to rail at him, not for sending me away—I understand why I have to go—but for being so cool while doing it. And for the danger I know he'll put himself in once I'm gone. The Gestapo have already questioned him once. They won't leave him alone until they get what they want, and when they don't get it, they'll arrest him.

The thought sends a chill through me and reminds me just how much is at stake. I must be brave and do my part for the Resistance, even if my part is to leave. But when he crushes me to his chest, I don't feel brave. I cling to him, clutching his shirt as tears spill down my face, the ache of missing him already too real.

Finally, he pulls away. "We have to go, but first, I need to give you something." He steps away briefly, retrieving the canvas satchel from the nearby chair. He fumbles a moment but finally withdraws a zippered case of smooth brown leather and puts it in my hands.

"I want you to take this."

I stare at it, at the initials A.W.P. stenciled in gold in the lower right-hand corner, and think of the handkerchief he loaned me the day we met.

"It's my shaving kit. My mother gave it to me the Christmas before she died. I want you to take it with you."

"But you'll need it."

"I'm pretty sure I can scrounge up a razor at the hospital. Take it. Please. And hang on to it until I'm home."

We lock eyes, saying nothing. He's making a promise. One we both know isn't in his power to keep, but I take the case, then reach into the pocket of my skirt and pull out *Maman*'s rosary. I take his hand and turn it over, letting the beads trickle into his palm. "They belonged to my mother," I say quietly.

He stares at the loop of garnet beads, the silver crucifix with its tarnished savior. "I didn't realize you were Catholic. I never thought to ask."

"We're not. We're not anything."

"Then why the rosary?"

I shrug. "Insurance."

"I can't take these, Soline. What if—"

I press a finger to his lips, unwilling to let him finish the thought. "I want you to take them—and bring them back to me."

He forces a smile. "We'll trade back when I get home."

My heart squeezes as I contemplate how long it might be before I see his face again—and the unimaginable possibility that this might be the last time. This man I have known for a handful of months has become the most important thing in my life, as necessary as the air that I breathe or the blood in my veins. And yet there are things I haven't shared with him, truths I haven't told. It seems wrong suddenly that we should part with a secret between us.

"Anson, there's something I need to tell you before I go, something about myself."

He smooths the backs of his knuckles along my jaw, smiling softly. "Are you going to tell me you're a Nazi? One of Himmler's spies?"

The question nearly makes me smile. "Of course not."

"A Communist?"

"Anson, please don't be silly. I need to tell you about my family. We're—"

He kisses me then, silencing me with his mouth. "Save it until I come home."

"But—"

He shakes his head, cutting me off again. "I know I love you. And you love me. Nothing else matters." He opens his palm, showing me *Maman*'s beads. "I'll give these back when I get home. And then you can tell me your secret. Deal?"

"All right, then. When you get home."

He pushes the beads into his pocket, acknowledging the pact we've just made. I place the shaving kit into the dress box and refasten the cord. We've said what we need to, promised what we can. And now it's time to go.

My contact is waiting as promised, the ambulance idling out behind the hospital mess, a Pole with a thin mustache and sharp, dark eyes, who gives his name as Henryk. He wears a uniform like Anson's, with the familiar AFS patch on his shoulder, but I'm certain I've never seen him before.

He says nothing as he opens the back door and helps me in. Anson stands off in the shadows, watching. I can feel his eyes in the darkened yard and will him to come to me, to say one last farewell, but I know he won't. We've done that part already. I sink my teeth into my lower lip, refusing to cry.

Henryk slams the door, and I find myself shut in. I feel a frisson of panic in that abrupt moment of blackness, the realization that I am now at the mercy of strangers. Everything I know, my home, Anson, even my name, has been stripped away.

And then we're moving, gears grinding noisily as the ambulance gathers speed. I fix my eyes on the back window in time to see Anson step from the shadows, legs apart, shoulders squared, and with *Maman*'s words echoing in my head, I will the image to burn itself into my brain as he recedes, then disappears from sight.

As long as you keep his beautiful face in your heart, he will never truly be lost.

TWENTY-THREE

RORY

July 12, 1985—Boston

Rory was already regretting her decision to venture across town in lunch-hour traffic. She eyed the orange leftover container on the passenger seat and briefly considered turning around. Her mother owned every piece of Tupperware they made. She wasn't likely to miss this one anytime soon. So why had she suddenly felt the need to return it now—on a Friday afternoon?

Nearly three weeks had passed since that prickly afternoon at her apartment, but things between them remained strained. Neither had mentioned the incident, but the few phone conversations they'd had since had been stilted and cool. Because that's how their relationship worked. They'd simply gloss over the episode as if it never happened. One of them would make the first move, some small gesture of conciliation, and the other would follow. Advance, retreat, advance again.

And this time, she would make the gesture. Because she'd glimpsed something that day in her kitchen that made her wonder if it might be possible to break the cycle. And because she'd spent the better part of the morning making her usual Friday calls about Hux, working her way down her list of contacts, hoping there'd been word, a sighting or rumor, some new trail being pursued. As usual, she'd come up empty.

Nothing new to relay. Doing everything we can. So very sorry.

She wasn't sure how it had become a Friday thing. She only knew that with each week that passed, the outcome was beginning to feel more and more inevitable. She wouldn't be the first to lose a fiancé. Women had been doing it for centuries, waiting for news that never came, weeping over news that did. Which would *she* be? How long could she keep hoping, when there wasn't a scrap of news to cling to? When did she move on? And what did that look like? Was she already doing it? Was that what the gallery was about? A stand-in for Hux? Camilla had once suggested it was. Now, with all her heart, she needed to hear that it wasn't true, that she was doing the right thing for the right reason—and that she shouldn't feel guilty.

She wouldn't stay long. Just long enough to return the Tupperware and maybe a cup of coffee.

The front door was unlocked. She slipped off her shoes in the foyer, then headed for the kitchen. By the time she heard the voices, it was too late. Her mother's high, tinkling laugh, Vicky Foster's nasal drone, and one more she couldn't quite place. She should have called first. She wasn't in the mood for chitchat with her mother's friends.

She was about to turn and leave when Camilla appeared in the doorway. "Aurora. I thought I heard the front door. Is everything all right?"

"Everything's fine. I just came by to return this." Rory held up the Tupperware container. "I didn't know you had company or I wouldn't have come."

"Don't be silly. It's only Vicky and Hilly. We've just finished lunch. Have you eaten? There's some bisque left and plenty of salad."

"I'm not hungry. And I'm not really dressed."

"Oh, no one cares about that. I know they'd love to see you."

Before Rory could protest, she was being steered toward the dining room. "Look who I found, ladies," Camilla announced as they sailed into the room. "She stopped by to return a leftover container, but when she heard you were here, she just had to come in and say hello."

Rory managed a smile. Vicky Foster and Hilly Standridge were members of the Women's Art Council and held prominent positions in Camilla's entourage.

Hilly smiled at her with sad eyes. "It's lovely to see you, dear. We were awfully sorry to hear about your young man, but we're keeping a good thought. Will you be joining us for dessert? I believe your mother's gone to bring it in."

As if on cue, Camilla reappeared with the dessert tray. "Your timing is perfect, Aurora. I made your favorite. Apple spice cake with brown-butter frosting."

"Thanks, but I really can't. I just stopped by to bring back your soup container. I've got tons to do, and traffic—"

"Oh, sweetheart, stay for cake at least. I'm sure you can spare a *few* minutes—and give your mother a chance to brag a little to her friends."

Rory shifted awkwardly, keenly aware of Hilly and Vicky looking at her with indulgent smiles. For a sickening moment she was eight again, wearing a yellow chiffon party dress, being hoisted up onto a piano bench at one of her mother's dinner parties, expectant faces all turned in her direction. Her little hands hot and sticky, frozen on the keys. Her mother's voice, high and tight from behind her camera. *Come now, Aurora, you don't want to embarrass Mommy in front of her friends.*

The photo now sat in a silver frame in her mother's curio cabinet in the living room, her humiliation captured for posterity. And here she was again, being called on to do her party piece.

Her vision began to smear as she stared at Camilla. *It's just the perfume,* she told herself, Shalimar and White Shoulders, mixed with her mother's Chanel No. 5. She blinked the moisture away and dropped her eyes to the cake. Perfection, as usual.

"Here, sit by me," Camilla said, pulling out a chair. "And I'll cut you a nice big slice."

Rory dropped into the chair obediently, watching as Camilla wielded the cake knife with the skill of a surgeon. Vicky filled four of her mother's pretty china cups. Four cups, not three. Her mother had known all along that she would get her way.

"Your mother mentioned an internship in Paris when you finish school," Hilly said, spooning sugar into her coffee. "You must be looking forward to that. We sent all our girls after graduation, though not for anything so exciting as an internship at the Musée d'Orsay."

"I'm afraid that's on hold for now," Camilla answered for Rory. "Aurora has decided to pursue interests closer to home."

Vicky nodded. "Oh, yes. Of course. But it's a shame to pass up such a wonderful experience after you went to so much trouble arranging it for her." She paused for a sigh. "But I suppose school can wait, and Paris isn't going anywhere."

Rory had been fiddling with her cake, content to let the conversation go on without her, but listening to her mother being painted as the *real* victim was a bridge too far. She put down her fork and turned to Vicky. "Actually, I've decided not to finish school, Mrs. Foster. I plan to open a gallery instead. With any luck, this fall."

"A gallery?" Hilly's mousy brows shot up. "Why, that's wonderful. Camilla, why didn't you tell us about this?"

Camilla lifted her coffee cup and sipped before offering a tight smile. "It's all still in the planning stages. I didn't want to jinx it."

"Well, this *is* exciting. Your very own gallery. You found a good location, I hope. You know what they say—location, location, location."

"As a matter of fact, I did. I found a wonderful row house right next to DeLuca's."

"On Newbury? How perfect—"

183

"Wait," Vicky interrupted, waving her fork. "Isn't that where the bridal shop was? The French woman with her magic dresses. Guaranteed all her brides a happy ending. Hilly, your daughter bought her dress there, didn't she, back before it burned? What was it called? Something catchy."

"The Charmed Needle," Hilly replied. "The woman did stunning work, and all by hand. Though I can tell you, we paid for every last stitch."

Rory leaned forward in her chair, cake forgotten. "Did it work? The magic, I mean."

Hilly smiled serenely. "Three grandbabies later, I suppose it must have. The doctors said she couldn't after she fell off that beast of a horse, but I am thrice a grandmother."

Vicky rolled her eyes. "Don't tell me you actually believe those silly rumors."

"I'm saying it never hurts to hedge your bet, darling. If I had to do it over again, at twice the price, I'd pay."

Vicky sniffed at her. "Whatever floats your boat, as they say. But it *was* a lovely shop. I remember the owner, I think. French and absolutely gorgeous. I seem to remember her being tapped to do a dress for one of the Kennedy girls. A cousin or niece or something. I can't remember which one, but I remember it being a very big deal. Heaven knows the Kennedys need all the luck they can get. And she certainly had the reputation for it. Whatever happened to her?"

"Died when the shop caught fire, I think," Hilly replied, fingering the strand of pearls at her throat. "My daughter was terribly upset when she saw it in the papers. They said she was asleep when it started. I'm trying to remember her name."

"Soline," Rory supplied. "Her name is Soline Roussel. And she didn't die. In fact, she's my landlady."

"Your landlady! Well, what do you know about that?"

"The building wasn't really for lease—it had been vacant for years—but when she heard I wanted to open a gallery for new artists, she agreed to let me rent it."

Vicky turned to Camilla, who had remained silent throughout the conversation. "You've been holding out on us, Camilla, dear. You never said a word about Ms. Roussel. And it sounds as if she has an interest in the arts. Perhaps we should invite her to join the council."

Camilla continued to stir her coffee, her expression carefully blank. "I'm afraid it's Aurora who's been holding out. I've never met Ms. Roussel, though I understand she's something of a recluse. Perhaps we could invite her to make a contribution instead."

Hilly turned to Rory. "Could you talk to her about joining our little group? Just, you know, feel her out?"

Camilla set her spoon down with a clatter. "Aren't we getting a little ahead of ourselves? Five minutes ago, you couldn't remember the woman's name. Now you're ready to invite her to join the council. Don't you think we should find out if she's our sort of person first?"

Hilly rolled her eyes. "For heaven's sake, Camilla. It's the 1980s, not the 1880s. No one thinks like that anymore."

Vicky sighed and laid down her napkin. "Personally, I'm bored to death with *our sort of person*. And in case you haven't noticed, Camilla, our membership numbers are in the loo, which means we can't afford to be snooty. Perhaps it's time to shake things up. She must know scads of people. Think of the buzz it would create."

Camilla looked genuinely astonished. She wasn't used to being countermanded, and certainly not at her own table. "I just meant it might be better to stick with people we know."

Vicky was undaunted. "Why don't you drop a few hints the next time you speak with her, Aurora, and see if she'd be interested in joining forces."

Rory reached for her coffee, uncomfortable with being put on the spot. "I really don't know when I'll speak to her again. I usually deal with her attorney on anything to do with the building. Which reminds me," she said, emptying her cup and pushing back from the table. "I'm due to meet my contractor at four. It was nice seeing you both again."

Camilla's face fell. "You're going already?"

"I told you I couldn't stay."

"But I hoped you'd help us brainstorm for the fundraiser. We seem to repeat the same old themes, and you always have such creative ideas."

"I'm sure you'll do fine," Rory said, turning to go. "You always do."

She was nearly to the door when Camilla caught her. "Aurora. You're not really going to talk to that woman about joining the council, are you?"

"Her name is Soline. But you know that, because we've talked about her. And why would it be so terrible for her to join your precious council?"

"For starters, we know nothing about her."

"Correction. *You* know nothing about her. I know quite a lot about her, and I like her."

"That much is obvious. Honestly, the way you went on in there. Like she's the patron saint of unknown artists or something."

"I didn't go on about her. I was asked about her—by *your* friends. I didn't come here to talk about her or to have cake. I came . . . Never mind. It doesn't matter."

"What doesn't matter? What were you going to say?"

"Nothing. I wasn't going to say anything. I'm just having a bad day. I didn't expect anyone to be here. I thought . . . we could talk."

"We can. I'll get rid of them, and we'll talk all you want. You can stay for dinner. We'll cook like we used to. Or we can go out. You name the place."

But it was too late for talk. Somewhere between kicking off her shoes and sitting down for cake, the need to pour out her troubles to her mother had evaporated. "I'm all right now."

"But something's wrong. I can tell."

"Something was wrong when I got here. I told you that, but I had to have cake with your friends and smile and make polite conversation, so you could play hostess."

"It isn't Matthew, is it? You haven't had news."

She shook her head wearily. "No. No news."

"Then what?"

"Go back to your guests, Mother. With any luck, they'll forget about Soline."

"I didn't mean—"

"Yes, you did. I saw your face. You hated that her name even came up. I don't know why, but you did. Or maybe it was me talking about the gallery that set you off. You twist my arm until you get me to stay. Then, when I commit the unpardonable sin of going off script, you get all huffy. You expect everyone to dance to your tune. Even me."

"That isn't true."

"But it is. It was true when I was eight, and it's true now."

"When you were . . . Aurora, what are you talking about?"

"Forget it. And don't worry—I won't mention your precious council to Soline. I don't see her fitting in, though not for the reasons you think."

Camilla blinked at her. "Meaning?"

"Meaning I don't see her wanting to be part of your court." Rory paused, jerking her chin in the direction of the dining room. "She isn't like them. And she certainly isn't like you. She sees me. Not the way she *thinks* I should be but the way I am. Maybe that's why I like her so much."

And with that, she turned and stepped into the foyer, trying not to think of an eight-year-old in a party dress, perched on a piano bench and frozen with fear.

TWENTY-FOUR

RORY

An hour later, Rory found herself standing on Soline's front step, a bag of takeout from Gerardo's in her arms. She had knocked four times and was about to knock again when the door opened a crack.

"Whatever you're selling, I'm not interested."

"It's me," Rory blurted. "I'm sorry. I should have called."

A waft of coffee drifted out onto the stoop as the door swung back. "Rory?"

She was barefoot and simply dressed: a plain white tee, jeans rolled up at the ankles. Her hair was pulled into a messy bun, her skin devoid of makeup. What was it about French women—even the middle-aged ones—that allowed them to roll out of bed, throw on the first thing they pulled out of the closet, and be ready for a photo shoot?

Her eyes narrowed perceptively, lingering on Rory's face. "What's wrong?"

"Nothing. Or maybe everything. Are you hungry?"

Soline eyed the bag and stepped aside. "Come through."

The kitchen was at the back of the house and much larger than she expected, with a high ceiling and tall windows that let in the afternoon sun. Here, too, was a room meant to be used, with ropes of onions and garlic on the wall, bottled vinegars lined up on a shelf above the stove, tomatoes ripening on the sill.

"Whatever it is smells delicious," Soline said as she began extracting the food from the bag. There was a container of pasta tossed with mushrooms, zucchini, and eggplant; another of salad; and a bag filled with fragrant knots of garlic bread. "Where did you get it?"

"There's a place near my apartment—Gerardo's. I order from there a couple times a week. Everything's delicious, and they deliver. Can I set the table?"

"It's a pretty day. Why don't we eat on the patio? Grab plates and glasses from the cupboard next to the stove. Silverware is in the drawer just below. I'll put the food on a tray and be out in a minute."

Rory located the necessary items and carried them out to a sunny patio scattered with potted herbs and tomato plants. There was a small wrought-iron table in one corner, tucked beneath a rose-draped pergola. It was a lovely spot, cool and shady with the mingled scents of roses and basil drifting on the late-afternoon breeze.

Soline appeared with the tray just as Rory was finishing the table. "Here we are. Help me, please. It's heavier than I thought, and my hands are trying to cramp."

Rory hurried to relieve her of the tray. "I'm sorry. I didn't think. I should have carried it out."

"I'm not an invalid, *chérie*. I do quite well for myself. Most of the time."

"Yes. Sorry. I didn't mean . . ." Rory set out the food, then dropped into one of the chairs. "Thank you for this. For letting me barge in on you. I hope I haven't ruined any dinner plans."

"Plans?" Soline barked out a laugh. "I haven't had plans in years. And certainly not dinner plans." She held out both hands—bare, since she hadn't been expecting company. "It's to do with the gloves mostly. They make me clumsy—especially when eating—and something of a spectacle in this day and age, an eccentric old woman stuck in the past."

Rory shot her a dubious glance. No one in their right mind could ever mistake Soline Roussel for an old eccentric. Even now, makeup-free and unprepared for guests, she looked beautifully chic. Like the effortlessly beautiful women in *Condé Nast Traveler*, her face spoke of glamour and exotic adventures, lives lived in faraway places.

"I've always loved gloves," Rory said. "I think they make you look chic."

Soline smiled unconvincingly as she leaned across the table to fill Rory's water glass. "Aren't you sweet. Now, tell me why you're here, and don't say it was your turn. You have a face like a rain cloud. What's happened?"

"Nothing, really. I just . . ." She shook her head, suddenly self-conscious. "It's nothing."

Soline arched a brow. "You knocked on my door because nothing happened? What kind of answer is that?"

Rory helped herself to a piece of eggplant, then poked disinterestedly at it. "I'm sorry. It hasn't been a good day, and I needed someone to talk to."

Soline's face softened. "So talk."

Rory shrugged. "It's Friday. That's the day I call to see if there's any news on Hux. There wasn't. I didn't really think there would be, but . . ."

"But?"

"I can't see how this ends, and it scares me. I'm afraid he's never coming back, and the gallery will be all I ever have. What if . . ."

"You turn out like me?" she supplied quietly. "It's all right to say it."

"No. It isn't that." *At least it isn't only that.* "It's something my mother said. She thinks I'm opening the gallery for the wrong reasons."

"Why would she say that?"

"Because Hux is the one who put the idea into my head. It was something I used to toy with when I got bored with school, one of those *what if* kind of things. But Hux made it seem possible. He said it was a dream worth chasing. So I chased it."

"And you think that makes it wrong? Because someone inspired you?"

"I was supposed to finish school, then do an internship at the Musée d'Orsay. When I told her I was leaving school to open a gallery, she said I was trying to prove something to someone who wasn't even here. Because I was scared."

"You're not, are you?"

"I don't know. I didn't think so then, but now . . . I'm just second-guessing everything. It's starting to feel like Hux is never coming home, and maybe I've known it for a while now. Why else would I decide to open a gallery right now, unless some part of me thinks it's time to move on?"

"Your mother said all that to you?"

"No. Not in so many words, but she knows how to get under my skin. She doesn't like it when I make plans for myself, so when I do, she has to undermine them. In twenty-three years, it's never occurred to her that I might actually know what I want."

"What *do* you want?"

Rory closed her eyes, fighting a hitch in her throat. "I want Hux to come home. Healthy and in one piece. I want to know what comes next. For me. For us."

Soline's smile was tinged with sadness. "Of course you do. But you can't, *chérie*. None of us can. We can only live the life we have right now, today."

"That's the problem. I don't have one. Not really. And part of me is afraid I'm making a huge mistake. My mother keeps reminding me that I don't have any experience at this and that eighty percent of galleries don't survive their second year. If I blow it, what happens then? If Hux

. . ." She paused, swallowing hard when her voice suddenly broke. "I don't think I can take losing anything else."

Soline put down her fork and met Rory's gaze squarely. "Rory, you must learn to separate Hux from the gallery. Right now, you're thinking of them as the same thing, as if one cannot exist without the other. But it isn't true. I had to learn this for myself—after Anson died."

Rory blew out a breath. "Please don't say you want me to get on with my life. My mother says that, and it makes me crazy."

"All right, I won't say it, but she's not wrong. You were a person before Hux came into your life. And you will go on being a person, even if he leaves it. It's not a choice. It's how it works. The question is what kind of person you'll be. What will you do with your life, your dreams, your art?"

Rory blinked at her across the table. "My art?"

"Yes, silly girl. Your art. You have a gift. You think you get those for nothing?"

"But I'm not—"

"If you're having second thoughts, we can tear up the lease. You don't have to go through with it."

Rory stared at her. She wasn't sure what she'd been expecting, but it certainly wasn't an offer to tear up the lease. The thought made her stomach lurch. "No, I don't want that."

Soline smiled knowingly. "I didn't think so. You're having—how do Americans say it—a case of cold feet. But if you want the gallery badly enough, you'll make it work."

"Like you did with your bridal salon?"

"I had nothing when I came here. I was a foreigner, broke and alone. It was a hard time, harder even than the war, because of what I'd lost. But I couldn't just lie down and die, even when I wanted to."

Rory watched as Soline tore a small bite from a garlic knot and slowly chewed. Her loss was still visible despite the patina of years. She had shared her story freely enough, but Rory couldn't help feeling there was more, some heartache she still kept to herself. "You told me you and Anson were separated because of the war and that you learned he'd gone missing. Were you still in Paris then?"

"No. I had to leave. I didn't want to, but Anson made me go. He was working with the Resistance, helping to get people out—people the Nazis were looking for. I began helping, too, until it became . . . problematic."

Rory stared at her across the table. "You were part of the Resistance?"

"In those days, if you were living in Paris, you were either a collaborator or you were part of the Resistance. There were a few who tried to walk the middle road, but sooner or later we all had to choose. We did what we could. I was a courier. Women could get away with more. Especially if they were pretty." She paused, smiling bitterly. "The Germans liked French girls. They were so busy flirting with us that they forgot to suspect us. But they found out about Anson and me—and they used me against him."

Rory put down her glass, breath held as she waited for more.

"One night on the way back from a run, Anson's ambulance broke down, and he was picked up by the Gestapo. They questioned him for hours. When he wouldn't cooperate, they told him they knew who I was. They said if he didn't give them the names they wanted, they would come after me. They used to do that, pick up wives and sweethearts and send them to terrible places. Prison camps and brothels. Anson refused to talk. They let him go eventually, but the next day he made me leave."

"Alone?"

Soline reached for her water glass but found it empty. She refilled it with shaking hands and took a long sip. "The work he did was critical," she replied finally. "None of the rest of it mattered if the men couldn't get out. He couldn't afford distractions. So he arranged to get me out with some of the others. I hated that he was making me go, but I understood."

"Where did he send you?"

"Across the border and into Spain. Eventually to England and then here, to America. It was the usual route, so I knew what to expect, but not how long it would take or how hard it would be. It was strange being on that end of it. Until then, I could only imagine what happened once the men were handed off. And then all of a sudden, there I was, being handed off myself."

Rory suppressed a shudder, imagining herself in Soline's shoes, leaving her home and the man she loved at the mercy of strangers. "Wasn't it dangerous? Traveling like that while the war was going on?"

"It was. But for many, staying in Paris amounted to a death sentence. We lost some, but there were more successes than failures, and that made the risk worth taking."

"I can't imagine it. To leave Paris and end up here in Boston. It must have been like landing in another world."

Soline went quiet, her hands still and white on either side of her plate. "I didn't come to Boston right away. I went to Newport first—to Anson's father. Anson wrote to say I was coming."

Rory was surprised by this. Soline had never mentioned Anson's family. "It must have been a comfort to be with his people, rather than all alone in a new place."

Soline shook her head very slowly, her eyes dark with memory. "No. It was not . . . a comfort."

TWENTY-FIVE

SOLINE

Whosoever shall misuse la magie *for selfish ends shall bring unhappiness on the family entire. Take care, then, to keep your needle true, and do not use your charms in pursuit of things not meant for you.*

—*Esmée Roussel, the Dress Witch*

22 September 1943—Newport

I arrive at the station in Newport on a chilly Wednesday morning, messy and creased after hours on the train. I'm as thin as a rake in my borrowed clothes, exhausted after weeks of seasickness and uncertainty. For days, all I've been able to think about is a hot bath and a real bed with clean sheets, but now, as I stand on the crowded platform, searching for a face that looks like Anson, my thoughts turn in a new direction.

I've done the best I can with my hair, but I didn't have enough pins to do it up properly. Hairpins are hard enough to come by these days, but they're especially hard to find on ships and trains and convoys full of men. I hate to think what I must look like. No hat, no gloves, no proper shoes. Not exactly the way a girl hopes to look when meeting her future father-in-law for the first time.

The crowd on the platform has begun to thin. I stand on my tiptoes, searching the remaining faces, but none of them seems right. A young man with a pinned-up sleeve. An old man clutching a rumpled paper sack. A pair of GIs in army green, carrying a trunk between them. But no one likely to be Owen Purcell.

My stomach turns over, wondering if there's been a miscommunication of some kind, a missed call or lost letter. And then I see a man moving toward me on the platform. He's wearing a plain black suit and a brimmed cap.

His brows lift as he eyes me up and down. "Would you be Miss Roussel?"

Relief floods through me. "*Oui*, I am—" I stop, reminding myself that I'm in America now. "Yes. I'm Miss Roussel."

"My name is Stanton. I'm Mr. Purcell's driver. If you'll just point out your bags, I'll take them to the car."

"I don't have any bags," I tell him, holding up my battered box. "It's just this."

He gives the box a dubious glance but manages a nod. "Very good, miss."

But when he reaches for it, I find myself taking a step back. It contains everything I care about in the world, and I haven't let it out of my sight in weeks. "I'll carry it, thank you."

"As you wish." His face is carefully blank, like *Maman*'s when dealing with a troublesome bride. "If you'll follow me."

He leads me to a great ship of a car, gleaming black with a shiny grille and tires with wide white sides. The sight of it makes my throat constrict. It reminds me of the Gestapo's cars, long and sinister, prowling the streets of Paris. I peer through the window, expecting my first glance of Anson's father, but the car is empty.

If Stanton notices my disappointment, he gives no sign as he whisks open the rear door. I step past him and climb in. It's warm inside and comfortable, and suddenly I'm so very tired. I let my head fall back against the leather seat and close my eyes, trying not to think about why Anson's father didn't come to the station to meet me.

When I open my eyes again, the car is easing up a long, brick-paved drive. I'm completely unprepared for my first glimpse of Anson's childhood home. It's a sprawling sort of edifice, three stories of cream-and-gray stone with diamond-paned windows on the upper floors and more gables and chimneys than I can count from the moving car. I run my eyes over the highest windows, the small panes turned to mirrors in the chilly morning light, wondering if Owen Purcell is standing behind one of them, awaiting my arrival.

I'm still fumbling with my box when Stanton opens the car door. I slide out, acutely aware of my shabbiness. Everything is so large and immaculate. The car, the house, even Stanton, towering over me in his somber black serge. He points me toward a set of double glass doors decorated with iron scrollwork, stoic as he steps past me.

The door swings back before I can ring the bell. Suddenly Owen Purcell is there, impeccable in a charcoal-gray three-piece that's almost certainly tailor-made. He's tall like Anson, with thick shoulders, a broad chest, and a middle that's just starting to go soft. He has a head full of silver-gold waves, and his eyes are the same liquid blue-green as Anson's. They miss nothing as they sweep over me, coming to linger briefly on my scuffed black shoes.

"Miss Roussel, here at last."

I manage a wobbly smile. "Good morning, Monsieur Purcell."

His eyes touch mine with no hint of a smile. "He said you were French." He looks past me then, out to the drive. "Stanton, please bring in Miss Roussel's things."

"She hasn't any things, sir. Only the box."

Mr. Purcell eyes me again, brows lowered as he examines the dress box dangling from my hand. "Very well, then. Come in."

I wipe my feet once, twice, three times before stepping over the threshold into a large entryway. The polished parquet floor makes the space feel more like a ballroom than a foyer. The walls are a soft, creamy yellow, the ceilings high and decorated with ornate plasterwork. A chandelier dripping with crystal pendants splashes small droplets of light on the walls and floor, and my head whirls as the lights dance around me. For a moment, I'm afraid I will crumple into a heap at my future father-in-law's feet.

"Are you unwell?"

I swallow the thick sensation in my mouth and try to shake my head. "I'm just . . . I've been traveling rather a long time."

"Yes, of course. Perhaps you should rest before lunch. I'll show you to your room."

There isn't time to protest. He's already heading for the staircase, not bothering to check that I'm following. He has a slight limp, a straight-legged gait that hinders his progress—likely the result of the war wound Anson told me about.

At the top of the stairs, a broad gallery lined with English hunting prints stretches in both directions. When I hesitate, he glances back briefly. "This way, please. The last door on the right." At the end of the hall, he pushes the door open and stands aside. "I've had the room aired and the bed made up. You have your own bath, just through there, if you care to freshen up before luncheon."

The drapes are drawn, the interior dim as I step inside. It's a small room with a double bed, a nightstand and lamp, a bare bureau, and a long oval mirror. The walls are papered with enormous cabbage roses on a background of dull green. The pattern is too loud for such a small room, making it feel faintly oppressive.

"Thank you," I say with all the politeness I can muster. "It's lovely."

He bows his head, clearly all the response I am to receive, and I find myself trying to make him out. He's handsome for a man in his fifties, high cheeks, broad forehead, a bit of a bump at the bridge of his nose—as if it might have been broken. But it's his mouth, full and yet hard somehow, that holds my attention—a mouth unused to smiling.

"Luncheon is served at twelve thirty. Someone will come to take you down."

He pulls the door closed then, leaving me alone. Like a lodger, I have been shown to my room and left to my own devices. I put my box on the bureau and slip off my shoes, then lie down fully dressed and close my eyes. Not once has Owen Purcell mentioned his son's name.

I've barely drifted off when I jolt awake again. The door is open a crack, an eye peering through, wide, watching. I sit up quickly, my head still muzzy. "*Vous pouvez entrer*," I call thickly, then remember my English. "Come in."

The door creaks open a few inches. A face appears, broad cheeks, blue-green eyes, a thick sheaf of wheat-colored hair. A younger version of Anson—and female.

"You're Thia," I say, smiling. "Anson's sister. Your brother told me all about you. How you like to paint and play the guitar."

She inches forward, shy but curious. She's eleven or twelve, but tall for her age and a little awkward, with large front teeth and a liberal dusting of freckles. Her lumpy sweater and ill-fitting skirt make her look shapeless and plain, but beneath the dowdy layers there is a beauty waiting to bloom.

"Are you really French?" she whispers with a kind of awe. "Daddy said you were. He calls you Anson's little French seamstress. What's a seamstress?"

I register the slight but choose to ignore it. Instead, I focus on Thia, the way she tilts her head as she studies me. She's Anson to a T, and I suddenly long to wrap my arms around her. "A seamstress is a woman who makes dresses," I explain. "And yes, I'm from Paris."

The corners of her mouth turn down. "They have the war there."

It seems an odd way to put it, though perhaps not to a child. America is sending its men to fight, but they have been spared the horrors of occupation and bombs. "Yes," I answer quietly. "They do."

She sits beside me, hands pressed between her knees. "Anson's there. He drives sick people around."

I smile, charmed by her innocence. "Yes, he does. And he's very good at it."

"Did he drive you around? Is that how he met you?"

"No. We met at the hospital where we both worked. I was sick on my first day, and he helped me."

She grins, wrinkling her nose. "Anson's always helping people. He's nice."

"I think he's nice too."

"Please don't tell my father I spied on you. He wouldn't like it. I was only supposed to knock and then bring you down to lunch, but I was hoping we could be friends."

I can feel my heart melting as I look at her face, shy yet hopeful. "Of course we can be friends. And you can come see me anytime. Is your room next to mine?"

"No." She stretches out an arm, pointing to the opposite end of the hall. "The family rooms are at the other end of the gallery. Mine's the first one on the right side, and Anson's is across the hall. Mummy and Daddy's room is way down at the end, but it's only Daddy's room now."

"Who lives at this end?"

"Oh, no one lives here. It's just where we put guests. Auntie Diane stayed in here when she came for Mummy's funeral. She's Mummy's sister, but Daddy says she's not really our family."

I nod, understanding. To Owen Purcell, family means blood. Sisters-in-law don't count. Neither do French fiancées.

"We'd better go down," Thia says. "Daddy doesn't like it when people are late."

Thia waits while I wash my face and attempt to pat my hair into place. My reflection startles me. I'm so very pale, the bones in my face sharp after weeks of meager meals and little sleep. I run a hand over my clothes. My skirt and blouse are shabby and horribly wrinkled after too many wearings, but I have nothing better to put on and no money to buy new.

I step out of the bathroom to find Thia at the bureau, running a tentative hand over the lid of my box. For a moment, I feel a frisson of panic, a territorial instinct.

Thia snatches her hand away, but an instant later her gaze returns to the bureau. She points shyly. "What's in there?"

I grin at her with a conspiratorial wink. "All my secrets. Let's go down, shall we?"

Downstairs, in the dining room, Owen is already seated at a long linen-clad table laid for three. He glances up as Thia and I enter, his lips thinning as he takes me in. "I thought you might have changed," he says coolly. "Were you able to rest?"

"Yes. Thank you. I'm feeling much better. Thia tapped on my door to let me know it was time to come down."

Thia beams her gratitude as we take our seats, but Mr. Purcell continues to scowl. "Her name is Cynthia," he says stiffly. "After my mother. We prefer not to encourage diminutives."

"I'm sorry. I didn't realize . . . It's how Anson always referred to her."

"Yes, well, my son has always indulged her. I suspect it's to do with the difference in their ages. Cynthia, your napkin."

Thia suppresses a scowl as she drags her napkin into her lap. I follow her example, wondering if his reproach was actually meant for me.

Seconds tick by without conversation. I run my eyes around the dining room, avoiding Owen's gaze. It's a beautiful room, everything white and gold and sparkling clean, and suddenly I feel conspicuous, like a dusty smudge amid all the loveliness.

A woman in a pale-gray uniform enters through a swinging door, bearing a soup tureen and a large silver ladle. Owen nods coolly as she sets the soup in the center of the table. "Thank you, Belinda," he says dismissively as he lifts the tureen lid. "Cynthia. Your bowl, please."

Thia holds out her bowl obediently, watching as her father ladles out a rich red bisque. She stares at it, nose wrinkled. "This is tomato, isn't it?"

"It is," he replies, filling his own bowl, then passing the ladle to me. "And you'll eat it. Everyone must do their part for the war, Cynthia, and you're no exception. That means making do with what we grow locally. Or would you prefer your brother go hungry halfway around the world?"

Thia's eyes go shiny with a sudden rush of tears, and I feel my anger flash, stunned that a father could be so unfeeling. "Actually," I say casually as I fill my bowl, "the Red Cross sends regular food shipments to the hospital where Anson works, and they've turned all the flower beds into vegetable gardens so they can grow their own tomatoes."

Owen gives me a hard look. "My son wrote that he met you at this hospital, but not much more. Were you a nurse there?"

"No, not a nurse. I was a volunteer."

"A volunteer. What does that mean?"

"We looked after the men's needs."

He regards me frostily over his soup spoon. "Indeed."

I ignore his tone and the unspoken suggestion that there was something inappropriate in the work I did. He was wounded himself in the first war. He knows very well what volunteers do. "We fed the men who couldn't feed themselves, bathed them, read to them, helped them write letters home."

"Very admirable, I'm sure. And so lucky for our boys. Tell me, how did you and my son become . . . friends?"

Friends.

I bristle at the word, clearly chosen to diminish my relationship with Anson. But before I can open my mouth to respond, Thia jumps in. "Oh, I know this! She got sick on her first day at the hospital, and Anson helped her."

Owen flicks a look at his daughter before returning his attention to me. "On your first day. Well, well, that *was* quick work. And it seems you and my daughter have become fast friends as well."

"She asked about Anson as we were coming down," I say, spooning up more bisque. "I'm sure she misses her brother."

He puts down his spoon and fixes me with a cold stare. "We both miss him, Miss Roussel. And we'll be happy to have him back home with his family—where he belongs."

I manage a smile but say nothing, unsettled by his use of the phrase *back home with his family*. Surely he doesn't think Anson and I will remain under his roof after we're married. I try to imagine it, living under those cold, watchful eyes, constantly trying to earn his approval—constantly failing. The thought actually makes me queasy.

Belinda reappears in her ghost-gray uniform, balancing three plates, which she serves without a word. I look at the food, a small green salad and a salmon steak topped with a dill-and-cucumber relish. After weeks of little more than bread and watery soup, it's an absolute feast, but as I stare at my plate, I find I'm no longer hungry.

TWENTY-SIX

SOLINE

*A bride must remember that in being bound
to her lover, she is also bound to his family,
and that we make no claims with regard to
the success of those relationships. Such is not
our work.*

—*Esmée Roussel, the Dress Witch*

5 October 1943—Newport

Two weeks after stepping off the train, things with Anson's father are no
better. He's civil when he has to be but rarely bothers to speak, even at
meals when I'm seated directly across from him. He's gone most of the
time, which is some small mercy, either working late, attending meet-
ings, or dining with clients at his club. And when he does happen to be
at home, he's in his study with the door closed.

The days stretch emptily, with nothing but the radio for company
while Thia is in school. I listen to the news with clenched insides, wondering where Anson is, praying he's safe and will be home soon. I wrote
several times along the journey and again when I got to Newport, letting him know I arrived safely. Weeks later, I still haven't received a
letter, and the waiting is making me restless.

I haven't left the house since I arrived, except to sit out by the pool or walk the small stretch of beach beyond the patio gate. The fresh sea air is good for my headaches and makes me feel less claustrophobic. I'm uncomfortable moving about the house, as if I'm somewhere I don't belong—a trespasser. But I'm not entirely alone. There's Belinda, who sees to meals, and a cleaning woman named Clara who comes in twice a week, but they treat me like a piece of furniture when they see me. And so I keep to my room with its hideous wallpaper and heavy gloom.

Thia is my one pleasure. She's such a delight, so hungry for attention and for love. She receives neither from her father. He isn't intentionally cruel; that would require more energy than he's willing to spend. He simply doesn't see her, which is a cruelty all its own. Perhaps that's why she's made me her special friend—her *sister-to-be*, as she calls me. I confess, it's a title I like very much.

She finds me each day when she arrives home from school, eager for her lessons. She has asked me to teach her French so she'll be fluent when she moves to Paris and becomes a famous painter. But today, she has come to my room with one of her sketchbooks under her arm. She drops down on the bed and waits for me to join her, then opens the book and slides it into my lap.

My throat catches as I look down and see Anson's face captured in three-quarter profile. "This is wonderful," I whisper, tracing the outline of his face with my finger.

"I miss him."

"Me too."

She tips her face up, trying to smile. "He's brave, isn't he?"

"*Oui, chérie*. He's very brave. The bravest man I know."

She blinks several times, her lashes spiked with tears. "I hope he comes home soon. Then you can get married and I can come live with you."

My heart cracks as her words sink in. At her age, I desperately wanted to leave *Maman* and live with *Tante* Lilou, to escape my cage as Lilou had and follow my own dreams. But this feels different, not the restlessness of a spirit who longs to spread her wings but the deep sadness of a child who knows she isn't loved.

I press a kiss to the top of her pale head and try to change the subject. "I used to draw when I was your age. Pages and pages of beautiful dresses I was going to make one day."

Her eyes go wide. "You did?"

"I was going to be famous once. Not for my drawings but for the dresses I would make. Dresses with my name on the labels."

"What happened to the drawings?"

"I had to leave them in Paris. They weren't as good as yours, but they didn't need to be. They were only ideas."

"Did you ever make the dresses?"

I smile wistfully. "I made one. But then the war started, and no one was buying dresses like mine anymore."

She sighs dreamily. "I wish I could have seen it. The dress, I mean. I'll bet it was beautiful."

I touch a finger to my lips, then go to the closet, pull out the box, and carry it back to the bed. Thia's eyes turn to saucers as I lift the lid.

"It's a fairy-tale dress!"

"Yes," I say softly. "It is . . . sort of. It's my happy ending dress."

She cocks an eye at me. "Your what?"

"It's something my mother and I used to say."

"Did you really make it?"

"I did."

"All the way from scratch?"

I smile at the turn of phrase. "All the way from scratch."

"It's the prettiest thing I've ever seen." She sighs, fingering the beads almost tenderly. "Did you make it to wear when you marry Anson?"

I think about how to answer as I fold the dress back into its box. The truth is, I started the dress long before I knew Anson, when all I cared about was proving myself to *Maman*. But even then, there had been the dream of someone like Anson. A prince of my own, kind and brave and handsome. Like Lilou's Brit.

"Yes," I say finally, softly. "I made it to marry Anson."

She looks up at me, eyes shining. "I can't wait till he sees you in it. You'll be the most beautiful bride ever."

I swallow past the tightness in my throat, surprised by the deep attachment I've come to feel for her. "And you'll be a beautiful bridesmaid. What color would you like for your dress?"

"Blue," she answers at once. "Mummy liked me in blue. She said it brought out my eyes. I had a blue dress a few years ago, with pretty puffed sleeves, but it doesn't fit anymore. None of my good dresses fit now. But Daddy says it's wrong to want new clothes while our boys are going without. We have to do our part."

I suppress a scowl as I return the dress box to the closet. I've heard Owen's mantra often enough now, and I recognize it for what it is—a way to keep his daughter in line. But an idea begins to form as I eye Thia's shapeless jumper and too-tight skirt, a way to help her without depriving American GIs, but I won't say anything until I speak to her father.

Owen is both surprised and annoyed to find me waiting when he comes home from wherever he's been. I'm seated on the cream-colored sofa, pretending to read a book I borrowed from his library. I feel all wrong sitting here, worrying about what I look like, how my legs are crossed, what to do with my hands, but he pretends not to see me as he goes about pouring himself a drink.

I watch mutely as he drops two cubes of ice into a glass, then adds a splash of amber liquid, and I find myself wondering how the ice got into the bucket. Belinda, I suppose. But Owen isn't the least bit curious about the ice. He's used to everything being exactly as he expects it to be. It's why he doesn't like me, because I'm not what he expected for his son.

Finally he turns, pivoting stiffly on his bad leg. I close the book, waiting while he takes a pull from his glass. At long last, he fixes me with a chilly stare. "What is it that has you up so late, Miss Roussel?"

Two weeks and he still refuses to call me by my first name, as if our relationship is a temporary one. "I was hoping to talk to you about Cynthia—about her clothes."

"Her clothes?"

"Girls are different from boys."

"You don't say."

There isn't a hint of humor in his tone, but I push on, determined to make my point. "Girls reach an age where they start comparing themselves to their friends. How they look. What they wear. They worry about fitting in. Cynthia is at that age now."

"There is nothing wrong with my daughter's clothes."

"Not wrong, no. They're just a bit . . . plain. And they don't fit her as well as they could."

"We've all had to do without a great deal since the war started. Gasoline. Cooking oil. Even paper. With the men off fighting, there's no one to cut down the trees. It's easy to take things for granted until you suddenly have to do without. It's a matter of sacrificing for one's country."

I stare at him, piqued by his platitudes. From where I stand, there is precious little the Purcells have gone without compared to the people of France and England. No bombs have landed on American soil, no businesses looted or seized, no oafish soldiers plundering their store shelves. It's true that their men are across the sea, fighting the Nazis, and that it's a great sacrifice indeed, but it isn't the same.

"We're well acquainted with sacrifice where I come from, Monsieur Purcell. We learned about it the day the Germans marched into Paris and hung their swastikas all over the city."

He eyes me coldly, but there's a glint of surprise in the look too. He isn't used to anyone talking back to him, and certainly not a twenty-year-old seamstress without a sou to her name. "How fortunate that my son came to your rescue when he did."

I smile meekly, pretending not to register the dig. "I was fortunate. Not only because Anson and I met and fell in love, but also that you've been kind enough to open your home to me. In fact, I've been thinking about how I might repay that kindness. I thought perhaps I could make a few new dresses for Cynthia. She's such a pretty girl, and a new dress or two would mean so much to her."

His eyes narrow, as if sensing some trap in the offer. "She put you up to this, did she?"

"No. It was my idea. She doesn't even know I was planning to ask. I wanted to be sure I had your approval before saying anything."

He takes another pull from his glass, eyeing me over the rim. "My daughter's dresses are perfectly suitable for the times, Miss Roussel. Good, sturdy clothes."

Ugly clothes, I think to myself.

"Actually, she's outgrown most of her dresses. She hasn't mentioned it because she doesn't want to be selfish. She understands that things are in short supply and that the war effort must come first, but I've had an idea."

He rattles the ice in his glass, signaling his impatience. "Have you, indeed?"

"In Paris, when the Nazis came, they went through our stores like a swarm of locusts, snapping up food, shoes, even books, until the shelves were bare. And then the rationing started. There were no clothes to be had and nothing to make clothes *with*. So we learned to make do. By the time I left, women were pulling apart their husbands' suits to make new clothes for themselves. So I thought, if you had some older things lying around, some things of her mother's perhaps, I could rework them for Cynthia."

"That won't be necessary. My secretary—"

"Just a few pieces," I persist. "Please. It would be so nice for her to have some of her mother's things—to remember her by."

Owen lowers his glass. For a moment, his face seems to soften. "There are still some of Lydia's things in her dressing room. I suppose you could take a few pieces. But only a few. And nothing too fussy or grown-up. She's eleven."

"Yes, of course." I swallow a smile, unwilling to let him see my triumph.

I've won this round at least. But there is truth in what I said to Owen. I do want to express my gratitude and to make myself useful until Anson returns. And I'll be making clothes again. Not bridal gowns meant to guarantee happy endings, but dresses that might perhaps bring about a new beginning for all of us.

TWENTY-SEVEN

SOLINE

For the novitiate, la magie *can be draining. One must be fully rested before beginning The Work and remember to take frequent breaks to replenish one's energy, lest her power become depleted and ineffective.*

—*Esmée Roussel, the Dress Witch*

22 October 1943—Newport

Once again, I find myself sewing in secret. Only this time it's for Thia instead of me. *Ma pauvre fille.* How can I not be worried for her? She was eight when her mother died, her father is little more than a ghost in her life, and her brother is half an ocean away. That leaves only me, her *sister-to-be*, to comfort her, and while I've come to adore her, I'm a poor substitute for a parent.

Things with Owen are no better. I had hoped our conversation about Thia might help thaw him toward me, but it seems to have had the opposite effect. He no longer takes his meals with us and is rarely home before midnight. I wonder sometimes if there's a woman somewhere he spends time with, a mistress who helps fill the empty space left by his wife's death, but it's hard to imagine any passion in the man or warmth of *any* kind.

But then this morning, as he was putting on his hat and preparing to leave for the day, he asked if I'd had a letter from Anson since I arrived. The question took me by surprise. He never mentions Anson to me. When I told him I'd written but hadn't had a letter back, his face darkened, and for a moment I almost felt sorry for him.

I tried to reassure him, explaining that Anson is very dedicated to his work and that I'd seen him go days without sleep when there was a rash of new casualties. I finished by reminding him that the French post is hopeless with overseas letters. He nodded to all of it, but the weight of Anson's silence hung heavily between us, because I've begun to feel it too. I'm also worried that there might be something wrong with me. I feel so tired all the time, weak and sick and unable to sleep, and with no word from Anson, the days drag on, empty and exhausting.

At least I have Thia's dresses to keep me busy. It was strange to find myself picking through Lydia Purcell's closet, through her everyday dresses and Sunday suits. They were hand-tailored, even the simple ones, tasteful but clearly expensive. It was from those that I made my selections. But there were evening clothes too. Jewel-toned satins, velvets trimmed with rhinestones, chiffon and lace and shimmering silver lamé. I peered at their labels: Worth, Dior, Lanvin. They were stunning things, the kind I used to dream of designing myself when I was a girl. But compared to Lydia's daytime clothes, they felt startlingly lavish, as if they belonged to another woman entirely, and I found myself wondering which dresses belonged to the *real* Lydia Purcell and which had been chosen for the woman Owen Purcell expected his wife to be. I've made a mental note to learn more about her when Anson returns home. Until then, I will focus on finishing Thia's dresses.

I've already completed two and should finish the third by day's end. I smile as I pick up my needle again. Thia is home from school and I can hear her banging around in the kitchen, letting me know she's there—and that she's still angry with me. I've said nothing about the dresses, letting her think I've passed on our daily French lessons to create something for myself. But tonight after dinner, I'll show her the dresses, and she'll finally understand why I've been so secretive.

Dinner is a plate of beef, potatoes, and carrots, swimming in a sea of oily gravy. Belinda has been making less of an effort since Owen stopped taking his meals at home. The greasy smell turns my stomach, but I push the food around my plate for show. Across from me, Thia pokes sulkily at a bit of carrot, hiding her face behind a sheaf of heavy blonde hair.

I lay down my napkin and turn to her. "Would you like to come to my room after dinner? I have something to show you."

Her head comes up slowly. "What?"

She's trying to look petulant, but I feel her curiosity. "It's a surprise," I half whisper.

"For me?"

For an instant, she looks so much like Anson it takes my breath away. "*Oui, ma fille.* For you."

"Oh! Yes, please!"

And just like that, we're friends again.

She follows me up the stairs and along the gallery. I make her close her eyes before I open the door and steer her to the bed.

"*Voilà!*" I say with a flourish. "You can look now."

She gasps when she sees the dresses laid out on my bed like life-size paper dolls. "Are they . . . for me?"

"Of course they're for you, silly girl. They certainly won't fit me."

She takes a tentative step forward, eyeing the dresses with wonder. There's a soft pink floral with a smocked top and puffed sleeves, a white eyelet A-line with a yellow silk sash at the waist, and my favorite, a navy-blue sailor's suit with a pleated skirt and crisp white collar. She reaches out but pulls her hand back at the last minute, as if touching them might make them disappear.

213

"Where did you get them?"

"They belonged to your mother," I tell her gently. "Your father said it would be all right if I made them over for you. I used one of the dresses from your closet for the patterns, so they might need a few tucks here and there, but I wanted to surprise you."

"That's why we haven't been having lessons?"

"*Oui, chérie*, that's why."

Before I can brace myself, she's hurtling herself against me. "Thank you! Thank you! I love them."

The feel of her arms around me sets off an unexpected longing, and for a moment I imagine what it would be like to have a daughter of my own, one with Anson's blond hair and blue-green eyes. "Which one will you wear first?"

Thia steps back to the bed, eyeing the sailor dress longingly, but in the end points to the pink floral. "That one."

"Really? I was sure you'd choose the navy."

"I wanted to, but I'm going to save that one for when Anson comes home. Would that be okay?"

I smile past a throatful of tears. "I think that would be lovely. We'll hang it—"

"Daddy!" Thia's head swivels toward the door. "Look!"

Owen stands with a shoulder braced against the doorjamb, a glass in his hand, staring at me with a blend of surprise and annoyance, as if he'd forgotten I live under his roof. I try to smile, but his sudden appearance has unnerved me. "I was just showing Cynthia her new dresses."

"I *assumed* you would show them to *me* first."

His words are thick and slushy, his eyes slow to blink. "I'm sorry. I didn't think you'd want to be bothered about them. I know how busy you are."

"Come look, Daddy!" Thia is pointing excitedly. "They're so beautiful."

Owen drags himself out of the doorway and pushes past me, coming to stand beside his daughter. Thia runs a hand over the pleated navy skirt, then cocks an eye up at her father. "This one's my favorite. Soline says it belonged to Mummy. Do you remember it?"

His face goes slack, and for a moment I think he won't answer. Finally, he nods. "Yes, I remember." But it's the white eyelet that has captured his attention. His throat bobs as he brushes a knuckle over the neckline. The touch is so intimate I nearly look away. Thia senses it, too, and reaches for his hand.

"I know you miss her, Daddy."

Owen looks up, as if just remembering his daughter is there. He pulls his hand free and looks at me. "These will do," he mumbles before tipping back his glass and draining the contents. "Thank you, Miss Roussel."

Thia catches his hand again as he turns to go. "Daddy, are there any dresses in Mummy's closet for Soline? She doesn't have anything nice, unless you count what's in the box, and she can't wear that until Anson's home."

He shakes free of her hand. "What box?"

"The one she brought with her from France." She turns to me with a toothy grin. "It's where she keeps all her secrets."

Owen pivots awkwardly. "A box of secrets?"

I smile past him at Thia. "It's a little joke we share. A secret between us girls."

"We're sisters-to-be, Daddy."

Owen stiffens. "It's past eight, Cynthia. Time for bed."

Thia wilts a little but makes no protest as she gathers her new dresses and slips out into the hall. Owen closes the door behind her. The room suddenly feels claustrophobic.

"My daughter is fond of you."

"She's a sweet girl. And so much like her brother."

"But she is *not* her brother."

"No," I say quietly, not sure what's coming.

"Cynthia is quick to form attachments. Unfortunately, she isn't always discerning in her choices. She's like her brother in that way—rushing in only to find he's misplaced his trust. Neither of them ever considers the possibility of being hurt."

I blink at him, stung. "You think I want to hurt your son?"

"I don't know you, Miss Roussel. I have no idea what you want."

"I love your son, Mr. Purcell. I want to be his wife."

"I'm quite certain of that," he responds dryly. "Or at least the last part. It's the *why* I'm not clear on."

It strikes me that somehow I have always known this was coming, that one day his suspicion of me would finally spill out. Still, the words chill me. "What is it you're accusing me of?"

"I'm not *accusing* you of anything. I'm just trying to understand. It isn't enough that my son decides to run off and join the Red Cross rather than enlisting in the US Navy, where he belongs. He compounds matters by sending me you, a seamstress-turned-nurse's-aide, whose name I've never once heard him mention and can barely pronounce, and writes to inform me there's going to be a wedding. It all seems a little rushed, don't you think? Convenient?"

I feel blood flood into my cheeks as my pulse ticks up. "You think sneaking out of Paris with the Nazis on my heels was convenient? Leaving my home? Leaving Anson?"

"It got you to the States, did it not?"

The room sways as a wave of nausea washes over me. I swallow thickly, shoving it down. "I came because this is Anson's home. Because his family is here, and I want you to be *my* family, too, when we're married—you and Thia."

"And your parents? Where are they?"

"My mother died last year."

"And your father?"

I touch the locket at my throat and think of Erich Freede, wondering, like *Maman*, about his fate. "I don't know," I say softly. "One of the camps, perhaps. Or dead."

His eyes narrow sharply. "You're Jewish?"

I see that the idea displeases him, and I find I'm savagely glad. "My father was Jewish. But it isn't only Jews they're sending to the camps. Anyone willing to stand against them is in danger of arrest."

"None of that is my concern at the moment, Miss Roussel."

"Yes, I can see that. But it's Anson's concern. Which is why he's still there—to stop it."

He looks back at me with a blend of contempt and annoyance. "By driving around Paris with a patch on his arm while others do the *real* fighting?"

His dismissiveness astonishes me. I open my mouth, prepared to defend the work Anson is doing, but catch myself in time. Instead, I lift my chin and meet his gaze head-on. "Do you truly think so little of your son? Because he's not on a ship somewhere, in danger of being blown to bits? You're disappointed that he won't come home with a chest full of medals—or in a box—but I'm not. The war has taught me that there are all sorts of heroes, and that almost none of them will ever have something shiny pinned to their chests."

He sways as he raises his empty glass in mock salute. "Pretty words. Quite . . . impassioned. But at the end of the day, it's what we *do* that counts, Miss Roussel. The mark we leave behind. And the Purcells have always been careful about the kinds of marks we leave. Our name is synonymous with respectability, with honor and service. I have a duty to protect that for the next generation, to preserve our traditions. That includes my son."

"Why do you never use his name?"

His eyes narrow. "What?"

"When you talk about him, you refer to him as your son or Thia's brother, but never as himself. Never as Anson."

"I'll refer to him in whatever way I choose. He's my son. And I didn't break my neck grooming him so he could throw his life away on the first woman who caught his fancy. He's got school to finish, and then I have plans for him."

"And those plans don't include a wife?"

He stares into his glass, giving the melting ice a swirl. "I assume they will—at some point. But when that time comes, my son will marry a woman who will know how to help him be successful."

"How do you know I can't help him?"

"Our way of life comes with a very specific set of rules, Miss Roussel. And there isn't room for someone who doesn't understand them. It's my job to make you see that."

A fresh wave of clamminess hits me as his words penetrate. He's telling me he has no intention of letting the wedding go forward. The roses on the wallpaper spin dizzily. I drop my eyes to the floor and reach for the edge of the bureau to steady myself. There are tears in my eyes, my throat.

"You've written to him, haven't you? To tell him you don't approve. That's why you asked if I'd had a letter. Not because you were worried. Because you expect him to write to me and break it off." He doesn't say anything, but I see that I'm right. "You're going to make him choose," I say quietly. "Between you and me."

"Life is choosing, Miss Roussel. And I intend to make sure my son chooses wisely."

"What happens when he chooses me over you?"

He smiles, a thin, unpleasant expression that sends a chill through me. "How long have you known my son? Six months? Seven? I've known him all his life. He's always had a soft spot for strays. He's like his mother in that way, always taking up for some cause or other. But he's been raised to know what's expected of him. He may have forgotten while in France, but he'll remember soon enough." The smile vanishes as he sets his empty glass on the bureau and turns to leave. "He won't choose you."

I stand there a moment, holding my breath until he's gone, then rush to the bathroom and bring up my dinner.

TWENTY-EIGHT

SOLINE

*The Work is our legacy to the world, the spells
we weave, the hearts we bind, and all the generations that come after. These are our gifts
made manifest.*

—*Esmée Roussel, the Dress Witch*

29 October 1943—Newport

It's a Friday afternoon, and the house is eerily quiet when I return
from my afternoon walk on the beach. Thia is home from school again,
though I haven't seen her for several days. Belinda will only say that
she's under the weather and that her father doesn't want her disturbed.
Owen has been scarce as well, locked away in either his room or his
study, leaving me to dine alone.

My mood has grown dark of late. I'm so isolated here, unmoored
from my own world and a stranger in Anson's. I have no friends here,
no means of filling my time or striking out on my own. The days stretch
before me with no horizon and no news from Anson on which to pin
my hopes. Thia is my one happiness, and I suspect I am hers. Owen
suspects it too, though he isn't above keeping us apart to hurt me.

As I climb the stairs, I find myself wondering what kind of woman could love a man like Owen Purcell, a man who treats his children like pieces on a chessboard, to be moved only when and where it suits him. Yet, in spite of her cold and dictatorial husband, Lydia Purcell managed to raise a pair of warm and wonderful children.

I'm nearly to the end of the gallery when I hear a faint rustling and realize the door to my room is ajar. I feel my spirits lift at the thought of finding Thia sitting cross-legged on my bed with one of her sketchbooks. Instead I find Owen standing over the bed, pawing through the contents of my dress box.

"What are you doing?"

He glares at me. There's no remorse in his expression, only annoyance that he's been interrupted. His jaw is peppered with pale stubble, and his eyes are puffy and bloodshot. He looks as if he's aged ten years, and grown smaller somehow, since our last conversation. And then I realize what has changed. It's the first time I've seen him in something other than one of his impeccably tailored suits. Instead, he's wearing a gray cardigan and trousers that look as though they've been slept in. The change is shocking.

"What does it look like? I'm going through your box of secrets." His words are slurred, his S's thick and wet. It's barely three o'clock, and he's clearly been drinking for hours.

I smother a curse when I see my dress—the one I'm meant to marry Anson in—lying at his feet, a froth of beads and white silk twisted around his ankles. I bend down and snatch it up, cradling it against me like a rescued child. "You have no right to go through my things."

His eyes glitter coldly. "You're living in my house, eating from my table, sleeping on my sheets. I'd say that gives me every right."

"What is it you expect to find?"

"You think you're so clever, landing on my doorstep like some war orphan, without two nickels to your name and everything you own in a cardboard box, claiming to have landed the most eligible young man in Newport. I'll say this for you, when you were shopping for a meal ticket, you didn't mess around. Not a decent pair of shoes to your name, but you managed to bring a wedding dress all the way from Paris. That's what I call planning ahead."

"It wasn't like that."

He takes a step forward, swaying a bit in his attempt to look menacing. "What *was* it like?"

I try to think of something to say, something that will make him believe me. But there's nothing. Because he doesn't want to believe me. When he looks at me, he sees what he wants to see—an opportunist who used her wiles to trick his son into a marriage proposal.

I drop my gaze, taking in the once-tied packet of letters, loose now and strewn across the spread. Several have been opened, their contents tossed aside. The sight makes me sick to my stomach. "You read my letters."

"I would have, but they're all in French. Lovers, I assume. Did my son know?"

There is no shame in his reply, no acknowledgment that he has trespassed where he has no business. Only icy accusation. I bend down to gather them, one at a time, hating that he's opened them, touched them at all. "They belong to me," I tell him sharply. "They have nothing to do with Anson."

I'm reaching for the ribbon that once bound them together when I see Anson's shaving kit lying facedown among the letters. Owen sees it too. I lunge for it, reaching it before he can snatch it away. I can't bear the thought of him touching that either.

His eyes glint dully, fury blunted by drink. "Where did you get that?"

"Anson gave it to me the morning I left Paris."

I'm surprised when his shoulders sag, as if all the air has left his chest. For a moment he seems on the verge of tears. "His mother gave it to him the Christmas before she died."

221

"He told me," I say softly.

"Give it to me."

I'm startled by the sudden change in his voice. I stare at his out-stretched hand, then take a step back. "No. Anson gave it to me. It's mine."

I don't see the slap coming, but all at once there's a dull crack in my head and a flash of bright light as his palm connects with my cheek. I taste blood as my head snaps back. Before I can get my bearings, the leather case is torn from my hands.

"Nothing here is *yours*," he hisses. "Nothing here will ever be yours. At least I can be sure of *that* now."

A blade of cold slices down my spine. Something about the way he says the last words, with an icy sense of satisfaction, thickens my blood. I watch as he reaches into the pocket of his trousers and pulls out a folded scrap of paper. When he tries to hand it to me, I shake my head, refusing to take it. He shoves it at me again. This time I take it, but I squeeze my eyes shut, unwilling to read the words I already know are there, unwilling to make them real.

Every mother, sister, wife, and lover has imagined what this moment might be like, rehearsing it in her mind while trying to pray it far away. And now it has come to me. I force my eyes open and feel my throat constrict when I see the words at the top of the page: *Western Union*.

25 October 1943

Mr. O. Purcell:

It is with deepest regret that I must relay the news that your son, Anson William Purcell, has been reported missing dated 19 October after failing to return from a transport mission. If further details become available, you will be promptly notified.

Charles M. Petrie

C.O. American Field Services

My lungs suddenly stop working, as if I've received a punch I didn't see coming. Not dead—*missing*. I stare at the word. It should bring me comfort, some frail thread of hope, but I've heard the stories. I know how rare it is for a missing man to turn up alive. Suddenly, something Anson said the night before he sent me away floats back . . . *If you're safe, it won't matter what they do to me.*

I tell myself I would know if he were dead, that I would have felt the loss instantly, like a part of myself being torn away. I haven't. But as I recall the words *Maman* spoke the night she died, I realize this was what she was trying to prepare me for. This day. This moment.

As long as you keep his beautiful face in your heart, he will never truly be lost.

But he *is* lost. I'm holding a paper that tells me he is.

I force my eyes back to the telegram, as if the words might some-how have changed. They have not. The final line blurs on the page as I read it. *If further details become available . . .*

Details.

I try not to think of him, lying somewhere, broken, bleeding. Or worse. But it's all I *can* think of. How many women have read those same words? And how many ever got their soldiers back—or even learned their actual fate? As a member of the AFS, Anson isn't actually a soldier. His Resistance missions aren't carried out in coordination with the military. They're secret and often spur-of-the-moment, mean-ing only a handful of people would even know where to look for him. Revealing such information could expose the entire cell, and the first rule of the Resistance is that the safety of one person must never be allowed to jeopardize the cell.

No one would talk.

I let the telegram fall to the bed, then frown as I notice the date: 25 October. I pick it up again, to be sure, then look at Anson's father through a scrim of tears. "This is four days old."

He stares back, mute.

"You've known for days, and you said nothing?"

"It was sent to *me*."

I'm stunned by his reply. "When were you going to show it to me?"

"I'm showing it to you now."

Once again, there is no apology in his tone, nothing that speaks of regret or empathy. Only an icy flatness I cannot comprehend.

Thia.

My chest tightens as her name pops into my head. Anson is her hero, the lone bright spot in this cold and unfeeling house. She'll need comforting, and I can't imagine her getting it from her father. I need to go to her, to help her be strong.

"Does Cynthia know?"

His eyes harden on me, a warning. "No, she does not. And she won't until I'm ready for her to know. Is that understood?"

I nod, because I haven't any say in the matter, though I'm not convinced it's right to keep the truth from her, or that she'll thank her father for his silence when she does find out. But maybe she'll never have to find out. There's still a chance Anson will be found safe and well, and she'll never have to know about the telegram. I grab hold of the thought like a lifeline.

"There must be someone we can call, someone at the Red Cross who might know something."

Owen regards me without emotion, but every muscle in his body seems clenched, as if he's willing himself to stay together. "I'm a well-connected man, Miss Roussel. I have an extensive network of well-placed contacts within the various branches of government, and I can assure you I have made every call there is to make."

"Did you call the hospital in Paris and speak to Dr. Jack? He's the chief surgeon."

"A surgeon?" He seems astonished by the question. "Young lady, my connections go all the way to the White House. Not that they did me any good. No one could tell me anything, except to say that my son failed to report back to the hospital at the expected hour and that his ambulance was found abandoned on some road where it had no business being. No one knows why. He isn't listed as captured or killed, which is something, I suppose, though I've been cautioned not to read too much into that. There was a substantial amount of blood in and around the vehicle, and two witnesses claim to have seen a pair of German soldiers leading a man fitting my son's description into the woods. They reported hearing gunshots a few minutes later. There's been no sign of him since."

His voice goes thick, his pain finally palpable as he picks up the telegram and slowly begins to fold it.

"The official line is 'presumed captured or killed,' though they think it likely that he died and was quietly buried. Apparently, even Hitler knows it's bad form to murder a Red Cross worker. Either way, in all likelihood, my son is dead."

My head swims as I reach for his hand. "I'm so sorry."

It's all I can think to say. I know it isn't enough, that no words will ever be enough, but I find that I'm strangely numb, as if I've somehow slipped my body and am watching it all unfold from a distance. I'm aware of that other me—the one still clutching the wedding dress she'll never wear, the one whose heart is splitting open, bleeding, breaking. I just can't feel any of it.

He jerks his hand free as if I've burned him. "Get away from me."

I sag limply onto the bed, his hatred suddenly more than I can bear. I thought that in this moment of grief we might find a way to comfort one another, but I was wrong. My comfort is not wanted. Nor am I to receive any. In this, too, I will be alone.

The nausea rises without warning, the prickly wave of clamminess so sudden that for a moment I fear I might lose consciousness. I barely make it past Owen and into the bathroom before I'm sick. The spasms are more violent this time, threatening to turn me inside out. I drop to my knees on the cold tile floor, retching so hard my vision goes dark, then crouch there, heaving, until finally there is nothing left to bring up.

My legs are unsteady as I stand at the sink and rinse my mouth. In the mirror, my face is chalk-white and sticky with sweat, and I'm suddenly reminded of the day Anson and I met at the hospital. How he steered me into the lavatory, then stayed with me while I cleaned myself up with his handkerchief. Because of a little smear of blood. But there was no blood today. No blood for a while now. Not this month or the one before. Suddenly, I realize what I've been ignoring for weeks.

I'm going to have a baby.

TWENTY-NINE

SOLINE

The Reading is the foundation of The Work and must always be the Spell Weaver's first undertaking. Some personal item shall be provided with the understanding that nothing seen will be used for the purposes of manipulation or harm.

—Esmée Roussel, the Dress Witch

I don't know when Owen left. I only know he was gone when I came out of the bathroom, leaving me alone with my grief and this terrible new awareness. There will not be a wedding, but there *will* be a baby.

Enceinte. Pregnant.

The word brings a lump to my throat, like a stone lodged partway down that I can't seem to swallow. Babies are meant to bring joy, but I feel no joy. In fact, I feel nothing. I have heaved myself empty and wept myself dry. I'm hollow, scraped raw. And yet strangely disconnected. Perhaps there's a limit to how much pain the heart can hold.

The room is dark, and I have no sense of time. I've slept a little, somehow. But I'm awake now in the yawning quiet, the taste of bile still sharp in my throat. It never occurred to me that a child might result from our single night together. *Maman* never spoke of such things, but

I always assumed it would be more difficult than that. Now I see that I've been naive. The headaches and queasiness, the endless fatigue. It began on the ship, nearly a month after leaving Paris. I thought it was *mal de mer*—seasickness. And then later, I thought it was just the toll the journey had taken on my body: days with little or no food, always on the move, the constant fear of being caught and arrested. I have been an *imbécile*.

I shield my eyes as I turn on the lamp and look around me, at the scattered letters, the dress box yawning emptily at the foot of the bed, my discarded wedding dress sprawled beside me, a ghost of the bride I once dreamed I was meant to be. Anson's shaving kit—the one thing I possessed of him and promised to keep—is gone.

I think briefly of *Maman's* rosary, my parting token to him, and wonder where it is now. In the hands of some SS officer who picked his pockets after shooting him? In a heap somewhere at one of the camps?

Presumed captured or killed.

I squeeze my eyes closed, but the images are still there, burned into the backs of my eyelids. Anson's face—his sweet, beautiful face, bloodied and still. Wide eyes, the color of a calm summer sea, open and unseeing.

He can't be gone. He mustn't be.

If only I could see his face again, as it was the last time I saw him, I could hold on to him the way *Maman* held on to my father—in her heart. My hand drifts to the locket, small and warm at the hollow of my throat. If only I had a photograph of him. I could carry him with me always, and one day share it with our child.

Before I can stop myself, I have slipped from my room and out into the hallway. The house is still, the silence as complete as the darkness. I hold my breath as I move down the hall, bare feet soft on the carpet. I have never been on this side of the gallery—the family side—but I know Thia's room is the first door on the right and that Anson's room is across from hers.

I pause outside Thia's door, listening. All is quiet. And for this moment, at least, I'm glad she doesn't know about the telegram, that when the sun comes up and she opens her eyes, she won't know what I do—that her beloved brother isn't coming home.

I turn around to face Anson's door, my pulse drumming in my ears as I try not to think about Owen stepping out into the hall, finding me skulking outside his son's room. Then I remember that the worst has already happened. If Anson is truly gone, nothing he can say or do can hurt me.

The glass knob is cool against my palm. I glance once more toward the end of the hall. No light, no sound. I let my breath out slowly and push inside. The smell of him is suddenly all around me, limey and clean and male, and for a moment his presence is so palpable, it feels as if I might reach out and find him in the dark.

I wait for the ache of it to subside, my back pressed against the closed door. Moonlight seeps through the sheer curtains behind the bed, washing the room in cool, angular shadows. There are no blackout curtains—probably because the room hasn't been used since Anson left for Paris, long before the Americans joined the war.

I move to the window and draw down the shade, then flick on the small bedside lamp. It's a simple room, not much larger than my own, decorated in shades of pewter and sand. There's a double bed covered in pale-gray brocade, a heavy chest of drawers, and a small desk and chair tucked into one corner. It suits him. Simple and neat, unfussy.

I feel like a prowler as I tiptoe about the room, opening drawers and peering in his closet, peeling back the layers of the life Anson lived before I met him. Being here, touching the things he used every day, is the worst possible torture, and yet I can't seem to stop myself. I'm hungry for him, desperate to connect with his memories if that is all I'm to have of him now.

I move on to the desk. The surface is bare except for a small lamp and a scarred leather blotter. I run my hand over the back of the chair, imagining him in it, studying or writing letters, then slide the center drawer open. A framed photograph stares up at me, the glass cracked down the middle. It's of Anson and Thia, smartly dressed in matching white sweaters, posed with their mother in front of a large sailboat. All three are squinting against the sun, grinning for the camera. Thia is missing a front tooth.

My heart tears as I try to guess Anson's age. Fifteen, maybe sixteen. He's thin, almost gangly, but he already towers over his mother. A tear slides down my cheek. I catch it with the back of my hand before it falls. It isn't exactly what I'd hoped to find—it was taken years ago—but it's more than I have of him now. I could cut it to fit the locket. But as I stand there staring at the three smiling faces, I can't bear the thought of cutting Anson out of a photograph with his mother and sister.

I ease the drawer open a little farther, preparing to return the photograph, then notice a book shoved toward the back. I tease it forward, then lift it out. The cover is coarse blue cloth decorated with a gold crest of some kind. The lettering on the spine reads: HISTORY OF THE CLASS OF 1941, YALE UNIVERSITY.

I carry the book to the bed and lay it open on my lap. I turn the pages slowly at first, scanning face after unfamiliar face, until they all begin to look alike. And then suddenly he's there, staring up at me from the heavy white page. Anson William Purcell. Sophomore.

I nearly smile as I trace the image with my finger. He looks so handsome in his suit and tie, his unruly blond waves carefully tamed for the occasion. The boyish softness in the earlier photo is gone, replaced with a brash, almost stubborn sense of purpose, a resolve to make his own way in the world, to be his own man.

A wave of rage shudders through me, a sob surging up from a well I thought emptied. For promises that will never be kept and good that will never be done. For a child who will never know its father.

My eyes are already raw from weeping. I close them and lie back against the spread, the yearbook hugged to my chest. I'm so tired suddenly. The baby, I think muzzily. The baby is making me tired. Anson's baby.

I come awake with a start, a bright light suddenly searing through my closed lids. I'm dimly aware of something thumping to the floor as I sit up, and that I'm not in my room. My eyes won't focus properly, but Owen's shape at the foot of the bed is unmistakable.

"What the hell are you doing in here?" he snarls.

I blink heavily, fumbling for a response. He has switched on the overhead light, and the glare hurts my eyes. "I'm sorry." My throat is thick from crying, my words a mere rasp. "I only wanted to see his room, to be near his things."

He moves to the desk, where I've left the drawer open, and picks up the broken frame, examining it. He has shaved since I last saw him, but he's wearing the same rumpled cardigan as yesterday, the cuffs rolled to his elbows. I push to my feet, watching as he bends down and retrieves Anson's yearbook from the floor. His hand hovers over the cover a moment, as if he might flip it open. Instead, he rounds on me, his face so close to mine that I can smell his stale hair tonic and unwashed clothes.

"You have no right to touch my son's things. Or to sleep in his bed. You've no right to be here at all. This is *not* your home."

I take a step back. His fury is terrifying, and his breath is sour from drink. "I was looking for a picture of Anson, and I found his yearbook in the desk. I sat on the bed to look through it and must have fallen asleep."

His eyes narrow, as if he's just thought of something. "What do you want with a picture of my son?"

"I wanted to see his face," I say softly, pleadingly. "And to have something to remember him by. His shaving kit was all I had, but you took it. So I thought—"

"Get out of this room," he barks, pointing to the door. "Or I'll drag you out myself."

My eyes blur, but I refuse to let the tears fall. "I'm going to have a baby," I say quietly. "Anson's baby."

His eyes slide to my belly, then back to my face, sparking with accusation. "I suppose I should have seen this coming. Now that you know there won't be any wedding bells, you've decided to play your ace. Did my son know?"

I shake my head. "I only realized it yesterday, after you showed me the telegram."

"Convenient timing, I must say."

His callousness astonishes me. "Your son isn't coming home, and I'm carrying his child. This is what you have to say to me?"

He glares down his nose. "I don't question the fact that you're carrying a child. Only a fool would lie about such a thing when time stands to expose her, and though I suspect you of being many things, a fool isn't one of them. But there's no way to say for certain *who* the father is." He pauses, raking his eyes over me. "For all I know, *you* don't even know."

The words wound in a way I never would have thought possible. "You don't believe that. You can't."

"Can't I?" His mouth curls unpleasantly. "There are names for women like you. Experts at luring our boys into marriage. It nearly worked too. You managed to get yourself all the way across the big blue ocean and install yourself in my home. You even have my daughter eating out of your hand. But you didn't plan for the telegram, did you?"

"It isn't true! None of that is true!"

"Spare me your outrage. It will do you no good." He moves to the desk, briefly studying the cracked picture frame before slipping it back into the drawer. When he turns to look at me again, his face is blank and hard. "You thought you were so clever, showing up on my doorstep with your box full of clothes. You assumed I would simply look the other way while you sauntered down the aisle with my son. But that was never going to happen. Now you think your belly will save you, that a baby gives you some kind of a claim on the Purcells. But you've miscalculated, *mademoiselle*. Your child will never be a Purcell—in name or anything else. There is no place for either of you here."

I stare at him as the reality of my situation creeps in. I am an inconvenience, a mistake to be corrected. The sooner the better. "Are you really so hard—so full of hate—that you could live with turning your back on your own grandchild? Could Thia live with it?"

He stiffens, hands fisted at his sides. "My daughter isn't to hear a word about you and your belly. Or about her brother. Is that clear? I've arranged for her to go away to school in Connecticut. She leaves the day after tomorrow. And until she does, you will stay well clear of her. By the time she returns, you'll be gone."

The thought strikes me with terror. I know no one here, have no money, no work. But my first concern is for poor Thia. "May I at least say goodbye?"

"You may not. I won't have you manipulating her further."

I have nothing to say to any of that. He's made up his mind. About me, about all of it. "What happens now?" I ask simply.

"Steps will need to be taken. Damage control. You have no money, I suppose?"

"Not much, and none of it American."

"There's a man I know in Providence, a doctor who works with women like you."

"Women like me," I repeat. "What does that mean?"

"It means unmarried, pregnant, no family or means of support. I'll call him today and get started on the arrangements."

I feel myself go pale. In Paris, there were women who specialized in such things, in medicines and . . . procedures. *Avorteuses.* I cross my hands over my belly, an instinctive act of protection. "What kind of . . . arrangements?"

"A place for you to go. A suitable family to take the baby. Help getting on your feet when you're done with all of it. What did you think I meant?"

I shake my head, unable to say the word out loud.

Owen drops his eyes to the floor, clearly uncomfortable. "I'm not a barbarian, despite what you might think. But I will not have your condition become public knowledge and create a scandal for myself and my daughter. No one knows about your *connection* with my son, and I intend to keep it that way. And if you're as clever as I think you are, *you'll* keep it that way. If this were the movies, I would just write you a check or set you up in a little business, and that would be the end of it. But this isn't the movies. In the real world, that kind of assistance could be mistaken for an admission rather than what it really is—a simple act of Christian kindness."

"This is your kindness? To treat me like some little schemer? When I've asked you for nothing?"

He moves to the door as if I haven't spoken. "This conversation is over. Except to say that if you decide to be troublesome, if you attempt to contact me or my daughter or ever breathe my son's name to a living soul, I will make it my mission to ruin you. In other words, Miss Roussel, I can help you or hurt you. The choice is yours."

I stand there with his ultimatum, studying the man I thought would one day be my father-in-law. How cool he is as he makes his plans to dismiss me, so steely and businesslike. A deal to be brokered. A mess to clean up. Anson once called him *formidable*, and he was right. His father has thought of everything.

But Owen is right too. I haven't many options. None, in fact. I'll need a place to live, somewhere clean and safe, until I can find work and make my own way. I will accept what he's offering, because I have no choice. But my baby will not need a family. I will be its family.

THIRTY

RORY

July 12, 1985—Boston

Soline sat with downcast eyes, clearly shaken by the story she'd spent an hour pouring out. Rory studied her, trying to imagine what it must have been like. A terrifying escape. A heartbreaking telegram. A baby she hadn't planned on. And a monster who had turned her out to fend for herself. How on earth had she survived it all?

How might *she* have fared in similar circumstances?

The question made her feel vaguely ashamed. She forgot sometimes just how comfortable her life had been. She'd been born with a trust fund and a name guaranteed to open doors and had never known anything close to hardship. In fact, before Hux's disappearance, her biggest challenge had been navigating her thorny relationship with her mother.

"You make me ashamed," she said quietly. "Most people would have given up after the things you went through, but you just kept fighting. And then there's me, showing up at your door with my bag of takeout, whining about how tough I have it. Why can't I be strong like you?"

Soline closed her eyes and let out a sigh. "Being strong for too long makes one brittle, *cherie*. And brittle things break easily." She looked away, dabbing at her eyes, then forced a smile. "There, you see? Not so very strong. Perhaps there's hope for me yet."

"I'm sorry to make you remember all that. Are you okay?"

Soline nodded, but her smile slipped as she pushed to her feet. "I'm fine. Just a little warm. Why don't we go in? I'll wash up the dishes, and then we'll have some dessert. I'll show you how to make *real* coffee, with a press. I promise you'll never go back to your drippy machine."

Rory did the dishes while Soline gave a tutorial on the virtues of a french press, declaring it the only civilized way to make coffee. She filled two cups and arranged madeleines on a plate, then carried the tray to the living room.

They settled on opposite ends of the sofa with their cups. It was a large room but comfortable, furnished with items chosen to please rather than impress. It was Soline to a T. Tasteful but without all the fuss of Camilla's perfectly styled home. She'd been right about the coffee too. In fact, everything here felt right.

She reached for a madeleine, nibbling thoughtfully as she watched Soline sip her coffee. She couldn't explain the connection between them. She only knew that it was real, that fate had somehow seen fit to weave their stories together. But why?

"Do you ever think about why we became friends?" Rory asked quietly. "The way I found the row house and then the box. It felt sort of . . ." She paused, searching for the right word. "Inevitable, maybe. Do you believe in that kind of thing? That certain things are supposed to happen?"

Soline was silent a moment, as if weighing the question carefully. "Once, perhaps," she said at last. "I believed Anson and I were supposed to get married, that he'd come home with my mother's rosary and I would give him back his shaving kit, and we'd live happily ever after."

Rory nodded gloomily, then frowned as she recalled something Soline had said earlier. "Wait. You said Anson's father took the shaving kit, but I remember seeing it in the box."

Soline shrugged. "He gave it back. I don't know what made him do it or even when he did it. I was gone within the week. The chauffeur drove me to the train station, and a woman named Dorothy Sheridan met me in Providence."

"Who was Dorothy Sheridan?"

"She ran the Family Aid Society, which is a pretty way of saying a home for unwed mothers. There were eight more like me there. Some were little more than girls, others claimed to be war widows, but we all had one thing in common—we'd gotten caught without a husband and had nowhere to go. I cried the whole first day. I couldn't believe Owen could hate me that much. But when I opened my box, there was Anson's shaving kit at the bottom. It's hard to imagine him feeling remorse, but perhaps he did it for Anson's sake. It certainly wasn't for mine."

"Did you at least get to say goodbye to Thia?"

Soline shook her head. "He sent her away the next day."

Rory was quiet for a time, trying to imagine the horror of it. Pregnant and grieving alone. "You have to be the bravest woman I know. To live through all of that and keep on going."

Soline looked at her hands, alternately clenching and flexing them, something she often did when she appeared lost in thought. "I kept going because there was no alternative."

"I know, but giving up a baby . . ."

"I didn't give her up," Soline said, looking away. "She died."

Rory went still, absorbing the words like a blow to the solar plexus. "I'm so sorry. I just assumed . . . What happened?"

"One morning I got out of bed, and there was a rush of water. I knew that happened, but it was too soon. I told them they had to stop it, that she wasn't supposed to come for another month, but they said she was coming anyway and I needed to pray. They brought me to a small room with no windows and a narrow bed with leather straps. There was a tiny crib, too, a hospital bed for babies. Then they gave me something—a needle in my arm and a mask over my face. I don't remember much after that."

Rory's eyes widened. "They put you under to have the baby?"

"It's how it was done in those days. Twilight sleep, they called it. So you wouldn't remember after. When I woke up, I felt as if I'd been beaten. There were bruises on my ankles and wrists from the straps. But I didn't care. I begged to hold her, to feed her, but they said it was too soon. She wasn't strong enough to nurse. I must have fallen asleep. I was so tired. When I woke up, the little crib was gone, and I began to holler. Someone finally came, one of the matrons, but she wouldn't look me in the eye. I knew then what was coming, but hearing her say the words nearly broke me in two. *Too small to survive. Lungs not developed. Gone to be with the angels.*"

Rory closed her eyes, unable to find adequate words of comfort. Language for that kind of anguish simply didn't exist. "I'm so sorry," she repeated feebly.

"I knew it would be a girl. I had already named her—Assia. It means 'one who brings comfort.'" She paused, struggling to swallow. "I heard her cry," she whispered. "When she was born, I heard her. I wish sometimes that I hadn't. If she'd been stillborn, lifeless from the moment she left my body, it might have been easier. But knowing she lived for even a few hours without her *mère*, that she died never knowing my touch, still breaks my heart. I asked to see her, to hold her, but they had already taken her away."

"Taken her where?" Rory asked, horrified.

"They called the coroner's office to come for her. It's the law, so they can verify cause of death for the certificate. They said because I was indigent, Assia would be buried in the county cemetery. There would be no service, no marker. I begged them to stop it, to give me time to find the money to bury her properly. I would have called Anson's father and begged, but they wouldn't let me use the phone. Three days later, they told me it was done."

Rory swallowed a throatful of tears. "Did they at least tell you where, so you could visit her grave?"

"No," she murmured. "But maybe that's a blessing. I know it sounds strange, but seeing her grave would have made her death too real."

"But it was real."

"Yes, it was. But when you love someone—truly love them—you're connected in a way that can never be severed. Even when they're taken from you, years later, you still feel them, like an echo calling back to you. And a part of you is just a little bit glad for those moments, even when they nearly double you up."

An echo calling back to you.

The thought washed over Rory like a cold breeze. Was that how it would be with Hux? No goodbye, no answers, just nebulous memories?

"I imagine that I see her sometimes," Soline said in a faraway voice. "Like I used to with Anson. I'll see a little face in the crowd and my heart goes still for the tiniest instant. She has eyes like her father's and a grin like her aunt Thia. But then she turns her head and the face is all wrong, and I remember that Assia is gone."

Rory sat silent for a time, overwhelmed by the totality of Soline's losses. She denied being brave, but she was wrong. Out of nothing but grief, she had forged a life. A woman, alone in a strange city while a war was raging and there was no real work to speak of, and yet she'd managed to build a lucrative career and, from the look of it, make a good deal of money in the process. What else might she have accomplished had a succession of heartaches not altered the course of her life?

"How long did you stay . . . after?"

"Not long. Once the babies were born, they wanted us out. A week later, Dorothy Sheridan came to me and said she'd found me a room and work. I was to pack my belongings and be ready to go the next day. When the work dried up in Providence, I moved to Boston, but when the men started coming back, it was impossible to find anything. I worked at a shoe repair shop for a while in exchange for room and board, and I took in sewing on the side. I had to share my meals with the mice, but I didn't mind them so much. They were hungry too."

"And you never spoke to Anson's father again?"

"No. I took him at his word when he said he'd ruin me if I tried to contact him. Besides, I wanted nothing from him. I would have liked to have seen Thia again, though, to explain why I left so abruptly." She paused, smiling wistfully. "And to tell her I finally got to make dresses with my name in them."

"I'm still in awe," Rory breathed. "To start with nothing and accomplish so much. How did you do it?"

"Like the heroines in all the best stories, I had a fairy godmother."

Rory grinned at her. "How do I find one of those?"

"You don't find them, *chérie*. They simply appear. Often, when you need them the most. And the *how* is different for everyone. Mine was named Maddy, and he was wonderful."

"Your fairy godmother was a man?"

Soline flashed a grin. "He was."

"All right, then, how did *he* find you?"

Soline's smile dimmed. "That is a story for another day, I think."

"I'm sorry; I didn't mean to push."

"You didn't, but I'm tired."

Rory looked at her watch, shocked to find it was after seven. She stood, collecting their cups and placing them on the tray. "I didn't mean to stay so long. I was supposed to be picking out light fixtures. I'll just help you clean up before I go."

Soline picked up the tray before Rory could grab it. "It isn't much. You go on. I want you to."

Rory reluctantly slid her purse onto her shoulder and headed for the foyer. "I really am sorry I made a pest of myself. You should have kicked me out hours ago."

"Don't be silly. What else had I to do?"

"Still, I promise not to barge in on you again. Thank you for the talk, though. I don't really have anyone I can talk to about Hux. No one who gets it, I mean."

"I meant what I said before, Rory. If you're having second thoughts, we'll tear up the lease and forget it. But I think your Hux was right—this dream does have your name all over it."

Rory blinked back the sting of tears, struggling against an impulse to pull Soline into a hug. "Thank you for that," she said instead, grateful as she stepped out onto the stoop, that this lovely and inexplicable woman had come into her life. As she reached the bottom step a thought occurred. She paused, looking back at Soline silhouetted in the doorway. "I just realized something."

"What's that?"

"You're my fairy godmother."

THIRTY-ONE

Soline

While it is fair to expect compensation for our craft, financial gain must never be considered when weighing whether or not to accept a particular client. Trust La Mère to provide in other ways and remember that our first and last consideration must always be The Work.

—*Esmée Roussel, the Dress Witch*

Rory's words stay with me as I close the door. I fear I'm a poor excuse for a fairy godmother, but hearing her say the words has warmed me in a way I haven't been warm in a very long time. And yet I find myself strangely melancholy. The house feels empty suddenly, and so do I.

I go to the kitchen and open a bottle of wine to keep me company, then take the plate of uneaten madeleines to my study. It's where I spend most of my evenings these days, sitting with my memories and getting tipsy enough to sleep without dreaming.

The madeleines are flavored with lemon. I pick one up and take a bite, letting it melt on my tongue. Suddenly I'm smiling. The tangy sweetness reminds me of Maddy, which is why I purchase them from time to time. They were his favorites and, in a roundabout way, the reason we became friends.

It seems like yesterday sometimes, at others, like a lifetime ago. I had only been in Boston a few weeks and was still looking for work. My accent remained very thick, and the dress shops didn't want a foreigner reminding their patrons of the war. With my money running low, I couldn't afford to be choosy, and so I began going from shop to shop, offering to do whatever might be needed.

One day, I walked into a little patisserie named Bisous Sucrés. *Finally*, I thought, *my accent will be an asset.* But it was late and I was so tired, and the smells of coffee and chocolate reminded me so much of home that when the woman behind the counter asked what I wanted, my eyes filled with tears and I couldn't get a word out.

She took pity on me, bless her, leading me to the back of the shop, then bringing me a plate of the most beautiful pastries I'd ever seen. I made a terrible pig of myself, though she pretended not to notice, and over several cups of coffee, I told her my story—or at least the parts I cared to share.

She was ten years my senior, but we had a lot in common. She had come over from Chartres with her parents at the start of World War I and learned her trade from her mother. She'd lost a brother at Normandy and a husband to drowning, and was struggling to raise a daughter on her own. She understood hardship and loss and the need for a woman to be able to make her own way. She couldn't afford to hire me, but she knew someone who might be looking for a girl who knew how to use a needle, a tailor who had recently lost both his assistants and was in rather a bad way.

She wrote his name and address on the back of an envelope and told me to go see him in the morning, to mention her name and not take no for an answer. Before I left, she gave me a pastry box tied with twine and told me to bring it with me—to sweeten him up.

And so, a little after nine the next morning, pastry box in hand, I knocked on the door of a smart brick row house on the corner of

Newbury Street with the word MADISON'S stenciled in clean gold letters across the front window.

~

4 August 1944—Boston

He answers after a second knock, a tall man in his fifties, wearing a rumpled robe of charcoal-gray silk and a pair of badly creased trousers. His hair is wavy and toffee-colored, threaded with fine strands of silver, and he wears a thin mustache that I suspect is tinted with brow pencil or wax, because it's several shades darker than his hair.

"No," he mumbles at me before I can speak.

I blink at him, not understanding. "Pardon?"

"Whatever you're selling. I don't want any."

"Are you Myles Madison?"

"Who's asking?"

He's so gruff, so completely dismissive, that I nearly turn and walk away, but I remember my instructions. *Don't take no for an answer.* "Claire Bruneau told me to come see you. She said you might need someone to sew for you."

He runs a hand through his hair, scowling. "Claire?"

"From Bisous Sucrés. She told me to bring you these."

His eyes are pale gray, heavy lidded with long golden lashes. They light on the box briefly, then shift back to me. "Madeleines?" he inquires warily.

"I don't know. She only told me to bring them—to sweeten you up."

He grunts but takes the box from my hands and turns away: an invitation to enter, I assume. I take it, finding myself in a dimly lit parlor furnished with deep leather chairs and dark, heavy tables. It feels the way I've always imagined a gentlemen's club would feel. Thick brocade draperies. Brass lamps with dark-green shades. A sumptuous Turkish carpet in shades of claret and sage. Everything burnished and tasteful.

"What is it you're after?" he asks in the same gruff tone he used when opening the door. He has untied the twine on the pastry box and is peering inside, treating me as if I'm a distraction.

"Work," I reply coolly. "Claire said you just lost both your assistants. My mother owned a salon in Paris until the war. I worked with her there."

"This is not a salon, young lady. I do not make dresses."

"Does the needle care what it stitches?"

He jerks his head up, cocking one eye at me. "What is your name?"

"Soline Roussel," I say, refusing to flinch under his sharp appraisal. "And you're Myles Madison, the finest tailor in Boston, or so Claire claims. I'm good, Monsieur Madison, quite capable of whatever task you ask of me—and I badly need the work."

His face softens a little, but his eyes are chilly as they take me in, inch by painstaking inch. My hatless head and oft-mended dress, my worn shoes, scarred handbag, and ringless finger. Like *Maman* assessing a potential client, he misses nothing.

"Yes," he says dryly. "I should think you must. What else did Claire tell you about me?"

I frown, not sure what he's asking. "Nothing."

"Nothing about why I lost both my assistants?"

I shake my head, unsettled by where he might be going.

"I assume you're not married?"

"No."

"No, I thought not. And you're what—eighteen?"

"I'm twenty-one."

"And little acquainted with the world, I imagine."

"I am well acquainted with the world, monsieur. Much more than I would like to be."

"Well, then," he says, wandering to a small bar in one corner and picking up a glass. "That makes two of us. Perhaps I should tell you my story before we go further." He splashes a few inches of clear liquid into the glass, stares at it a moment, then turns as if suddenly remembering his manners. "Forgive me. Might I interest you in a drink?"

My eyes slide to the clock on the mantel. It's not yet ten. "Thank you, no. I generally prefer coffee at this hour."

"Suit yourself." He lifts his glass in a mock toast, then takes a deep swallow, wincing as it goes down. He turns away, topping off his glass, and I wonder if he's forgotten me again.

"You were going to tell me your story," I remind him.

"Yes, yes, my story. All right, then. I cater to a very affluent clientele, Miss Roussel—or did. The Brahmin, as they style themselves. Important men in important jobs. Men with money and power and names that go back to the bloody peerage. They also have secrets. But not from me. I see my customers in every state of undress—like a doctor. It's a relationship that tends to lead to certain . . . *confidences*. I know whose health is failing, who's in financial difficulty, who's had a bit of luck in the market, who's leaving his wife for his mistress—and who's cheating on his mistress with the handsome new instructor at the tennis club."

He pauses, waiting for me to blush or become flustered. When I don't, he continues. "As you might guess, I'm seldom in social settings with the kinds of men I dress. They're well above my station. But a few weeks ago, I was at the bar in the Statler Hotel with friends and happened to run into a new client of mine, a political type with a society matron wife and plans to move up."

He pauses, striking a melodramatic pose and a voice to match. "Lawrence Tate, of the *Mayflower* Tates, thank you very much. Needless to say, I was surprised to see him there. Though not nearly as surprised as he was to see me."

"Why?"

He regards me with open amusement, his smile blatantly sexual, and I realize he's handsome, or was not so long ago. "Because, my pretty girl, as a rule, the club I'm talking about isn't frequented by ivory-tower types seeking young ladies of good breeding. They like their lovers on the masculine side and rarely bother with last names."

I say nothing.

"Do you understand what I'm telling you?"

"*Oui*," I say evenly. "I do." I glance at the clock again, growing impatient. I came for a job. If the answer is no, I need to get back out on the pavement. "Will you hire me or not, monsieur?"

He empties his glass and turns once more to refill it. His hand shakes as he pours, and for the first time, I see through his bluster to the frailty beneath. He's shattered, and quite possibly ill. The last thing he needs is more alcohol.

"Don't drink that," I say, capturing the glass before he can lift it. "Let me make you something to eat instead, and you can tell me about the job."

"I am a homosexual, Miss Roussel."

I blink at him, my face blank. "Are you hoping to shock me into going away?"

He rakes a hand through his hair, exasperated by my response. "Do you know the word? What it means? What I am?"

"Yes."

"And do you know what people do to men like me when they find out? They ruin us. With lies and accusations. Until we've lost everything. And I have, my dear. I've lost everything. My clients. My reputation. Everything I've worked for, gone. That's why my assistants left. No one will even work for me."

"I will."

"Didn't you hear me? There *is* no work. Maybe it's different where you come from, but here, men like me are pariahs."

I tip up my chin, eyeing him squarely. "Where I come from, monsieur, men like you are rounded up and put in camps, where they are beaten and starved and murdered. No one has arrested you. No one has killed you. If you're alive, you can start again."

"How?" He shakes his head slowly, his pale eyes vacant. "There's nothing left."

I make a show of glancing about the elegantly appointed room, mentally comparing it with my last glimpse of *Maman*'s shop the morning I left Paris, and suddenly I'm furious.

"You have no idea what nothing is," I reply coldly. "But I do. In two weeks, my money will run out, and I'll be on the street. Do you have a job for me, yes or no?"

He glares at me, his face flushed with annoyance. "There *is* no job—for you or anyone—because there is no business. Do you want to know why?"

I don't, but I see that he's going to tell me.

"The day after our chance meeting, Mr. Tate came to the shop claiming to need a pair of trousers altered. I wasn't surprised. In fact, I'd been wondering how long it would take him to call on some pretext or other, to explain away his presence at the Statler. *I had no idea it was that kind of place when I went in. I feel so silly; I was there to meet a friend. How could I know?* I brought him to the back, to one of the fitting rooms, and asked him what it was he wanted done. He answered by pushing me against the wall and shoving his tongue down my throat."

My mouth drops open. There isn't a woman alive who hasn't been on the receiving end of an unwanted advance, but I've never thought of a man being accosted in that way.

He barks out a laugh. "So you can be shocked after all."

"I'm not shocked. I just expected the story to end differently."

He waggles his brows wolfishly. "So did he, my dear. He had an arrangement in mind. Very discreet, of course, and lucrative if I played my cards right. When I declined, he went home and told his wife I'd made an advance. Me! As if I could ever be interested in such a parasite. Word spread like a brushfire. That woman he married, blabbing to anyone who'd listen. *Myles Madison is a lecherous old queen who can't keep his hands off his customers.*"

He pauses, running his fingers over his mustache. "Mark me, one day the joke will be on that mouthy old cow. Men like her husband invariably embarrass themselves in some public way. And then we'll see who the pariah is. This puritanical town will turn on him like a pack of dogs."

He's swaying slightly, and his words have become slurred. I run a chilly eye over him. "Cold comfort, I should think, if you're broke when it happens."

"I'll never be broke. Money may be the only thing I have, but I have plenty of it."

"How very lucky for you," I reply coolly and start for the door. "Good day, monsieur."

"Where are you going?"

"I'm going to look for a job. Because, unlike you, I do *not* have plenty of money."

"Is it your habit to knock on a man's door at the crack of dawn, start an argument, then simply depart?"

"It is *not* the crack of dawn, which you would know if you were not already half-drunk. And I did not come to start an argument. I came because I need to work, but not here." I glare at him openly. "Claire said not to take no for an answer, but I think I will. Self-pity is a luxury I cannot afford, and I'm afraid yours might rub off on me. I'm sorry to have disturbed you."

"You're a child," he growls. "What do you know?"

"I am young, but I'm not a child. I've seen things no one should see. Countries overrun with evil. Entire families imprisoned and murdered. Men shot to pieces and women who have lost everything they hold dear. There are many tragedies in the world, monsieur. I do not count gossip among them. You boast that you will never be broke, but you are clearly *broken*—because you choose to be."

And with that, I tuck my handbag into the crook of my arm and head for the door, eager to be gone. My hand is on the knob when he finally speaks.

"Fine," he sighs with a pained air. "But if I hire you, you must promise to stop calling me monsieur. I loathe the French."

My heart gives a little gallop. "What shall I call you, then, instead of monsieur?"

"My friends call me Maddy."

I make eggs and strong coffee, and we eat together in his small, sunny kitchen. While he smokes, I tell him my story, leaving nothing out. Because I know somehow that I can trust him with my secrets and that nothing I say will ever shock him. I tell him about *Maman* and Anson and the Resistance. He tells me about Richard, the love of his life. How they fell in love the night they met. How Richard died in his arms after a ravaging bout with cancer. And how Richard's family barred him from attending the funeral. I tell him about Dorothy Sheridan and Assia, how they took her away to bury without telling me. We cry, holding hands over our empty plates, and we become family, kindred spirits bound by loss and loneliness.

The clock on the mantel chimes softly, tugging me away from my memories. But I'm not ready to let them go. I tip back my wineglass and reach for the framed photo at my elbow, taken the day my name was stenciled below Maddy's on the front window. He's grinning for the camera, looking especially dapper in navy pinstripes, shoulders back, chest out, proud as punch of his *little bird*, as he called me.

It had been a happy day with cake and champagne, followed by dinner at Marliave, a swishy French restaurant Maddy claimed to detest, though he seemed to know the name of every waiter in the place. We drank too much wine and danced until dawn, in celebration of Madison's resurrection from the ashes.

The turnaround had been swift, thanks in part to the addition of a line of women's evening dresses. Maddy had been shameless, touting me as *a couturier from Paris who has created wedding gowns for some of the most discerning women in Europe*. I didn't care that it wasn't true, because in my heart it was. Finally, I was making the kinds of dresses I always dreamed of.

He referred to himself as my fairy godmother, a private joke between us, but it was true. I learned so much from him, about clothes and business and life. How to merchandise and accessorize, how to charm suppliers and manage cash flow, how to create an illusion of exclusivity that would have clients clamoring for my designs. I soaked up his lessons like a sponge.

And then came the day that changed everything. Mrs. Laureen Appleton came in for a fitting and happened to announce that her granddaughter Catalina had just gotten engaged. Maddy, never missing an opportunity to expand our business, casually suggested that an honest-to-goodness couture gown would make her granddaughter the envy of Boston. He also whispered, just loud enough to be overheard, that word around Paris was that a Roussel gown virtually guaranteed the bride a happy ending.

Once word spread that one of the season's biggest weddings would feature a Roussel gown, orders began to trickle in. There was no *magie* in the beginning. We needed the work too badly to turn anyone away. I designed gowns for anyone who could pay and had just enough luck with my brides to perpetuate the rumors Maddy shamelessly continued to spread. Soon, I had a waiting list of brides willing to submit to a reading if it meant going down the aisle in one of my dresses. Like *Maman* and her rosary, they wished to hedge against *malchance*. Somehow, without meaning to, I had become *la Sorcière de la Robe*—the Dress

Witch—and I was strangely glad. Perhaps because I'd come to understand just how rare happy endings truly are.

Eventually, Maddy set up a small salon for me on the second floor, along with my very own workroom. A year later, the salon took up the entire second floor, and I had to hire two girls to handle patterns and fittings. In a small way, at least, I was living both my dream and *Maman's*.

Then, a few years later, Maddy developed a cough, the result of smoking nearly two packs of cigarettes a day. I had picked up the habit, too, by then. It relaxed me and gave me something to do with my hands when I wasn't working. Maddy's cough grew steadily worse, and soon his beautiful suits began to hang on him. I saw *Maman* when I looked at him, and I knew what was coming. Not that knowing made the truth easier.

I did what I could to keep him comfortable toward the end. I bought him a television, which he claimed to hate, though he watched it incessantly. I read him the paper each night after supper. I even smoked for him now and then, when he would beg me to *share a smoke*. I would lie beside him in the dark, blowing pillars of blue smoke into the air above his head, so he could enjoy it secondhand. His doctor would have had ten fits, but I didn't care. I owed him everything, and he deserved some enjoyment in his last days.

He died on a Sunday, leaving me the shop and every cent he had in the world. He also left a note containing a few scribbled words. *It's your nest now, little bird. Time to spread your wings and fly, fly, fly.* Two months later, only my name remained on the window, along with the words L'Aiguille Enchantée in pretty gold script.

I still miss him terribly.

He was my champion—father, mentor, and a dear, dear friend. I knew his secrets, and he knew mine. I drove him crazy, and he made me laugh. I gave him back his will to fight, and in return he gave me a future.

THIRTY-TWO

RORY

September 7, 1985—Boston

Rory set her purse on the dresser and sagged onto the bed, aware of Hux's eyes on her as she began to unlace her boots. She reached for the framed photo on the nightstand and laid it in her lap, seized by a pang of loneliness so sharp it nearly took her breath away. Was this all she was to have of him now? An image trapped behind a rectangle of glass?

He'd been missing nearly nine months, without a scrap of news. What was the appropriate length of time for giving up on happy endings? A year? Two? And what then? What shape did her life take when Hux was no longer a part of her hopes and dreams?

She would have the gallery and an ever-changing stable of artists to promote. But could she make a life out of that? Or would she end up like Soline, walled off from the world with her grief? Hux wouldn't want that. He'd want her to move on—in *all* aspects of her life. But was that what *she* wanted? She couldn't imagine anyone ever filling the empty place Hux's disappearance had carved in her. And she wasn't sure she wanted to. Her heart belonged to Hux and would for a very long time. For now—for a very *long* now—the gallery would have to fill her days. Like Soline with her shop.

And things were finally beginning to take shape on that front. The painters had started work today, and she'd stayed late, eager to see how the slate gray she had chosen for the walls looked after the second coat. She'd ended up covered in paint after bumping into a ladder and knocking a roller out of its tray, but the color was perfect. And to top it off, she'd set up a meeting with Kendra Paterson, an artist whose stunning sea glass sculptures had caught her eye last year at an art fair in Portsmouth. If all went well, her pieces would be the focal point of the opening.

Unfortunately, she was going to have to call her mother and explain why she couldn't make brunch. Again. She stripped off her paint-spattered clothes, started the shower, then grabbed the cordless on the way to the laundry room.

"Hey, it's me," she said, cringing when Camilla answered. She'd been hoping for the machine.

"Let me guess—you're not coming tomorrow."

"I can't. I'm sorry. I'm heading to Freeport first thing in the morning to meet with an artist."

"Is there a shortage of hippie artists here in Boston?"

"She's not a hippie, Mother. It's 1985. No one's a hippie anymore." She paused, measuring detergent into the washer with her free hand, then dropped the lid with a hollow clang. "She works full time and teaches classes on the side. This is the only time she could do it."

"What on earth is that noise?"

"The washer. I was a klutz and got covered in paint today."

"You do know there are people you can pay to do that sort of thing, Aurora. It's not as though you have to do this on a shoestring."

"I am paying someone. Several someones, in fact. But I wanted to see how the color turned out. I'm afraid I made a nuisance of myself, but they were great about it."

"So things are coming along?"

"Swimmingly. It's actually starting to look like a gallery. You could come by sometime, you know, and see for yourself."

"I know, and I will, but I've been frightfully busy. I'm glad things are on schedule."

"Ahead of schedule, actually. I'm hoping to set the date for the opening next month. That reminds me, I promised to invite Vicky and Hilly. I'll need their addresses for the invitations. And for anyone else you think I should invite."

"I'd include Maureen Cordeiro and Laura Ladd. Oh, and Kimberly Covington Smith. They're younger and have loads of connections. They'll be good allies."

"Thank you," Rory said, pleasantly surprised. "And what about you? Do you want to be invited?"

"Well, of course I do. Why would you even ask?"

"I was giving you an out. I know you're not crazy about the idea. I didn't want to put you in a position of either having to grit your teeth and go or find a polite way to say no."

"What a thing to say. I'm your mother, Aurora. Of course I want to be part of your big night. Speaking of which, have you given any thought to who might cater? I could make a few calls, maybe work out a finger food menu. It's one less thing for you to worry about. Also, there's entertainment to consider. The right entertainment can make an event—or break it. There was the time Laurie Lorenz made the mistake of hiring a pianist, sight unseen. The man crooned Barry Manilow tunes all night. I offered to contact a wonderful harpist, but she insisted on doing everything herself. It was a disaster."

Rory bit her lip. Under no circumstances would there be a harpist at her opening. There was no denying that Camilla Grant knew her way around an event, but the only fingerprints on this event were going to be hers. "Thanks, but I've been working on some ideas, and I'd really like to do this on my own."

Camilla sighed breezily. "Suit yourself, but I'm here if you change your mind. How about letting me give you a makeover instead?"

Oh, good grief. "I do not need a makeover, Mother."

"Sweetheart . . . How do I say this without sounding mean? With so much on your plate, you've let yourself get a little . . . shabby."

"You make me sound like a bag lady."

"All right, I'm sorry. But you have to admit that you've been focused on other things these last few months. You could do with a little . . . sprucing up. If you won't let me help with anything else, let that be my contribution. We'll get you a new outfit, something smashing, and maybe do something with your hair."

"I don't need something smashing. It isn't going to be that kind of night—or that kind of gallery."

"Fine. We'll find you something less than smashing. We can do it next Saturday. I'll make an appointment with Lorna for your hair, and a manicure, too, I think. We can grab lunch at Seasons afterward."

"We'll see. I have to go. I've got the shower running."

"So . . . Saturday?"

"I'll call you later in the week."

Rory was still smarting over her mother's use of the word *shabby* when she returned to the bathroom. Was she . . . *shabby*? She wiped the fog from the mirror and peered at her face. Her cheeks and forehead were smudged with paint, and flecks of gray speckled the wheat-colored waves that had escaped her ponytail. She pulled the elastic free, shaking out the unruly mass. It fell well past her shoulders now, her bangs so long they nearly obscured her eyes. She couldn't remember the last time she'd had a haircut, and her highlights had grown out a good three inches, creating a subtle but discernible line of demarcation.

Perhaps her mother had a point. She *had* let herself go. She'd never been a girlie girl, with drawers full of makeup and a twice-a-day skin-care regimen, but she'd never completely stopped caring about her appearance. Maybe it *was* time for a change. Nothing elaborate, just enough to signal the start of her new role as gallery owner.

She turned off the shower, padded back to the bedroom, and opened her closet. Her wardrobe was another area she tended to neglect, partly because the thought of shopping for clothes made her break out in hives. Nothing ever seemed to fit her properly, as if every piece of clothing in the world had been made for someone else. She wasn't petite like her mother. She was tall and long-limbed with broad shoulders and narrow hips. A swimmer's body.

She peered toward the back, where her *good clothes* hung. Gifts from her mother, mostly, intended to feminize her boyish daughter. Eggshell, beige, taupe, and ivory, with the occasional pastel thrown in, many still bearing their original tags. And if she agreed to go shopping with her mother next week, she'd have one more beige elephant to add to her collection.

On impulse, she located Soline's number and dialed.

"Hello?"

"Is this the fairy godmother hotline?"

"Rory? Is something wrong?"

"No, but I need a favor. I need help with an outfit for the opening. My mother wants to take me shopping. She's planning this whole makeover thing."

"And this is a problem?"

"I hate shopping. As in, I'd rather have a root canal. Throw in my mother criticizing everything I pick out, and there isn't enough Novocain in the state of Massachusetts. The thing is, she's a little bit right. I do need to change my look if I'm going to be at the gallery every day. I was hoping you could give me some pointers."

"You want me to go shopping with you?"

"No. No, I didn't mean that. Just . . . tell me what to wear. And how to wear it. And where to buy it. Better yet, help me figure out what I already own that will work, so I don't have to shop at all."

"When do you want to do this?"

"The sooner the better. If I can tell my mother I'm set with an outfit and promise to get my bangs trimmed, maybe she'll let me off the hook. I'm not talking full-scale makeover. I just need help putting a few things together, and you always look so chic. I'll even cook if that will sweeten the deal."

"Maybe you should let your mother take you shopping, Rory. It might ease some of the tension between you. Maybe she wants that too."

"Trust me—what she wants is to make sure I don't embarrass her in front of her friends."

"Are you certain you're being fair? I'm sure she just wants it to be a special night for you."

"I'm not trying to be unfair. I just don't want a big fuss. Say you'll help me."

"All right, I can come tomorrow. But you don't need to cook."

"Oh, you're wonderful! I'm meeting an artist in Freeport in the morning, but I should be home by three. We'll order a pizza."

"All right, pizza. But none of that pineapple nonsense."

Soline arrived a little after four, looking effortlessly chic in slim-fitting black slacks and a soft gray tunic. As usual, she was flawless, perfectly accessorized with pointy ballet flats and black gauntlet gloves.

Rory eyed the ensemble with a pang of envy. Only Soline Roussel could pull off kid gloves in September. "Thank you for helping me with this. I hated to ask, but I'm clueless when it comes to fashion. And let's face it, I'm not exactly runway material."

"Let me be the judge of that," Soline replied briskly. "Show me your closet. So I know what I'm working with. Then we'll talk a little."

Rory led her to the bedroom closet and pushed back the bifold doors. "There it is. Everyday stuff here, dressier stuff at the back. My mother bought most of it."

Soline flicked through the hangers with military efficiency, pausing now and then to study a collar or a sleeve, clucking and tsking as she went. Finally, she pivoted to look at Rory. "A nightmare," she pronounced flatly.

"Aren't they hideous?"

"On the contrary. They're quite lovely. Your mother has exquisite taste."

"I thought you said they were a nightmare."

"*Oui.* For *you*, they are a nightmare. I see why you haven't worn most of them. These clothes are meant for *une femme menue*—a petite woman. *You* are not petite."

"Yes," Rory said, ducking her head. "I'm aware."

"It's not meant as a criticism, *chérie*. Only the truth. And when it comes to clothes, we must always tell ourselves the truth."

"I'm one of those people who's just not meant to wear nice clothes."

"Everyone is meant to wear nice clothes. Most just get it wrong. They chase fashion rather than style."

"What's the difference?"

Soline looked crestfallen. "Oh, Rory."

"What?"

"Look," Soline said as she began pulling pieces from the closet and tossing them on the bed. "This skirt. Beautiful, but too short for you. And that flounce at the bottom—you'll look like you're wearing a lampshade. This jacket with the nipped waist. Cute, as the teenagers say, but not on you. This blouse with the puffy sleeves and little pearl buttons. No. No. No. These are someone else's clothes—someone else's *style*. You must find your own."

"What if I don't have one?"

"Don't be silly. Everyone has a style. Most women just never bother to find it. It's easier to open a magazine or turn on *Dynasty* and copy someone else. That's why everything in the stores looks the same. Because everybody is trying to look like everybody else. They're happy being vanilla. But you're not vanilla, Rory. You're lovely and exceptional, with a flavor all your own. But you've been hiding in those boyish clothes for so long that you can't see yourself anymore."

Rory felt color rise in her cheeks. It was true. Or maybe she'd never been able to see herself. "So what do I wear? I hate fussing with outfits. Not that it matters. Whatever I put on looks wrong."

"Ah, but when you buy the right clothes, you don't have to fuss. It all works together. Like the pieces you'll choose for your gallery. You want them to say something to the people who see them. You're after a theme, a statement. Clothes are the same."

Soline took her by the shoulders, turning her to face the mirror. "Look at your shoulders, strong and square. The long legs and narrow hips. You're lean, but not stringy like those silly models. You exude power—or you will when we dress you properly. You need pieces that play up your shape instead of hiding it. Tailored shirts and blazers. Wide-legged trousers to balance the bottom with the top. Pinstripes. Checks. Yes, and tweed, I think. Jewel tones will work wonderfully with your coloring too. No more beige. And absolutely no lace of any kind." She smiled secretively as she caught Rory's eye in the glass. "Unless it's underneath."

Rory stared at her reflection, trying to mentally swap her Red Sox T-shirt and lumpy sweatpants for anything remotely resembling what Soline had just described. "In twenty minutes you figured all that out?"

Soline shrugged. "I've been dressing women for forty years. We'll go shopping next week."

"*We* as in . . . both of us?"

"Unless you don't want to."

"No, I'd love it, but are you sure?"

"Yes. But only this once, as a kind of training exercise. Next time, you'll do it on your own. Or with your *maman*. No, don't shudder. Once you know what works for you, you'll have confidence to choose for yourself. That's what style does for a girl." She paused, squinting at Rory's reflection. "Have you ever thought about cutting your hair?"

Rory scowled at the mirror. "I know, I need a trim. It's on the list."

"No, I meant short, like this." She reached around, gathering Rory's hair to the crown of her head. "You have beautiful cheekbones and a lovely neck. Wearing it short would show off those beautiful eyes too. And you have such good hair. Paul would love to get his hands on it."

Rory found herself grinning. "My mother would have seven fits. She thinks I'm half a boy as it is."

"You wouldn't look like a boy, *Aurore*. You'd look beautiful. Chic."

"Chic," Rory repeated softly, catching Soline's eye in the glass. "Me?"

"*Oui, chérie*—you."

Rory stared at her reflection, trying to imagine her mother's reaction to the kind of cut Soline was suggesting. She'd asked to cut her hair short once, when she first started swimming, because it was such a pain to stuff it into her swim cap, but her mother had been adamant. *Young ladies do not lop off their hair for the sake of convenience.* She hadn't thought about cutting it since. But she was definitely thinking about it now. It would have to be a surprise, though. If she breathed a word to her mother, she'd wind up getting talked out of it, and she was pretty sure she didn't want to be.

Soline caught her eye in the glass. "What do you think?"

"I think I might want to. But I'm not telling my mother until it's done. She won't be happy, but by then it will be too late."

Soline said nothing, but the corners of her mouth turned down.

Rory shot her a sheepish grin. "I know. I seem to be taking up an awful lot of your time lately. What's the going hourly rate for fairy godmothers these days?"

"It isn't that," Soline said, letting Rory's hair spill back down around her shoulders. "I'm happy to help."

"Then what?"

"I can't help thinking your mother is going to resent me for the new you. From what you've said, she doesn't seem the type of woman who'd appreciate another woman's interference. And were I in her shoes, I might feel the same."

Rory thought about that. She made a valid point. Soline was the last person her mother would want giving her fashion advice—or anything else—but she really did need guidance. In so many things. And from someone who knew what it was like to have to reinvent herself after life had knocked her down. Camilla had never been anyone but who she was right now. Stolid and perfect and in control of every facet of her life.

"Then we'll just have to make sure she doesn't find out," Rory said finally. "I'll tell her it was all my idea. Now, how do I find this . . . Paul, was it?"

"If you're really sure, I'll phone him tomorrow and get you in."

It was all Rory could do not to throw her arms around Soline. "I'm so excited. Thank you."

Soline's mouth twitched, as if she were about to say something, but she bit her lip instead. "What are fairy godmothers for?"

THIRTY-THREE

RORY

September 14, 1985—Boston

Rory held her breath, silently repeating Soline's words as another shower of hair fluttered into the lap of her black nylon cape. *When it comes to hair, Paul Ramone and the staff at Bella Mia are as good as it gets.* No doubt, it was true. But as she sat there, surrounded by a puddle of freshly cropped locks, she prayed she hadn't made a mistake she'd regret for months.

She had green-lighted Paul's suggestions for lowlights and a sassy pixie cut and had held her breath as he set to work. An hour and a half later, she'd been foiled, shampooed, moussed, and blow-dried, and was now in the process of being *debulked*—whatever *that* meant—while Soline pretended not to watch from behind her magazine.

It had already been a full day, beginning with a visit to Neiman Marcus. Soline's personal shopper, Lila, had done the legwork in advance, so that when they arrived, an entire rack of carefully curated pieces had been waiting. All she had to do was try on and give the thumbs-up or -down.

The final tally was more than she'd spent collectively on every scrap of clothing she'd ever owned, but the new pieces made her feel stunning. In fact, she'd been so excited with her updated look that she'd decided to wear one of the outfits out of the store.

She'd ended up leaving with only a handful of bags, as the bulk of her purchases had been left for alterations. She had initially balked at the idea, until Soline explained that beautiful clothes, like beautiful women, deserved to be shown to best advantage, which meant they must fit properly.

Ironically, the only thing they hadn't nailed down was an outfit for opening night. But Lila had asked for another chance, promising to come up with a winner in plenty of time. Rory had been only too happy to agree. She had to admit, for someone who'd never cared for fashion, she was certainly enjoying the Cinderella experience.

It took a moment to realize Paul's scissors had gone quiet and that he was standing back, studying her head with narrowed eyes. After a moment, he shook his head. "No. Not yet."

Rory slid worried eyes to Soline, who was nodding. "Shorter over the ears, I think. And soften the fringe."

Rory wasn't sure what surprised her more, the words *shorter over the ears* or the fact that Soline was telling one of Boston's most sought-after hairstylists how to do his job. "Can I *please* look now?"

Paul's and Soline's "no!" came simultaneously. Paul also admonished her to hold still if she didn't want to end up like Van Gogh. She closed her mouth, cringing as the *snick-snick* of his scissors resumed. *It'll grow back,* she reminded herself. *Eventually.*

Twenty minutes later, Paul removed the black nylon cape and gave Rory's chair a spin until she faced the mirror. "*Voilà!*"

Rory blinked at the woman staring back at her from the glass, familiar but a stranger too. Her eyes looked larger, her cheekbones more sculpted. She ran her fingers through the short waves, admiring the subtle lowlights Paul had added. She touched the bare skin at the back of her neck, her exposed ears. She felt naked. And strangely liberated. She already knew what her mother would think, but what about Hux? She looked nothing like the Rory he'd left behind.

"I look . . ."

"Chic," Soline supplied, appearing over her left shoulder. "And polished. And beautiful."

Rory blinked at her reflection. "Do I?"

"Like a proper gallery owner."

Rory turned to beam at Paul. "You're a miracle worker."

He shrugged, waving off the remark. "Who would guess that under such a mop lurked an absolute beauty? But promise me you won't put either one of us through that again. I'll see you in five weeks. And then every five weeks after that. Short hair requires upkeep. And mousse." He handed her a tall silver canister. "A dollop the size of a golf ball. No more or you'll be crunchy. Nod so I know you understand."

Rory nodded obediently. "How much do I owe you?"

"For today? Nothing. I'm happy to do this favor for Ms. Roussel. God knows I owe her a thousand more. And please, put your tip money away. I don't want it." He paused, shooting her a wink. "This time."

Paul and Soline exchanged hugs and a few quick words while Rory gathered her purse and shopping bags. Soline smiled at her when they finally met up at the door. "You're gorgeous, *ma petite*."

"I don't know how to thank you for today."

"You don't need to thank me. It's what we fairy godmothers do."

"Just the same, I'm treating you to lunch. Even fairy godmothers need to eat. There's a place down the block called Seasons. We'll order something decadent, and then I'll take you home."

It was nearly four by the time they reached Seasons, and the lunch crowd was long gone. The hostess showed them to a patio table, commenting when she saw Rory's shopping bags that someone had spent the day cleaning out the stores.

They ordered lemonades and browsed the specials, opting for the shrimp flatbread and a salad to share. When the waitress returned with bread and their drinks, Rory lifted her glass to propose a toast.

"To the best fairy godmother any girl could ask for."

Soline smiled as she raised her glass, but the gesture seemed like an effort. Rory lowered her glass, suddenly aware that in her excitement she had been inconsiderate. "I'm sorry. You're tired. We'll tell her we're going to get it to go, and I'll take you home."

"Don't be silly. We're here. I'll just go to the ladies' room and tidy myself up."

Rory felt a pang of guilt as she watched Soline disappear into the restaurant. They'd been having such a wonderful day she hadn't wanted it to end. But she'd forgotten that Soline had forty years on her, and they'd been going hard for nearly six hours.

"Aurora?"

Rory's hand flew reflexively to her freshly cropped hair when she saw Camilla making a beeline in her direction.

"My god. What have you done to your hair?"

"I cut it."

"Please tell me Lorna didn't do that to you."

"No. Paul."

"Who on earth is Paul?"

"He owns Bella Mia, and I love it, so please don't criticize."

Camilla snapped her mouth closed, confirming that she'd been about to do just that. Instead, she narrowed her eyes on the striped linen suit Rory had opted to wear out of the store. "And the clothes?"

Rory smiled, determined not to take the bait. "You wanted me to spruce myself up, and I have." She paused, pointing to the collection of bags at her feet. "I've been shopping all day."

"So I see. Since when do *you* go shopping?"

"Since you called me shabby. You were right, though. It was time for a makeover."

"And you picked these things out for yourself?"

Rory resisted the urge to squirm in her chair. "What are you doing here, Mother?"

"I've just been to Cartier to pick up my watch. I knocked the stem out a few weeks ago, and they called to say it was ready." Her gaze slid to the table, resting briefly on the second place setting. "And you're having lunch. Who with?"

Rory was about to reply when she spotted Soline making her way back to the table.

Camilla saw her too. "Who is that?"

"That's Soline."

"That's who's been helping you shop?"

"Yes."

"And the hair? That was her idea too?"

"I wanted something new. Something . . . different."

"Well, you certainly found it."

Camilla fell silent as Soline approached. The silence spooled out as the two women stood staring at each other. Finally, Rory cleared her throat. "Soline, this is my mother, Camilla Grant. Mother, this is Soline Roussel."

"Ah, yes," Camilla drawled with a sugary smile. "The landlady I've been hearing so much about. We meet at last."

"Yes," Soline replied with a polite nod. "At last."

"Isn't it funny? I was running some errands and just happened to be walking past. I remember they used to do the most delicious lobster salad here. In fact, Rory and I were just talking about it the other day, weren't we? And now here you both are having lunch."

Soline indicated the empty chair beside her. "You're welcome to join us."

"Oh, I don't know. I hate to push in." But even as the words were leaving her mouth, she was pulling out the empty chair. "Still, I can't pass up a chance to lunch with the infamous Soline Roussel."

Soline's brows slid up. "Surely not infamous."

Camilla's charm bracelet jangled as she shook out her napkin and laid it in her lap. "I only meant that my daughter has told me so much about you. And your shop. Such a pity about the fire."

Soline reached for her water glass, clearly rattled by the mention of the fire. "She's told me about you too," she said after a brief sip. "In fact, she speaks of you quite often."

Camilla held Soline's gaze a moment longer than necessary. "Does she?"

Rory's stomach roiled as she watched them spar, painfully aware of what was being said—and what wasn't. She needed to divert the conversation before her mother's tone escalated from passive-aggressive to just plain aggressive.

She was about to blurt out that she'd settled on the light fixtures for the gallery when their waitress appeared, balancing a tray on her shoulder. She blinked at Camilla, then at Rory. "I'm sorry. I didn't realize you were expecting a third. Let me just set this down and I'll grab a menu and some silverware."

Camilla waved a perfectly manicured hand. "No need. Just bring me a nice chardonnay and a plate of that lovely lobster salad if you still have it. Oh, and the dressing on the side if you don't mind." She ran an eye around the table when the waitress was gone, surveying the freshly delivered food. "Doesn't that look delicious. And you're sharing. How nice. Please, don't wait for me. I'm sure my salad won't take long."

Rory silently fumed as her mother took a piece of bread from the basket, then reached over to borrow her knife to butter it. She was being punished, she realized, for her disloyalty. As Camilla had punished her husband each time one of his affairs came to light and embarrassed her in front of her friends.

"Aurora tells me you've been helping her shop," Camilla said between bites of bread. "It's awfully kind of you, though I must say, I was surprised to hear it. My daughter has never been one for fashion. Not that I didn't try. But she was such a tomboy growing up. Always up a tree or kicking a ball around. I couldn't keep the child clean."

"The *child* is all grown up now," Rory muttered. "And sitting right next to you, in case you forgot."

Camilla didn't miss a beat, addressing Soline as if Rory hadn't spoken. "The hair is . . . interesting. Was it your idea?"

"Rory thought that with the opening coming, it might be time for a new look."

"Well then, she succeeded beautifully. I raised her, and I nearly walked right past her. Can you imagine?" She turned to look at Rory then, holding her gaze for an uncomfortable beat. "It's rather disconcerting to not recognize your own daughter."

Rory stared back, startled by the brief flash of pain in her mother's eyes. Not anger. Not jealousy. Pain. And she'd put it there. She'd been so caught up in the magic of the afternoon that she hadn't given a thought to how her mother would feel about being cast aside for Soline—again. Soline had warned her that this might happen. And now here they were, face-to-face, looking petulant and uncomfortable.

"The haircut was my idea, Mother. I asked—"

Camilla turned back to Soline, cutting Rory off midsentence. "I couldn't help noticing, you call my daughter Rory."

"It's what she calls herself."

"Her father and I always preferred Aurora."

"Yes, she told me. Is it a family name?"

"No. Just one we liked. We never cared for the shortened version. It's so boyish, don't you think?"

"Oh, I don't know . . ." Soline cocked her head, studying Rory with a little smile. "It's young and fresh. I think it suits her. "

It was all Rory could do not to bark out a laugh. Soline was apparently quite capable of holding her own. "Actually," she said, sliding a slice of flatbread onto her plate, "it was my father who started calling me Rory. He wanted a boy but got me instead." She paused for a dramatic sigh. "My poor parents. I couldn't seem to please either one of them."

Camilla tossed her head with a little laugh. "Really, Aurora. What a thing to say."

Rory swallowed her response as the waitress appeared with Camilla's order and place setting, and for a few minutes the table went quiet. Camilla picked up her fork, poking suspiciously at the scoop of lobster meat on her plate. Rory eyed her warily while she nibbled her flatbread, grateful for the cessation of hostilities, if only temporarily.

Soline was extricating bits of red onion from her salad and relegating them to the edge of her plate. When the silence began to grow stale, she turned to Camilla. "Rory tells me you're president of the Women's Art Council, Mrs. Grant. It must make you proud to see her dreams for the gallery taking shape."

"Well, yes," Camilla said, clearly annoyed by the question. "Of course I'm proud. Aurora was brought up with art. So was I. It's in her blood. I had hoped that she would finish her degree and then go on to Paris to complete her internship, but she's young and there'll be time later."

"She means there'll be time after I *fail*," Rory threw in caustically. Because that's what Camilla always meant. Sooner or later, she'd muck things up and realize she was in over her head, forcing her back to a more prudent path. *Prudent* was her mother's favorite word. Mustn't stray outside the lines. Mustn't be messy. And above all, mustn't be an embarrassment.

Camilla sighed, offering one of her long-suffering looks. "I did *not* say that. But we have talked about this, Aurora. There's no future in the kinds of things you're talking about. Tomato soup cans and inflatable balloon rabbits. They're fads—here today and gone tomorrow." She paused, dabbing daintily at her mouth. "Art is about the preservation of culture, the expression of beauty, not shocking the public. That's why the masters are *still* the masters. And why fifty years from now, no one will remember Andy Warhol's name. Because *real* art endures. Wouldn't you agree, Ms. Roussel?"

Rory smothered a groan. "Please don't drag Soline into our argument, Mother."

"No one's arguing, sweetheart. We're just having a conversation. And the French do know a thing or two about art. They gave us Monet, Degas, Renoir, and Cézanne, to name a few."

"And there you have it," Rory said, aiming her reply at Soline. "If it isn't a Renoir or a Monet or some other thing painted by a dusty old man, it isn't *real* art."

"Go ahead," Camilla replied curtly. "Make fun. But I happen to know a little something about the subject, Aurora. The art world has a way of culling those who stray too far from good taste."

"And who decides what constitutes good taste? You?"

"The experts decide. Historians. Collectors. Critics. Their opinions can make or break an artist—or a gallery owner."

Soline had been silent for some time, pushing her food around her plate. She put down her fork very carefully and looked at Camilla. "During the war, the Nazis labeled art they didn't like as degenerate. *They* decided. They claimed it had to do with unsuitable subject matter, but we all knew better. The *boche* cared nothing about decency. It was to do with the artists themselves: who they loved, what they believed . . . what their last names were."

She paused, closing her eyes briefly. "Artists were arrested and questioned. Some—Jews, mostly—were even killed. One night, they built a bonfire in the gardens of the Galerie Nationale, burning entire collections to ash. Picasso. Dalí. Miró. All lost. Works by your Renoir and Monet survived because they were snapped up—stolen—by Nazi officers, while the rest burned. Because *they* were the ones to decide."

Camilla's cheeks had gone a mottled shade of pink, as if they'd just been slapped. "Are you comparing me to the Nazis, Ms. Roussel?"

"I'm merely pointing out that letting one group decide what is and isn't worthy can have terrible consequences. Art, like all things, should be left to the beholder, *n'est-ce pas?*"

Camilla squared her shoulders, like a bird fluffing its plumage to appear more threatening. "It's a lovely sentiment, Miss Roussel, but I think it wise to stay in one's own lane, particularly here in Boston, where the lanes tend to be narrow. We may look like a great big city, but underneath it all we're frightfully conventional, and tend to distrust anything flashy or foreign."

Rory stared at Camilla in horror. She'd seen her mother take people down before, coolly and surgically and without batting an eye, but on those occasions it had been deserved. This was something else entirely. The dismissive tone and thinly veiled antagonism, the stilted body language that only served to amplify her disdain. And the look on Soline's face, ashen and dazed, as if she'd just been ambushed. She needed to step in, say something to deflect her mother's hostility, but what? Defending Soline would only make things worse.

She was almost relieved when Soline grabbed her handbag and pushed back from the table. "I just remembered, I left my lipstick in the ladies' room. Please excuse me."

Rory waited until she was sure Soline was out of earshot before rounding on Camilla. "What do you think you're doing?"

Camilla stared at her with wide eyes. "Doing?"

"Don't give me that look. You know perfectly well what I mean. You were angry with me, and you took it out on Soline. Didn't you see her face? You hurt her feelings."

Camilla blinked at her stonily. "I hurt *her* feelings."

"Yes. And you . . ." Rory went still, her words falling away as she caught sight of Soline, heading not for the ladies' room but for the patio exit. "Damn it." She shot to her feet, nearly toppling her chair. "Soline! Wait!"

Soline gave no indication that she'd heard. Rory scrambled after her, winding through the maze of tables and out onto the sidewalk. She'd gone half a block when she finally spotted her at the curb, ducking into a bright-yellow taxi.

Fuming, Rory returned to the restaurant to find Camilla calmly sipping her wine. "I suppose you're pleased with yourself."

Camilla managed to look stunned. "What did I do? We were having a conversation, and the next thing I know she's off in a huff, without so much as a good afternoon. It's downright rude, if you ask me."

"I'll tell you what's rude. Horning in on a lunch you weren't invited to. Referring to Soline—my friend—as *the landlady*. The nonsense about staying in her lane and then slipping in the word *foreign*, as if she wasn't supposed to know exactly what you meant? Why?"

"For heaven's sake, Aurora, lower your voice. Why must you always be so dramatic?"

"I'll be as dramatic as I like. It's my table. And you've got a lot of nerve calling me dramatic after the show you just put on. You hate my hair. I get it. But it was my decision, not Soline's."

Camilla drained her glass, then set it down very carefully. "You think that's why I'm upset? Because you cut your hair?"

Rory blew out a breath, both annoyed and stung by her mother's petulance. She knew it wasn't her hair, but she was too angry to concede the point.

Camilla removed her napkin from her lap, folding it with great care before laying it aside. "I asked you to let me do this for you, Aurora, to go shopping and get your hair done, but you said you were too busy. You're always too busy."

"Because I *am*. The gallery—"

"You weren't too busy for *her*. I suppose you already had this little outing planned when I called."

"I didn't."

"I see. You liked the idea; you just didn't want to go with me."

"That isn't it."

"Then what *is* it? Explain it to me."

"I just didn't want a big ordeal, and it would have been, because it always is. You hating everything I pick out and me eventually giving in because I'm tired of arguing. I wanted to do it myself, to just pick something out and be done with it, but I'm clueless when it comes to clothes, so I asked Soline for some tips. She took one look at my closet and decided she'd better go with me."

"Did she?" Camilla reached for her handbag, fishing about blindly until she located a lipstick. After a quick touch-up, she snapped the tube closed and dropped it back into her bag. "How very kind of her."

"It *was* kind," Rory shot back. "Because that's who she is. A kind woman who wanted to help me. Why does she make you so crazy?"

"She doesn't make me crazy. I just don't understand your fascination with her. An old woman, and a recluse to boot. And those silly gloves, as if she's just come from a wedding or a parade. And now you're taking fashion advice from her, because once upon a time she used to make wedding dresses. It's odd, that's all."

Rory stared at her. "When did you turn into this person?"

"What person?"

"Never mind. We've been over this. Soline is my friend, and today you purposely made her uncomfortable. She may not be Boston blue blood, but she doesn't deserve your disdain. She's been through a lot."

"We've all been through a lot, Aurora. *Life* is a lot. But we get on with it if we don't want to become an object of pity."

"An object of pity," Rory repeated, bristling. "Soline losing everything makes her pitiful. Is that what you think of me too? Because Hux is missing and I refuse to just *get on with it*?"

"I never said—"

"Yes, you did. Maybe not in so many words, but it's what you've always meant. You have a spine of steel, Mother, and you're terribly proud of it. But a mother is supposed to have a heart, and I sometimes wonder if you do."

Rory gathered her shopping bags and her purse, then reached into her wallet and counted out several bills. There was nothing left to say, nothing that would ever make her understand. "That should cover the check."

"Aurora, sit down. We're not finished."

"Yes, we are. In fact, I'll save you a call. I won't be there for brunch tomorrow. After twenty-three years, I think it's time we admit we just don't like each other very much."

THIRTY-FOUR

SOLINE

There are times for holding on in this life and times for letting go. You must learn to know the difference.

—*Esmée Roussel, the Dress Witch*

My hands are still shaking as I pour a large glass of wine. I should have come straight home after Bella Mia rather than going to lunch. Not that what happened at Seasons was Rory's fault. Her mother turning up was an unwelcome surprise for us both.

The instant our eyes caught, the ripple of . . . what was it? Wariness? Distaste? Yes, both of those, but something else too. To her, I'm a rival, her daughter a prize to be won or lost. I've been encroaching on her territory, and she wants me to know that she isn't going to stand for it.

And there was my own reaction, the immediate wave of recognition I felt as I took in the carefully coiffed gold hair, the high cheeks and wide mouth. The resemblance to her daughter was inescapable, a reminder that I am an outsider—that Rory is not mine.

And yet I've grown so close to her in such a short time. Me, who prefers to keep the entire world at a distance. But she's become a part of my life now. A surrogate, I suppose, for the daughter I lost. From that very first day, when she walked into Bisous Sucrés, hugging my battered dress box to her chest, I've felt the connection, as if fate were somehow winking at the two of us.

She seemed to me a kind of angel that day, the gift I never knew I wanted—or needed. And perhaps I've been that for her too. She calls me her fairy godmother, and I'm glad to have had a hand in making her dream come true. My contribution was leasing her the row house, and I've already made arrangements with Daniel to gift it to her, as Maddy once gifted it to me.

She has asked me to be at the opening, and I would like very much to be there, but I see now that it would be a mistake to go. I would happily play second to Camilla were I welcome. Clearly, I am not, and I will not embarrass myself by pushing in where I don't belong. I've had my little run, as they say. Any *tragédienne* worth her salt knows when it's time to exit the stage. As does any decent fairy godmother. She'll have this last gift from me, the row house for her gallery, and that will be the end. I will have done my bit of good and will back away quietly.

I tell myself I'm fine with it all, but it's a lie. What was I thinking? To let a stranger into my life, after so many years of self-protection, to feel again after the blissful numbness. Like my hands after the fire, when the nerves began to regenerate. The pain was so excruciating that all I wanted was to be numb again.

Today felt like that.

I saw it the instant Camilla's eyes locked with mine. She'd taken her measure of me and found me wanting. The flared nostrils and tilted chin, the thin smile that made me go cold all over. It was the way Anson's father used to look at me, like an interloper who had overstepped her bounds. I didn't belong in his son's life, and I don't belong in Rory's either.

I look at my fingers as they close around the stem of my wineglass, curling and shiny pink, and recall Camilla's casual mention of the fire—as if I need help remembering. For as long as I'm alive, I will always remember.

22 July 1981—Boston

I haven't had a moment's peace since word leaked that L'Aiguille Enchantée has been chosen to create a gown for one of the Kennedy cousins. The phone rings all day—brides who read the society pages and are suddenly desperate for a Roussel gown. And then there are the curiosity seekers who wander in off the street or stand gawking on the sidewalk, as if expecting to see the bride-to-be having her hem pinned in my front window.

I understand why everyone is *très agité*. The Kennedys are the nearest thing to royalty Americans are ever likely to have, which means even a distant cousin is treated like a fairy-tale princess. And if I have my way, her gown will be worthy of a fairy tale. It's a stunning thing, perhaps my best work ever. Ivory shantung embellished at the hem with silver embroidery and pale-pink crystals. But there is still the bow to attach and the beading on the sash to finish, and time is growing short. I've been working day and night to complete the dress on time, but I cannot work without sleep. Not even for Boston royalty.

It's nearly 2:00 a.m. when I climb the stairs to my rooms on the third floor. I need only an hour or two, and then I will go back down. But I'm too wound up to sleep. I go to the kitchen and make a small pot of chocolate, add a splash of bourbon, the way Maddy used to drink it, then carry it back up to bed.

I think about having a cigarette, but I've left the pack downstairs in my workroom, and I'm too weary to go down after it. The chocolate will have to be enough, and I can already feel my eyelids beginning to droop. Two hours. That's all I need.

I have no idea how long I've been asleep when I awaken with my throat on fire. The room is dark and thick with smoke. I roll from the bed and onto my knees, in search of air as I crawl in the direction of the stairs. I cling to the rail as I go, disoriented by the thickening smoke and eyes rendered useless. The heat is savage, searing my throat and chest. *Keep moving*, my brain screams. *Keep moving!* But I freeze when I see the ruddy glow at the back of the house and hear the sickening crackle of flames, feeding, consuming.

My workrooms. My work. On fire.

Frantic, I find my feet, hurtling toward the hideous glow rather than away from it. The heat is like a wall, knocking me backward as I reach the largest of the workrooms. Shelves stacked with spare bolts of fabric are completely engulfed, the curtains, too, and the surface of the worktable where a few hours earlier I had been pinning a pattern. It's what I always imagined hell to look like.

And then I see them, three nearly finished gowns in various stages of completion, their shadows stretching grotesquely along the back wall so that they appear to be dancing. I watch, horrified, as flames lick up the side of a skirt, then leap to the sleeve of the gown beside it, feeding on lace, buttons, beads.

I hear a wail from somewhere, muffled in the greedy rush of flames. A siren, I think dimly. Someone must have called the fire department. But no, the sound is coming from me, raw and desolate—a mother grieving for her imperiled children.

Without thinking, I stagger forward, wrapping my arms around the waists of two dress forms, weeping and gasping as I drag them to the door, tripping over skirts and trains as I stumble down the final set of stairs, making blindly for the door and the safety of the street.

It isn't until I spill out onto the steps that I register the searing pain in my left arm. One of the gowns I rescued is crawling with flames, and they've caught the sleeve of my cardigan. I drop the dresses and let out a shriek, swatting at the spreading flames as they lick their way along one wrist, then catch the other as well. The pain is like nothing I've ever felt, blinding and bone deep. The flames continue to spread in spite of my flailing. There are sirens then, deafeningly real, and suddenly everything goes black as I'm shoved to the ground and smothered in a blanket.

Hours later, I wake in the burn unit, dry mouthed and groggy from the morphine. Both of my hands are bandaged to the elbow. Third-degree burns, the doctor explains, the left hand worse than the right. He speaks slowly, as he might to a child, and I feel like a child, helpless and confused.

The last thing I remember is the blanket swallowing me up. I have no memory of being loaded into the ambulance, where they put tubes in my arms, or the emergency room, where they had to cut the singed cardigan away from my flesh. The doctor has to tell me what happened, and I still can't remember. A combination of shock and strong opiates, he explains, and not uncommon given my injuries.

I ask him about my shop. He can't tell me anything. But he does tell me what will happen next. Debridement, skin grafts, exercises, scarring, contracture—and pain. So much pain.

He keeps saying I'm lucky to be alive, lucky to have gotten out when I did, lucky the burns aren't worse. But all I hear is that I'll never sew again, that the life I've built for myself is gone. The Roussel curse at work again, *Maman* would say.

My glass is empty. I refill it and go to the study for my box. Suddenly I want my things around me. It's silly to care now, after so much time without them, but when so much has been uprooted—so many things lost—one must seek comfort in the familiar.

I carry the box back down the hall, holding it in my arms the way one holds a found child, closely, fiercely. And for an instant, as I move past the mirror, I see her looking back at me—the girl who dreamed of princes and believed in happy endings. But a moment later, the girl is gone, replaced by the woman I've become. Worn and alone. Dreamless. Scarred.

For a time—a handful of months—I actually thought I might make something of the time I have left, that I might even be happy again. But I see now that it was only a trick of the light, a shimmery mirage that upon closer inspection falls away. Another loss for my collection. Another unhappy ending.

I strip off my clothes and then open the drawer to the nightstand. The pill vial is there. I take it out, hold it in my fist. A long sleep is what I need. Oblivion. I struggle with the lid, but finally it comes free, and they spill into my palm, small and white. I count them. There are seven. It doesn't seem like enough. I want to sleep for a long, long time.

I swallow two pills with the last of my wine, then fall back against the spread. A clock is ticking somewhere, distant and oddly muffled. I pull the box close. It's just us again. My box of memories and me. I close my eyes, welcoming the darkness, where everything is quiet and the memories can't find me.

I have always grieved the ends of things.

THIRTY-FIVE

RORY

September 18, 1985—Boston

Rory pulled up to the curb and cut the engine. The knot in her belly tightened as she stared at the bright-red door. It wouldn't be the first time she'd shown up on Soline's doorstep unannounced, but the circumstances had changed. Four days had passed since their disastrous lunch, and she hadn't heard a word from Soline, in spite of at least a dozen phone calls. Not that she blamed her. But she needed to apologize—not only for her mother's behavior but for sitting there and letting it happen—and if that meant pounding on the door until she answered, so be it.

The curtains were still drawn, the front steps strewn with a trio of newspapers still in their clear plastic bags. She rang the bell several times, then tried the knocker. "Soline, it's Rory."

A woman walking a pair of overweight beagles slowed as she passed by, eyeing her suspiciously. When she finally moved past, Rory fished an envelope and pen from her purse and scribbled a quick note. *Please call me. I need to talk to you. —R* She knocked one last time, then wedged the note between the door and the jamb, crossing her fingers that it would stay there until Soline discovered it.

But on the drive back to the gallery, her thoughts took a dark turn. What if Soline wasn't just holing up in her house, nursing hurt feelings? What if she were ill or hurt?

She tried Soline's number once more, letting it ring eight times before hanging up and immediately dialing Daniel Ballantine's office. As usual, his receptionist put her right through.

"Rory, good to hear from you. I trust the gallery's coming along."

"It is. Thank you. But I do need a favor."

"Shoot."

"Could you give Soline a call and make sure she's okay?"

"Why wouldn't she be?"

Rory bit her lip, wondering how much to say. "It's kind of a long story. We were having lunch the other day, and the conversation turned . . . unpleasant. The next thing I knew, she was walking away from the table. Now she isn't answering her phone, and when I went over and knocked on her door just now, she didn't answer. I'm worried."

He blew out a breath. "How long ago?"

"Four days," Rory said quietly. "I'm worried that something might have happened to her. The curtains were still closed, and there were newspapers piled up on the steps."

"Yeah," he said, drawing out the word. "She does that sometimes."

His casual tone surprised Rory. "Does what?"

"Pulls a disappearing act. Goes into hiding. Something sets her off and she just withdraws."

"You think she's just mad?"

"*Mad* probably isn't the right word. Certain things set her off, things she'd rather not deal with. Hiding is how she deals with it. I've seen her go more than a week."

"So what do you do, just wait her out?"

"Usually. She doesn't do it for attention. She genuinely wants to be left alone."

"But what if it's *not* that? What if she's sick or hurt?"

"Based on what you just told me, I'm betting she's neither. She'll resurface when she's ready."

"Could you try calling her? Or maybe go by? Maybe she'll answer the door if she knows it's you."

"Don't bet on it."

"Please."

"All right."

"And if she does, could you ask her to call me? I need to talk to her."

"I'll pass it along if I get the chance, but don't expect me to change her mind if it's already made up. She's a stubborn old bird when she wants to be. I'll see what I can do and let you know."

The next afternoon, Rory returned home from the gallery to find her answering machine blinking. The sight always made her pulse skitter, a mix of hope and dread that had become all too familiar in recent months. But none of the messages were about Hux. There were two from her mother, who she hadn't spoken to since the fiasco at Seasons, and one from Daniel asking her to call him back.

She dialed his number and was put on hold, treated to a tinny rendition of Christopher Cross's "Sailing" while she waited for him to end another call. Finally, there was a click, and Christopher Cross was gone.

"Rory?"

"Did you get hold of her?"

"No. I tried her several times last night, then went by today at lunch and rang the bell. No answer."

Rory's grip tightened on the phone. "We need to call the police and have them go by. Something's wrong."

"I don't think so. I think she's just holed up. Was the trash can out front yesterday?"

Rory closed her eyes, trying to remember. "No. I don't think so."

"Well, it's there now. And the newspapers were gone."

"Was there a note? I left a note in the crook of the door. Was it still there?"

"I didn't see it."

Rory's shoulders relaxed slightly. "Is there someone who does those kinds of things for her? A cleaning lady or helper of some kind?"

"No. There's a kid who does the lawn, but that's it."

"So what do we do?"

"We wait."

"For what?"

"For her to call one of us. But we're on *her* time. This may only be the halfway point."

"You promise you'll let me know if she calls?"

"*When* she calls," he corrected gently. "And yes, I promise."

An hour later, Rory was stretched out on the bed with a slice of cold pizza and a stack of catering menus when the phone rang. She grabbed the cordless so quickly, she nearly dropped it. "Hello?"

"I've spoken to her."

Rory closed her eyes as relief flooded through her. "And she's okay?"

"Cranky as ever. But that might have something to do with me climbing over the back hedge and sneaking up to the kitchen window. She was making coffee, and all of a sudden there I was. She screamed blue murder, I can tell you. She finally let me in, but she wouldn't give me any coffee."

"But she's okay? You're sure?"

"She's looked better, I'll admit that. But she claims she's fine. She's been having some trouble with her hands again, and the pain meds make her sleep."

"Did you tell her I've been trying to reach her?"

"She knows," he said after a slight hesitation. "She heard you when you came to the door."

"And the note?"

"She read it."

"She's not going to call, is she?"

Another pause, longer this time. "She thinks it would be better if she didn't."

"I see."

"I'm not sure you do," Daniel said quietly. "I'm not even sure I do. She's so protective of her past, but I know some of what she's been through. It wasn't easy, but she made her peace with what was left of her life after the fire by numbing herself. Then you came along, and she suddenly stopped being numb. She changed. Now something's happened. I don't know what. She didn't say. But she's crawled back into her shell."

"It was my fault. That's what I've been trying to tell her. That I'm sorry."

"She isn't angry, Rory. She just thinks it would be best if she didn't see you anymore. She asked me to thank you and to wish you well with the opening."

Rory closed her eyes, absorbing the finality of the words. "Will she change her mind, do you think?"

"Not if you push her. Give her some space. Focus on the gallery for now, and maybe try again after she's had some time. In the meantime, I'm here if you need anything."

Rory felt miserable as she ended the call. He was probably right about giving her space, but the thought of losing Soline's friendship was startlingly painful given their relatively short acquaintance. She'd been a lifeline in the beginning, a kind of mirror in which to see herself, but she'd become so much more. A friend and confidante. Her fairy godmother.

Kindred spirits.

That's how Soline had described their relationship. Strangers who shared a common past. The words had sent a chill up her spine then. Now they made her sad. It would seem the benefit of their paths crossing had been all on one side. She had received empathy and understanding when she needed it most, but in offering them, Soline had been forced to relive the loss of the only man she'd ever loved. And she'd done it without so much as a photograph for comfort.

Suddenly, the seed of an idea began to form, a way to thank Soline for her many kindnesses. But she was going to need some help.

At nine the next morning, Rory sat sipping her coffee, waiting for Doug Glennon to pick up. He was a sportswriter for the *Globe* and had married a friend of hers from Tufts a few years ago. He was a great guy, a jock with a heart of gold, and absolutely crazy about Kelly. She didn't know him well, but they'd hung out a handful of times, and Kelly had assured her he'd be willing to help and had promised to mention it when he came in last night.

"This is Doug."

"Doug," Rory blurted, startled after being on hold so long. "It's Aurora Grant—Rory. I don't know if you remember me, but I was one of Kelly's bridesmaids. I spoke to her yesterday, and she said I should give you a call."

"Rory. The swimmer, right? Kelly said you called. What can I do for you?"

"I was hoping you could do me a favor. I have a friend who lost someone in the war—an ambulance driver she was engaged to marry—and I found out she doesn't have a picture of him. I was hoping I could find one and frame it for her as a gift."

"We're talking Vietnam?"

"World War II."

Doug whistled softly. "Forty years. How old is this friend of yours?"

"I know. It's been a long time, but I thought there might be one in some archive somewhere. I know it's not your usual thing, but I know reporters have access to lots of old records. He was from a prominent family in Newport. They made boats, I think. Racing boats. So I'm hoping there's a shot of him in an old newspaper or something."

"Why not just contact the family and ask for one?"

Rory bit her lip. "Let's just say they're not inclined to be helpful."

"Right. Got it."

"I don't want you to do anything that would get you in trouble at work, but I'd love to be able to do this for her. Do you think you can help me?"

"What's the name?"

"Purcell," Rory blurted before he could change his mind. "Anson Purcell. Middle initial *W*. He was a driver with the AFS, if that helps."

"It might. Anything else that could help me narrow it down? Date of birth? Relatives?"

"No to the date of birth, but his father's name was Owen, and he had a sister named Cynthia."

"Owen and Cynthia Purcell of Newport, Rhode Island. Okay. I'll see what I can do. There might be an old yearbook photo somewhere or a graduation photo. Give me a few days to do some digging. I'll be in touch when I know something."

Rory left her number, thanking him profusely before hanging up. She would do what Daniel said. She would give Soline space while she concentrated on the opening, and then in a few weeks, she'd write a letter and send it with the photo of Anson. As a token of friendship—or a parting gift if she preferred.

THIRTY-SIX

RORY

September 23, 1985—Boston

Rory walked through the door of her apartment, exhausted but happy. She'd taken the early ferry to P-town to meet with Helen Blum, a modernist bronze artist recommended by Kendra Paterson. It was one of the things she loved most about budding artists, their unfailing generosity toward other members of their community. Without it, she'd still be trying to scrape together enough artists to open her doors next month.

She kicked off her shoes and made a beeline for the phone. It had been three days since her conversation with Doug, and she was beginning to worry that no news might be *bad* news—as in no photo. The message light was flashing. She pushed "Play." The first message was from her mother, another invitation to dinner, and still no mention of the lunch. Apparently, she was still trying to pretend it never happened.

The second message was from Doug. *Call me. I think I've got what you're looking for.*

She dialed his number at the paper, then punched in his extension, hoping he hadn't already left for the day. She hated the idea of bothering him at home, but she wasn't sure she could wait until tomorrow.

"Doug Glennon."

"Hey, it's Rory. I got your message."

"It took a little doing, but I finally hit the jackpot. I've got two headshots. One's a college yearbook photo; the other is him in uniform, taken by the local paper right before he shipped out. Clean-cut, all-American type. You want the current stuff too?"

"Current stuff?" Rory repeated with a sinking feeling. He'd found the wrong guy. "The Anson Purcell I'm talking about died in World War II, probably somewhere near Paris. He was an ambulance driver for the AFS."

"Yeah. That's the guy. But he didn't die in France. Or anyplace else, for that matter. He's alive and well, and quite the philanthropist, apparently."

"No. That's impossible."

"Impossible or not, I'm looking at an article that says he made a sizable donation to the ADL in March. Sounds like he's loaded, and a hero to boot. Captured, it says. Badly wounded. The dates fit; I can fax it over if you want, but I'm telling you, it's the guy."

Rory sagged onto the bed, her head suddenly full of white noise. There'd been some kind of mix-up. Perhaps Thia had a son and had named him after her brother. But the dates . . . "I don't have a fax machine," she replied finally. "How long will you be there?"

"I should already be gone. We're having dinner with Kelly's folks, and I can't be late again. I could put it all in an envelope, though, and leave it at the front desk on my way out. Would that work?"

"I'll be by within the hour to pick it up."

Rory sat staring at the phone after she hung up. It couldn't be true. But what if it was? How would Soline take the news? Not well, if her current seclusion was any indication. The only thing more agonizing than a lost love was one that had been purposely thrown away.

Forty-five minutes later, she was sitting in the parking lot of the *Globe* building in Dorchester, staring at a manila envelope with her name penned in heavy black marker across the front. It had taken every ounce of willpower she possessed not to open it right there in the lobby, but she'd managed to make it back in the car.

She clicked on the dome light, then fumbled with the string clasp and slid the contents out into her lap. There were several Xeroxed newspaper articles. The first was the piece Doug had mentioned, praising the Purcell Foundation for its history of philanthropic endeavors, including a recent seven-figure donation to the Anti-Defamation League. The next article had to do with being given a Lifetime Service Award by the New England Leadership Council, and offered a bit more background:

> Since ending his tenure as the director of financial resources for the International Federation of the Red Cross (IFRC), Mr. Purcell continues to serve the organization as a policy consultant and negotiation specialist, is associated with numerous humanitarian organizations, and sits on the boards of several NGOs and charitable trusts. He is also currently a member of the board of directors for Purcell Industries Ltd., where he serves along with his sister in an advisory capacity. In 1941, prior to the United States joining the war, Mr. Purcell left Yale for France, where he volunteered with the American Field Service (AFS), driving an ambulance and working at the American Hospital in Paris, until he was gravely wounded during the successful extraction

of a downed RAF pilot. He was captured and held in a German prison camp for nearly five months, where he struggled to recover from his injuries. When the war ended, Purcell spent two years with specialists in Switzerland, learning to walk again. As an only son and heir to a sizable fortune, he could hardly have been blamed had he opted to step into his father's shoes as CEO of the family business, along with all the perks the position entailed. Instead, he chose a life of service and philanthropy, earning the gratitude of the Leadership Council of New England and of this publication.

Rory laid the article aside, staring at the grainy photos beneath. She had never laid eyes on Anson Purcell, and yet the young man looking back at her seemed eerily familiar. She couldn't remember Soline ever describing him in any detail, but somehow his face felt . . . right. Pale eyes and a wave of fair hair, a mouth that was at once sensuous and serious. He was wearing a dark suit with a narrow tie. Below the photograph, she could make out part of a blurry caption—ANSON WILLIAM PURCELL, CLASS OF 1941.

He was dressed in khakis in the second photo, a leather jacket slung rakishly over one shoulder, like Van Johnson or Tab Hunter, the handsome, wholesome American hero. This was what he had looked like the first time Soline laid eyes on him. And the last time.

There was one more photograph, a five-by-seven color shot taken fairly recently. Rory stared at it, a hand to her mouth. For a man in his sixties, he was still strikingly handsome, with an athletic build and a head of silver-gold waves men half his age would envy. But he wasn't the young Anson of the yearbook photo or the dashing Anson in uniform. Deep lines fanned out from his eyes, and the once-square jawline had softened with time.

And there was something different about the mouth. The earlier sensuousness was gone, leaving a firm, almost grim line in its place. Not a mouth used to smiling, Rory concluded. There was pain there, old pain that had hardened over the years. But then, after what he'd endured at the hands of the Nazis, he was probably entitled. And yet, he'd dedicated his life to good works.

A barrage of questions assailed her as she continued to stare at the photo of present-day Anson. Captured and held for five months. Two years in Switzerland, learning to walk again. What had gone through his mind when he returned to find Soline gone? What had his father told him about her—and about the baby? And more importantly, why had he not come looking for her? Or perhaps he had looked and hadn't been able to find her. That seemed unlikely, though, given his obvious resources. Was it possible time and events had simply blunted his feelings for her?

The last question sent a prickle of dread through her. Perhaps because it struck too close to home. For months, she'd been fixated on Hux coming home to her, safe and sound and whole. Not once had she let herself imagine him returning a changed man, broken and tormented by what he might have endured at the hands of his captors.

Rory shoved the thought down as she gathered the photos and clippings and slid them back into their envelope, preferring to focus on the matter at hand. She had asked Doug to dig up a photo of a dead man, and instead, he'd managed to dig up the man himself. And now she was going to have to figure out how to tell Soline that the man she'd been mourning for more than forty years was very much alive.

One thing was certain. She wasn't breathing a word about any of it until she'd looked Anson Purcell in the eye and gotten some answers. Soline deserved at least that much.

THIRTY-SEVEN

RORY

September 24, 1985—Newport

Rory pulled into the parking lot and cut the engine, then glanced at the Post-it note stuck to the dash one more time. *Purcell Industries Ltd., 6 Commercial Wharf, Newport, Rhode Island.* This was the place. Not an ideal venue for the kind of conversation she was about to have, but it was the only address directory assistance had.

She grabbed her purse and headed up a meticulously landscaped walk toward a pair of smoked glass doors. It was a massive building of dark red brick, with a steeply pitched roof and arched windows that gave it the look of an old mill or railroad depot.

She hesitated as she reached the door, noting the elaborate matching logos etched into the glass. Was she really doing this? Ambushing a stranger at his place of business and demanding to know why he wasn't dead? And when all was said and done, what did she think she was going to accomplish? Perhaps the whole thing was better left alone. Except she was here now, after a nearly two-hour drive, with a long list of unanswered questions. If he refused to talk to her, all she'd have lost was half a day and a tank of gas.

She pulled back the door, stepping aside to let a man in navy shorts and deck shoes exit. The interior was clean and open with a high blue ceiling meant to mirror the sky and gleaming floors of honey-hued teak. There was a tall glass reception desk, where the Purcell Industries logo was again on display. Rory cleared her throat as she approached, hoping to convey the kind of confidence her mother displayed when entering a room.

The receptionist lifted her head, smiling. "Good morning. How can I help you?"

"I'm here to see Mr. Purcell."

The woman's smile slipped as she peered at Rory over half-moon glasses. "Mr. Purcell?"

"Anson Purcell," Rory clarified, realizing there might be more than one.

She smiled politely but with the slightest shake of her head. "I'm sorry, Mr. Purcell doesn't work in this office. If you care to tell me what it is you were hoping to discuss, I might be able to direct you to the correct party."

She was the gatekeeper, Rory realized, strategically positioned to prevent random women from wandering in off the street to ask impertinent questions. "It isn't business-related. I'm here about a friend of his. An old friend of the family, actually," she added, thinking of Thia. "Do you know how I might get in touch with him?"

"I'm sorry. I can't give out that information, but if you'd like to leave a contact number, I could pass it along to his assistant."

Rory did her best to maintain her smile. "Is Thia here, by any chance?"

The receptionist's brows lifted, a blend of wariness and surprise. "Thia?"

"Anson's sister, Cynthia. I've come from Boston, and it's quite important that I speak to one of them as soon as possible."

The woman regarded Rory again—and then the barest of nods. "What is your name, please?"

"Aurora Grant."

"Thank you. If you'll just give me a moment."

She reached for the phone and punched in a number, twirling a pen while she waited for someone to pick up. "Yes, it's Paulette," she said, sitting up a little straighter in her chair. "I'm sorry to disturb you, but there's a young woman here asking to see Mr. Purcell. When I explained that he doesn't work here, she asked to talk to you. She's from Boston. She says it's about an old friend of the family."

She paused, covering the mouthpiece, and glanced up at Rory. "She wants to know who the friend is."

Rory hesitated, weighing how much to say. She'd do herself no favors by being indiscreet with the family's secrets. "Tell her it's a very close friend of her brother's—from the war."

Paulette repeated Rory's words verbatim, listened a moment, then nodded pertly. "Yes. Thank you." She hung up the phone and reached for a notepad, jotting down an address and a hastily scribbled map. "Ms. Purcell says you're to come to the house. This is the address. Someone will meet you at the gate."

Rory tried not to look astonished as she took the slip of paper and dropped it into her purse, as if this were exactly what she'd expected to happen. "Thank you so much for your help, Paulette."

It took less than fifteen minutes to reach the address on Bellevue Avenue. She turned into the drive, coming to a halt before an ornate iron gate. A woman in faded overalls and a wide-brimmed straw hat scrambled up off her knees, abandoning her garden and her pile of weeds. She tilted her sunglasses down, peering at Rory.

"My name is Aurora Grant," Rory called as the woman approached. "I'm here to see Cynthia Purcell."

"Paulette said you came from Boston."

Rory ran her eyes over the woman, registering the similarities. The silvery-gold curls peeking out from beneath the straw hat, the pale eyes and wide mouth. "Are you Thia?"

She brushed off her hands and parked them on her hips. "Why are you here?"

"I was hoping to speak to your brother about his fiancée."

She adjusted her hat to better shade her eyes. "My brother doesn't have a fiancée."

"But he *did* have one during the war. I'd like to talk to him about Soline Roussel."

"Right," Thia replied with a peculiar crispness. "You'd better come inside."

Rory parked at the top of the drive, trying to imagine Soline, fresh off the boat from war-torn Paris, taking in the grandeur of the Purcell family home. It was just short of palatial, three stories of cream-and-gray-colored stone with high mullioned windows and a dizzying number of gables.

If not for the interference of Owen Purcell, Soline might be mistress of this house. She would have been here when the news arrived that Anson was, in fact, alive. And when he came home, she would have been here to help him recover from his injuries. There would have been a wedding and children. Happiness instead of sorrow. Joy instead of grief.

If not for Owen.

Thia said nothing as she led Rory to the mudroom at the back of the house. She kicked off her shoes, hung her hat on a peg just inside the door, and headed for the kitchen sink. "Let me scrub up, and I'll pour us some lemonade."

Rory tried to be inconspicuous as she studied Anson's sister. She was somewhere in her fifties, tall and earthy with sun-kissed cheeks and heavy wheat-colored waves that fell past her shoulders. That she was related to the man in the photographs couldn't be denied, but there was something else, some quality she couldn't put her finger on, that, in spite of the uncomfortable nature of her visit, put Rory at ease.

"Thank you for agreeing to see me," she said as Thia filled a pair of tall glasses with ice and lemonade. "I know this must be . . . awkward."

Thia handed off one of the glasses, then sipped from her own, her pale eyes meeting Rory's over the rim. "Perhaps we should go into my study, where we won't be interrupted. Nadine's here today doing the blinds, and the woman has ears like a bat."

It suddenly occurred to Rory that Thia might have jumped to the wrong conclusion about why she'd come. "I'm not here to cause trouble, Ms. Purcell. I don't want anything from you, if that's what you think."

"I know why you're here. I've known since Paulette phoned. Come with me."

Thia's study was at the back of the house, an airy room with interesting art on the walls—her own?—and an antique writing desk positioned dead center. Behind the desk, a pair of french doors led out to a small patio. Thia closed them, then pointed to a peach-colored sofa, indicating that they should sit.

She settled across from Rory, her grass-stained overalls and bare feet strangely at odds with the room's feminine decor. "Where should we begin?"

Her matter-of-fact tone was a little unsettling. Rory took a sip from her glass to regroup, then met Thia's gaze. "With Soline."

Thia nodded. "I've thought of her over the years, wondering if she were still alive and if she ever found happiness." Her voice was thick with remembered fondness. "How is she?"

"Life has left her a bit fragile, but she's managed to cope. She told me she lived here once."

"When I was a girl, yes."

"And she left abruptly. Do you know why?"

"My father drove her away." She paused, staring into her glass. "No, that's not true. He *sent* her away. She and my brother were going to be married when he came home, and then . . ."

"The telegram came."

"That he'd gone missing, yes. They found his ambulance all shot up. There was blood everywhere, but no body. Just his jacket in the road with a bullet hole through it. Someone—a farmer, I think—saw the Nazis marching him into the woods. It wasn't unusual for them to shoot someone and drag their body into the woods to bury. Sometimes they just left them for the animals. My father didn't tell me about any of it until Anson was safely in Switzerland."

"But no one ever told Soline your brother was alive."

"No, he'd sent her away by then. I was shuffled off to boarding school a few days after the first telegram and was still there when the second arrived. Conveniently out of the way."

"Because he never meant for them to be married. Not from the minute she set foot in this house."

Thia's eyes narrowed. "You seem to be in possession of a lot of information, Miss Grant. What, may I ask, is your connection to Ms. Roussel?"

"I'm a friend," Rory replied, hoping it was still true. "And I lease a building from her for a gallery I'm opening next month. That's how we met. I found some things of hers when I took possession and offered to meet her to return them. One of the items belonged to your brother, a shaving kit with his initials on it."

Thia closed her eyes briefly, lower lip quivering. "She kept it all these years."

"You remember it, then."

Thia nodded. "My father took it from her. He didn't want her to have anything of my brother's when she left—and certainly not anything with his initials on it. I thought it was terribly mean of him, so

I snuck into his room and found it, then slipped it into her box when she went down for breakfast."

"It was you," Rory said, smiling. No wonder Soline had adored her. "She assumed it was your father. She thought he might have been sorry about the way he'd treated her."

Thia's mouth thinned. "My father didn't believe in guilt, Miss Grant. Or love. To him, they were signs of weakness."

"Do you know *why* he sent Soline away?" Rory asked quietly. "The *real* reason?"

Thia stared into her lemonade. "I didn't then. But I know now." She glanced up, sighing. "I know a lot of things now. I suspect you do too."

"The baby, you mean."

"Yes. The baby."

"Her name was Assia," Rory said softly, remembering that the child would have been Thia's niece. "It means 'comforter.' Soline wanted so much to have a piece of your brother to hold on to, to keep his memory alive through their daughter. When she died . . ."

Thia set down her glass and clasped her hands tightly in her lap. "There are pieces of the story you don't know, Ms. Grant. Pieces no one knows except me. And even I didn't know them until recently. Soline's baby didn't die."

Rory stared at her, confused, then horrified. "What are you saying?"

"I assumed you knew and that was why you were here."

Rory shook her head, struggling to digest what she'd just been told. "How could I know? How is it even possible?"

"My father paid people to lie," Thia replied evenly. "To say the baby died so Soline could never come back and make a claim on my brother. He didn't care what happened to either of them when he thought Anson was dead. He just wanted them off his hands. But when that second telegram arrived, he knew Anson could never know about the child. He had to be sure there was no chance of her ever turning up with a baby in her arms. So he wrote a nice fat check—to arrange for a discreet adoption. Then he wrote to Anson in Switzerland, saying Soline had run out on him, that she had refused to tie herself to a cripple. He needed my brother to hate her so completely that he'd never even think about looking for her."

A wave of disgust washed through Rory as she listened to Thia lay the details end to end. "Your father thought of everything."

"Yes."

Rory dragged a hand through her hair. She had no words for what she was feeling. Rage. Loathing. Raw grief. None of it seemed adequate. To steal a woman's child and sell it to strangers. His own flesh and blood. It was unconscionable. And it would fall to her to break the news to Soline.

"I haven't even told Soline that Anson is alive. How am I supposed to tell her this?"

Thia's brows shot up. "You came here without telling her?"

"I just found out yesterday, and before I said a word, I needed to understand what happened and why. Soline's been through so much over the years, and it's left her fragile. I was worried about how she'd take the news that the man she loved with all her heart came home from the war and never bothered to look for her."

"It wasn't Anson's fault," Thia said abruptly. "When my father told him Soline left because she didn't want him if he was going to be a cripple, it broke something in him. It's why he opted to stay in Switzerland for his rehabilitation—and because my father persuaded him it was the best place for him. And he did learn to walk again, but he came home so broken and bitter I hardly recognized him."

"But you told him the truth when he finally came home, didn't you? About the baby and what your father had done?"

"How could I tell him? I didn't know myself until my father died and I had to go through his papers." She stood, crossing to a nearby closet, and threw open the door, revealing a stack of cardboard storage boxes. "This is what putting your father's affairs in order looks like.

Anson was out of the country when he died—naturally—so it fell to me. I had no idea the man was such a pack rat. I threw out tons. And then one day, I came across this."

After a few moments of poking around, she produced a dark-red ledger book held closed with a pair of heavy rubber bands. "It was headed for the throwaway pile until I looked closely at the entries—and what else I found inside."

"What is it?"

"The truth," Thia replied as she pulled off the rubber bands and handed it to Rory. "It's all there. All the payments and the paperwork, everything my father needed to erase Soline and the baby from our lives. I need you to look at it before I say more."

The words felt vaguely ominous, hovering between them like a threat. Rory held her breath as she opened the book. The name *D. Sheridan* nearly leapt off the page. She remembered Soline mentioning her, but seeing it here, presumably in Owen's handwriting, made her sick to her stomach. There were other names too: a Dr. Marcus Hartwell, an Elliot Mason, Esq. A doctor, a lawyer, and the Family Aid Society.

Thia hovered as Rory began turning the pages, scanning long lists of entries. Charitable contribution. Medical expenses. Charitable contribution. Charitable contribution. Court fees. Documents. Charitable contribution. The first entry had been made on October 24, 1943, the last on August 12, 1972. Dates. Dollar amounts. It was all so neat, so careful, as if the entries were mere business expenditures.

"Twenty-eight years," Rory breathed, still staring at the book. "The entries become more sporadic over time, but some of these payments are five figures."

"Hush money," Thia said matter-of-factly. "At least that's my guess. He would have been ruined if word got out that he'd paid to get rid of his own grandchild. And there was Anson to consider. He knew the Purcell dynasty would topple if Anson caught so much as a whiff of this.

Not that it mattered. Anson never wanted it to begin with. I'm sure my father's spinning in his grave as we speak, knowing I'm mistress of his house and running the family business."

"Anson didn't want it?"

Thia shook her head sadly. "My brother hasn't spent a collective month under this roof since he came back from Switzerland. Not that I blame him. There was always so much unhappiness here after my mother died. My father was never a kind man, but he got worse when he lost her. You'd think the idea of a grandchild would have softened him."

"How long have you known about all of this?"

"Four months, give or take."

"And Anson still doesn't know?"

"No."

Rory struggled to keep her tone even. "You didn't think your brother should know he and Soline had a daughter?"

"Of course I did." Thia's eyes pooled with tears. "I've thought of little else since I found that book. I had no idea what to do with what I'd learned. I tried to tell him once, when he called from London on my birthday, but he threatened to hang up and never call again if I so much as mentioned her name, and I believed him." She shook her head, chin quivering. "Soline isn't the only one left fragile by all of this. What happened during the war changed my brother. Coming home finished him."

"But he knew her, Thia. He loved her. I don't understand how he could believe your father's lies about a woman he loved."

"He didn't at first. In fact, they fought like sailors over the things my father would say about her, that she'd always been after his money, but in the end, even that hadn't been enough to make her stay if it meant pushing her husband around in a wheelchair. It was like he was punishing Anson for loving her. There were times when I was afraid they would come to blows over her."

"So what changed?"

"I don't know. One day it was as if someone flipped a switch. All of a sudden, Anson refused to even say her name. And he didn't want anyone else saying it either. It's still that way. Anytime I've tried to talk to him about it, he's ended the conversation. It's like she poisoned him."

"That must have made your father happy."

"I suspect it did. He got what he wanted. But then, he usually did. Even if it meant destroying the people he was supposed to love. He certainly destroyed Anson."

"And the baby," Rory replied. "He just gave her away. His own grandchild, and he had no idea where she was or what happened to her."

"Oh, he knew." Thia's eyes slid away. Her voice had taken on that ominous quality again. "The woman who ran the Family Aid Society sent him a copy of the adoption decree, proof that his money had been well spent. That's the kind of monster he was. No concern for the child, just his plans for Anson and the Purcell empire."

"How very tidy."

"That was my father, determined to get what he wanted at any cost. And Dorothy Sheridan was only too happy to help—for a fee, of course. I did some checking when I found the ledger. It appears the police got wind of Miss Sheridan's enterprise in 1972. That's why the entries in the ledger stop. She disappeared, and my father was finally off the hook."

Rory felt cold all over. "It's inconceivable. Soline has spent forty years grieving a daughter she believed dead and buried, and she's been out there the whole time. How could a woman do something so despicable to another woman?"

Thia studied her through narrowed eyes. "You seem awfully protective of her. Driving all this way. Asking all these questions."

"Yesterday a friend of mine, a reporter who was helping me dig up a photo of your dead brother, unearthed one taken two years ago. I think questions are in order."

"Why did you want a picture of Anson?"

Once again, Rory felt she was being accused of something, and it irked her. "I wanted to frame it and give it to Soline as a gift. Because she's my friend. She was your friend, too, once."

"Yes. She was."

Thia's voice was softer now. Rory felt herself soften too. "She told me about your sketches and the dresses she made for you, how you wanted to live in a garret and paint. It broke her heart that she never got to say goodbye, but your father wouldn't let her."

Thia pulled her arms around herself protectively. "He sent me to some horrible all-girls' school. When I came home, she was gone. I thought she'd abandoned us—abandoned me. By the time Anson came home, I'd grown to hate her. Not only for leaving me but for leaving him too. My brother and I were close once, but when he came home he was so cold and withdrawn. I thought if I hated her, too, it would make us close again, but it only made him angrier."

"He used you," Rory said softly. "Your father, I mean. He made you hate Soline, and then he used that hate to fuel your brother's pain."

Thia's eyes flicked to hers. "I told you he was a monster."

"I'm sorry. I realize this is hard for you too. I just wanted a picture. I never meant for it to turn into all this."

Thia blew out a long breath. "I think it's time for you to see the family photos." She rose and went to the closet, returning a few moments later with a pair of leather-bound albums. "My mother was a fanatic about family photographs. She kept an album for each of us. This is Anson's."

Rory laid the album open in her lap, the yellowed pages crackling as she flipped through the usual milestones. First Christmas. First steps. First haircut. Eventually, the chubby toddler became a schoolboy. Anson at eight or nine, in a baseball uniform, freckles, and a gap-toothed grin. There was another of him in a football uniform, down on one knee, squinting against the sun. A few pages later, he stood grinning in a dark suit and crisp white shirt, a white carnation on his lapel. Prom night.

And finally, on the next-to-the-last page, dressed in uniform khakis, his fair hair cropped close and combed back from his forehead: a boy no longer.

It was strange to see him grow up that way, a page at a time. In her mind, he'd been little more than a ghost, and now, here he was in black and white—and somewhere in the world, very much alive. She stared at the young man in the photo again, square-jawed and movie-star handsome.

"No wonder Soline fell head over heels. Your brother was gorgeous. And I can see the family resemblance. You have the same nose and cheekbones."

"We both look like our father. The same hair and eyes." She paused, folding her hands carefully in her lap. "Who do you take after?"

Rory blinked at her. "Me?"

"Would you say you look like your mother?"

It seemed a strange question, though she supposed Thia was entitled to a few questions of her own. "I have my mother's coloring, and we have the same nose, broad and straight, but she's not nearly as tall as I am. I think I must have gotten that from my father's side."

Thia opened the second album and slid it into Rory's lap. "I think you should have a look at this."

Rory found herself staring at a little girl of five or six in footie pajamas. She had a pair of perfectly matched dimples and a head full of pale ringlets. "Look at those curls. How adorable."

Thia's face remained carefully blank. "Look at the next photo and tell me what you see."

Rory squinted at the photograph, taken several years later. A ruffled party dress and lace-trimmed socks, the curls tamer now, pulled up into a messy bun pinned with tiny white flowers, like a princess or a fairy. And strangely familiar. "This is you?"

"Yes."

"My mother has almost the same picture of me. She dressed me up to play the piano for her friends, but I froze. I can't get over how alike they are."

"Who is your mother? Was she originally from Boston?"

Rory was still staring at the photo. She looked up. "I'm sorry . . . what?"

"Your mother. What's her name?"

"Camilla Grant."

"And her maiden name?"

"Lowell. Why?"

Thia slid a folded sheet of paper from beneath the remaining albums and handed it to Rory. "It's time you see this."

Rory scanned the document warily. The paper was heavy and yellow with age, neatly typed, and stamped at the top with the word *COPY* in red ink. It was dated January 17, 1945, had the words CERTIFICATE OF DECREE OF ADOPTION at the top, and was signed at the bottom by the clerk of the Circuit Court. But at that moment, there was only one word on the page that mattered—Lowell.

THIRTY-EIGHT

RORY

Rory felt her heart skitter against her ribs, like a stone skipping down the walls of a bottomless well. There was nothing to get hold of, nothing to break the sudden sensation of falling. Why was her mother's name on this piece of paper? And what was the paper doing among Owen Purcell's things? She was dimly aware of Thia beside her as she scanned the page again.

State of Rhode Island and Providence Plantations
Department of Vital Records
Certificate of Decree of Adoption.

Maiden name of natural mother: Soline Louise Roussel
Name of natural father: Unknown
Name of child at time of birth: n/a
Name of adoptive mother: Gwendolyn Lucille Lowell
Name of adoptive father: George Edward Lowell
Name of child after adoption: Camilla Nicole Lowell

Rory laid the paper in her lap and stared at it, head spinning. Her mother's name—and her mother's mother. What did it mean? Finally, she looked up at Thia. "I don't understand."

"Yes, you do."

"She's . . . You're saying . . ." She broke off again, pressing the flats of her fingers to her eyes. "I don't understand."

Thia pulled in a breath, as if gathering her words. "Your mother is the baby listed on the adoption decree, Rory. Which makes Soline your grandmother. And my brother your grandfather."

"It has to be a mistake. One of those weird coincidences you read about in the tabloids. There are Lowells all over Massachusetts."

"Look at the picture again. It's not a mistake. Or a coincidence. You can demand a blood test if you need confirmation, but I knew the instant I saw your face. You're a Purcell—because your mother was a Purcell. Or should have been."

"My mother," Rory repeated, recalling something Camilla had said once about how she'd been trained to live up to the position she'd been given as a Lowell. *Given.* It had seemed an odd word at the time, but Camilla had ended the conversation before she could delve further. Was it possible her mother knew the true circumstances of her birth and how she'd become a Lowell? And if so, why would she have kept it a secret all these years? Either way, it all led back to Soline.

Rory felt as if the floor were shifting beneath her feet, her world suddenly turning inside out. Nothing made sense. Or maybe, finally, *everything* did. Maybe there was a reason she'd felt such a strange affinity for the row house the first time she saw it, and to Soline the first time they met. Fate had pushed them together somehow. But was such a thing even possible?

She looked at Thia, sitting quietly beside her with her hands in her lap. "You're saying that after all these years, Soline and I managed to cross paths . . . by chance?"

Thia answered with a strange smile. "I never said it was by chance. I mean, it couldn't be, could it? Chance is one of those things we pull out when we have no other explanation for what's happened. But there are all kinds of things we don't understand. Forces we can't see. That doesn't mean they're not at work. And there's always been something special about Soline. Something . . . otherworldly."

"You're saying all this is the result of some kind of magic?"

Thia shrugged. "Magic. Kismet. Some fluky psychic connection. I really don't care what it is. I only care that it's happening. When Paulette told me you were asking about an old friend of my brother's, I assumed the friend was Soline. And then I saw you and I thought about those adoption papers and . . . I knew. I thought maybe you did, too, or that Soline had sent you because she suspected. Did she never mention that you look like my brother?"

"No," Rory said softly. "Never."

It was too much to absorb at one time, an avalanche of questions and emotions tumbling at her so fast there wasn't space to sort them out. Soline, her grandmother. Anson, her grandfather. Suddenly there were tears in her eyes.

She ignored them, trying to wrap her head around the implications of what she'd been told. Her mother, the proudest woman on the planet, had apparently been walking around with a phony pedigree and would soon be forced to confront the truth—that she'd actually been born out of wedlock to a woman who'd recently compared her to the Nazis. It wouldn't be an easy conversation to have. But the conversation with Soline would be worse. To learn her child had been stolen from her, that all this time she'd been right here in Boston, would be the cruelest cut of all. And after their disastrous lunch . . .

"My god, Thia. How am I supposed to tell either of them about all this?"

"I've been thinking about that, and I don't think you should. At least not straight off. My brother may still come around when he knows what really happened. In fact, I'll make sure he does. Soline has gone forty years without knowing the truth. If there's a chance that some good can come from all of this, some healing for them both, isn't it worth waiting a few more weeks?"

Rory considered this. A little time to process might be a good thing for her as well, before she tried to break the news to anyone else. Soline had to be told. But she would need someone to help hold her together when the time came, someone who understood the history and could help pick up the pieces. At the moment, they weren't even speaking. Waiting might allow her to repair the rift between them and to navigate the prickly relationship between her mother and Soline. Neither of those things was going to happen overnight.

"All right. I'll wait. When will you talk to Anson?"

"I was thinking more along the lines of you talking to him."

Rory gaped at her. "Me?"

"He's made it quite clear that he doesn't want to hear it from me. Every time I've tried, he's shut me down. He's good at that, shutting out things he doesn't want to deal with. And people. He's been alone so long, he doesn't remember what it's like to let someone into his life."

"Anson never married?"

Thia shook her head. "There's been no place in his life for anyone since Soline. Not even me. We speak at Christmas and on my birthday, but it's always very stilted. I hoped things would get better when my father died, that he might even come home, but . . ." She broke off with a shrug. "I don't even know where he is most of the time, usually out of the country. It's as if he's trying to stay one step ahead of the memories."

"And you think a total stranger is suddenly going to thaw his heart?"

"A stranger? No. His granddaughter? Maybe." Thia tapped a finger to her lips, eyes narrowed thoughtfully. She glanced at her watch. "I should still be able to catch her."

Thia stepped to the desk and picked up the phone, punching in a number with cool efficiency. "Paulette, can you check with Cheryl and see where my brother happens to be this week? Thank you."

Rory felt a bubble of panic forming in her throat. Whatever Thia Purcell had in mind, it was happening way too fast. She opened her mouth to protest, but Thia had grabbed a pen and was speaking to Paulette again.

"Yes, I'm here. No, I don't need a phone number, just his hotel." Her gaze flicked briefly to Rory. "I'm sending him something."

THIRTY-NINE

RORY

September 25, 1985—San Francisco

Rory dropped her tote and overnighter on the bed and wandered to the window, gazing out over the San Francisco skyline, the sprawling city, the glistening bay, the iconic Golden Gate Bridge just visible through a scrim of fog. It was breathtaking, like a postcard she'd received once, but she hadn't come to enjoy the sights. She was on a mission to upend a man's life.

Eight hours ago, she'd been in Boston, still trying to think of a reason not to go through with what she was about to do. And then the boarding call had come and the decision was made. She'd debated the wisdom of staying at the Fairmont. Knowing Anson was just four floors above her felt vaguely stalkerish. But her time was short. It made sense to stay where travel time was limited to an elevator ride.

On the plane, she had tried to prepare herself for what she was about to do. She had practiced her opening lines, what she would say first, what she would say next, how she would lay out the facts, like a lawyer during summation. A tidy argument for why he needed to make things right with Soline. What she hadn't prepared for was coming face-to-face with the grandfather who, until twenty-four hours ago, she hadn't known existed.

How did one bridge that kind of gap? Twenty-three years without a grandfather and suddenly there was Anson Purcell. Absorbing the news that Soline was her grandmother had been hard enough, but at least they had formed a bond before she learned the truth. There was no bond with Anson, nothing but Soline's memories to connect them. She'd heard the stories, people feeling an instant affinity upon meeting a newly discovered relative for the first time, others feeling nothing at all. Which would *she* be? She honestly couldn't say, and for now she needed to stay focused on the mission at hand.

Returning to her tote, she pulled out the ledger Thia had sent with her—the proof she would need to convince Anson of his father's deception. She had the photographs too: the one of young Thia in her party dress and the one of her, taken the day of her impromptu recital. She had borrowed the latter from her mother's curio cabinet while Camilla was at her weekly bridge game last night. She'd been careful to rearrange the remaining objects on the shelf, so as not to leave an empty spot. With any luck, the frame would be back where it belonged before her mother noticed. Once she knew where Anson fit into the picture, she'd break the news to both her mother and Soline.

She glanced at her watch, still set to Boston time, and subtracted three hours. Almost 6:00 p.m. in San Francisco. She'd booked her return ticket for tomorrow afternoon, in order to be back in time for the final walk-through with Brian. That gave her twenty-four hours to do what she'd come to do. She checked Thia's note for Anson's room number, then picked up the phone and asked for room 903. A male voice answered on the third ring.

"Mr. Purcell?"

"Yes."

"My name is Rory Grant. Your sister, Thia, told me where I might reach you."

"What can I help you with?"

His voice was intimidating, crisp and all business. Suddenly every word she'd practiced during the flight seemed lodged in her throat. "I'm a friend of Soline Roussel's," she blurted finally. She held her breath, waiting for a click. It didn't come. "Mr. Purcell?"

"What is it you want?"

"She doesn't know I'm here or that I've spoken to your sister. I'd like to talk to you about what happened after Paris. There are things you should know. Things I think you'd *want* to know."

"There's nothing you can say that I want to hear, Miss Grant. Good night."

"No! Wait! Please let me talk to you in person. What I have to say won't take long, but it's not the kind of thing that should be said over the phone."

Another yawning silence. But he hadn't hung up.

"Please, Mr. Purcell. It's important. I'm here at the hotel, but I'll meet you wherever you say. Whenever you say." She bit her lip, breath held as she waited.

"The bar downstairs. Thirty minutes."

Rory arrived early and took a table in the corner. It was a small bar connected to the hotel restaurant, subdued yet elegant, with creamy lighting, creamy carpeting, and creamy marble pillars framing the doorways. Piano music tinkled over the low hum of conversation, Cole Porter's "Night and Day." It was soothing and pleasant, but she couldn't relax. Her eyes were trained on the door.

She was glad to see that most of the tables were full. Less chance of a scene. She ordered a glass of chardonnay. Not because she wanted it but because she needed something to occupy her hands. She was about to take her first sip when Anson appeared. She knew him instantly. Tall and square-shouldered, with a head full of silver-blond waves, a handsome man despite his sixty-some years.

Her grandfather.

The realization brought an unexpected lump to her throat. *Not now, Aurora. Don't start blubbering, or you'll never get through this.* But the sight of him, just a few yards away, made it hard to breathe. She gulped a mouthful of wine, her hands suddenly clammy. She wasn't sure what she'd expected, but it wasn't this gut-tightening reaction.

He was still hovering in the doorway, running his eyes around the tables. She held her breath, waiting for his eyes to connect with hers, then lifted a hand. He made no attempt to smile as he approached, his face set in what Rory suspected was a perpetual grimace. He had a noticeable limp, but walked like a man who'd lived with it a good many years and had learned to compensate.

He avoided her gaze as he pulled out the chair across from her and sat. Before a word was spoken, a waitress appeared with a highball glass that looked to be a gin and tonic with two lime wedges. He nodded his thanks. She eyed Rory with a measure of curiosity, then turned back to Anson. "Will you be needing menus, Mr. Purcell?"

"No, thank you, Ellie. We won't be here that long."

A regular at the hotel, then, with a regular drink order. And he'd just made it crystal clear that her window of opportunity was a narrow one.

When Ellie was gone, he picked up his glass and leaned back in his chair, eyeing her coldly. If there was even a flicker of recognition, he gave no sign. "All right. Why am I here?"

"I'm a friend of Soline's."

"You said that on the phone."

His icy tone was intimidating, and he knew it. "She speaks of you often."

316

"Does she?"

"About how you met at the hospital and the work you did there—the work you both did—for the Resistance. And how you made her leave to keep her safe. Because you loved her."

He stared at her, unblinking. "Did I? It's all so fuzzy now."

There it was. The bitterness Thia had talked about. Pain hardened into hostility and sarcasm. And yet there was an edge to his nonchalance, a sullenness that told her Anson Purcell wasn't nearly as detached from his memories as he pretended.

"She told me about your last night together," Rory said, watching him closely. "How you asked her to marry you, and how she watched you through the back window of the ambulance until it turned the corner and you disappeared."

"You're quite the storyteller."

"It didn't happen that way?"

Anson stared down into his drink. "I don't remember."

"I think you do. So does your sister."

"What is it you want from me, Miss Grant?"

"I want you to remember how much you loved her and how much she loved you. Before you came home and your father poisoned you against her. There are things you don't know."

He took a sip from his glass, swallowing hard. "Here's what I do know. I know I pulled every string there was to pull to get her to the States. I greased every palm, called in every IOU, and when none of that worked, I threw my father's name around to keep her safe. I also know that when she found out I was laid up in Switzerland with a hole in my gut and a pair of legs that might be hacked off any day, she bolted for greener pastures. I've got to hand it to her, though, most women would have hung around for the money. I guess she let me off easy."

"Don't do that," Rory said, more sharply than she'd intended. "Don't remember it that way. It isn't true."

317

Anson set down his glass with a heavy thunk. "But it is, Ms. Grant. It gives me no pleasure to admit it, but I let myself be taken for the oldest ride in the book. My father, on the other hand, got a great deal of satisfaction out of being proved right."

Rory reached for her wineglass, sipping slowly. It was painful to hear him say such horrible things about Soline, but equally painful to realize he actually believed them. "Your father lied to you."

Anson stiffened, bristling now. "Miss Grant—"

"He lied," she said again. "About why Soline left and where she went. It was all a lie. She didn't leave you. Your father kicked her out. Thia knows. She didn't then, but she does now. That's why I'm here—to talk about what *really* happened."

Anson sat very still, his face devoid of emotion. "This is what you needed to discuss with me? This ridiculous, cooked-up story?"

"Do I look familiar to you?" Rory asked, realizing there was only one way to make him understand. "Look at my face. My eyes. My nose. Do I remind you of anyone?"

Anson's eyes narrowed warily. "What is this?" His whole body was coiled for an attack, his jaw rigid. "I don't know what you're playing at, but I can tell you it isn't going to work."

"I'm not playing at anything. And I think you should start calling me Rory. Or Aurora, if you prefer."

"I have no intention of calling you anything." He shoved his chair back and pushed to his feet. "This conversation is over."

Tiny needles of panic prickled through Rory's limbs. If he walked out now, she'd never get another chance. "Soline had a baby," she blurted. "Your baby."

Anson froze.

"Assia," she added quietly. "Your daughter's name was Assia."

He pivoted stiffly, dropping back into his chair, as if the weight of what he'd just heard was too much for his legs. Rory pulled her tote into her lap, withdrawing the photos and setting them side by side on the table. "Do you know what these are?"

Anson studied the photos a moment, then returned his gaze to Rory. "They're pictures of my sister. A birthday party, I think."

Rory nodded. "One of them is." She pointed to the photograph on his right. "This one. But this . . ." She paused, pointing to the photo on the left. "Is a photo of your granddaughter—your daughter's little girl—when she was eight. She'll be twenty-four in January."

Anson sat stonily, arms folded. "Until fifteen minutes ago, I'd never laid eyes on you, but you expect me to believe this on your say-so?"

"Not just mine." She reached into her tote for the ledger and placed it in front of her on the table. "Your father's."

He eyed the book warily. "What is that?"

"Thia found it among your father's things after he died. Lucky for us, he was meticulous about keeping records. And they line up perfectly with what Soline told me. He arranged for her to go to a home for unwed mothers. And by arranged, I mean paid. Only, when the baby came, they told Soline she died. Then they gave her to a wealthy couple from Boston. Their name was Lowell. They renamed the baby Camilla. Eventually, Camilla married a man named Geoffrey Grant and had a daughter of her own—a daughter named Aurora, Rory for short."

It took several seconds, but eventually her words seemed to penetrate. "It isn't . . ."

"But it is. It's why you thought both these photos were of Thia. I look like her because I'm her grandniece. I also look like you . . . because I'm your granddaughter."

His face grew dark. "If you think you're going to get a cent—"

Rory slid the ledger to his side of the table, effectively cutting him off. "It's all there. Every penny your father spent, including what look to be blackmail payments. There's also a decree of adoption naming Soline as the birth mother. The father's name is listed as unknown, but the date of birth lines up perfectly with your last night together in Paris."

Anson closed his eyes, as if the mention of that night brought him physical pain. After a moment he opened them again and cleared his throat. "My father lived by his own set of priorities, Ms. Grant, and nothing got in his way. He had plans for me, and those plans didn't include a wife unless she had the Owen Purcell stamp of approval. I don't doubt he did what you're accusing him of. In fact, it sounds just like him. But in this case, he had good reason to doubt the sincerity of my . . . fiancée."

The way he pronounced the word *fiancée* made Rory's blood simmer. "How can you say that? She was pregnant with your child when he sent her away."

"I don't suppose it ever occurred to you that I might not have been the *only* man in Soline's life. And that there might be a very simple explanation for why the father is listed as unknown—she didn't know herself."

Rory stared at him, stunned by his feigned indifference. And it *was* feigned. She could see it in the set of his jaw and in the way he gripped the base of his glass, so tightly his knuckles went white. He couldn't let himself believe the truth because it meant he'd thrown away too much.

"You don't believe that," she said evenly. "I know you don't."

A muscle ticked along Anson's jaw. "I think I should be the judge of what I believe and what I don't. She's convinced you that she's some kind of martyr, but I happen to know better. It doesn't matter how; I just do. So let's dispense with the fairy tale that she's spent the last forty years nursing a broken heart."

"She never married."

Anson lifted his glass, nearly empty now, and stared into the dregs. "That's no business of mine."

"Isn't it?"

"Do I need to point out the obvious? She didn't come looking for me either."

"Why would she look for you? She thought you were dead."

Anson's head came up sharply. "Dead?"

Finally, she seemed to have his attention. "Your father had already sent her away when news came that you were alive, and he was perfectly fine with letting her go on believing you were dead. And to let you believe she'd walked out on you. He didn't just send her away. He made sure she'd have no reason to ever come back."

Anson met her gaze with strained calm. "That's quite a story."

"Your sister can verify what I'm saying if you don't want to take my word. She was crushed when Soline left, but she only knew what your father told her—the same thing he told you. Then she found the ledger and started putting the pieces together. She tried to tell you, but you wouldn't let her. She thought you might listen to me."

For an instant, Rory thought she saw something flicker in Anson's eyes, a chink in his icy armor, but it was gone almost instantly. "I understand my sister having a blind spot. They were close once. But I'm curious. What is all this to you? After all these years, why do you care? You're a bit old for piggyback rides and camping trips with Grandpa. What is it you see happening here?"

"Why do I care?" Rory echoed, stung to the point of tears by his cavalier response. "Soline is my grandmother. And even if she wasn't, she's still my friend. I don't want *anything* from you. I'm just trying to right a forty-year-old wrong. Because I know what she went through when you went missing, the hell of not knowing if you were alive or dead, to never know what happened or even say goodbye. I know what that feels like. I know it firsthand." She turned to wipe the tears from her face, mortified to have veered into such personal territory.

"Ms. Grant . . ."

When she looked up, Anson was holding out a crisply folded handkerchief. The monogram was in dark blue now, but it was there. A.W.P. She took it, blotting her eyes. "I'm sorry. I didn't mean to get emotional, but this is a lot to digest for me, too, and I really do know what it's like to lose someone the way she did. To never know . . ."

His entire bearing seemed to change as he leaned forward, arms folded on the edge of the table. "Your husband?"

The lines around his mouth and eyes had softened, making him look younger—and so much like Camilla that she felt herself relax. "My fiancé, Hux. Sorry, his name is actually Matthew, but his last name is Huxley so everyone calls him Hux."

"What happened?"

"He's with the MSF—Doctors Without Borders—in South Sudan. He's a pediatrician. There was a raid early one morning at the clinic where he was working. A truck pulled up and abducted him and two others. It's been nine months, and no one seems to know anything."

"I'm sorry. That's a tough part of the world right now, so much unrest and so many factions with their own agendas. But don't give up. His abductors, whoever they are, know any chance of getting what they want begins and ends with keeping their hostages alive. It may feel hopeless, but I have some experience here. The IFRC works with governments all over the world to bring our guys home. Not hearing anything doesn't mean nothing's being done."

"Thank you for that," Rory murmured, grateful for the words of comfort. "It's hard to hold on when there hasn't been a shred of news, not knowing how long is too long to hold out hope. I can't imagine living this way for forty years. I guess I hoped . . ."

"That after forty years apart, Soline and I would ride off into the sunset while the credits rolled?" He settled back in his chair, as if needing to put distance between them. "That we'd all become one big family, with birthday parties and Sunday dinners? I'm afraid it's a little late for that."

Rory felt her cheeks go hot. In some tiny corner of her heart, it was exactly what she'd hoped. And for a moment, she'd glimpsed a side of him that might have made it possible. The man who had offered his handkerchief to a woman in distress. But that Anson had vanished the moment they returned to the subject of Soline.

"You don't believe in happy endings?" she asked quietly.

"Not for a very long time."

"Is that why you never married?"

He stiffened. "I fail to see how that's relevant—or, for that matter, any of your business. But if it helps, let's just say I'm privy to certain facts that you're not."

Rory folded the handkerchief and handed it back. "I don't know what that means, but if you'd just come to Boston—"

"There is no chance of a happy ending here, Miss Grant. Sometimes things are just too far gone to be saved." He stood then with a cool nod. "If you'll excuse me, I have an early day tomorrow." He tossed a handful of bills on the table. "I'm sorry about Matthew. I hope it turns out well for you both."

Rory's heart sank as she watched him go. She hadn't let herself believe the years could have hardened him enough to turn his back on the woman he'd loved so deeply all those years ago, or slam the door on a possible relationship with his daughter, but they clearly had.

She dropped the photos into her tote, then picked up the ledger and pushed to her feet. He hadn't even bothered to look at it. If he had, he might . . .

Yes . . . he might.

Heads turned as Rory slung her tote up onto her shoulder, narrowly missing her wineglass, and scurried out of the bar. She paused when she reached the hotel lobby, glancing frantically in both directions. She saw him finally, disappearing around the corner toward the elevators. She quickened her pace, nearly running now, desperate to reach him before he stepped into the elevator and was whisked away.

"Anson!" Her voice ricocheted appallingly in the empty corridor. "Wait! Please!"

He had just stepped into the elevator when he saw her. He stiffened briefly, then began to jab at the control panel in an attempt to close the door. Rory threw out an arm as the door began to close. It bucked, as if confused, then slid open.

Anson stared at her, too astonished to react as she shoved the ledger against his chest and stepped back out of the elevator. He would probably throw it in the trash as soon as he reached his room, but she had done all she could do. The rest was up to him.

FORTY

RORY

September 26, 1985—Boston

Rory flipped the wipers to high, wishing she had stayed home and climbed into the bathtub as planned. But when she'd returned home from the airport, there was a message from her mother on the machine. It was another invitation to brunch on Sunday—which she had no intention of accepting—but she'd also mentioned having theater tickets for this evening, which meant if she hurried, she could slip in and return the borrowed photo before her mother realized she'd taken it.

She was exhausted after a night of no sleep. She'd been naive enough to hope Anson would go back to his room, take one look at the ledger, and suddenly change his mind. He hadn't. She tried his room while waiting for her breakfast to arrive, to make one final plea, only to be told by the front desk that Mr. Purcell had already checked out. She'd called Thia with the news before leaving for the airport and had agreed to give her a few more weeks to work on her brother. In the meantime, she'd say nothing to her mother and do what she could to repair the rift between herself and Soline.

The house was dark as she swung into the drive, with only the foyer light showing through the sidelight curtains. There was no sign of her mother's car either. She located her old house key, grabbed her tote from the passenger seat, and headed up the walk.

She felt like a burglar as she let herself in, groping about with just the light from the foyer, but she would only be a minute. Then she could sink to her neck in a tub full of bubbles with a snack and Heather Graham's latest release. Or maybe she'd just skip the bath and go straight to bed. Tomorrow was going to be a full day.

In the living room, she navigated the sofa, then a pair of wingbacks, finally making her way to the curio cabinet in the corner. She had just turned the tiny key and was pulling back the door when the living room lamp snapped on.

"Aurora, what on earth are you doing skulking around in the dark?"

Rory's mouth worked soundlessly as she racked her brain for an explanation.

Camilla frowned at her. "I saw your car in the driveway when I pulled in. Is something . . ." Her voice trailed off when she noticed the picture frame in Rory's hand. "What are you doing with that?"

"I was just . . ." Rory ran her eyes around the room, as if there might be an excuse lurking in one of the corners. There wasn't. "I thought you were going to the theater."

"I've been, but my allergies are kicking up, so I left at intermission." Camilla set her handbag on the arm of the sofa and peeled a shimmery beaded shawl from her shoulders. She gave it a shake, sending a shower of rain droplets flying, then laid it aside. "Aurora, what's going on? You haven't returned any of my calls, and now I find you slinking around in the dark. Is there something I should know?"

"Like what?"

"I have no idea, but something's going on. If you wanted to borrow a photograph, all you had to do was ask."

For a moment, Rory considered lying, but she'd never pull that off, not when her mother knew how much she'd always hated this particular photo. "I wasn't taking it," she said finally. "I was putting it back."

"Back from where?"

"I came by the other night while you were out and sort of . . . borrowed it."

Camilla looked genuinely baffled. "Why?"

"I've just come back from San Francisco. And before that, I was in Newport."

"I don't understand. What do San Francisco and Newport have to do with a photo of you as a little girl?"

Rory closed her eyes, letting out a long sigh. She was going to have to tell her—all of it. "It's not just to do with me. It's about you too."

"You're not making sense, Aurora. What are you saying?"

Rory dropped her gaze. She wasn't prepared to have this conversation now. For starters, she'd given the ledger and adoption paperwork to Anson. She had no proof for the claims she was about to make. But there was no walking it back now. Her mother was waiting for an answer.

"I'm saying we need to talk."

She looked wary suddenly. "About what?"

Rory took a deep breath, letting it out all at once. "Your parents."

Camilla sagged onto the sofa, her eyes bent on the carpet. When she finally lifted her head, she looked tired and strangely relieved. "How did you find out?"

Rory stared at her, trying to wrap her head around the response. She hadn't asked, *What about my parents?* She had simply conceded the point. "You knew about the adoption?"

Camilla nodded.

"For how long?"

"I was ten. I wasn't supposed to know, but my mother let something slip one day when I made her angry. She said she should have known better than to think I'd ever be a Lowell, that I'd always be trash and she should have packed me up and sent me back when she had the chance. I had no idea what she meant, but a year later, she and my father were arguing, and I heard her say it again. *Trash.* I don't know where I ever found the nerve, but I threw the door open and marched right in, demanding to know why she kept saying it. She slapped me so hard, my ears rang for an hour. She was furious that I'd been listening, but deep down I think she enjoyed telling me I wasn't hers. My father didn't speak to her for weeks."

Rory's throat went tight as she imagined it. Hearing the woman she thought of as her mother refer to her as trash, being told point-blank that she'd never be good enough. No wonder she never spoke about her childhood.

"All these years, you've been keeping this from me. Why?"

Camilla's eyes remained downcast. "I never told anyone. Not even your father."

"You never told Daddy?"

"My mother was determined to see me married well. She didn't care to whom, so long as the boy was from a suitable family. She told me to choose someone and get the business done. I chose your father, threw myself at him, really. He married me for my name. And for my inheritance. And I didn't care. I would have married him on any condition. But my mother had conditions of her own. She made it clear that if I ever told your father about the adoption—if I ever breathed a word to anyone—she would cut me off without a cent, and that would be the end of my marriage. She would have done it, too, if I had crossed her." She looked away, shaking her head. "I never cared about the money, but I couldn't lose your father."

Rory let the words sink in, wondering if she'd heard them correctly. She'd always thought of her parents' marriage as a kind of devil's bargain, with both parties being compensated in some nebulous way in exchange for enduring a loveless union. Had she been wrong? Was it possible that her mother had actually been in love when she married Geoffrey Grant?

"But that was years ago. Are you saying that after everything, all the arguing, all the women . . . Are you saying you were in love with him once?"

Camilla managed a smile, her eyes suddenly shiny with tears. "I was in love with him always, Aurora. Always and always."

Rory shook her head as she digested this bit of news. How had she not seen this love that was suddenly written all over her mother's face?

You have no idea what I've lost.

Her mother had uttered the words once in a heated moment. They hadn't made sense then, but they did now. As a child, Camilla had been cast aside by her mother, then later, as a woman, she'd been cast aside by the man she loved. Again and again, while her friends looked on and felt sorry for her.

"I'm sorry you felt like you had to carry that around by yourself all these years, that you didn't think you could share it with me."

She shrugged. "I was ashamed, I suppose."

"Ashamed? Of what?"

"Of being unlovable," Camilla said, blinking the tears from her lashes. She reached for her handbag and fished out a tissue, dabbing at her eyes. "And I'm the mother. You're supposed to lean on me, not the other way around. I'm glad you finally know about the adoption, though. I was always worried that it would come out in some terrible way. Some health thing would rear its head, and they'd need my family's medical history, and I wouldn't know what to tell them." Her eyes narrowed suddenly. "How *did* you find out?"

"By accident." Rory glanced at the framed photo in her hand. Without meaning to, they seemed to have circled back to the original topic. "How much *do* you know about your birth parents?"

Camilla shook her head slowly. "Only that I was a war baby and that my mother gave me up because she wasn't married. It wasn't uncommon back then. So many boys were killed, leaving sweethearts and babies behind. My father finally told me, not long before he died. My mother—Gwendolyn—had lost three babies and was ashamed of being childless when all her friends had houses full of children, so he quietly arranged for the adoption. I was her consolation prize."

"Did he ever mention the name of your biological mother?"

"Oh, no. Adoptions were very hush-hush in those days, especially when the mother was unmarried. Things are much more open now, but back then, the whole subject was taboo. My mother was adamant that no one know I wasn't really theirs. They went abroad for a year—on her doctor's advice, or so the story went—and lo and behold, they came back blooming and healthy, with a daughter in tow. If anyone suspected, they never let on. But of course, they wouldn't dare if they wanted to stay in the Lowells' good graces. And everyone did."

"And your father? I mean, your birth father."

"No one ever mentioned him, but I always assumed he'd been killed in the war." She pressed her fingers to her lips, shook her head, as if to apologize for her display of emotion. "I loved George Lowell dearly. He was a kind and loving man, but he wasn't strong. At least not when it came to my mother. He wasn't able to . . . protect me from her. When he died, I remember thinking he'd finally found a way to be free of her. I couldn't begrudge him that, but it left me at her mercy. That's when I started daydreaming about my real father. I used to imagine what he looked like. Tall and handsome, like a knight in a fairy story. A hero to his dying breath. I used to wonder if he knew I'd been born and if he ever thought of me. I needed so much to believe he did."

The words seemed to hum in the silence that stretched between them. Rory dropped down next to Camilla, the photograph in its silver frame balanced on her knees. Her features, but Anson's, too, and Thia's, and Camilla's. But Soline was there, too, in the heart-shaped face and high cheekbones, the long neck and pointed chin. The blending of bloodlines—so obvious now that she knew the truth.

She pressed the photograph into Camilla's hands, meeting her puzzled gaze squarely. "This started with you asking me what I was doing with this old photo. I told you I'd just come back from San Francisco. And now I need to tell you the rest."

Camilla stiffened almost imperceptibly. "The rest?"

"I've found out something else. Something I didn't expect. I asked an old friend—a reporter with the *Globe*—to help me dig up an old photo of Anson. I wanted to surprise Soline with it. A few days later—"

"Who's Anson?"

"He's the man Soline was supposed to marry."

"Ah, the ambulance driver who was killed in the war."

"Except he wasn't."

"Wasn't what?"

"Killed. He was wounded, badly, and spent time in a prison camp, but he didn't die. He's been alive all this time, and two days ago, I met his sister in Newport."

Camilla was frowning, clearly confused. "Have I missed something? What does Soline's fiancé have to do with a picture of you when you were eight?"

"I'm getting to that," Rory promised. She understood her mother's impatience, but it was a lot to tell, and it needed to be told carefully. "I originally went to Newport to see Anson but wound up talking to his sister, Thia, instead. She showed me a photo of herself as a child. One so much like this one that it was like looking at twins born thirty years apart. She also showed me some things she found among her father's papers after he died. An old ledger book and a copy of an adoption decree. That's why I flew to San Francisco—to meet Anson and explain all this. He's been walking around for forty years hating Soline because he believed she left him when she learned about his injuries. But it was a lie. His father sent her away because she was going to have a baby. I had to see him, to prove to him what I already knew—that the baby girl Soline bore all those years ago was you."

Camilla went pale, her expression rigid. "It isn't true."

"It is," Rory said gently. "I've seen the adoption decree, and George and Gwendolyn Lowell's names were there in black and white. Soline's was there too. And yours. The father was listed as unknown, but there's no doubt the baby was Anson's. His father paid a woman named Dorothy Sheridan to tell Soline you died shortly after being born. And then they gave you away."

"No."

"She named you Assia," Rory said, ignoring the repeated denial. "It means 'one who brings comfort.'"

Camilla shook her head, her eyes wide and glazed. "What you're saying is impossible, Aurora. After all these years . . . the chances of it being her . . . of all people."

"I know this is a lot to digest. It was for me, too, but it's true. The woman who gave birth to you is alive and well and living right here in Boston. You had lunch with her last week."

Camilla stood suddenly, sending the silver frame thumping to the floor. "Why are you saying this? Do you really need her in your life so badly that you'd swallow this preposterous story? Or is this my punishment for misbehaving the other day?"

Rory stared at her, stunned. "You think I'd make up something like this out of spite?"

"I'm saying I think you want to believe it, no matter how outlandish it seems. You barely know this woman, but in your mind, she's some kind of saint."

"You sound like Anson. He said the same thing last night."

Camilla seemed almost relieved at this news. "Anson doesn't believe it either?"

"It isn't a matter of believing. I laid the proof out for him. I even left him the ledger. But he made it perfectly clear that he isn't interested in a family reunion."

"And Soline?" Camilla asked coolly. "What does she have to say about this miracle?"

"She doesn't know any of it. She's not speaking to me at the moment. Won't take my calls or answer the door since the day at Seasons."

"And that's my fault, I suppose."

"I didn't say that, but you have to understand Soline. Withdrawing is how she protects herself. What happened the other day felt like an attack—because it was. You didn't hear yourself, but I did. And so did she. And I hear you now. Through some weird twist of fate, you've been given a chance to know your real mother, and instead of embracing it, you accuse me of wanting to punish you. I don't understand you."

Camilla nodded stiffly. "This is a lot to process, Aurora. I'm sorry if I'm not doing it quickly enough to suit you. Perhaps Soline will do a better job of it." She bent to retrieve the fallen frame and walked it to the curio cabinet, where she spent a few minutes making space for it among the others. When she turned to face Rory again her features were arranged in a kind of bland resignation. "When will you tell her?"

"Not for a while yet. Thia is still hoping to bring Anson around, so I promised to wait. It won't do any good, but I'll need time anyway, to smooth things over with Soline."

"How will she take it, do you think?"

"Not well, I'm afraid. Losing him again—this way—might shatter her. Throw in the fact that the daughter she's grieved for forty years is also alive but wants nothing to do with her, and I'd say you've got the makings of a perfect nervous breakdown."

"Aurora . . ."

"I'm tired, Mother. I'm going home."

Camilla looked stricken. "You can't just leave. We have to talk."

"I'm done talking tonight. I'm exhausted, and I need some sleep."

"Will you come to brunch on Sunday? Please don't say you're busy."

Rory had been about to say just that. Instead, she searched Camilla's face. She looked tired, too, or maybe *shaken* was a better word. It *was* a lot to process. An entire family had suddenly been dropped in her lap, along with some pretty messy baggage. And tonight, she'd been given a glimpse into just how much baggage her mother was already carrying. Perhaps like Anson, she was simply unwilling—or unable—to carry more.

"I don't know," Rory replied finally. "I think right now we both need time to digest all of this."

"Please don't leave angry, Aurora."

"I'm not angry, Mother. I'm disappointed. Soline isn't just my friend now. She's my grandmother. I shouldn't have to choose between you, but after lunch the other day, I realize you expect me to. Part of me wanted to believe this news might change that—that we'd have a chance at a do-over. Not just for my sake but for yours and Soline's. You have no idea how much losing you cost her, but I do. All I could think about was she'd finally have her daughter in her life, and you would finally have the kind of mother you deserved—the kind who never stopped loving and wanting you. And I would have you both, like a real family. But I guess Anson was right. There isn't going to be a happy ending here."

She turned then and headed for the foyer before glancing back over her shoulder. "If you're still curious about what your father looks like, I have a fairly recent photograph."

Camilla folded her arms close to her body, as if suddenly vulnerable. "Maybe you could bring it with you on Sunday."

"Maybe."

FORTY-ONE

SOLINE

La Mère has a plan for each of her chosen, a unique path carved out especially for us. We must therefore be wary of the echoes of past generations and guard against making their echoes our own. Ours is not to repeat the past but to learn from it.

—*Esmée Roussel, the Dress Witch*

27 September 1985—Boston

The phone begins to jangle at eight o'clock sharp. I sip my coffee and let it ring, cursing myself for forgetting to leave it off the hook after calling the grocer. I snatch it from the cradle. At this time of morning, I already know who it is. "Yes. What?"

"Good morning. This is the Daniel Ballantine answering service calling for Ms. Soline Roussel."

"Very funny. What do you want?"

"I just had a call from Camilla Grant—Rory's mother."

The name catches me off guard. "I know who she is. What did she want with you?"

"To get to you, apparently. Rory obviously mentioned my name at some point, because she tracked me down. She wanted your number. I offered to pass hers along to you instead. She didn't say what it was about, but she was pretty determined, kind of agitated."

"I'm not calling her."

"Have you spoken to Rory yet?"

"No. Why? Did she say something was wrong?"

"No, but Camilla sounded kind of emotional. She said it was important that she speak to you. Maybe you should give her a call just in case."

In case . . . what? What could she want with me? I've backed away as she wanted me to, retreated to the solitude of my lair, and here I shall stay. I will not lay myself open to another scene.

"I'm not talking to that woman," I inform him icily.

"What the hell happened at that lunch anyway?"

"Never mind."

"Fine, just take down her number so I can get back to work. But maybe you want to just check in. Like I said, she sounded a little wound up."

"Give me the number."

I grab a pen and pad from the drawer and scribble down the number, though I have absolutely no intention of using it. But after I hang up the phone, I stare at it, wondering what Camilla Grant could possibly want with me.

I arrive at Camilla's, already regretting my decision. Coming was probably a mistake, but when I finally broke down and phoned Rory's mother, I found myself unable to decline her invitation to brunch. She asked for a do-over, which is American for second chance. When I hesitated, she asked me to come for Rory's sake. I couldn't say no to that. Now, two days later, part of me wishes I'd said no. The other part of me is wondering what all this is about.

There's a knot in my stomach as I ring the bell, like I used to get when I was learning the craft at *Maman's* knee, an echo I can't interpret. I want to turn and go back down the walk. But before I can step away from the door, it opens, and she's there, creamy perfection in gauzy linen and long strands of coral beads that reach nearly to her waist. She tries to smile, but it quickly falters.

"Ms. Roussel, thank you so much for coming. Please come in."

She steps back from the door, allowing me to enter, and for a moment my eyes are drawn to her wrist, to a bracelet studded with gold charms. The sound it makes reminds me of the day at Seasons, the way it jangled when she shook out her napkin.

"Shall we go out to the terrace?"

She closes the door with another metallic jangle and sweeps me through a series of pale, meticulous rooms. It's just as Rory described, immaculate and unlived in—sterile. For a moment, I'm that other Soline, the one just off the train with the scuffed shoes and mussy clothes, painfully out of place.

The kitchen looks like something from a magazine, stainless and stone with a collection of pretty pitchers above the stove that I sense are just for show. She offers me coffee. I nod my thanks, awkward and not at all sure what I'm doing here.

She fills two cups and puts them on a tray, along with cream and sugar.

"This way," she says with another attempt at a smile. She feels awkward, too, I realize, surprised that this cool, elegant woman should feel awkward in my presence.

She nods toward an open set of french doors. I follow her out onto a slate-paved terrace. There is no sign of Rory, but a pretty little table has been set for three. The view from the terrace is breathtaking, with a lovely glimpse of the river and a wide swath of greenway.

I feel Camilla's eyes on my back and turn to find her standing behind me, studying me. She shifts her gaze when she realizes I'm looking at her and points to a chair.

"Please, won't you sit down?"

She attempts another smile as she settles into her own chair. I choose the one farthest away and take my cup from the tray, conscious of my gloves and still not sure what all this is about.

"Thank you for coming." It's the second time she's said it, and I find myself feeling sorry for her. She looks almost frightened, vulnerable and anxious. "I asked you to come early because I wanted to talk to you before Aurora arrived. She told me the two of you haven't spoken since that day at lunch, and I'm afraid that's my fault. We got off to a bad start." She pauses, shaking her head. "No, that's not right. *I* got off to a bad start. I was so awful to you that day, and I wanted to explain, to . . . apologize."

I can tell by the way she struggles with the last part that she isn't used to apologizing. This is difficult for her, and because it is, I feel myself softening. I sip my coffee, waiting.

"I don't know what came over me. I could hear the words coming out, but I couldn't seem to stop them. It was like my mother was talking instead of me."

Her eyes dart from mine, as if she's said more than she intended. "I'm sorry I blurted out that bit about my mother. It's just that I sometimes find myself channeling her when it comes to Aurora. We don't always . . . We see things differently. Almost everything, really. And then when Matthew . . . Hux," she corrects. "When Hux entered the picture, I handled it badly. I didn't know anything about him, and I worried that he wasn't . . ." She sighs and goes quiet again. "I swore I'd never be like her. That when I had a daughter of my own, I would be different, and it turns out I'm just like her."

"You're speaking of your mother again."

She nods, the corners of her mouth turned down like a child's. "I was never the daughter she wanted, and she made sure I knew it." She pressed a hand to her lips. "I'm so sorry. You didn't come here to listen to this, but there's not really anyone I can talk to about it, and you're . . . you and Rory have grown so close."

I watch as she bends her head to sip her coffee, knowing my next words will hurt her, knowing, too, that the things we need to hear often do. "Rory said the same thing once," I say quietly. "That *she* wasn't the daughter *you* wanted."

Her head comes up slowly, and I see that the remark has shaken her. "Aurora thinks . . ." Her eyes pool with tears. "But it isn't true. I'm so proud of her. *So* proud. She's brave and beautiful and knows exactly what she wants to do and be." Her words thicken, and she blinks away her tears. "She's the me I wish I'd had the courage to be when I was her age."

"Why doesn't *she* know that?"

The question stings, but it needed to be asked. She puts her cup down and wipes beneath both eyes, careful of her makeup. "I've made so many mistakes. I've held on to her too tightly. To protect her, I told myself, but that wasn't it. That was *never* it. I tried to clip her wings and keep her close. So I would . . . have someone. When Hux disappeared, she withdrew from me, from everything, really. I tried to pull her back, to reach her, but she just kept getting further and further away. And then she met you, and it was like she was alive again. And the gallery . . . all of a sudden that was back on, and she was talking about her art. I know how petty this must sound, but it felt like you were trying to take her away, and she's all I have. That's why I acted the way I did, because I was jealous. And afraid."

Her eyes drift from mine, sliding toward the horizon. I study her, her profile so familiar I feel as if I've always known her. She is so much like Rory, and yet she's different too. On the outside she's cool and polished, but beneath all that perfection there are layers of pain. I feel my heart take a step toward her.

"No one can take her away from you, Camilla. She's your daughter. You're bound for life, and by something that runs much deeper than blood and shared memories. You're bound by your echoes."

She turns back, a little crease between her brows. "Echoes?"

I smile, because she looks like she needs a smile. "It's something my mother used to say. She believed we each possess an echo, a kind of spiritual fingerprint, and that those echoes connect us to the ones we love, binding us forever."

Her eyes hold mine, wide and still shiny with tears. I can't read what's in them, but I feel a kind of yearning in her, a need to speak, and yet there's a reluctance. "Do you . . . believe it?" she asks finally. "The part about the echoes binding us forever, I mean?"

Her voice is thick, choked with emotion, and I realize with a start that she has laid herself bare to me, like a child. There's a sudden ache in my throat, a tightness that makes it hard to breathe. I'm confused, almost dizzy, but she's still looking at me, still waiting for a reply.

Before I can think of how to answer, Camilla sets her cup down abruptly and pops up out of her chair. She looks nervous, almost guilty. "That's the door. Aurora's here."

She's preparing to step away when Rory suddenly appears in the doorway. She looks vaguely stricken as our eyes meet, both glad and afraid, and I realize her mother hasn't told her I'd be here. She's holding a large manila envelope. She tucks it beneath her arm and shoots Camilla a look. "What's going on?"

"Oh, good, you're here," Camilla says, managing to sound both flustered and pleased. "Soline and I were just having a little chat."

Rory glances in my direction, then narrows her eyes at her mother. "We talked about this."

"No, no. We were just getting to know one another. You know, girl talk."

"Your message said to get here as soon as I could. I thought something had happened."

"Only because I knew you'd want to see Soline. I thought it would be nice for the three of us to get together for brunch."

"Except we talked about this. What are you up to?"

Rory has lowered her voice, but her words carry on the breeze. She's angry. Camilla turns, peering at me anxiously over her shoulder. She tries to smile and once again misses. I can't help feeling there's a conversation involving me taking place, one to which I am not to be made privy.

"Please." Camilla catches Rory's hand, holding it in both of hers. "I'm trying to make things right, Rory. I remember what you said. I remember every word. I just want us to be . . ." Her voice trails as she lets go of her daughter's hand. "I want us all to be . . . friends. Good, good friends. Now, go talk to Soline while I serve up the food."

Rory still looks wary as she slides the envelope from beneath her arm and hands it to her mother. She lingers a moment, watching Camilla disappear into the house, then joins me at the table. "I had no idea you were going to be here. Did she trick you too?"

"She called Daniel, and he called me. She felt bad about lunch and invited me to join you today. She was very determined. She wouldn't take no for an answer."

"I'm so sorry. She's always been a force of nature. How have you been?"

"Well enough."

"You know, I tried to call you. Then I came over and knocked on your door. When you didn't answer, I left you a note."

"And then you sent Daniel snooping around my kitchen window."

"I was worried. You were so upset when you left that day. I wanted to apologize, but you wouldn't answer your phone. I'm so sorry about what she said and how she was."

"Why are you apologizing for your mother's actions? They were hers, not yours. And she had her reasons for behaving as she did."

Rory's eyes widen. She's surprised, and perhaps a little hurt that I have taken her mother's side even a little. "You're defending her now?"

"She was afraid, *chérie*. People lash out when they're afraid."

"Afraid of *you*?"

"How a person behaves toward us is never about *us*, Rory. It's about them. Your mother acted as she did because she felt threatened. You're hers, and she wanted me to know it. Because she's afraid of losing you—and of being alone."

Rory scowls at the open french doors. "Then she should stop doing things to drive me away. She acts like I don't deserve a life of my own, like everything I am and do is about her. My art, the gallery, even who I choose to be friends with."

I feel her anger in my bones, the tug-of-war between mother and daughter. It's a clash as old as time itself, for there have always been mothers who knew best. Just as there have always been daughters who knew better. It's a contradiction that is part of every woman's journey—the need to shape in one's own image versus the aversion to being shaped at all.

I smile sadly. "It's a hard thing for a mother to relinquish her *bébé*. You've been a part of her life for a very long time, her whole world, and now all of a sudden, you're grown up with a life of your own. She's lonely."

"How on earth can she be lonely? There isn't a blank space on her calendar. She's always flitting off to some luncheon or card game or going to the theater. She has an actual entourage. Especially since my father died, not that he was ever much of a companion."

"One doesn't have to be alone to be lonely, *chérie*. They're not the same thing. We all cope with loss in our own way, inventing ways to fill up the emptiness. That's why her calendar is full. And why she's been so possessive. She wants to be part of your life, but she doesn't know how."

Rory folds her arms and lets out a sigh. She looks so young and petulant, sitting there with her arms crossed. It chafes to hear me defend her mother. But the rift between these two must be mended before it hardens into something cold and permanent. Perhaps that's why fate has thrown me into their lives. To broker peace.

"In France we say, *tu me manques*. It means 'you are missing from me.' Not *I* miss *you*—the way Americans say it—but *you* are missing from *me*. The part of *you* that is a part of *me* . . . is gone. This is how it is for her. There's a void in her life where you used to be, and she doesn't know how to fill it."

Rory sinks into the chair beside me, silent. She's determined to cling to her anger.

"She knows she's made mistakes, Rory. That's why she asked me to come today, to make amends. Not just with me but with you. And I think you should let her."

"You don't know her."

"No. But she thinks the three of us should be friends, and I think so too. We've been brought together somehow. I don't know how or why, but you can't deny it. Perhaps we're meant to help each other in some way, to fill each other's empty places."

She looks at me so strangely, as if I've said something earth-shattering and she's about to correct me. For the tiniest moment, I'm afraid of what she'll say, afraid our newly formed circle is about to be broken, and suddenly I don't *want* it to be.

And then I hear the tinkle of Camilla's bracelet as she approaches with a tray full of food. "Isn't this just lovely," she says, beaming. "The three of us, together at last."

FORTY-TWO

RORY

October 18, 1985—Boston

Rory stared at the expanse of blank wall with a blooming sense of dread. Forty-eight hours ago, Dheera Petri had called to explain why, ten days before the opening, her pieces still hadn't arrived for installation. She'd had a call from an interior designer who wanted all but two of her paintings for a new office building she'd been hired to decorate. She felt terrible putting Rory on the spot so close to the opening, but would it be possible to get out of their agreement so she could sell her pieces?

They'd agreed to schedule something in the future, and Rory had wished her well. She couldn't, in good conscience, stand in the way of an offer like that, but she had no idea how she was going to fill the spot on such short notice. To top it off, Camilla and Soline were due to arrive any minute. It would be the first time either of them had seen the gallery, and she'd been looking forward to giving them the full tour. Instead, she was fretting about the prospect of a glaringly empty space on opening night. Not exactly a good omen.

She'd been so pleased with how it all turned out. Brian had done an amazing job, coming in both under budget and two weeks ahead of schedule. The color scheme she had settled on, soft layers of charcoal and slate, gave everything a slightly industrial feel, but careful lighting and reclaimed art deco fixtures added just the right amount of glamour. Even the installations had gone off without a hitch. Until Dheera called with her terrible good news.

"Aurora? Honey? Are you here?"

Rory started at the sound of Camilla's voice. She hadn't heard the entry chime, but apparently it was showtime. "I'll be right there."

The sight of Soline and her mother hovering in the doorway instantly lifted her spirits. They looked nothing alike—Camilla had inherited Anson's pale eyes and blond hair, while Soline's coloring was dark—and yet there was an inexplicable similarity as they stood side by side, an invisible cord that seemed to tether them.

A month ago, she couldn't have imagined them spending time together, but in the weeks since her mother's surprise brunch they had grown surprisingly close.

It was good to see Soline getting out again, and she was both thrilled and surprised by how quickly her mother's cool beige persona had morphed into something vibrant and almost playful, thanks to a trip to Bella Mia and a series of consultations with Lila at Neiman Marcus. Apparently, Soline had become Camilla's fairy godmother too. And Camilla had been happy to return the favor, inviting Soline to luncheons, shopping excursions, even a ballet performance last week.

Soline had filled a hole in Camilla's life that even *she* hadn't known existed, easing her need to cling and manage, which had allowed Rory time to focus on the gallery. And it appeared they were going to become a regular threesome for Sunday brunch.

It was more than even Rory had hoped for, but what would happen when they finally told Soline the truth? Not all the news would be bad— she would be reunited with her daughter and granddaughter—but even then, there would be bitterness over all the lost years. And of course, the news about Anson would be devastating. Would their newfound closeness be enough to pull her through the aftermath?

Camilla was starting to grumble about feeling disingenuous, and Rory worried that one day her mother would simply blurt out the truth, a gaffe almost certain to end in disaster.

She had agreed to give Thia time, but as of their last conversation, there'd been no movement on that front. Anson had gone abroad soon after their meeting in San Francisco and wasn't returning calls. She wasn't surprised, but a tiny part of her *had* hoped Thia might be successful, that the scales would suddenly drop from Anson's eyes and there would be a happy ending after all. But with every day that passed, that was looking less likely.

"So," Camilla said, clapping her hands eagerly. "We're here for our tour. We said eleven, right?"

Rory pasted on a smile. "Yes, we did."

Her gaze shifted to Soline, who was surveying her surroundings with an open mouth. It was the first time she'd been back since the night of the fire four years ago, and Rory had been worried about her reaction. Her last memories of the place could hardly be good.

"This is astonishing," Soline murmured at last. "I worked and lived here for thirty-five years, and I barely recognize the place. It's all so beautiful. And you left the original stair railing. How wonderful."

Rory felt herself relax. "I'm so glad you like it. I wanted to leave some of the details as an homage to the building's history. We still need to tweak the acoustics a little because of the bare floors—there's quite an echo when the place is empty—but overall, I'm thrilled with how it all turned out."

Camilla had just returned from a quick circuit around the front room. She peered at Rory's face, frowning. "What's wrong? Something is, isn't it?"

"No. I'm just a little tense about the opening. And tired. The last few weeks have been such a blur, getting the invitations out, organizing the food and the music, working with all the artists to get the installations just right. It's been a lot."

"But you're finished now. And just look at it. I can't believe what you've done here. The colors and clean lines. The way you've used light to create a mood. It feels so . . . dramatic and yet calm too. You've managed the perfect blend of elegant and artsy."

Rory waited for the inevitable *but*, followed by a list of things she would have done differently. *But it's a little . . . Perhaps you could have . . . Did you ever consider . . .* They didn't come. Her mother just stood there, smiling.

"Thank you. Are you ready to see the rest?"

"Lead the way. We want to see everything."

Rory walked them through each of the seven collections, referring them to Plexiglas wall placards featuring each artist's bio and photograph. Along the way, she pointed out her favorite pieces, explaining the specific types of media and techniques used to create them. It was good practice, and she was happy to find the talking points she'd memorized came easily.

She ended with her favorite collection, Kendra Paterson's sea glass pieces, which turned out to be her mother's favorite, too, particularly the large wave sculpture titled *Crest*. It was an absolute showstopper—an ocean wave created from thousands of sea-weathered shards ranging in color from frosty white and pale foam green to inky kelp and every shade in between.

"It's just breathtaking," Camilla sighed. "And such clever work. I can't imagine the patience something like this requires, not to mention the pure skill involved. I've never seen anything quite like it."

Rory was beyond pleased with her mother's reaction to what she considered the pièce de résistance of all seven collections. "That's what

I thought too. I found her by accident, through another of my artists, and I'm thrilled to have her on board for the opening."

Soline was moving slowly around the plinth, her gloved hands clasped before her, as if to stop herself from reaching out and touching. "The longer you look at it, the more it seems to be moving, like an actual wave. Does the artist know how many pieces of glass she uses for each sculpture?"

"She used to, but she's stopped counting as her pieces got larger and more involved. But every shard of glass is collected by hand by her and her husband. They travel to beaches all over the world. You wouldn't believe her studio. It's filled—"

"Aurora? Honey?" Camilla's voice drifted from the other side of gallery. "What's supposed to be here?"

Her mother had wandered off while she and Soline were talking, but Rory knew without turning that she was referring to the blank wall where Dheera Petri's acrylic pieces should have been. "I had an artist pull out the day before yesterday."

"Oh no. That's terrible. And not very fair so close to the opening."

Rory shrugged, trying to play down her disappointment. "She got an offer from a decorator for all but two of her paintings, and I couldn't stand in the way of the sale. So now I have a wall to fill with just eight days to go. I could probably fill it with one-offs. I'd have to take out one of the pod walls and shift the installations, then change all the lighting, but I can get it done in time. It's just not what I wanted for the opening. I've got a few more days, though, so I haven't completely given up."

"You know," Soline said, eyeing the empty wall thoughtfully, "I know an artist whose work would be perfect. Very . . . original. It's short notice and she's terribly busy right now, but I think I might be able to twist her arm. She owes me a favor."

Rory nearly shouted for joy. She had no idea Soline had connections in the art world. Her fairy godmother was about to come through again. "Is she local? Please say yes."

"Quite local."

"Could you call her? I'll meet her anywhere she wants."

Soline offered one of her quizzical smiles. "I'm talking about you, Rory, about *your* art. It's exactly the thing for that wall, a perfect segue from the sea glass pieces. And you wouldn't have to move anything."

Rory let out a sigh, like the air going out of a tire. "I thought you were serious."

"I am serious. I was serious the last time I said it too. You remember, don't you?"

Rory did remember, but she'd chalked it up to kindness. "But they're not . . . They don't belong here, next to all of this."

"Oh, *ma pêche*. Don't you see? This is *exactly* where they belong. This woman backing out wasn't an accident. It was precisely what was supposed to happen."

"But it's only five pieces for an entire wall."

"Perfect," Camilla said firmly. "They'll have room to breathe."

Rory turned to look at her in astonishment. "*You* think I should do it?"

"I do. Soline is right, sweetheart. This *is* what's supposed to happen."

"But you always said—"

"Forget what I said. I should have encouraged you a long time ago, and I'm sorry I didn't. But I'm encouraging you now. Not because you're in a pinch. Because your work is beautiful and original and belongs on these walls. Please say you'll do it. Or that you'll at least think about it."

Rory managed a smile, touched by this unexpected declaration, but she didn't need to think about it. She had enough on her plate without the pressure of wondering how her work would be received when seen side by side with real artists.

"Well, you've had the tour, unless you want to see upstairs."

Camilla shot Soline a wink as she hooked an arm through Rory's. "Actually, Soline and I have a surprise for you."

Rory wasn't sure she liked the sound of that. She'd had enough surprises for one week. "What kind of surprise?"

"Really, Aurora, stop being so suspicious. It's a good surprise. We promise."

Up front, Soline retrieved a Neiman Marcus shopping bag from beside the door and handed it to Rory. "For you," she said with a catlike smile. "From both of us."

Rory carried the bag to the front counter and removed a large, flat box. Her breath caught as she lifted the lid, revealing a suit of claret-colored silk. It was cut like a tuxedo, with black velvet lapels and a single-button closure. She stared at the label. *Valentino.*

"This must have cost a fortune." She ran a hand along one velvet lapel. "It's gorgeous."

"It's for the opening," Soline told her. "Unless you've already purchased something."

Rory shook her head as she folded the suit back into the box. "I hadn't given it another thought, actually."

Camilla threw her head back with one of her tinkling laughs. "You see? I told you. She's never given any thought to clothes. When she was little, dressing up for Halloween meant shoulder pads and a helmet or a conductor's hat and overalls. Never a princess or a fairy like the other little girls. And now look at her . . ." She broke off, blinking rapidly, as if caught off guard by her emotions. "All grown up and an artist with her very own gallery." Her fingers crept to the strand of pearls at her throat, twisting awkwardly. "You had a dream, and you chased it. Not many can say that, but you can, and I'm happy for you. You deserve this, Rory."

It was Rory's turn to be caught off guard. *Not Aurora . . . Rory.* That was new.

"Thank you," she said thickly. "Thank you to both of you. I can't tell you how happy it makes me that you'll both be at the opening."

"Just try and keep us away." Camilla leaned in to drop a kiss on her cheek. "We're off to lunch now and then a little shopping. Soline's going to help me pick out a pair of boots. I'm thinking suede."

Rory walked them out, lingering in the doorway until they had melted into the crowd of pedestrians along Newbury Street. Lunch and boot shopping. That was new too.

Rory was exhausted by the time she got home. She'd spent the rest of the afternoon on the phone trying to find an artist to fill Dheera Petri's wall. Of the five artists she'd managed to reach, four said they'd be able to ship a piece or two in time for opening night, but none would be available to attend the opening on such short notice. It was looking like she'd have to settle for a selection of one-offs rather than a single collection. Unless she went with Soline's suggestion.

She padded down the hall and flipped on the light in the spare room. Her eyes went immediately to the piece hanging behind the desk, the towering granite lighthouse standing defiant in a storm. It was the largest of all her pieces and one of her best. The four in the closet would make a total of five. She pulled them out, lining them up side by side. It might work until she found another collection to replace it. She just needed one more piece for balance.

She wandered over to one of the frames near the window, running a hand along the unfinished piece clamped between the stretcher bars. A winter harbor scene with a scrim of white fog sliding across the water. All it needed was the sky: the glimmer of a watery sun struggling to break through low shredding clouds. Pewter silk, periwinkle moiré, slivers of soft gray flannel. The light would be tricky. Maybe pleated silver tissue. She was pretty sure she had some scraps in one of the bins, and she still had a week to work. If she started tonight, she might be able to finish one more in time to have it mounted.

The thought set off a flutter of wings in her belly. Was she actually considering this? Her mother's words had touched an unexpected chord in her this morning. Not just her declaration of pride but her reference to *both* of them—Soline and Camilla united in support of her, like a family. They were three women who'd been thrown together by a series of events none of them could explain, across seas and years and so many losses. Three separate strands woven to make one whole. Fragile alone but stronger now, because they were together.

And they would need to be strong when the time came—to help Soline through what was coming. The opening was eight days away. Once that was behind her, she was going to need to talk to Thia about an end date. She'd waited as long as she could in good conscience. Dragging it out only added to Owen's lies, and there'd already been too many lies. It was time the truth came out, let the chips fall where they may. She only hoped that when they did, Soline would take comfort in her new family and continue to rebuild her life.

FORTY-THREE

RORY

October 26, 1985—Boston

Rory checked her watch, then took three more deep breaths. The doors were scheduled to open in an hour, and they were as ready as they were going to get. A bar had been set up near the front, offering a selection of wines and imported beers; platters of cold hors d'oeuvres had been arranged on a small buffet toward the back; the classical guitarist she had hired was setting up in a discreet corner; and all seven artists had arrived on time and were clustered up front, chatting and waiting for the doors to open.

Her mother and Soline were upstairs, pretending to powder their noses while they gave her some space. She was grateful for that. The week had been a blur of manic creativity and last-minute details, leaving little time for sleep, let alone reflection. Now, with nothing left to do but turn the OPEN sign around and unlock the door, she needed a few seconds of quiet to ground herself in the moment.

It felt almost surreal standing in this place that she had created out of thin air, as if she'd stepped into the middle of someone else's dream. And in a way, she had. A few months ago, the row house had been abandoned, gutted but not empty. Her grandmother had dreamed here once and had left a little of her magic behind, like bread crumbs for her to find one day. And she *had* found them. Or perhaps they had found *her*. Now, whatever the sign above the door might say, Soline Roussel's echoes would continue to live within these walls. And so would hers.

She stared at the acrylic placard for the gallery's newest collection—Dream Wave by Aurora Grant—and blinked back the sting of tears. Suddenly she was with Hux, staring at her work through the window of Finn's, hearing the words that had set it all in motion.

Dreams are like waves . . . You have to wait for the right one to come along, the one that has your name on it . . . This dream has your name all over it.

"Look what I did, Hux," she whispered softly. "Look where I'm standing. It did have my name all over it. And now it's real. Because of you."

"I think it's time, sweetheart."

Rory batted away the last of her tears as she turned to look at her mother. She was wearing a calf-length skirt, a vest of plum-colored crepe, and gray suede boots with pencil-thin heels. Not a stitch of beige in sight. "Have I told you how amazing you look tonight?"

Camilla dropped her chin, smiling shyly. "Thank you. I think we have the same dresser. And look at you—the suit fits like a glove. You look beautiful. And so does everything else. You've done an amazing job with all of it. And I'm so glad you decided to hang your work. It deserves to be seen and appreciated."

"It's so strange. For months, I've been trying to imagine what this night would feel like, and now . . ."

Camilla reached for her hand. "Oh, honey, what is it?"

"Nothing. I was just thinking about Hux. How none of this would be happening if it wasn't for him believing in me. I wish he were here to see it."

"He will be, sweetheart. He'll come back, and he'll be so proud when he sees what you've done. But right now, we need to get you out front. Your public awaits."

The words sent a flurry of butterflies skittering against Rory's insides. "I don't *have* a public. What if no one shows up? We'll be eating stuffed cherry tomatoes and roasted red pepper crostini for a week."

Camilla barked out an uncharacteristic laugh. "Now you're just being silly. We mailed over two hundred invitations. Both papers covered the opening in their weekend sections, and I've told literally everyone I know—twice. My guess is there won't be a tomato or a crostini to be had by the time you close the doors tonight. Now, march. There's a party waiting to get started."

"Where's Soline?"

"Still upstairs, but she said she'd be right down. I think she's a little nervous about being around so many people."

Rory knew exactly how she felt, but she managed to put one foot in front of the other anyway, dimly aware of her mother beside her, shooting a crisp nod to the tall brunette standing behind the bar, another to the redhead manning the food table, and a third to the guitarist, who instantly picked up his guitar. Soft strains of The Beatles' "Blackbird" filled the air, and the artists scattered to take their places with their collections.

"You're ready," Camilla whispered close to her ear. "I'll man the door. Your job—your *only* job—is to smile, mingle, and look like a gallery owner. And remember to pace yourself. It's going to be a long night."

A draft of crisp autumn air wafted in as Camilla pulled back the door. Within minutes, several clusters of women entered and were exchanging hugs and air kisses. Friends of her mother, she realized with a rush of gratitude.

Camilla really was quite fabulous in action, completely in charge of the moment, pulling invisible levers with a nod or a glance, and making it all look effortless, and Rory found herself wondering if she was capable of developing such skills. She was still mulling the question when her mother and her gaggle of friends began heading in her direction.

"Oh, there she is. My word, what have you done to yourself? You're simply stunning, Aurora!" It was Laurie Lorenz, treasurer of the art council, running heavily made-up eyes down the length of her. "I barely recognized you without your hair. You look so chic, like you just stepped off a Paris runway."

Hilly was nodding enthusiastically. "It is divine, isn't it? Will you look at those cheekbones? Just like her mother's. And I can't get over what you've done with this place. We bought my daughter's wedding dress here four years ago, and now look at it. No one would ever guess it nearly burned to the ground."

"Thank you," Rory said awkwardly, hoping Soline wasn't in earshot. "The damage wasn't as bad as originally thought, and I found a wonderful contractor. We managed to save quite a few of the original fixtures and the staircase, which I've fallen in love with."

The ladies followed Rory's gaze to the staircase, nodding in unison. As if on cue, Soline appeared at the top of the stairs, magnificent in black silk palazzos and an embroidered silver jacket. She paused briefly, running an eye over the crowd, then began to descend, one black-gloved hand sliding along the railing.

No one spoke. Rory could scarcely blame them. She was breathtaking, and so graceful her feet seemed not to touch the ground. She paused again on the last step, and for a moment, Rory was afraid she might turn and bolt back up the stairs. Instead, she squared her shoulders and looked out over the crowd until her eyes connected with Rory's.

Rory lifted a hand, aware of the curious stares of her mother's friends. Camilla was aware of them, too, and appeared poised to rush to Soline's defense if necessary. But Soline threw them both a reassuring smile as she approached. She looked amazing with her smoky eyes and scarlet lips, her hair swept back on one side with a jeweled comb.

Camilla hooked her arm through Soline's, drawing her close. "Ladies, I'd like you to meet my dear friend, Soline Roussel."

There was a brief pause, followed by a ripple of polite murmurs. It was Hilly who finally spoke up. "Madame Roussel! This was your shop once. You made my Caroline's wedding dress. Caroline Walden. I'm sure you don't remember, but she and her husband have three lovely children now, thanks to you. And people still talk about that dress, the way the bow—"

Camilla cut her off with a wave of a hand. "I'm sure Soline doesn't want to spend the evening talking shop, Hilly. But perhaps you and Vicky could speak to her about the art council. I need to get back to manning the door, and Aurora needs to circulate with her guests. Be sure to sample the hors d'oeuvres and let me know what you think about using Aurora's caterer for New Year's Eve. She's fabulous."

Rory ran her eyes around the room, surprised at how quickly it was filling up. She'd been worried that no one would come. Now she wondered if there would be enough wine. But it was good to see so many familiar faces. Kelly and Doug Glennon were just arriving; Daniel Ballantine and a pretty blonde she assumed was his wife were browsing the food table; and Brian, who had traded his contractor's clothes for neatly pressed khakis and a brown tweed jacket, was sipping a beer and chatting with a couple she recognized as friends of her mother.

She felt herself relax as she began to circulate. She was thrilled to see guests chatting with the artists, discussing media, technique, and sources of inspiration.

At some point, her mother had pressed a glass of chardonnay into her hand, and then later, she had grabbed another. A mistake, she now realized. The evening's excitement, coupled with a week of little or no sleep, seemed to hit her all at once, and she suddenly felt herself winding down. Camilla must have realized it, too, because she appeared with a plate of hors d'oeuvres, suggesting it might be time to eat something.

She felt better after a little food. And even better after selling one of her pieces to a local surgeon and her husband. By the time the last guest left at ten thirty, they had sold a total of four pieces, booked two commissions, and had a promising lead for Kendra Paterson's *Crest*. All in all, a successful night. And now that it was over, she was going to crawl into bed and sleep like the dead.

She looked up to see her mother wandering toward her with two glasses of wine. "They're breaking down the bar, so I figured I'd better grab one for each of us. Soline went up to your office about an hour ago. Tonight was a lot, but I think she did well. I offered to run her home around nine and come back, but she was determined to stay. Here." She pressed one of the glasses into Rory's hand. "I thought we'd round off the evening with a toast."

Rory eyed the glass warily. "I'm not sure I should. I'm dead on my feet, and I have to drive home."

"Just a toast. We didn't get a chance before."

"All right. But just a sip."

Camilla raised her glass, waiting until Rory followed suit. "To the young woman I'm lucky enough to call my daughter. I haven't always been particularly good at letting you know how proud I am of you or of trusting you to know what's right for you, and I'm sorry for that. I *am* proud. Not just tonight but always, and I promise to do better in the future."

"Thank you," Rory murmured, moved by her mother's unexpected declaration. After a sip, she lifted her glass again. "And now it's my turn. To the woman who taught me what grace under fire looks like. You were wonderful tonight, keeping your eye on everything, including me. I'm not sure I could have gotten through it without you." She cleared her throat, dismayed to find herself choking up. "I haven't always given you credit for how much you do—and for how well you do it, and I promise to do better too."

Camilla lowered her lashes as they touched glasses. "You're going to make me cry."

"You started it," Rory shot back before taking her obligatory sip.

"Fair enough. I'm going to the kitchen now to see if there are any of those little crostini left; then I'm going upstairs to find Soline so I can go home and soak my feet." She paused, pointing to her new boots. "These heels are going to take some getting used to."

Rory couldn't help smiling as she watched her mother head for the kitchen. It had been a night of surprises, starting with a pair of high-heeled boots and ending with a moment of honesty and mutual respect she couldn't have imagined just a few weeks ago. It was the perfect ending to a nearly perfect night, but she had to admit, she was glad it was over.

She took one last turn around the room, on the lookout for plates or glasses the caterers might have missed, and collected stray cocktail napkins. She had just bent down to pick up a rumpled brochure when she heard the entry chime. Apparently, no one had thought to lock the front door.

She straightened, reaching for a polite smile. "I'm sorry. I'm afraid . . . Oh my god."

No. Not now. Not like this.

"Anson—what are you doing here?"

He stood just inside the door, stiff and unsmiling, his hands fisted at his sides. "Thia told me your opening was tonight. I need to talk to you."

"You can't be here!" Rory hissed. "Soline is upstairs, and she doesn't know that you're . . ." She paused, throwing a frantic glance up the staircase. "Please! You can't be here!"

"Aurora, I packed . . ." Camilla's words trailed off when she saw that Rory wasn't alone. "I'm sorry. I didn't realize anyone was here."

"This is Anson," Rory explained stiffly. "He was just leaving."

Camilla's face went momentarily slack, her mouth parted in a silent O. Eventually, the spell lifted, and blankness was replaced with something Rory couldn't name. "You look like your picture," she said coolly.

Anson took a step forward before catching himself. He stood stock-still, his eyes riveted on Camilla's face. "Are you . . ."

"Yes, I am. And you have to leave. Now."

"I need to speak to your . . . I need to speak to Rory."

Camilla arched a frosty brow. "Not now you don't. Whatever you have to say has waited forty years. One more night isn't going to change anything."

"Please," Rory pleaded. "Go. And give us a chance to talk to Soline. She can't find out like this."

The words were barely out of her mouth when she heard the rasp of an indrawn breath from somewhere overhead, followed by the dull thump of an embroidered silk clutch tumbling down the stairs.

FORTY-FOUR

SOLINE

*There is a grief worse than death. It is the grief
of a life half-lived. Not because you don't know
what could have been but because you do.*

—*Esmée Roussel, the Dress Witch*

It can't be, yet it is.

He has aged, the years softening his once-hard body, adding lines
to his face and threads of silver to his hair, but I would know him
anywhere.

For forty years, I've dreamed of seeing him again, knowing it was
impossible but dreaming it still. And now, somehow, he's here. Alive,
and staring up at me like *I'm* the ghost. My throat is suddenly full
of tears and answered prayers, but when I open my mouth, nothing
comes. Because I see that something is wrong. Terribly, terribly wrong.
I see it in the way Rory is looking up at me, like she's apologizing for
some unforgivable crime, in Camilla's folded arms and rigid stance, as
if she is preparing to do battle. And in the icy blankness that has stolen
over Anson's face. In the space of an instant, I have become a stranger
to him. No, not a stranger—an enemy. But how? Why?

"Anson?"

His eyes connect with mine, hooded and hard. I can't see their color, but I can feel their coldness, like a steel blade between my ribs. It is a look he used to wear when speaking of the *boche*. And now he's aiming it at me.

Somehow, I make my legs move, managing to take one step, then another. But he's backing toward the door now, holding up a hand, as if to ward me off. And then he's gone, out into the street, leaving the door hanging open behind him. For a moment, I'm in Paris again, sitting in the back of an ambulance, watching him disappear through a small square window.

My legs go then, and I fold down onto the step like a felled bird, too stunned to utter a word or even cry. Rory is at my side, taking my hands, murmuring again and again that she's sorry, so very sorry, as if what just happened is her fault. I look at her, trying to make sense of what I see in her face. Sadness. Pity. And . . . is it guilt?

"I was going to tell you. After the opening, we were going to tell you everything."

We?

I look to the foot of the stairs, where Camilla is staring up at me, clutching the newel with both hands, and I see it there too. The same guilt. But I can't make sense of it there either.

"Going to tell me what?"

"That Anson was alive. I've known for a while now, and—"

"How long?"

"A few weeks. Maybe a little longer."

I drag my eyes back to Camilla. "You knew too? And said nothing?"

"We wanted to tell you," Rory blurts before Camilla can get a word out. "We were just waiting for the right time to break the news. I'm so sorry. I never dreamed he'd show up here. When I left him in San Francisco, he made it clear that he didn't want to see you."

"You went to San Francisco? To see Anson?"

She drops her head, nodding. "But first I went to Newport. Thia told me how to get in touch with him."

Newport. The word sends a shiver through me. And Thia. The name is strange after so many years. But my mind is too crowded with questions. I trip over them, teetering on the brink of panic. My world has been upended, and I don't understand anything.

"I found out by accident," Rory says, as if that makes a difference. "I asked a reporter friend of mine to look for an old photo of Anson as a surprise for you. Except I was the one who ended up surprised. One of the photos he dug up was only two years old. That's why I went to Newport, to find out if it was the right Anson. Then I went to San Francisco to talk to him. I needed to understand what happened after the war, why he never came looking for you. I thought I could convince him to come to Boston to talk to you, but he wouldn't budge. When I told Thia, she asked me to wait a little before telling you, and I agreed. We thought he might change his mind. We never dreamed he would just show up like that."

I close my eyes, as if that will erase what has happened. The tears I wasn't able to cry a moment ago are suddenly flowing as the truth slams into me. Anson—my Anson—has been alive these forty years but wanted no part of me . . . and still wants no part of me.

"There's more," Camilla says gently from the bottom of the stairs. "You need to know the rest."

"I don't want to know the rest," I say, pushing to my feet. "I want to go home. Please call me a taxi."

"I'll take you home," Camilla protests. "But first we need to talk. There are things—"

"I don't want to talk." My voice is strangely flat, hollow and unfamiliar. "I want to be alone." I blink to clear my vision, but the tears keep spilling down my face. "Please. The taxi."

From the corner of my eye, I see Camilla throw Rory an imploring look. She's determined to keep talking, to explain away the secret they've kept, to somehow make it all better. But it will never be better. Rory sees it, too, and answers her mother with a faint shake of her head. She knows nothing they say now will make a difference.

The staircase tilts precariously as I move down the steps. I hold tight to the railing, afraid my legs won't hold me. I brush past Camilla and then Rory, then stoop down to retrieve my handbag and make my way to the door.

"I'll wait outside."

I feel their eyes on me, waiting for me to break into a million tiny pieces. But I can't. Not yet. Because this time when I break, I will break forever.

FORTY-FIVE

Soline

*Always be mindful of the Rule of Three. Three
times your deed return to thee. Work ill and
thrice ill winds shall come. Work love and
thrice love finds a home.*

—Esmée Roussel, the Dress Witch

30 October 1985—Boston

Four days.

That's how long I've been hibernating, living on coffee and toast
because I haven't the energy to do more, wandering bleary-eyed from
room to room or curled like a fetal thing, with Anson's shaving kit
clasped to my chest.

I've taken the phone off the hook again. I don't want to hear it ring.
Don't want to wonder who it is or what they want. I already know, and
I want no part of their placations. I don't doubt that Rory meant well in
keeping the truth from me. It's not in her to be cruel. But she sees me
as fragile, a brittle old woman unable to endure one more blow. And so
I am. Perhaps she had good reason to worry about whether I'll recover
from this. I'm not certain I will.

I keep telling myself it doesn't matter, that the fact that Anson is alive somewhere in the world changes nothing. But it isn't true. Everything *has* changed. Because I've lost him all over again. Except this time, it wasn't the *boche* who took him from me. It was his *choice* to stay away.

His proposal had come out of nowhere, at a time when our emotions were running high. Had he come to regret it once we were apart and been secretly relieved to return home and find me gone? Did he know about our daughter? That she left the world the same day she came into it? That I never even got to hold her?

My Assia.

All this time, I've imagined her with him, that somehow, somewhere, they were together. But she's been alone all this time. He probably has children of his own, perhaps grandchildren—and a wife. Even now, all these years later, the thought doubles me over, and yet my eyes are dry. It seems I'm out of tears at last.

I've lost all sense of time, and the clock on the stove hasn't been right in two years. I lift the kitchen blinds and peer out. The sky is the color of lead, and a steady rain spatters the panes. I give up caring and go to the refrigerator, pulling out eggs and butter and mushrooms. The spinach in the crisper has gone slimy at the edges, but there's a tomato on the sill that isn't too far gone. I don't actually want food, but my head aches, and my insides feel hollowed out. I need to eat, and an omelet requires little skill.

I've just put the pan on the stove when the doorbell rings, and for one wild moment, I feel a bolt of hope tear through me. Could he have changed his mind? I flip off the burner and creep past the living room curtains, to the foyer, and wait.

It's not him. It can't be him.

The bell rings again, followed by the sharp rap of the knocker. I hold my breath, willing whoever it is to go away. It's Rory, of course. Or Camilla. They've come by three times already, and three times I've ignored them. Or perhaps it's Daniel, braving the drippy weather to come check on me again. I don't want to see him either. He knows too much of my story as it is. I have no wish to be cross-examined for the rest.

"Soline?" A woman's voice, muffled through the door. "Soline, it's Thia."

Thia. After all these years. My heart thunders in my ears, the saliva suddenly thick in my mouth. I lean close to the door, a hand on the knob. It's a mistake, I know, but I'm weak.

"Are you alone?"

"I can be," comes her answer. "If you want me to be."

I turn the knob and pull the door back a few inches, glimpsing a narrow slice of unfamiliar face. A full mouth, the bridge of a too-wide nose, skin that shows the wear and tear of someone who spends too much time in the sun. And an eye. Pale blue-green, with flecks of gold around the iris. The same as Anson's.

I open the door and stand with my hands at my sides, stunned to find her on my front steps, stunned by all of this. Even now, the similarities between them are impossible to ignore. But there's something else, too, that keeps my eyes fixed on her, something just outside my grasp.

"Why are you here?" My throat is rusty from disuse and too many tears.

"I want to talk to you," she says, her voice low and steady, as if addressing an animal that might skitter away. "About what happened after you left my father's house."

I keep my hand on the knob, pleased that the cold drizzle is slowly soaking through her shirt. Suddenly I'm very angry with her. "I know what happened. Your brother came home, and no one told me."

"Please, can we all just sit down and talk?"

All? My chest tightens as I register the word. "Is he . . . Who's with you?"

"Just Rory and Camilla. They're in the car. I know you're angry and hurt, and you have every right to be both, but there are things you need to know, Soline. *Other* things."

There's an ominous tone to her voice now, and I feel my stomach knot. "What . . . other things?"

"Please. I'm standing in the rain, and the steps aren't the place to have this discussion. Let us come in."

I drop my hand from the knob and step back. Thia looks down the street and waves, a signal for them to come. I catch a glimpse of myself in the foyer mirror as I turn away. I'm a ghost, pale and disheveled, my eyes heavy and shadowed with grief. I drag a hand through my hair, trying to tame it, then realize I'm wearing nothing but the robe I've had on for four days.

"I'll need a moment to dress."

They're in the living room when I return. Rory and Camilla are on the sofa. Thia is perched on the edge of a chair, her hair clinging damply to her forehead and neck. She looks me over, clearly relieved that I've tidied myself up. I've run a brush through my hair and traded my robe for a cardigan and slacks. Thia's eyes linger on my white cotton gloves before sliding away. But there's something else in the way she's looking at me, the way they're all looking at me. Pity mingled with discomfort, and I find myself wishing I hadn't let them in.

"All right, you're here. Say what you came to say, then go."

"We think you should sit down," Camilla says, patting the sofa cushion beside hers. "Here, between us."

"I don't want to sit." I sound petulant now, like a cranky child.

Rory looks at me, eyes pleading. "Please, Soline. We have something we want to show you. Something that might help make all of this . . . easier. Please come sit down."

I drop down beside her, sitting stiffly with my hands in my lap. Whatever this is, I want it over with.

Rory reaches into a black nylon tote, pulling out what looks like a photo album. I steel myself for something; I don't know what. And then she presses the album into my hands. "Open it."

The gloves make me clumsy as I attempt to turn back the cover. Rory reaches over to help me, and then I'm staring at an old black-and-white photograph. A tiny girl with pale curls and wide-set eyes, dressed in boots and a puffy snowsuit. She's three, perhaps four, and familiar, though I have never seen the photo before. I glance at Rory, not sure what's happening or what's expected of me.

"It's Thia," she explains. "When she was a girl."

I look at Thia, who is strangely still. I still don't understand.

"Turn the page."

It's another photo of the same girl, but she's older now, wearing a party dress dripping with ruffles. I can see Thia's features clearly now, the broad cheeks and pointed chin, the dusting of freckles on the bridge of her nose. I look up at three carefully blank faces and feel my patience wearing thin.

Camilla touches my arm. "Go on. Go to the next page."

The page's plastic cover crackles as I turn to the next photograph. It's Thia again, roughly the same age, but wearing a different dress. But something else is different. Her face is thinner, her cheekbones higher and sharper. And there it is again, that elusive tug of memory, like a loose thread I can't get hold of. I'm annoyed and confused—and suddenly frightened.

I narrow my eyes on Thia. "Why am I looking at old photos of you? What have they to do with me?"

"Look closely," she says quietly. "That one isn't me."

I study the photo again, then flip back to the previous page. The photographs are nearly identical, but on closer inspection, I see that the second one was taken more recently. The nebulous thread, unraveling now. Impossible. And yet . . .

"Who is this?"

The question hangs in the air, untouched as the seconds tick by. No one speaks or breathes. Finally, I feel Rory's hand steal over mine.

"It's me."

My eyes are still on the photo, taking in each curve and bone of the face looking back at me. *Aurore.* Yes, I see it now. I flick a glance at Thia, then Rory, then look at the photo again.

"I don't understand. How . . ."

Rory still has hold of my hand. She squeezes tightly. "We're related," she says very carefully. "Thia and I . . . are related."

Static fills my head, a scratchy white noise crowding out my thoughts. I can't wrap my brain around what she's just said, can't find the questions I need to ask. Why won't Rory let go of my hand? Why does Thia look like she's afraid to exhale? And why is Camilla crying?

"Related . . . how?" I manage finally.

"I'm her grandniece." She sits blinking at me, waiting for me to say something. When I don't, she presses me. "Do you understand what that means?"

"No." I shake my head, strangely numb. The thread is there, waiting to be pulled, but I can't—or won't. I shake my head again and keep shaking it. "No."

"Anson is my grandfather, Soline. Which makes *you* . . . my grandmother."

I stare at the photo, unable to breathe. "It isn't possible."

"It is," Rory says and turns the page again. "Your little girl didn't die. They took her."

I peer down at the new page. It's a photocopy, creased but legible enough. CERTIFICATE OF DECREE OF ADOPTION. In one of the boxes is the name Soline Roussel, in another, the name Lowell. And then farther down, Camilla.

I turn the names over in my mind, like tiles in a game of Scrabble. They mean something—they must—but I can't connect them.

"Lowell was my maiden name," Camilla supplies through a fresh rush of tears. "Camilla Lowell is the name I was given by the couple who adopted me. Before that, I had another name."

I stare at her until my eyes fill with tears and her face begins to blur. It can't be true. And yet her face—all their faces—says it *is*. "You're . . ."

"I'm Assia," she whispers. "Your daughter."

I cover my face, the rush of sobs so sudden, it threatens to choke me. I feel arms around me—I don't know whose—and then I'm rocking and keening, a high, thin gush of grief and inexplicable joy. I try to stop, to quiet myself, but the sound keeps welling up, pouring out of me like a storm. I'm making a fool of myself, and I don't care. In fact, I don't care about anything. Not that Anson didn't love me enough to look for me. Not even that I've lost forty years with the daughter who should have been mine. She's here now. And so is Rory.

I think of *Maman*, of her teachings when I was a girl at her knee, and know that somewhere, she is happy too. We cannot undo what has been done, but we can move forward—three generations bound by blood and echoes, making up for all the lost years.

I feel a tissue being pressed into my hand, and little by little, my sobs stutter to a halt. I mop my face, trying to pull myself together. When I look around, everyone's cheeks are wet, but it's Camilla's face that holds my gaze. I devour it, every line and precious contour, as if seeing them all for the first time.

"All this time," I whisper. "All this time, you were right here. My Assia."

Rory disappears briefly, returning with an entire box of tissues, and for the next few hours, I hold my daughter's hand and listen to Thia explain how far her father had gone to poison his son against me.

He's dead now, and good riddance. I'll never forgive him for what he took from me—or forgive his son for letting him do it. That Anson could believe me capable of such a betrayal is the bitterest pill of all. Because I see now that he was never the man I thought him. I lost that man the morning I climbed into the back of an ambulance and watched him disappear. That he has suddenly turned up alive all these years later changes nothing. Anson—*my* Anson—is dead.

FORTY-SIX

SOLINE

Lovers wound one another for many reasons, but in the end, fear is always at the root of it. It's a hard thing, perhaps the hardest of all, to trust when we're afraid—to open ourselves to the risk of forgiveness. But forgiveness is the greatest magick of all. Forgiveness makes all things new.

—Esmée Roussel, the Dress Witch

They've gone, and I'm back in my robe after a long, hot shower, alone with this strange new reality. I'm curled up on the sofa, combing through the album of old photos Rory and Camilla left for me. I've been through it a dozen times already, but I can't seem to stop turning the pages, savoring the details of each and every childhood photo, as if I'm trying to engrave their little faces on the blank places in my memory.

Assia—alive. And Rory.

For the second time in a handful of days, someone I loved has come back from the dead. It seems impossible, like the ending of a fairy tale, where the princess receives a kiss and the spell is suddenly broken. The long, dark sleep is over at last. The Roussels have been taught that fairy tales are for other people. But something has set this strange chain of events in motion. It can't be mere chance that brought Rory and Camilla into my life or me into theirs.

We will have much to talk about in the days ahead, stories I must eventually share—about *la magie* and the legacy that has always been a part of them. It will be a strange conversation, or perhaps not. From the beginning, I have sensed something special in Rory, and of course Camilla—my Assia—will have inherited the gift too. What they do with it will be up to them, but they will know about the Spell Weavers who came before them—Esmée, Giselle, Lilou, and all the rest.

I think of *Maman* and her belief that we are irrevocably connected to those we love. That our echoes will always tether us. Across years and miles and even death. Is that what's happened? A collision of echoes? I suddenly realize it doesn't matter.

I close my eyes, my limbs deliciously heavy, and let the events of the day wash over me. There is so much to think about, so much lost time to make up for, but I'm content to leave those things for tomorrow. Outside, the rain is still falling, heavier now, and the wind has picked up, buffeting the windows in uneven gusts. One of the shutters sounds as if it has come loose. I can hear it thumping against the house. No . . . not a shutter. The door. Banging on the door.

I bolt up from the sofa, my head muzzy. Rory promised to check on me later, but the phone is still off the hook. Surely she hasn't come back out in this.

I scurry to the foyer, fumbling with the chain, then the bolt. A sharp gust of wind catches the door as I pull it back, spattering me with a wall of cold rain. I see him then as I push my hair out of my eyes. Anson.

His silhouette fills the doorway, unmistakable despite the years, but I can't see his face. He's backlit by the streetlamp, his shoulders hunched against the blowing rain. I stare at him, my breath tight and shallow. For forty years, I've imagined this moment, what it would be like to see him just once more, to say the things I wished I had said before we parted. And now that he's standing on my front steps in the pouring rain, I find I can't manage a word.

He runs a hand over his face, wiping the rain out of his eyes. "I need to come in. It won't take long."

I back away, leaving him to follow me into the foyer. When I hear the door close, I turn quickly, afraid he's left instead, but he's still there, standing with his arms stiff at his sides. His jacket and shirt are sopping, his hair slick with rain.

I remember my bare hands suddenly and shove them into my pockets, painfully aware of my robe and bare feet. The seconds tick by as we stand looking at each other, and I find myself wondering what he sees. Forty years is a long time, but it's an especially long time for a woman. Does he still see the girl he met in the halls of the American Hospital, or have the years made me a stranger? It shouldn't matter, but it does.

"I'll get you a towel," I say thickly.

When I return, I'm wearing white cotton gloves. He's hovering at the edge of the foyer, just off the carpet. I hold out the towel and back away.

He blots futilely at his shirt, then scrubs it over his hair before giving up. When he tries to hand it back, I keep my hands in my pockets. "Just leave it on the chair."

"You've lost some of your accent," he says without expression.

"I've lost a lot of things." It hurts to see the blankness in his eyes, but I force myself to meet his gaze. Has he come to apologize? To explain? No. I can see that it's neither of those. Whatever he's come to say, I need him to say it and leave. "What is it you want?"

"To end this."

"I don't understand. What is there to end?"

"Don't play a scene with me. You're not twenty anymore. Whatever this farce is that you've been playing—it ends now."

His voice is just as I remember, the same husky timbre that set my nerves jangling the first time we met, but it's tinged with contempt now. For me. "Whatever there was between us ended forty years ago, Anson. In Paris."

"Did it?"

I can't answer. I can't even breathe. I focus on the small scar above his right eye. It wasn't there before. There's another just below his jaw, on the left side. Also new. And still one more near his hairline. I'm memorizing his face, I realize. Making a new memory to superimpose over the one I've been carrying around—for when he's gone again. Only I don't want to remember this Anson.

"Rory said she flew to San Francisco to see you, and that she told you . . . everything."

"She did. I must say, it was quite a surprise. It isn't every day a man becomes a father and a grandfather all at once."

"You didn't *just* become a father, Anson. You've been a father for forty years. And I had nothing to do with her visit. I didn't even know—" I stop abruptly, angry that I'm explaining myself to him. I feel the beginnings of a sob and swallow it down. I will not cry in front of him. "I left your father's house thinking you were dead, that the *boche* killed you and buried your body in the woods. And then last night, I see you standing at the foot of the stairs. Can you imagine what that felt like? And you just stood there, glaring up at me. At *me*! Like *I* did something wrong. Did it never occur to you that I'd want to know you were alive? That even if you didn't want me, you owed me at least that?"

"It never occurred to me that you'd be interested."

His reply stuns me. "We were going to be married."

He flicks cold eyes over me and shrugs. "And what would you have done? Dropped everything, I suppose, and run back to Newport to play nurse to a man facing the possibility of life in a wheelchair?"

Yes! I want to scream at him. *Yes, that's exactly what I would have done. I would have done anything to have you back.* But it's too late for

375

such melodrama. I turn away, moving to the small bar in the corner to pour myself a cognac. *Liquid bravado,* Maddy used to call it. I'm in need of some bravado just now.

My back is still to him as I fumble with the decanter. I feel his eyes between my shoulders as I empty the glass in two quick gulps. The heat tongues its way down my throat and into my belly. I reach for the decanter and pour another.

"I used to think I could hear you calling me," I say, with my back still to him. "Your voice on the breeze. In the rain. In my sleep. Just my name, over and over again, as if you were reaching out to me from wherever you were. Silly, isn't it?" I wait a beat, until the silence grows awkward. "Can I offer you something? A cognac? Something stronger, perhaps?"

"I don't drink anymore."

The hesitation before the word *anymore* is almost imperceptible, but it's enough to make me abandon my drink and turn to face him. Once again, I'm struck by the change in him. Not in his looks—he's still a handsome man—but in his manner and the way he carries himself. Time mellows most of us, wearing down our sharp edges. But it's done the opposite to Anson. It's made him callous and eerily emotionless, reminding me again that this is not the man I loved.

I think about the time he got tipsy at dinner on a single glass of wine. It was one of the few times I ever saw him drink. "I don't recall you *ever* being much of a drinker," I say to fill the silence, then immediately wish I hadn't. I don't want to talk about how he *used* to be.

"I got better at it," he replies flatly. "A lot better, in fact. Medicinal purposes. Or so I told myself. Good for the pain. And remarkably effective if you start early enough in the day. Until you start losing whole days at a time. Then it gets tricky."

"The pain . . . It was from your wounds?"

He looks at me for a long time. So long, I think he won't answer at all. "Sure," he says finally. "Let's go with that."

There's no mistaking his meaning. I'm to blame. Not his father. *Me.* Because of the lies his father told him. Lies he chose to believe. Still, the rawness of his response finds a chink in my defenses. "Will you tell me what happened to you?"

He eyes me coldly. "Why?"

I lift my shoulders, feigning indifference. "I thought it was part of what we're supposed to be doing—like an autopsy to determine the cause of death." I sound like Anson as I throw the words at him, flat and unfeeling, and I'm not sorry. "We both know how it started; we were there. Then we went our separate ways, and things get a little fuzzy. After forty years, don't I deserve the rest of the story?"

He drops down onto the arm of the nearest chair, right leg extended stiffly, and I'm briefly reminded of Owen. "I was on the way back from a drop one night. It happened so fast, I never saw it coming. I caught one in the side, another one in the shoulder. They dragged me out of the truck and into the woods. I figured they'd kill me. Instead, they shot me through both legs and left me there. I don't know how long it took for me to drag myself back to the road, but it finished me. I closed my eyes and made my peace. When I came to, there was a Nazi in rubber gloves digging around in my shoulder. Apparently, Red Cross workers made excellent bargaining chips, though I never did find out who they traded me for."

He looks away then, eyes clouding. "It's a pretty shitty way to get out when you figure how many guys don't. You're on your way home and they're still just a number on a list, part of the daily tally—because their fathers don't have the right last name."

I suppress a shudder, remembering talk of the stalags: starvation, forced labor, grueling interrogations, and electrified fences. I'll never forgive Owen Purcell for the harm he has caused—to me, to my daughter, to Anson—but I can't fault him for pulling every lever in his power to bring his son home.

"How long were you held?"

"Six weeks in the hospital before being transferred to the camp at Moosburg for three and a half months. I was *kriegie* number 7877."

"You were . . . what?"

"A *kriegie*. It's the shortened version of the German word for POW. We all had numbers. Mine was 7877."

There's an ache at the center of my chest, the stirrings of an old wound. I've been living with his death for so long, but somehow this is worse, knowing what he endured, and that he feels guilty for having survived it.

"Your father . . ." I stop, pull in a breath, then start again. "There was a telegram saying you'd gone missing. Your father called everyone he could think of, but no one knew where you were. They said you'd been ambushed and that you were likely dead. And then your father sent me away—knowing I was carrying your child. He never told me you were . . ." I close my eyes, fighting tears. "I didn't know, Anson. If I had, nothing would have kept me away."

"Not even Myles Madison?"

Maddy's name brings me up short. And there's a new edge to his voice, harder and colder, as if he's caught me at something. "What does Maddy have to do with us?"

"Not us—you."

"I don't understand."

"I think you do."

He's staring at me, reproaching me for something, but I don't know what. "Please tell me what you're talking about."

He folds his arms again, his smile so cold it raises the hair on my arms. "What if I told you I *did* look for you? That when my father claimed not to know where you were, I paid an investigator—a Mr. Henry Vale—to find you? And he did."

All the air seems to go out of the room. It can't be true. It mustn't be. If he's known where to find me all this time . . . I take a step back, then another, until I'm backed against the bar. "You knew I was here? The whole time? And you stayed away?"

He shrugs. "Three's a crowd. The pictures were nice, though. I thought you made a lovely couple. A bit old, but maybe you prefer them distinguished. Some women do. Where is he now?"

I shake my head, confused. "Are we talking about Maddy?"

"Was there more than one?"

My nerves are taut, like an over-tuned violin string. He's not making sense. "More than one what, Anson? What pictures?"

"The ones Mr. Vale took."

I go still. "Of me?"

"Of both of you, actually. One of you in the kitchen, making breakfast together in your robes. Very domestic. Another of him feeding you some sort of pastry at a café. You were practically in his lap in that one. But I think the two of you dancing was my favorite. His arms draped all over you, your cheek against his. I certainly got my money's worth. I'm guessing he did too."

I'm so stunned, and so furious, that I don't know what to respond to first. "You paid someone to find me? To spy on me? With a camera?"

"It's not like finding you was hard. Took less than a week, as I recall. But when he told me you were in Boston, shacked up with a man old enough to be your father, I told him he'd made a mistake. The woman I was looking for was in love with *me*. So he brought me proof."

I throw back my head and laugh. The events of the day have made me a little hysterical, I think, or perhaps it's the cognac, but suddenly I find the whole thing very funny. "You think I was *shacked up* . . . with Maddy? That he and I . . ." Another snort of laughter. "So much for your proof!"

His face darkens. He's angry that I'm amused. "I'm not blind, Soline."

"I'm afraid you are, Anson. Quite blind. Myles Madison was my boss and my friend. He was also gay. He gave me a job when . . . after

Assia was born. And a place to live. I was at the end of my tether, as they say, and he came to my rescue. We fought like cats and dogs and we loved each other madly. But we were never lovers. And even if he had been straight, there could never have been anything between us. I was still in love with you."

"Except, as far as you knew, I was dead."

I stare at him, stung by the absurdity of his remark. "Do you think that's all it takes? Dying? There was only ever one man in my life, Anson. The fact that you don't know that stuns me. But the fact that you would take your father's word against mine, that you were so quick to think the worst of me, stuns me more. He took my daughter—my baby girl—and let me believe she was dead. When I had already lost you, he took her from me, and paid someone to give her to strangers. He took her from *you*, too, Anson. But instead of asking about her, you've come to throw Maddy in my face. And you sounded just like your father when you did it."

I go quiet, waiting for him to say something, but he just stands there staring with his hands fisted at his sides. His silence makes my throat ache. "Back then, it seemed impossible that you could be his son. Now I see that there's more of him in you than I realized." I swallow my tears, determined to keep my voice even. "Perhaps fate did us *both* a favor."

I see his shoulders tighten and realize I've struck a nerve. I'm glad. We eye each other silently, the quiet brittle. It seems there's nothing left for either of us to say.

He pushes to his feet slowly, as if his legs have stiffened. "I'll go."

I nod, not trusting my voice. I want him gone so very badly, and yet the thought of him walking back out of my life fills me with a grief I'm not sure I can bear.

He moves toward the door, then turns back. "I nearly forgot," he says, reaching into his pocket. "The reason I came."

After a moment of fumbling, he holds out his fist and pulls my hand from my pocket. I resist briefly, then look down at the puddle of garnet beads he's left in my gloved palm—*Maman's* rosary.

A sound catches in my throat, the beginnings of a sob, as I remember the moment I gave it to him. A pledge made the night our daughter was conceived. I look up, searching his face. "You kept them?"

"I promised I would bring them back. Now I have. The end."

The finality of his words hits me like a dousing of cold water, and I suddenly understand what he meant when he said he'd come to *end this thing.* He meant he'd come to fulfill his part of our bargain. Before I can stop myself, I'm weeping. It's as if he's spent forty years planning the best way to cut out my heart. On this day of all days, when I've just learned our daughter is alive, he's come to reopen a different wound. So be it.

"Wait here," I say thickly. "I have something for you too."

He's standing near the sofa when I return, flipping through the photo album Rory made for me. I jerk it out of his hands. "I'd rather you not touch that."

"They both look so much like Thia."

For an instant, there's a tenderness in his face that belongs to the Anson I used to know. "They look like you," I say softly. "Especially Rory."

His lips curl briefly, an uncomfortable smile that fades almost immediately. "I always imagined our daughter would look like you. I guess nothing worked out the way I thought it would."

"No," I say, shaking my head. "Nothing did." I put down the album and hand him his shaving kit. "This belongs to you."

He takes it, turning it slowly in his hands. Finally, his eyes lift to mine. "You've had this . . . for forty years?"

"You know exactly how long I've had it," I tell him flatly. "I would have returned it sooner, but you were dead."

"Soline . . ."

I turn my back, weary of sparring, but he catches me by the wrist, pulling me around to face him. For the first time, he seems to register the fact that my hands are not bare. He goes still, his face unreadable. "Why are you wearing gloves? What's wrong with your hands?"

"There was a fire," I say, forcing myself to hold his gaze. "Four years ago now. I was trying to save a dress, and my sweater caught fire."

"You were . . ."

"Burned. Yes."

The lines around his eyes soften and I feel his grip relax. "I'm sorry. I didn't know."

The warmth of his fingers is bleeding through my glove, making it hard to think. I pull my hand free. "There's a lot you don't know."

"Soline . . ."

"Oh, please, won't you go?" It comes out like a sob, desperate, broken. "You've said what you came to say and done what you came to do. What else do you want?"

"I want to know why you kept my shaving kit."

"We had an agreement. Remember?" My throat is full of broken glass as I force myself to meet his eyes. "You came here tonight to hold up your end, and now I've held up mine. *C'est fini.* Finished."

"Is it?" he asks softly. "Is it finished for you? Because it isn't for me. I wanted it to be. When I came home and found you gone, when I saw the pictures of you with another man and thought . . . I would have given anything for it to be done." His breath comes hoarsely, and a tiny pulse has begun to beat at the hollow of his throat. "I tried to drink you away, but that just made it worse. You were like a poison, your face, your voice, running in my veins. Even now . . ." He breaks off, raking a hand through his still-damp hair. "There hasn't been a day in the last forty years that I haven't thought of you, Soline. Haven't wondered if there wasn't a way—"

His voice breaks then, and he closes his eyes, as if taken unaware by a sudden sharp pain. When they open again, they're red-rimmed and dull. "Before, when you asked what happened to me, I told you about lying in the road, waiting to die. I said I made my peace, but I didn't say how."

My throat tightens. I don't want to hear any more, don't want to imagine him bleeding and broken—afraid. "Please, Anson . . ."

"I pulled the rosary out of my pocket and said your name over and over, out loud, like a prayer, until I could see your face. Because I wanted it to be the last thing I saw. If I could just see you, it would be okay. I could . . . let go. When I came to in the hospital, the rosary was lying next to me. And it felt like you were too. That's why I kept it all these years. Because as long as I had it, I felt like I was still connected to you, that what we had in Paris never really ended. When you handed me this . . ." He looks down at the shaving kit and shrugs. "I thought maybe you'd kept it for the same reason."

My eyes are dry in the wake of his declaration. I want to believe him, to trust him. But the pain of forty years remains lodged in my chest. "Why did you never come to me, Anson? I was here. All that time, I was right here, learning to make a life without you. You say you wanted to see my face, but you never saw my heart if you believe I could betray your memory with another man. There was never anyone but you. Not then, not now, not anywhere in between. We could have been together, but you let your father win. He wanted you to hate me, and you did."

"No. I never hated you. I wanted to. I tried to. But I *did* hate myself. Who I became after the war and the hospitals. Bitter. Hard. Lost in a bottle most of the time. You were right when you said I was like him. I let that happen. I used the war as an excuse—and you. Until I looked in the mirror one day and saw *him* instead. Everything I hated about him staring back at me. That night I went to my first AA meeting. I've been working my way back ever since."

"Back to what?"

"To this," he says hoarsely. "To you."

I resist the words. Words are easy. "But when Rory went to San Francisco . . . When she told you . . ."

He looks away, as if pained by the memory. "Twenty years sober, and I never needed a drink like I needed one that night. I can tell you, club soda isn't much help for that kind of news. It was like she ripped the scab off all of it. My mistakes and my bitterness, my goddamn pride, everything I'd thrown away, and I couldn't bear to look at it. She was asking me to own it, and I wasn't ready."

"And now?"

"Now everything's changed. Last night, I saw your face, and all the poison came rushing back. I thought I'd come here tonight to end it, that I'd hand you back the rosary and it would be over. Now I realize it's never going to be over, and I don't know what to do with that, except to finally own it—and say I'm sorry. About the years we lost. About our daughter. About believing my father's lies." He reaches for my hand, stroking the back of my glove with a tenderness that makes my breath catch. "And about this."

When I don't resist, he raises my hand to his lips. I feel the warmth of his mouth against my knuckles, and I turn my hand, cupping his face as if it's the most natural thing in the world, as if no time has passed at all. The memory can play tricks. The heart too. And I marvel at how the simple touch of a cheek, the landscape of a face, can erase years of loss and pain—and leave you vulnerable.

He covers my hand with both of his, as if afraid I might pull away. "Tell me what you want, Soline, and I'll do it. If you want me to go, I'll walk out that door and you'll never see me again. But if you want me to stay, I'll spend the rest of my life trying to give you back the years we missed."

My eyes pool with tears until his face begins to blur. "We can never get those years back, Anson. They're gone."

He nods and lets his hands fall, stepping away from my touch. "I suppose they are."

My throat closes as I watch him move toward the door, and I think of the morning I left Paris. If I had known then that forty years would pass before I saw him again, would I have allowed us to be separated? Can I allow it now?

As if in answer, *Maman*'s words drift back to me. *There are times for holding on in this life and times for letting go. You must learn to know the difference.*

And suddenly, I do know.

He's turning up his collar, preparing to duck out into the downpour, when I catch his arm. Because I don't have another forty years to waste, and neither does he. "We can't get those years back, Anson, but perhaps we can make something of the ones we have left."

FORTY-SEVEN

Soline

·

31 October 1985—Boston

We wake together with the sun streaming in. Anson smiles sheepishly as our eyes meet, and for a moment it's as if no time has passed. We're the same people who met in a busy corridor of the American Hospital, a handsome hero and a frightened volunteer. But we're not those people. Time has left its scars on us both and made us into *different* people. People who will have to work hard to discover one another again. But we've decided to try.

There are gaps to fill, empty years and hollowed-out dreams, and we have begun to fill them. I have told him about the Roussels and our strange vocation, and he has told me about the faces that still haunt his dreams and sometimes jolt him awake in the night—ghosts from his time in Moosburg. There is more to tell, of course, for both of us. We have each collected our share of shadows over the years, but there have been bright places, too, and eventually we will get to it all.

We lie amid the tangle of sheets, flushed and awkward, tripping over our tongues as we endeavor to navigate this new reality. It's been a long time since either of us has awakened to a lover's touch. The sharing of a bed and our bodies, and of all that comes after, is unfamiliar ground.

Now and then, one of us will go quiet and simply stare at the other, or venture some small touch, reassurance that all of this is real, and I suddenly realize that this is how it would have been—*should* have been—after that first night all those years ago. We would have risen with the sun, young lovers with a newfound wonder for the world and each other. We were cheated of that morning, but we have been given a do-over, as Rory calls it, a chance to do it differently, to do it better.

We get up finally, and I make coffee while Anson uses the phone in my study to make a few calls. Later, I take him to Bisous Sucrés for croissants, and we walk the few blocks to the Common. The trees are nearly bare, the ground littered with papery leaves, and there's a bite to the morning air. We stroll around Frog Pond and eventually find a bench in the sun. We've been talking nonstop, filling in the blanks left by forty years apart, but suddenly there's a lull in the conversation. I watch as a child of two or three toddles after a pair of ducks, her mother close behind.

"I love it here," I say with a sigh. "It reminds me of Paris, when we used to sneak away to the park for lunch. I used to come here every Sunday with my coffee and my croissant. Because it reminded me of us. That's why I wanted to come today. To show you."

"I've been here before," he says, his tone suddenly somber.

"To the Common?" It never occurred to me that his business might have brought him to Boston, though I suppose it should have. "When?"

His eyes cloud, and he looks away. "Sometimes," he says heavily, "when I was home and missing you so much I was afraid I might drink, I'd get in the car and come here instead, walking for hours, thinking maybe I'd catch a glimpse of you."

The confession stuns me. "Did you?"

"No."

"And if you had?"

He shrugs. "I don't know. I'd like to think we would have ended up on this bench, that somehow we were always going to end up here, but I don't know, and it scares me a little to think about it."

I weave my fingers through his, holding his gaze. "Rory asked me once if I believed that certain things were meant to happen. I wasn't sure then, but I am now. Somehow, against all odds, we've found each other again, with the help of a granddaughter neither of us knew existed. I can't explain it. I only know that we *are* here on this bench. The rest of it doesn't matter."

He answers me with a kiss, and I feel like a teenager again, with flushed cheeks and a belly full of butterfly wings.

He's grinning one of his boyish American grins when we finally pull apart. "I must remember to thank our granddaughter," he says huskily. The grin slips then, and he checks his watch. Suddenly he looks very somber. "Speaking of Rory, I never told you why I turned up at the gallery the other night. I came to see Rory, but then . . . there you were." He pauses to touch my cheek, but his face has gone serious. "At the risk of ruining the moment, I need to get back to my hotel. I'm expecting a call, and then I'm going to have to talk to Rory. In person."

FORTY-EIGHT

RORY

Rory sat down at her desk with a fresh mug of coffee and opened her planner. With the opening in her rearview mirror, she'd finally been able to settle into the day-to-day activities of running the gallery. Business was slow and would be for a while, but she planned to use the time to expand her stable of artists and get a jump on plans for several spring events she wanted to hold. And she could do with a little downtime after the excitement of the last few days.

She had just scribbled a reminder to buy thank-you notes when she heard the soft peal of the entry chime. She grabbed a sip of coffee before heading down. No need to pounce. Give them time to get inside, look around. But when she reached the landing, instead of customers, she found Soline—and Anson.

Her initial reaction was panic, but the longer she looked at them, the more she realized everything was fine. Quite fine, in fact. Anson had a hand at the small of Soline's back, as if it belonged there, while Soline looked up at him with soft, wide eyes. *Is she blushing?*

Rory started down the stairs toward them, unable to suppress a grin. "Unless I miss my guess, something's happened since I last saw the two of you."

Soline reached for Anson's hand. "Quite a lot, actually."

It was impossible to miss the change that had come over Anson since their first meeting. He looked almost boyish standing there with Soline's hand in his, as if forty years had suddenly lifted from his shoulders. She had no idea what had transpired between them. She only knew it felt right, like a circle finally closing.

"Should I call you Grandpa now? Or Gramps? Pops, maybe?"

Anson cleared his throat awkwardly. "We'll talk about that later. Right now, we need to talk about other things."

Soline's eyes flicked to Anson, then back again. "There's been some news, Rory. About Hux."

"News . . ." The room seemed to wobble as she repeated the word. "What . . . kind of news?"

Anson let go of Soline's hand and came to stand in front of Rory. "The night we met in San Francisco, you mentioned your fiancé had been missing for some time. I remembered his name, so the next day, I decided to make a few calls."

Rory clutched at the stair railing, her palm suddenly sticky.

"After the war," Anson continued, "when the doctors finally finished putting me back together, I went to work for the International Red Cross, as a prisoner advocate. They have people all over the world who specialize in negotiation and extraction. Some of them are friends. So I picked up the phone to see who might have a useful contact."

"And someone did?"

Anson narrowed his eyes at her. "Maybe you should sit while we talk."

"No. Just tell me. Please."

"A few months ago, the State Department received a tip. Someone claiming to have spotted two men and a woman in a village just outside

Atbara in the company of two armed men. They were washing clothes at a pump in the center of town. When they finished, they were waved into a green panel truck with no markings. Our guys were skeptical, and not without reason. I doubt there's a soul in Sudan who doesn't know about the kidnapping—and the reward. Liars come out of the woodwork when there's cash up for grabs. The source was a shaky one, and the lead looked like another dead end. But there was one guy who wouldn't let it go, and it paid off. They found him, Rory. They found all three of them—alive. That's all I knew when I came here the other night. That he was alive. But since then, one of our negotiators managed to broker terms for release. A friend of mine called a few hours ago. They were released last night. They'll need to be checked out, but barring any serious medical issues, Hux should be on his way back to the States in a week or so."

Rory sank to the bottom step, burying her face in her hands. The tears came silently at first, catching in her throat until she thought they would break her open.

Alive. Safe. Coming home.

Finally the sobs broke free, welling up from the dark place she'd been trying not to look at for so long. *Home.* The word seemed to sing in her veins, over and over again. Hux was coming home—after ten months of god only knew what. She'd heard the stories, everyone had, men so damaged their lives were never the same. She lifted her head, dragging her sleeve across her eyes. "Did they say . . . Do you know if he's . . ."

"I don't. But if there was anything serious, they would have said. That doesn't mean he won't go through some things. There's always a period of adjustment. Some rockier than others. But there are people who specialize in that kind of trauma. And more importantly, he'll have you."

She nodded mutely as the tears came again. He would have her—and *she* would have him. Together, they would work through whatever came.

In time, Rory became aware of Soline sitting beside her on the step. She mopped her face again with her sleeve, smiling weakly. "He's coming home."

"*Oui, ma petite.* He's coming home. You will have your happy ending at last."

"I still can't believe it. Part of me was starting to think it might never happen, and now it has. I know he'll have some things to deal with, but I can't wait for you to meet him and for him to meet you and Anson. And to show him the gallery. So much has happened . . ." She paused for a breath, then smiled sheepishly. "Sorry, I know I'm rambling, but this feels like a miracle. And speaking of miracles . . ." She tipped her chin toward Anson, who had wandered over to one of the exhibits, presumably to give them some space. "How did *that* happen?"

Soline smiled mischievously. "That, *ma petite*, is too long a story for now. And we don't know where it's headed yet. What we do know is that we're willing to find out."

Rory felt a fresh wave of happiness wash through her. After all the years and all the heartache, a reconciliation. "I'm so glad, Soline. He's never stopped loving you. It's written all over his face."

Soline's smile widened as she watched Anson move from painting to painting with a furrowed brow. "We're certainly going to have a lot to tell your mother."

Rory nodded, sniffling noisily. "You can call her from my office, if you want, and fill her in. I'd like a minute alone with Anson, if you don't mind."

She waited until Soline reached the top of the stairs, then went in search of Anson. She found him standing in front of one of her pieces. He turned when he heard her approach. "These are amazing."

Rory managed a watery smile. "Thanks."

The silence stretched as they stood looking at each other, and for a moment she was afraid she was going to cry again. "I sent Soline upstairs to call my mother because I wanted a minute to talk to you, to say thank you for what you did for Hux. And for me. I didn't exactly endear myself the first time we met, but you still—" She broke off, swallowing a fresh rush of tears. "I don't know how to thank you. I'll never know."

"I was only a tiny piece of the outcome, but I'd say we're even."

"You mean you and Soline?"

Anson lit up like a boy with his first crush. "It could just be that getting ambushed in the bar of the Fairmont Hotel was the best thing that ever happened to me."

Rory felt herself flush. It had worked out pretty well for her too. And for Camilla. That night at the bar, he'd told her bluntly that there was no chance of a happy ending. He'd been wrong about that, and she was glad. "I'm still not sure how it happened, but I seem to have gone from having no grandparents to having a full set. Do you think I could maybe . . . hug you?"

The request seemed to catch him off guard. He swallowed hard, then nodded. "I'd like that too."

She stepped into his arms, breathing him in—soap and citrus with a hint of shaving cream underneath. It was subtle yet masculine: the smell of comfort and safety. How had she lived all these years without smelling this smell? Something told her she was going to enjoy having grandparents, though she really was going to have to think of something else to call them.

Moments later, they heard the tap of Soline's heels as she approached. "Look at you two, already making up for lost time."

Rory shot Anson a wink. "I'd say we all have a bit of that to look forward to. So did you call her?"

"I did."

"And you told her everything? Not just about Hux but all of it?"

"Well, most of it."

"And she was happy?"

Soline answered with a smoky laugh. "What do you think? She was going to call Thia, and then she was coming right over. She says we need to start planning your engagement party. And then the wedding."

Rory let the words sink in. The wedding. *Her* wedding. The thought made her want to pinch herself. Hux was coming home, perhaps not unscathed but home—to her. Yes, there would be a wedding, though not right away—he would need time to recover—but she would wait as long as he needed her to wait. And they would figure out the rest together.

The thought filled her with a quiet joy, like ripples spreading across the surface of a pond, slowly widening, until they eventually lapped the shore. She broke into a grin. "I suppose at some point, I'm going to need a dress," she told Soline, then turned to look up at Anson. "And someone to give me away."

It still seemed impossible. Such an inexplicable confluence of events. Lives intersected. Hearts reunited. Families mended. Because of a box she'd found under the stairs of a burned-out building. A box full of happy endings—and perhaps a touch of *la magie*.

EPILOGUE

SOLINE

A new and specific binding charm must be composed for each client bride, conceived for her and her alone. The charm will be hers in perpetuity and may never be reused.

—Esmée Roussel, the Dress Witch

17 May 1986—Lyman, Massachusetts

At long last, there is to be a wedding.

I stand at the window, gazing out over sloping lawns and perfectly manicured hedges, gardens filled with blushing pink peonies, and a sky so blue it hurts my eyes. I blink away the sting, afraid I'll muss my makeup. There's a pretty gazebo out by the lake, dressed in yards of ivy and frothy white tulle, and several rows of folding chairs. It will be a small, intimate affair, limited to family and close friends.

Camilla had hoped for something grander, the ballroom at the Park Plaza with a string quartet and swags of fragrant white lilies, but she was overruled and had to content herself with a garden ceremony on the grounds of a small estate just outside Boston.

I check the clock. There's still a little time. Rory is with her mother, getting dressed; Hux has taken Anson off somewhere to handle a boutonniere mishap; and I'm alone with my thoughts for what feels like the first time in weeks.

I've learned firsthand what a taxing business planning a wedding can be. Doubly so if one also happens to be designing and overseeing the making of the dress. I was nervous about trusting someone else to handle the sketches, but I was pleased with the way they turned out, and I'm even happier with the finished product—a flared A-line in ivory satin, tea length with a wrapped bodice and tulle underskirt. Not a dress fit for a princess, perhaps, but certainly one fit for a happy ending.

I think of the charm I managed to work into the left side seam. Two weeks with my stiff and achy hands, and not nearly as pretty as I would have liked, but it is done. Under the circumstances, I think *La Mère* will not deduct points for neatness, though I cannot be so sure about *Maman*.

She has been on my mind these last few days, her voice in my ear, reminding me of all the Roussels stretching back through time. Cursed in love, or so the story went. We were told from an early age what we were allowed to have—and what we weren't. Told not to long for what others have, because somewhere along the way, one of us had broken someone else's rules.

But I've come to believe we create our own curses and carry them through life because we've been told it's our lot. We're taught to relive our mothers' heartaches, to accept their sufferings as our own, and pass them on to the next generation, again and again, until one of us at long last says *no*, and the curse is finally broken. Because we've discovered a new kind of magick—the kind that comes with choosing for ourselves, with saying I will *do* something else, *be* something else, *have* something else. This was the lesson *Maman* was trying to teach me the night she slipped away. There are no curses. Only patterns meant to be broken. Dreams to chase. Hearts to hold. Magick to make.

Another glance at the clock. It's time. I repeat the charm once more for good luck, the words so similar to the ones I composed so many years ago, for another dress.

> Over distance, over time,
> Whatever trials might come,
> May the echoes of these once lost hearts
> Be forever joined as one.

My heart is full as I pull on my gloves and pick up the flowers from the box at the foot of the bed. I'm all but floating as I step into the garden. Rory is beaming and absolutely beautiful. She blinks back tears and places a hand on her heart. Beside her, Hux grins like a man who knows he's hopelessly blessed. And why shouldn't he, when fate has seen him safely home to the woman he adores and his new practice is set to open next month.

Camilla pushes to her feet, already blotting away tears. Thia signals the musicians, and the first notes of Pachelbel's "Canon" fill the air. I take a step and then another. And then I see Anson, smiling at the end of the narrow slate path, his eyes locked with mine as I close the distance between us. The man I have loved for forty years, and the only groom I've ever wanted.

The music fades as I slip my hand into his. *Maman*'s voice is suddenly there, like a whisper against my cheek. *As long as you keep his beautiful face in your heart, he will never truly be lost. There will always be a way back.* And at long last, we have found it. It has taken us decades to get to this place, but that doesn't matter. Because we know now that neither of us ever really let go. Somewhere, in the most carefully guarded corners of our hearts, we held on.

La fin.

ACKNOWLEDGMENTS

And now, for the hardest part of writing any book. Saying thank you. Seriously, after the year that was, where do I even begin? With every book, there are people to thank, those who support our vision and hold our hands, dry our tears and keep us fed, but I'm always horrified by the thought that in the heavy fog that always descends at the end of a project, I might leave someone out, and holy smokes, this list is a long one. So here goes . . .

To my incredible agent, Nalini Akolekar, who threw me a lifeline when I was ready to jump ship. Thank you for keeping my head above water and reminding me to breathe. And of course, a huge shout-out to the entire Spencerhill team—you guys seriously rock.

To my editor, the extraordinary Jodi Warshaw, who understands that sometimes life gets in the way and also makes that okay—my gratitude knows no bounds. For your patience, support, enthusiasm, and generosity, so many, many thanks. Ditto for Gabe Dumpit and Danielle Marshall and every single member of the Lake Union / APub team, who are without a doubt the best in the biz.

To my developmental editor, Charlotte Herscher, who pushes me to go that extra mile—and then to go one more after that. Thank you for your eyes, your expertise, your love of story, and for always knowing what I'm *trying* to say—even when I'm not sure how to say it—and for helping me finally get there.

To the book bloggers, whose love of the written word has been the wind beneath so many writers' wings this year, including mine, your support and dedication to authors mean everything. Special thanks to Susan "Queenie" Peterson, Kathy Murphy (a.k.a. the Pulpwood Queen), Kate Rock, Annie McDowell, Denise Birt, Linda Zagnon, and Susan Leopold.

To my fabulous tribe at Blue Sky Book Chat: Kerry Anne King, Jane Healey, Patricia Sands, Alison Ragsdale, Marilyn Simon Rothstein, Bette Lee Crosby, Peggy Lampman, Soraya Lane, Lisa Ann Braxton, Lainey Cameron, and Loretta Nyhan, thanks for the fun and the friendship and for your wonderful generosity.

To my wonderful brothers and sisters: Todd, Gina, David, Scott, Nanette, Tom, and Shelly, without whom I would never have made it through 2020. My love always, and more gratitude than you can possibly fathom. I'm pretty sure I offered several of you a kidney. The offer still stands.

To my mom, Patricia Crawford, who has always been and always will be my biggest and loudest cheerleader. Thank you for being someone I could always look up to, for teaching me to work hard every day and to always be kind. I love you.

And finally to Tom: husband, best friend, beta reader, and soul mate. There are simply no words, but then we never *did* need words.

BOOK CLUB QUESTIONS

1. Throughout the story, there is significant friction between Rory and Camilla, much of which stems from Camilla's need to manage her daughter's life. In what ways, if any, do you feel Rory contributes to the chronic tension between them?

2. Soline's mother, Esmée, believes that each of us creates a unique echo in the world and that those echoes are constantly seeking their match—in order to become complete. Do you believe such a thing is possible?

3. One of the threads running through the book touches on the tendency of daughters to repeat their mothers' mistakes, especially in relationship matters. Have you or someone you know experienced this in real life? If so, was the pattern eventually recognized and broken?

4. The theme of chasing one's dreams figures prominently in the journeys of both Rory and Soline. From an early age, Soline was taught that the work they did was a sacred vocation for which the Roussels had been especially chosen, and Hux once told Rory that the dream of opening an art gallery had her name all over it. Do you believe we

are each given a calling in life, a talent or gift that feeds our soul and benefits others?

5. "Everything happens for a reason" is a commonly used axiom, particularly when events suddenly turn our lives upside down. Throughout the book, Rory's and Soline's lives are upended by a series of seeming coincidences, causing them to wonder if some unseen hand might be at work. Do you believe that certain things are meant to be? That some benevolent force is trying to guide us to our highest good? Or is everything random?

6. Rory tells Soline that she and Camilla push each other's buttons. Soline understands, but at times she seems to side with Camilla, perhaps because she had a similar relationship with her own mother. What parallels did you note in the relationships between Soline and Esmée and Rory and Camilla?

7. By the end of the book, it seems obvious that Soline has come into Rory's life for a reason and that the reverse is also true. In the end, each has irrevocably altered the other's life. Have you ever had someone come into your life, even briefly, who you feel came to teach you a lesson or help you find your path?

8. On her deathbed, Esmée tells Soline about the father she never knew, a man Esmée loved dearly but sent away out of obedience to her mother. She speaks to her daughter about a grief worse than death—the grief of a life half-lived. How do you think these revelations affect Soline's choices when Anson suddenly reappears in her life?

9. One of Esmée's quotes is about forgiveness. She says forgiveness is the greatest magick of all and that it makes all things new. Do you believe in the power of forgiveness? If so, is it true in all things, or are there certain things that can never be made new?